Praise for *Somebody's Perfect*

...it was sooooo worth the wait! Kallypso Masters puts her heart and soul in all of her books and this one is no exception.... Savannah and Damián now have a battle not only in the courts but in Savannah's mind. I laughed and cried and worried. I also felt like I was catching up with old friends and wanted to stay after the epilogue ended.

~ ~ ~

Loved loved loved this book. So much love gui in every page.

~ Donna Kemp, Goodreads Review

~ ~ ~

I loved this book.... There were ups and downs, there were what the hell moments and there were teary moments. It will keep you locked in until you can't put it down until you finish it.

~ LaWanna Lewis, Goodreads Review

~ ~ ~

I love that they have all come together as a family and I am excited to see the new couples that are forming and cannot wait to see what happens with Grant and of course Mari and her friend Aidan.

~ Toi, Goodreads Review

~ ~ ~

An emotional touching story of overcoming abuse and torture and finally facing the demons both in the mind and in a court of law.

~ Cindi, Goodreads Review

Somebody's Perfect

(Seventh in the Rescue Me Saga)

Kallypso Masters

Somebody's Perfect
Seventh in the Rescue Me Saga
Kallypso Masters

Copyright © 2018-2019
Ka-thunk! Publishing
Print Edition
E-book ISBN: 978-1941060322
Paperback ISBN: 978-1941060339

Original e-book version: December 27, 2018
Last updated e-book version: February 24, 2019
Print version: March 29, 2019

ALL RIGHTS RESERVED
Edited by Meredith Bowery and Jacy Mackin
Proofread by Christine Mulcair
Cover design by Linda Kuhlmann of Two Trees Studio
Cover images licensed through Shutterstock
and graphically altered by Linda Kuhlmann
Formatted by BB eBooks

This book contains content that is NOT suitable for readers 17 and under.

To discover more about the books in this series, see the *Rescue Me Saga* section at the end of this book. For more about Kallypso Masters, please go to the About the Author section. Or visit her web site directly at kallypsomasters.com.

Dedication

To all my fellow survivors who weren't able to experience their own justice, and to

Cassandra Dawn, who inspired a scene in the epilogue of *Somebody's Perfect* when she told me about it more than seven years ago. I immediately knew it had to be told in Damián and Savannah's continuing story and finally found the perfect place for it!

Acknowledgements

This book took longer than any other book I've ever published, including its predecessor, *Nobody's Perfect* (Rescue Me Saga #3). Now let me take a moment to thank the many people who helped me make Savannah and Damián's continuing story the best it can be.

As you know, research and accuracy are important to me. This book required legal expertise in a number of scenes because there is a major legal component to the story of Savannah obtaining justice. **Rhonda Copley** and **Glenda Edwards** provided criminal law advice, and Glenda also gave me the idea of having George Gentry testify in the narrative, which just blew the trial scenes out of the water. (I doubt any of you will have predicted that and I love providing something new and different than other authors might have done.) I also received legal expertise from several California attorneys familiar with San Diego County courtrooms and procedures, including **Lauren Weidner**, **Leslie A. Braun-Winet, Esq.**, and several who wished to remain anonymous.

Anytime I have a birthing scene to write in one of my books, I run to **Kim Bollinger**, a labor-and-delivery nurse, for help. And with this book, I had to call in a new type of expert—a hypnotherapist to help with the Alive Day scene and the hotel scene during the trial. **Traci Kanaan** was recommended to me by **Tymber Dalton** and provided great insights and advice. And of course, I received more help on the BDSM scenes from **Trish Bowers**, **Tymber Dalton**, **Iliana Gkioni**, and **Ekatarina Sayanova**.

Jack and Kay B. provided feedback and helpful information about the inside of a California detention center and read over those scenes multiple times until I got them right.

Several mentions of US Marine Corps traditions brought **Top Griz (Jeff Griz)** back to help on uniforms and SERE training. **Christine Mulcair** brought in her son to help with the USMC uniform question, and the two of them plus **Meredith Bowery** and her contacts helped me avoid a significant mistake there.

As always, my incredibly patient beta reader team helped me get the story facts straight from start to finish. A special thanks to **Barb Jack**, who not only beta read it, but also gave it another look at the last minute when she was still recovering from an illness to help me polish it before it went to the line editor.

My thanks always to **Margie Dees, Iliana Gkioni, Carmen Messing, Ruth Reid**, and **Lisa Simo-Kinzer**. Ruth and Lisa provided help with the psychology issues that ran throughout the pages of the book. And to **Charlotte Oliver**, my assistant, for compiling multiple files from betas into a single document of the first part of the story, which made it much easier for me to follow and compare.

The content edits for this book were done by **Meredith Bowery**, who was a major factor in helping me revise this story to my satisfaction—and kept me sane when the writing/revising process became daunting at times. Anytime I stumbled, Meredith was there with her superb analysis of the characters and their motivations and always helped get me back on track. Meredith and **Carmen Messing** also did a brainstorming session with me to work out some logistics problems when doing a rewrite of the Alive Day scenes at the club.

Jacy Mackin of Red Ink Editing, LLC, provided excellent edits on punctuation and overused words, as always, but her pointed comments about where I'd dropped the ball also helped keep you from hating Damián and Savannah at one part in the story. Some last-minute revisions and corrected motivation made this book even better. (It takes a village!)

To my proofreader, **Christine Mulcair**, for catching even more things we missed! Any remaining mistakes were probably made after my editors and proofreader signed off—and I take full responsibility! Thank you to

Trisha Bordenkircher, Annette Elens, and **Amy Jackson** for finding the few things I missed in advance of the print version.

And last, but not least, to the readers in my Rescue Me Saga Discussion Group on Facebook who kept me writing by answering research and character questions without stopping to look them up. Usually, they have my answers within half an hour. **Jessica Kelly** of that group also provided me with the URL for the image of the couple on the cover. It took some work for my graphic artist, **Linda Kuhlmann**, to morph two images of the couple together for the final version, but it totally rocks!

I also ran several contests during a birthday party for Damián there in February 2017 that resulted in one person being named here. **Eva Meyers** suggested that Damián and Savannah would live in the University Hills section of Denver, and that was perfect. And **Sarah Moody** for being the first to guess they might use one of Damián's parents' names for the baby. I did run some other contests for things that didn't end up in the book, but appreciate all who made suggestions and engaged with me there!

As always, all new and remaining typos and errors are solely *my* responsibility. So if you see something, please let me know via FB Messenger or email at kallypsomasters@gmail.com. If I don't respond to you, try again because it will mean I didn't get the message.

Author's Note

I hope you'll agree that this book has been worth the wait! I know for some of my fellow survivors of child sexual abuse, this is going to be a difficult story to read, but I hope sharing in Savannah's justice will help ease your own pain if you're like me and never got to experience that.

If you're experiencing emotions and feelings while reading that you need help to process, please reach out to a trusted friend. If needed, here are some web sites that can provide you with someone to talk, too.

Rape, Abuse, and Incest National Network (RAINN):
www.rainn.org

Crisis and Suicide Prevention Services (United States):
www.suicidepreventionlifeline.org

Please don't try anything you read about in a book without consulting experts. Wax play, for instance, requires that special care to be taken when used on a pregnant woman. And hypnosis can be dangerous without some training, even in a fun BDSM scene. Please ask a kink-friendly doctor or knowledgeable mentor in the community before you attempt anything you read about in this or any other book.

Lastly, while I did consult with numerous legal minds on this story, please remember that this is fiction and that time frames are truncated to fit the story. Justice is rarely swift in our judicial system, so please read those scenes with that in mind.

For timely updates, sneak peeks at unedited excerpts, and much more, sign up for my e-mails and/or text alerts!
www.subscribepage.com/kallypsomastersnewsletter

Chapter One

S avannah Orlando numbly pressed the button to end the call with the district attorney's office before laying the phone on the coffee table.

Lying on the sofa, she wrapped her arms protectively over her well-rounded belly. Bile threatened to escape her rapidly closing throat, and she swallowed several times to keep it down. She hadn't thrown up since the third month of her pregnancy but wasn't sure she'd make it through today without doing so.

Hearing that George Gentry's trial date had been set for December—barely two months away—had thrown her for a loop. She hadn't expected to be in her eighth month of pregnancy when she confronted him again. Even though Gentry couldn't possibly know she was pregnant, she couldn't help but feel he'd done this because he couldn't wait to torment her again. While he'd originally pled not guilty by reason of insanity, he'd been declared competent to stand trial over the summer. Gentry would no doubt make sure she'd be humiliated and beaten down again with verbal and emotional assaults at every turn. She could easily imagine the hatred he'd built up for her after being thrown in jail last spring.

Am I ready to face him again so soon? Will I ever be?

Chiquita whimpered as she padded across the room to where Savannah sat on the sofa and placed her front paws and head in Savannah's lap, staring up at her with soulful eyes. "Don't worry, girl. I'm not upset with you." The fast-growing four-month-old puppy seemed to sense the moods of those around her and always tried to comfort anyone who might be having issues. When they'd first brought Chiquita home, Savannah had noticed the rescue puppy had an uncanny way of knowing when Damián was about to have a PTSD episode or nightmare. But

Chiquita also tuned in to her and Mari's moods, often lifting their spirits or calming them down when distressed. She was in service-dog training now, along with Adam and Karla's dog and Chiquita's littermate, Hero. They'd only had their puppies since the family picnic at Luke & Cassie's last August, but couldn't imagine life without them now.

Chiquita's attempt at distraction was appreciated but short-lived as the other part of the DA's news came to her. Savannah picked up her phone to check the time. 2:18. When did Damián say he'd be home from the Patriot Riders' funeral detail? Knowing him, he'd stop by his Harley shop to check on things after being away all day. But Damián rarely missed a chance to sit down with them for dinner. He'd probably text when he took his helmet off to give her a heads-up on his arrival.

That could be hours from now, though. How would he react to the news that absolutely nothing pertinent to the charges relating to her mother's and John Grainger's murders had been discovered on the hard drive she'd stolen from Gentry's home office the night she'd escaped?

All that had been found on the drive were humiliating videos of her in the penthouse. While they'd found a copy of the sex-slave contract Gentry had held over her head that last year she lived with him, it wouldn't be allowed, even if relevant, because it wasn't signed.

To her horror, they did find photos of her brand.

Damián had worked so hard with her to change her mindset about the GG brand on her labia, which was originally intended to mark her as George Gentry's slave. In her mind now, the GG had come to mean she was Damián's *good girl*. Much of the shame associated with its origins now gone, she still wasn't ready to have that time in her life discussed in a public courtroom with Gentry watching for her response. At least she'd be spared that.

If her obstetrician even allowed her to attend the trial so late in her pregnancy. Every fiber of her being wanted to be there to confront that arrogant, evil beast, but travel might be an issue. So far, she had a low-risk pregnancy, and Doctor Palmer saw no reason to restrict her travel. However, no one had anticipated such a trip just seven weeks before the baby's due date.

While she'd waited decades for this long-overdue justice against the bastard who had stolen her mother away from her in such a brutal way, this baby's health outweighed everything else.

Even without her live testimony, surely the police and forensic evidence would put him away forever for the murders of her mother and John Grainger, not to mention for kidnapping and torturing Savannah last March.

Nausea continued roiling in her stomach at the thought of facing that monster again.

Perhaps she could submit a videotaped testimony telling the DA and the court what she remembered. Or a two-way video interrogation and cross-examination with her still in Denver might be admissible. Not as satisfying for her as facing her nemesis should be, but safer for the baby.

Who was she kidding? She wasn't brave enough to do this. She never had been. Savannah had simply run away from him before—twice. That wasn't an option this time.

Regardless of right or wrong, she needed to opt for the safest choice for the baby while not jeopardizing the DA's case.

She wished Damián was here to talk over her options with. Knowing it could be hours before he returned, Savannah stood. A stabbing pain behind her eyes had her pressing her fingertips to her forehead as counter-pressure, but it persisted. She shuffled toward the kitchen to check on dinner. After seeing the last of her Tuesday clients at noon—her short day at Doctor McKenzie's clinic—she'd come home to flesh out the fantasy Damián would ask her about later. They'd been working on it for a while to help overcome her past. While creating the scenario before the call came, she'd filled the slow cooker with the ingredients for chicken tortilla soup, Damián's favorite. The rich, spicy aroma soothed her as she entered the room, if only for a second or two.

Please hurry home, baby. I need you.

Damián had a way of putting things into perspective and making them less daunting. Although she wasn't sure he could help her today.

Boots rubbed against her ankle, meowing for a treat or some love. After stirring the soup and lowering the temperature, she replaced the glass lid and bent to pick up Mari's almost one-year-old kitten just as the front door opened. Savannah jumped, and the skittish Boots scampered out of her hands, sensing her momentary panic.

"I'm home, Savannah!" *Damián!* Her body sagged against the counter. He always announced himself, hoping to quickly allay her fears that someone had invaded their home. Perhaps she'd overcome her post-traumatic stress from the kidnapping one of these days, but she hadn't managed to do so yet.

Savannah stood a little straighter before the man she loved more than life itself entered the room. She hadn't expected him so soon but was grateful he'd come home early. When he entered the kitchen, Damián opened his mouth to speak, but his smile faded the moment he met her gaze. He glanced at her belly then back into her eyes.

"What's wrong?" He closed the gap between them in a second and stroked her upper arms, soothing some of her tension immediately. "Is it the baby? Marisol?"

She shook her head, unable to speak past the lump in her throat. The mixture of hormones and emotional waterworks had been threatening to overwhelm her since the phone call. Damián read her mood in an instant.

He wrapped his arms around her, cocooning her between his rock-hard body and the counter, giving her the much-needed assurance of safety that had been stripped away by the DA's call. Damián had provided asylum to her and Mari during one of the most frightening ordeals of their lives, later risking his own life and suffering a gunshot wound to save Savannah from her father's hands. No, Gentry's. He would never be a father to her. Damián had made her feel safe from the very first time he'd rescued her from Lyle at the age of nineteen.

"*¿Qué tienes, savita?*"

Tears streaked down her cheeks as she hugged him back, still unable to speak.

"Shh. I'm home now. Everything's going to be okay."

If only the day would come when she could believe his words. But she couldn't. They still had unfinished business with Gentry, and until that chapter in her life ended, she'd never truly feel in control.

He stroked her hair. "Tell me what's wrong, *bebé*."

Without another word, Damián guided her into the living room and sat down on the sofa then eased her onto his lap. Resting her head against his shoulder, she tried to let go of the fears threatening to engulf her as he stroked her arm and the side of her face reassuringly.

Tension and anxiety ebbed from her body. When he was with her, she felt safe. But he couldn't always be with her or able to protect her from every challenge. She'd have to take the stand and testify alone. Maybe she should consider doing a videotaped deposition after all.

He placed a kiss on her forehead. "Better?"

She took a deep breath and let it out. She couldn't lie to him.

"Talk to me, *querida*." His firm Dom voice removed any hope of putting him off or downplaying her anxiety.

"The DA called. A date has been set for Gentry's trial to begin."

"Good. That bastard doesn't stand a chance when you testify."

She shook her head. "No, you don't understand. The trial starts on the fifth of December."

"*This* December?"

She nodded. "Do you think Gentry pulled some strings with the judicial system to get the trial on the docket so quickly?" she asked.

"Where would he get any money to bribe judges now that your *maman's* money has been awarded to you?"

"You don't know him. Lyle must have put something aside for just such a contingency."

"That chickenshit Gibson copped a plea after Gentry's competency hearing. I'm sure the DA offered him a deal in exchange for his testimony against his old boss."

The thought of facing her former handler at the same trial made her stomach roil.

Why now?

"Did the DA say anything about the hard drive?"

She shook her head and let out a puff of air in frustration. But leave it to Damián to zero in so quickly on the other reason she freaked out today. "They've completed their search and analysis," she whispered.

His hand's movement faltered momentarily. "What did they find?"

She mentioned the obvious—videos of her liaisons with Gentry's clients, a second set of accounting books that might get him in trouble with the IRS, and an unsigned copy of the sex-slave contract. "She said there are…photos of my brand."

He cupped her chin until she met his gaze. "Whose brand?"

"Your brand, Sir. I'm your good girl." The words were almost rote now, yet she remained unsettled about the mark Gentry had left on her. She tried to glance away, but he held her focus with his intense Dom stare. "I know, Sir, but that's private and only between us. I won't share that, but I also don't want anyone to see that mark projected on the screen in the courtroom."

"Why would they want to show that to the jury? The defense wouldn't, because it won't help Gentry's case in any way to portray him as a sadistic bastard toward his own daughter. And the DA isn't going to exploit those early traumas, because they aren't pursuing charges about what he did to you as a child and young adult."

"That's not all that's on there. There are all those videos of me with those clients in the penthouse."

"What scares you most about that?"

"I stole the hard drive in the first place, hoping to protect you. I didn't want him to see you and fire you."

"Well, we know how that turned out," he said with a lopsided grin. He didn't seem to regret being fired in any way whatsoever, but that had led to his joining the Marines and losing his foot. She regretted that consequence. However, he'd helped her to see it wasn't her fault.

Damián leaned forward to place a tender kiss on her lips. "But I thank you, *querida*, for protecting me and having my back. Now, what scares you about the other videos?"

How could she admit this to him? She laid her head on his shoulder so he wouldn't notice how ashamed she was. "I'm sure…Gentry will…choose to show some of the videos of scenes in which I…"

She didn't want to say *came*. That was a term she used when she was with Damián to describe something beautiful. Not what those men forced from her.

"When you what?" Damián stroked her arm, coaxing the words out of her.

"Sometimes they did things to me that made my body respond in embarrassing ways."

"We've talked about that, too. Your body can respond to unwanted sexual stimulation. Doesn't mean you consented or wanted to be tortured or abused. Or that you mentally found any pleasure with them. What they did to you caused a natural physical response beyond your control."

Heat rose into her cheeks. "What if Gentry acts as his own attorney and shows those videos to paint me as a whore? And makes me watch his sick response to them? I don't think I can bear watching him get off on my humiliation."

"I don't think even Gentry would be that stupid, with or without an attorney's counsel. Besides, he's up on kidnapping charges. If he brings up your past, wouldn't he be opening up a can of worms he might not want to have brought up, namely the abuse and rape of his own daughter?"

What Damián said made sense, but Gentry didn't always use logic. "I just don't think I can stand the thought of him winning—not this time."

"Stop worrying. He won't see freedom for a very long time. If there's any justice left in this world, he'll never see freedom again."

Damián sounded so sure, but Gentry consistently managed to evade justice. If only he could be held accountable for the decade of child sexual abuse that began the night he'd killed her mother and John Grainger. Or for the year he'd trafficked her body against her will to his clients for their depraved sexual acts.

The DA chose not to file those charges, because she didn't think it would be as easy to prove them. However, finding the bodies of Maman and Grainger buried on Gentry's property would be difficult for him to explain away. Her mother's and John Grainger's deaths needed to be avenged, and Savannah was the best person to do it.

But what if I can't get it done?

Damián stroked her belly in gentle, circular motions. "Working yourself up about the trial is only going to cause you and the baby distress."

"I know. I've been spending time every day meditating and journaling to center myself. I want to stay healthy and strong enough to be there to testify, provided Doctor Palmer says it's okay for me to travel safely."

The thought that *she* might not be there to testify set her heart to racing again, and tears stung her eyes. But if she went, would Gentry find a way to torture her and exert his control over her life again?

He was doing an effective job of it even from a thousand miles away and behind bars. Her hand covered his momentarily before sliding onto her belly protectively. Did Gentry know she carried another of Damián's babies? He couldn't. Could he? She shuddered at the thought of him doing anything to hurt her baby.

"No doubt Gentry thinks he's going to beat this rap," she whispered, "because he's gotten away with every evil thing he's ever done."

"Let's not worry about what might never happen and focus more on what we know will. Like you having to testify for the prosecution and being cross-examined by the defense if you choose to be at the trial."

She stiffened as she tried to imagine what the trial experience would be like. Facing Gentry and all those strangers—

"Breathe, *savita*."

Savannah took a ragged breath. "How can I be sure what I say will be enough to convict him?" His hand stroked her belly as if to calm the baby and Savannah.

"You're one big piece of the puzzle, *querida*, but remember that the DA has forensic evidence to be presented by others for the murders. It'll be impossible for the jury to find him anything but guilty on all counts."

"You make compelling arguments, but the thought of having him outside prison walking free in this world again makes me sick." She swallowed hard to keep from losing her lunch all over Damián's lap.

"Don't worry, *bebé*. He's not going to get away with it this time."

Please, God, let Damián be right.

But he was definitely right about one thing. She'd never forgive herself if she didn't do everything in her power to make sure he'd be found guilty.

* * *

Damián needed to do something to take her mind off the trial. He hadn't noticed she'd been stressing about it until that phone call had rattled her.

Savannah shuddered against his shoulder. That settled it. Damián took her by the upper arms, pulling her upright and staring directly into her eyes. "We can work on ways to prepare you for the trial, but I won't let you jeopardize your health or the baby's by going to California if there's even a chance you might have problems. You'll be nearly eight months along by then."

"You know I would never do anything without thinking of the baby first." She tried to avoid his gaze, but he held hers by sheer will. A spark of defiance flashed. "But I can't let him get away with what he's done. This might be my only chance to bring him to justice."

"He's never going to harm you again. I'll take him out myself this time if he so much as tries to come near you." He realized he'd probably said more than he should. She knew nothing about what he and Dad had done to the bastard and Lyle Gibson after Savannah was taken to the hospital following her kidnapping—and he didn't want her to hear about it now, either.

"But Karla talked Doctor Palmer into letting her attend our wedding in Solana Beach, and they thought she carried twins at the time."

"It'll still be the doctor's call," he repeated.

She nodded. "You have my word that I'll only go with Doctor Palmer's approval."

He needed to make sure the trip and the stress of the trial wouldn't cause harm to their baby. Savannah seemed conflicted about being there, though, and he doubted it was entirely because of the baby. Her fears were two-fold. She was committed to ensuring justice was served but worried about what type of impact the stress of this process would have on the baby. But what if the doctor gave her the go-ahead? Would her fear of facing that monster paralyze her into using her pregnancy as an excuse? And would that leave her with lifelong regrets? He wanted her to have closure and put this behind her so they could live the life they deserved.

"Oh!" Her eyes opened wider before she smiled.

Damián felt the baby kick his hand at the same time and stroked her more firmly. "Baby Orlando agrees." Leaning down to her belly, he added, "There, there. Don't worry, little one. We're going to take good care of you before, during, and after your birth."

Savannah drew a deep breath, and the baby seemed to calm. He needed to get some advice from Dad about how he might best work on Savannah's issues with focusing and staying in the moment. Then he could help prepare her to withstand whatever they might throw at her during the trial. Maybe he'd find an opportunity to talk with Dad alone soon. Dad might know of some ways Damián could increase perceived pain levels without him actually getting as physical as he used to with Savannah.

Savannah was the strongest person he knew. She'd found the courage to escape her prison and her abusers when she'd discovered she was pregnant with Marisol. Father Martine and Anita had provided her with a refuge. And yet, for the next eight years, she hadn't stopped looking over her shoulder, fearing her abusers would find her at every turn. Thank God she'd run to Damián last December. Who knew what Gentry and Gibson would have done if they'd caught them. Damián shuddered to think of a life in which he never knew Marisol or married Savannah.

Worse yet, he couldn't imagine missing out on the opportunity to create another life with Savannah and to be there through it all. She carried his child—again. Only this time, he'd had a major role in her pregnancy beyond conception. While he'd seen lots of photographs of Savannah's first pregnancy and Marisol's birth and early years, to be a part of *this* baby's life from the get-go had been incredible. He didn't intend to miss a minute of it.

"We'll decide when it's closer to the trial date, after talking with Doc Palmer, of course." Damián pressed her head against his shoulder again, stroking her arm in soothing motions. Her body relaxed as they cuddled together. Her body grew heavy, and he wondered if she was drifting off to sleep when he realized the house was awfully quiet. "Where's Marisol?"

"Adam and Karla's. She wanted to help with the babies again. I hope she's at least helping."

Damián grinned. "Karla certainly has her hands full. I can't imagine dealing with triplets." His hand caressed her belly in rhythmic circles. "But we would welcome however many babies we were blessed with."

"I agree. But one at a time would be a lot easier." She was quiet a moment, then said, "Soup's in the slow cooker. I told Karla I'd bring it and the tortilla chips over at dinnertime since I had the afternoon off. We can all eat together before bringing Mari home."

"Everyone loves your tortilla soup." He did appreciate the time she spent in the kitchen, having never been one to cook much for himself. But with the few hours alone they now had, he wanted to cook up something different with his wife.

He'd found many creative ways to accommodate his wife's developing carnal desires in safe, obstetrician-approved ways. In fact, Doctor Palmer insisted they continue a healthy sex life knowing it would help alleviate Savannah's anxiety, which wasn't good for her or the baby.

His hand crept upward until he cupped her breast. "So," he dragged the word out as his thumb and finger pinched her nipple through her blouse, "that means we have a couple hours to ourselves, *querida*."

He knew just the thing to take her mind off her worries.

"We have at least two hours. I think there's a load of wash in the dryer to be sorted and folded, if you'd like to join me."

His hand ventured up to her chin, and he tilted her head until their gazes connected. "Tease." Her pupils dilated before his eyes. "That's not the kind of activity I have in mind for you, *savita*, and you know it. Unless you've come up with some new fantasy involving you on top of our new washing machine during its turbo-spin cycle—with my tongue pressing against your hot little clit until you scream your release."

Her breath hitched as she imagined the fantasy he'd just planted in her head. "Hmm," she said with a smile, as if contemplating his suggestion. "I hadn't considered that one—yet. So many fantasies, so little time."

Chapter Two

Savannah's heart skipped a beat in anticipation. Damián had been working on her for months to strengthen her skills at fantasizing, beginning with her journal exercises and now conjuring up forbidden, risqué scenarios each night after they tucked Mari in bed. While there was a lock on their door that they used often, they had also been blessed with a child who slept well at night.

Thank God Mari's life had been relatively trauma-free, unlike her mother's.

Damián's hand cupped her breast and pinched her nipple, grounding her once more as her body responded to his touch immediately. The buds bunching, stomach flip-flopping, lungs constricting. He always left her wanting—no, needing—so much more.

In her first trimester, she'd have screamed bloody murder if he'd squeezed them that hard, but as her pregnancy neared the end of its second trimester, she found them to be sensitive but not painful.

Or perhaps she'd learned to enjoy the pain more. Damián knew just how much she could take, although he also liked to push the envelope a little further each time.

"If you weren't so pregnant, I'd take you into the laundry room right now to try that out." He leaned forward, lowering his voice. "But instead, I'm thinking we'll continue this in the bedroom." His whispered promise sent a thrill through her as he placed a firm kiss on her lips.

Focus. Her clit throbbed. She still stumbled over words like clit, even in her thoughts. But she'd stopped hiding behind euphemisms like *chiquita* to refer to her...pussy...after Mari chose to name their new puppy Chiquita. Chico, the silly name Damián had given his penis, had gone by the wayside as well. But they'd served their purpose in helping her through her aversion to talking about her genitalia.

Her entire body craved intimacy. Savannah had never been hornier than during this pregnancy. Hormones might be the culprit, although she decided having Damián in her life made the biggest difference. She'd been so shut down, physically and emotionally, during Mari's pregnancy and hadn't wanted anything to do with sex or men back then.

Damián was the only man she'd ever wished to be intimate with. From their first visit to her cave at Thousand Steps Beach to today. Only Damián. The beach cave held a special place in her heart for many reasons, the most important of which was that both of her children were conceived there.

Damián, solid and protective, had opened up a world of sexual delights to her that he promised they'd only just begun to explore. They still had to maneuver around her hang-ups and triggers, but she trusted him more each day. She wanted to say she'd reached the point where she believed he'd stay with her one-hundred percent, but her insecurities still got the best of her at times. Still, he'd shown his love and commitment to her despite monumental sexual inhibitions resulting from so many years of sexual abuse at the hands of Gentry and his business clients. That said a lot about his capacity for patience and love.

Damián grabbed her hair and pulled her head back to open her mouth wider before his tongue plunged inside, demanding her complete attention once more. Why was she having so much trouble focusing today? He fueled the flames inside her into a raging inferno, sending Savannah to her submissive place in seconds. She loved when Damián took control of her. His dominance made her feel safe—free to explore her sexual self in ways she'd never imagined even a year ago.

Damián pulled away, smiling. She stared up at him numbly, automatically licking his taste from her lips as she struggled to keep from allowing her thoughts to stray again.

"Take a bathroom break then meet me in the bedroom."

Blinking back to awareness, she rose to her feet with his help. Savannah couldn't wait to find out what he had in mind as she hurried to the hallway powder room, not wanting to waste a second. Undoubtedly, whatever he came up with would take her mind off the trial and everything else, at least for a little while.

Coming out of the bathroom, she walked upstairs to join him in their bedroom. Seeing Damián silhouetted against the window in his leather pants—bare chested, hands on hips—set her heart racing. All she could think about now was what her Dom, her husband, her lover wanted to do to her. She awaited his instructions, but didn't have long to wait.

"Tell me what you *have* been fantasizing about today, *savita*."

She drew a deep breath. "I'm in my bedroom, undressing in front of the window." She let today's fantasy fill her mind again, one she'd played with since leaving the clinic. She hadn't completely fleshed it out yet, the phone call having derailed her earlier.

Slap!

The sting of his bare hand against her butt spurred her to focus and begin the scene.

Ahem. "What happens next, *bebé*?" he asked.

Hearing him clear his throat, she regained her focus, frustrated that she was so uncentered today. While it still embarrassed her to share her fantasies aloud with him, she couldn't deny his direct question. If she kept delaying, she'd be disciplined—not harshly, but she hated disappointing her Dom. However, she'd always be much harder on herself than Damián could ever be.

"I glance down at the neighbor's driveway where I see the Harley Fat Boy parked." She smiled. "I haven't been able to resist a man on a Harley since I was nineteen."

"Stand in front of the window, facing out." The sheers were drawn, so their new neighbors wouldn't be able to see anything.

Damián went to the closet to retrieve his toy bag. Her breathing became shallow with her growing excitement as she heard him set the bag on the mattress.

She waited, listening as he rummaged through his toy bag for whatever he intended to play with as they acted out this afternoon's fantasy. *Plink-plink-plink.* Plastic clothespins? They'd long since replaced wooden ones for the stronger plastic ones in her ever-increasing need to experience higher levels of pain. He still used the wooden ones in conjunction with his bullwhip, but he definitely didn't have room to throw a whip in their bedroom.

No doubt, he'd save that pleasure for a session at the Masters at Arms Club. Nothing could obliterate the world for her better than her Dom and his whip. But tonight, they had dinner plans at the Montagues.

He stood in front of her and placed a sleep mask over her head. Having her sight blocked still scared her a bit, but she'd come to trust Damián. She took a slow, calming breath as he'd told her to do so many times before when something frightened her and grounded herself deeply into the scene about to play out.

"That's my good girl."

I'm Damián's good girl.

He returned to the bed behind her, and she could hear him going through the toy bag again.

The swoosh of the cane slashed through the air, which brought her back to the moment in a hurry. Not her favorite implement, but Damián controlled what he wanted to play with now. An over-the-knee spanking wasn't possible at this stage in her pregnancy, but nothing would prohibit him from swinging a cane at her ass, albeit not as hard as he might have five or six months ago.

Yes, it would sting like the devil, but it also would provide her with the catharsis she needed today. Her stress over the earlier phone call completely dissipated, though, just thinking about it.

Focus.

"Remove your pants, *savita*..."—his voice came from her left—"as you continue to describe your fantasy."

Without her having to ask, he stepped to her side and guided her hand to his shoulder to steady her as she kicked off her slippers. Smiling, she shimmied her slacks down one leg at a time, careful not to touch her panties. She'd learned the hard way to only go as far as he specifically commanded her to do.

The smell of leather assailed her nostrils a second before he pressed something hard against her chin and firmly tilted her head backward. The crop? Or the handle of a tawse perhaps? A shiver went through her. They both delivered their own delicious level of pain.

"Remove your blouse slowly as you imagine him staring at you through the window."

A brief smile crossed her lips as she began undoing the top button of her blouse to merge fantasy with reality, feeling only Damián's eyes on her. She loved showing off her breasts to him now, because they were so much larger than they'd been at any time she'd been with him. He'd always loved her breasts, although lately he'd become equally fixated on her belly.

Her fingers paused on the third button as she remembered he liked to hear what fantasy was playing out in her head. "I wonder if I'm being watched by the mysterious Latino who moved in a week ago." In her mind, he was none other than Damián. She slipped the button from its hole. "Of course, I'm not pregnant in this fantasy. Not even married yet."

The sound of the curtains opening froze her fingers before she could undo the last button. She swallowed hard. The house next door actually was occupied by three college-aged boys attending the University of Denver, judging by their sweatshirts. What if one actually *was* watching her undressing now?

In the past, Damián had only required her to do "public" scenes at the club, surrounded by the owners and their subs. Never from their bedroom window. Of course, she still wore her blouse and panties.

She wasn't surprised that undressing in front of the open window made her uncomfortable, because it brought back memories of being on display for Gentry's business clients. But this was her fantasy. She'd merely have to find ways to control where her mind went and her reaction to it.

Besides, the cool air on her belly, visibly swollen with Damián's baby, assured her that no other man would find her sexy enough to take a peek.

"What's going on in my naughty girl's mind?" he whispered as he nuzzled her ear, sending a shiver down her spine. "Spare me no details."

Pulling herself together, she remembered her discipline and who she was doing this for.

Damián.

"I open my blouse to reveal my bra, and my neighbor's hand moves to stroke his crotch." Her panties grew damp as she spread open the panels of her blouse. "I can see a huge bulge."

Soon she'd reap the rewards of this slow tease with the bulge she imagined inside Damián's leathers right now. She couldn't wait.

*   *   *

Damián caught the telltale hitch in her breathing that signaled her surrender. It had taken her longer today than usual, probably because of the state of mind he'd found her in when he'd gotten home. But this was lightning fast compared to the struggles for her to let go even four or five months ago.

He tossed the crop onto the bed and unhooked the tawse from his belt carabiner before standing beside her. He admired her swollen belly, wanting to stroke it, but they hadn't moved that far in this fantasy yet.

Savannah's face glowed now, just the way people always said a pregnant woman's face did.

Until this afternoon.

He took a deep breath of his own to keep from letting his emotions get the better of him. Fucking Gentry would pay for everything he'd done to harm his sweet Savannah. Right now, though, Damián's job as her Dom was to take away any thoughts of that *cabrón.* To achieve that, he needed to maintain his focus on her and this scene.

Don't waste this bonus bedroom time together.

To help them both stay focused, he smacked her ass cheek with the tawse. Damn, he'd never grow tired of that sound. Both cheeks would soon be red, which brought a smile to his face.

"I asked you to continue describing your fantasy, *savita*," he reminded her.

The hand-tooled leather toy he'd made himself delivered maximum pain with minimal impact, which was perfect during her pregnancy. Taking her to her pain limit would help her forget about the phone call and everything but him and what he was doing to her body.

"Y-yes, Sir. Well, m-my new neighbor is quite handsome and totally ripped." Her shoulders relaxed again as she wrapped herself in her fantasy. "Rich, brown skin, a neatly trimmed goatee, and long, black hair pulled into a ponytail streaming halfway down his back. He usually wears leather pants and a jacket with the Harley Davidson logo on it."

"Sounds familiar." He smiled, self-satisfied that he held the starring role in her fantasy. Perhaps he should carry this scenario a little farther and turn it into a role-play.

"*Madre de Dios*, I can't take my eyes off this beautiful *chica* undressing in front of her window. How did I get so lucky as to move into this neighborhood and find the woman of my dreams next door?" He couldn't resist adding, "That she doesn't close her curtains concerns me, though. Perhaps I should go have a talk with her about privacy and personal safety."

Savannah inhaled deeply before picking up where she'd left off. "Suddenly self-conscious, I close the curtains." She smiled as she moved to do just that, probably thinking she'd outsmarted him, but he halted her wrist with a slap of the tawse.

"Hands at your side," he commanded. After she assumed the position, he continued. "This woman's high, firm breasts inflame me. I must remove that bra and touch them, lick her nipples." Damián paused several moments then knocked on the wall. "My dick throbs as I wait for her to answer her door."

Savannah cocked her head slightly but held her arms still. "Who could that be at this hour? I walk down the stairs to the front door, check through the peephole, and see it's my hot neighbor. I open it." She made a door creaking noise and gasped for dramatic effect. "What are you doing here? His gaze roams down my body before slowly rising to look into my eyes once more." Her breathing grew more shallow and rapid. "I find myself becoming…wet as I take in his muscular, near-perfect body and ask, 'How may I help you?'"

Always so fucking refined. He hoped to cut through to her earthy core soon. "*Chica,* it is I who has come to help you."

Her eyebrows rose above the blindfold as she cocked her head slightly.

"*Sí*. I am quite concerned that you are exposing yourself to me and the rest of the neighborhood from your bedroom window. That isn't very wise in this day and age. You never know who might be looking in."

"Are you a peeping Tom?"

"I would hardly be a man if I did not want to drink in your beauty."

"Well, thank you for pointing out the error of my ways. I'll be sure to close the curtains next time."

"What is your name?"

"Savannah. But I don't know your name."

"You can call me Sir." He continued, "Is there a man in your life to take you in hand and guide you, Savannah?"

She lifted her chin up. "I am a professional woman and don't need a man for anything. I can take care of myself."

His mind flashed back to when he'd first found her again, working at the clinic in Solana Beach where he'd taken Teresa for treatment after she'd been raped by her father. Savannah had had to fend for herself for so long.

He reined in his own errant thoughts. "I am sure you can. But I could also make your body burn with an internal fire that would leave you consumed, a fire that could only be quenched by me."

"I don't know. We've only just met."

"Ah, but I know you. I've been watching you through your bedroom window for almost a week now. In fact, I know you quite intimately, even though this is the first time we've met."

Again, he heard that hitch in her breathing as excitement kicked up another notch for her. "I have a confession to make, Sir."

"What is that?"

"I knew you were watching me. Our bedroom windows face each other. It wasn't prudent for me to undress in front of that window—in front of you—but I did so anyway. Every night, I hear your Harley pull into your drive and know that, within fifteen minutes, you're going to be stripping off your clothes and heading to the shower."

"I see. Well, I guess you've seen a lot of me, too."

She nibbled her lower lip as if wondering if she should say something else.

"What are you thinking, *querida?*"

"That I'd love for you to…take me for a ride sometime."

He drew a fingertip from her earlobe across her cheek and down her neck, stopping short of her breast and admiring the trail of gooseflesh he left in his wake. "You'd like to warm the back of my bike, little one?"

She pursed her lips into a pout, and it was all he could do not to bend down and kiss her before moving this to the bed. "Among other places, Sir."

He grinned. "Then, by all means, we'll have to take the hog out together sometime." Was Savannah missing their rides? She hadn't been on his hog since her first trimester, mostly because he refused to let her due to safety reasons. But they'd get back out there again when the doc gave her okay after the birth of the baby.

"I'd like that, Sir."

"There's something you should know about me before we go any further."

"Yes, Sir?" She swallowed hard, nibbling her lower lip in a teasing sort of way.

Muy caliente. "I like my women submissive. As in totally surrendering to my authority."

She tilted her chin up. "I'm strong-willed and independent. I'm not sure I can submit to any man."

"But haven't you ever wanted to let a man take away the burdens of your day and pamper you?" His voice had grown husky as he became more turned-on.

"Every working woman I know fantasizes about that. But that's only temporary submission—and this isn't a fantasy."

"Isn't it?" His finger trailed up to her shoulder and down her bicep and forearm. "Place your hands at the small of your back, but if you feel any tingling or discomfort, tell me. It is my responsibility to keep you safe." He waited until she complied. "What's your most deeply hidden fantasy…something so taboo you have hardly admitted it to yourself, Savannah?"

"I'm curious about…"

"Yes?"

"Having sex on the back of your bike."

His dick jerked against his zipper. "That sounds fucking hot. I'd totally reward my good girl with anything she desired."

"What if I'm naughty?"

"I'd discipline you when needed. If you consented to a Dom/sub relationship, of course." A pink flush crept from her neck into her cheeks. "Breathe, *savita*," he whispered.

"I've never allowed a man to take charge of me to that extent." Again, her defiant little chin poked out. "I'm *not* submissive," she reiterated in a breathy voice with much less conviction.

"But I am a Dom, and I strongly suspect you have a submissive streak. I'm not interested in a vanilla relationship, so we would negotiate. Can you entrust your body into my care, Savannah?"

Any residual tension released from her, and she smiled. "I can try."

"Thank you. That's all I ask. Now, remove your blouse." With only a slight hesitation, she let it slide down her arms, leaving her in only a bra and panties. He stepped closer, his chest brushing her shoulder blades as he wrapped his arms around her, sliding his hands below her belly as he nuzzled her neck. "Because someone needs to correct this wanton behavior of yours before you get hurt flashing the wrong man."

"I leave my training in your hands, Sir."

He moved his free hand up to her breast and squeezed before sliding the tawse down her side and around the back to slap against her ass, bringing the blood to the surface in both cheeks. Her little gasp made him smile. He liked catching her off guard.

"Why don't we continue this in your bedroom?" He whispered in her ear.

"Sounds perfect."

To cut to the chase, rather than parade her around the room pretending to walk to her bedroom, he turned her so that her back was to the window now. "Nice room you have."

"Thank you. What would you like me to do, Sir?"

"Stand just as you are, and let me look at you." *Look?* Who was he kidding? He positioned himself behind her, cupping one breast as he pinched her nipple through her bra. She moaned, letting her head tilt backward and sucking in a breath as he squeezed harder.

"*Ay, güey.*"

"Translation, please, Sir?"

"Roughly, *Oh, man.*"

"Ah. I love your Mexican colloquialisms. They sound exotic and sexy as hell. But, Sir, I've been waiting for *you* all week."

"You don't know how I've longed to do this for days now." He gave her nipple one last pinch. "I need to see more of you, *savita.*" His little Savi. "Remove your panties." He stepped around her to watch from her side. How had her fantasy world gotten him so hot, so fast? They made love almost every night, so it wasn't like he'd been deprived. Perhaps he enjoyed the idea of another man admiring his woman—as long as Damián was the only one reaping the rewards and it was pure fantasy.

"Yes, Sir." With a shaky breath, she slipped her panties down her legs and stepped out of them.

Damián's gaze zeroed in on the curve of her gorgeous ass. He shifted to ease the ache in his pants as his dick continued to strain against his leathers. He'd never grow tired of her body.

Grinning, he closed the gap between them again while placing the tawse back on the carabiner. He released the bra hooks and slid the straps down her arms before tossing it on the opposite side of the bed. Slipping his hands around her, he cupped her heavy tits and squeezed her nipples, pressing his cock against her ass, until she moaned. She so loved pain.

"I need to remember that I'm not pregnant in this fantasy," she said, coming out of the fantasy.

"Focus, *querida.*" Savannah took a deep breath to ground herself again. "It's mind over matter." He leaned closer, inhaling her scent and trailing kisses along the slim column of her neck.

"You smell good enough to eat."

"I think that could be arranged." When he broke contact with her, her lips were pressed together as she fought back a grin.

Perhaps a little fantasy within a fantasy. "Even now, I can feel my tongue circling the folds of your clit, lapping at the juices flowing from your sweet pussy as you lie over the seat of my Harley with your ass in the air."

She opened her mouth to draw in more air. "What kind of spell have you cast on me, Sir? You make me so hot thinking about what you plan to do to my ass. And I'm not the kind of girl who invites strange men into her house."

Her sexy mix of teasing temptress and reluctant virgin had him teetering on the brink of sanity. Time to take charge if he wanted to last long enough to give her the release her body sought. While orgasms weren't the goal in this afternoon's session, he knew what would take her mind off her problems.

"Which reminds me. I came over here to talk with you about endangering your safety in front of your bedroom window. You might not be so fortunate as to find someone like me watching you next time. That is a behavior I would like to correct. Now." He unhooked the tawse again and let it skim over her round ass. "Give your Dom your prettiest presentation pose, *savita*."

Without hesitation, she spread her legs to where her ankles were even with her shoulders and clasped her hands at the small of her back. She held her head high and straight. He couldn't see her eyes, but if she hadn't been blindfolded, no doubt they would have been cast downward. He walked around her, admiring every inch of her beautiful body.

"Lovely. Now, naughty girl, tell me if there have been any other lapses in judgment or behavior that might require the attention of your newfound Dom."

"I masturbated last night, thinking of you standing beside my bed and watching."

Since he'd been in bed with her the entire night, this was still part of her fantasy. His dick pressed against his leathers as he remembered the times he'd watched her masturbate, all the way back to that first time when he'd had to tie her to the gyno table at the club. "Masturbation itself isn't a problem, and I wasn't your Dom last night."

"But it felt naughty to be doing something against my upbringing."

"Fair enough. From now on, this is *my* pussy"—he cupped and squeezed her mound—"and you are not to touch it without my permission."

"Yes, Sir."

"Anything else I need to be aware of?"

She bit the inside of her lower lip, and her brow furrowed as she considered her response. "Nothing that I can think of."

As naughty girls went, she had a long way to go. But he wasn't meting out a true punishment.

"What do you feel would be a fit punishment for these lapses?"

"I need a strong Dom to provide discipline so that I can improve my behavior."

"Sí, *you do*." This would only be a disciplinary spanking in their fantasy. *Mierda*, he could remember a time when she'd have avoided pain at all costs, but now her body craved and welcomed it.

"I need to be spanked, Sir. With your tawse, if you like."

He slapped the implement against the palm of his hand and smiled when she jumped. "It's time for your punishment, *savita*."

Chapter Three

S avannah's heart pounded as she waited for Damián to position her for her punishment. Would he use the tawse as she suggested? The anticipation was killing her. She needed to feel the delicious bite of that or some other toy. Psychologically, she knew her love of pain had come from years of conditioning by Gentry and Lyle, but Damián had turned something sordid and humiliating into an intimate, sensual act between the two of them that totally set off every ounce of pleasure her body could muster.

He walked around her, occasionally slapping the three hard, leather strips against his hand or leathers. The first few slaps made her jump. "Each time you change your position or fail to obey, there will be consequences. *¿Comprendes?*"

"Yes, Sir."

"Now, Savannah, tell me why you're being disciplined."

"I put myself in danger by exposing myself to someone I didn't know."

"Are we forgetting something?"

"Oh, *Sir*! I'm sorry, Sir!" While she was a rookie in this fantasy, she couldn't believe she'd forgotten to address him the way she did during their playtimes.

"And I also was pleasuring myself. It's been so long since I've invited a man into my—" Without warning, a half-second after she felt the heat of his body on her breast, he sucked one tender nipple inside his mouth while pinching the other. "Oh, God, yes!" Her womb clenched in anticipation, and her knees nearly buckled with need. She clamped her hands around his ears to hold him in place.

Suddenly, his teeth and hand released her. "What happened to the pretty pose you're supposed to be giving me?"

She quickly returned her hands to the small of her back and positioned her shoulders so that her breasts would be completely accessible to him again, but she no longer felt the heat of his body. A sense of loss overtook her, bringing a sting to her eyes. She bit into her lower lip as she waited for him to touch her nipples again.

He hadn't used nipple clamps on her since she'd discovered she was pregnant, because her breasts had been hypersensitive. She wished he would today, though. Perhaps if he chose the tweezer type and didn't tighten them overly much, she'd find heightened pleasure and release. But first he would have to deal with her inability to hold her position despite distraction, something else they'd been working on. Focus.

"Ow!"

The tips of the stiff leather rhythmically struck her nipples, slowly at first then faster. Savannah flinched, but this time held her position. She couldn't catch her breath as the tawse swiped across her nipples dozens of times, stinging more than when he used a flogger on them, the sensation more intense than his tongue and fingers. Jolts of pain shot up her chest and neck. Faster, they came. When her chest expanded with her inhalations, he sometimes hit her areola or the fleshy part of her breast instead, but his precision with this toy was as accurate as with the whip. He probably landed each strike exactly where he intended.

All too soon, the barrage of slaps against her nipples and breasts came to a halt, and she drew a deep breath to prepare for what was to come.

"Thank you for disciplining me, Sir."

He chuckled. "Who said that was part of your punishment? I just enjoy watching your nipples engorge when stimulated."

Her sex grew wet thinking there was more to come.

"However, your break in protocol will require added discipline."

"Yes, Sir." Her nipples burned from the tawse, and her chest heaved as she tried to control her breathing.

"I know you were caught up in the moment and are new to this, though, so I'll go easy on you. Fifteen strokes for all offenses up to now."

Only fifteen? Would that be enough?

"You will count and thank me for each one."

Anticipation warred with a bit of trepidation. She loved the feeling after the endorphins hit, but always was a little nervous just before the beginning. After all, it did hurt! And Damián could make that leather toy sting far worse than the whip. From experience, the initial slaps would be the worst, but then she would be transported to the place of euphoria she needed to be in right now.

Don't go back there.

"Because you're so fond of my Harley, I want to bend you over the bed to deliver your blows. You're to imagine yourself bending over the seat of my Harley."

Oh dear Lord. Just the thought of fulfilling that fantasy nearly made her come.

He wrapped his arm around her back to lead her toward the four-poster bed. A couple of months ago, Damián had added a second mattress on top of the box springs making the bed the perfect height for their new favorite position—her bent over the bed—perfect for this stage in her pregnancy. But she hadn't realized it was the perfect height to imitate his Harley during her fantasy.

"Bend forward at the hips."

One hand cradled her breast as the tawse pressed into her upper back, and she leaned toward what she expected would be the mattress. Her head came down on a pillow, but she could smell leather nearby, reminding her of the Harley seat. In her mind's eye, she was totally in the garage bent over his bike.

"Hands at the side of your head. Grip the bike's seat and prepare for your punishment, my naughty Princess Slut." His voice came from behind her, delivering her favorite endearment when they played. Anxious to feel the sting, she complied quickly, pretending the pillow was the bike's seat.

His terse commands helped settle any remaining nerves. The tawse lightly tapped the backs of her thighs. He lightly smacked both ass cheeks with his hand a few times to bring the blood to the surface. "*Muy caliente, savita.*"

She held her breath, waiting. Waiting. When was he going to start? Suddenly, he laid it across both cheeks.

"Ow!" The force of the sturdy blow took her breath away, but when she could think again, she smiled. Fifteen like that, and she'd be right where she wanted to be in no time.

"Is that how you count and thank me, *savita?*"

"No, Sir! One, Sir. And thank you!"

His next slap landed on her upper thighs near where her ass met, a sweet spot for delivering maximum pain. She hissed upon impact, although it wasn't delivered as hard as the first one had been. "Two. Thank you, Sir."

For the next two, he placed one resounding crack on each cheek. Her hands gripped the pillow, and he paused after her next thank you to squeeze her cheeks, intensifying the pain.

"Oh, God! Yes!"

His fingers easily slipped between her folds. "So wet for me."

Only for you.

Still eleven blows to go. He landed the tawse loudly over her upper thighs again, much harder this time.

She screamed as the pain shot down her legs and up into her butt. "Five! Thank you, Sir."

The leather toy gently stroked her ass and thighs, eliciting a moan from her. Before she could prepare herself to continue, the leather lifted away from her skin and impacted both butt cheeks. The pain receded more quickly now.

"Six, Sir. Thanks."

While she heard herself counting out and thanking him for the next three, her mind began to drift. She was aware of Damián—his body, his words, his tawse—but nothing else mattered as she started to float and feel...*bliss.*

*   *   *

Damián's cock nearly sprang from his pants looking at her reddened ass and thighs. Too bad this wouldn't end with him burying himself inside her wet pussy. He paused a moment to regain his focus. He leaned over her and slid the sleep mask up to her forehead so he could assess her current state. She blinked her eyes open, staring blindly at him with a dreamy smile on her face. When he moved his hand, though, she still tracked him. Not quite there yet. But close. It took so little for her these days, her trust in him had become that deep.

"That's it, *bebé*. Float for me." He brushed her lips lightly with his and returned to his strike zone to take her the rest of the way home. He intended to deliver the remaining six strokes with lessening force. Just enough to reach subspace.

After three more strokes, she whispered, "Number twelve. Thank you…Sir." He suspected she was deep in subspace by that point.

"Spread your legs for me, *savita*."

She followed his command without hesitation. *A little eager, maybe?* He took the stiff leather and sawed the edge back and forth along her pussy's crack, eliciting a long moan followed by a hiss when he wiggled the leather against her clit.

"You do not have permission to come."

With only a slight delay, she said, "I won't, Sir."

Wanting to take her the rest of the way on his own, he slapped the tawse against her pussy with a loud thwack.

Savannah didn't scream but drew a deep, sucking breath. She did so love pain. And he loved that it distracted her.

"Are we forgetting something?"

She was probably close to forgetting her name at this point, but still managed to squeak out, "Thirteen. Thank you."

Damián decided to excuse her lapse in using his title this time. He delivered another blow to her pussy, making sure the strips of leather in the tawse impacted her mound and clit hood. This time, she screamed, "Son of a bitch!" After breathing rapidly a few moments, clenching her fists into the pillow, she added, "I mean, Fourteen, Sir. Thank you."

Savannah rarely cussed. He had her at her most primal self now. For the final blow, he raised his arm and delivered it down the crack of her ass, no doubt giving her asshole a jolt she felt to her core.

"Oh, yesss! Fifteen. Thank you, Sir." He wasn't sure if her excitement was because the spanking was over or because of the sensation, but didn't care to explore that right now.

Setting the tawse on the steam trunk at the foot of the bed, he removed the blindfold. "Ready, Savannah?"

Savannah moaned, keeping her eyelids closed. "Eyes, *savita.*" She blinked several times, disoriented and unfocused, lost halfway between reality and euphoria. Pupils dilated evenly. Not tracking. Hell, yeah, definitely in subspace.

He pinched both nipples dangling temptingly unsupported at the edge of the mattress, smiling when she winced.

"You are mine and mine alone, *savita.* Your body. Your heart. And your mind."

"Yes. All yours, Sir," she mumbled, her eyelids half-closed.

Worried she might dehydrate after such an intense session, he went to the nightstand to retrieve a water bottle and held it to her lips until she finished half of it. Then he guided her toward their aftercare chair, bringing the bottle with them. After settling himself first, he took her hand and tugged her gently onto his lap and covered her with an afghan her friend and mentor, Anita, had made for them as a wedding gift.

Savannah rested her cheek against his shoulder with a sigh, and he placed his chin on her head, holding her tight in the circle of his arms. He'd let her float a while before they finished with two much-needed orgasms.

His mind wandered to the upcoming trial and what he'd need to do to prepare Savannah to face the monster from her past. While Damián would be present in the courtroom, she'd have to leave his side at some point and take the stand. He anticipated a churning up of brutal memories for her as the trial grew closer, erasing all the progress he'd made with her this year. If he could have done anything over, he'd have shot the bastard when they rescued Savannah last March. Then she would never have had to face him again.

But if Gentry did anything to hurt her, their unborn baby, or Marisol, he'd find a way to take him out and rid the world of the *cabrón* once and for all time.

Savannah moaned, and he stroked her arm to soothe away any thoughts that might intrude upon her euphoria. She was an empathetic, sensitive person and might be feeling his own tension right now.

She sighed and relaxed against him again. "That's it, *bebé*. Just float. I have you."

Savannah, Marisol, and the baby were his whole life. He'd protect them no matter what so that nothing bad happened to them ever again.

A half-hour stretched to an hour, and still Savannah was lost in her space. Chances of them having sex before heading to Dad's were nil, but they had tonight. And a lifetime more of days and nights to enjoy each other's bodies.

After an hour, though, he decided he ought to bring her back out of it so she would be able to function tonight. She often described the state she was in as being drunk without any alcohol. And she sometimes acted a little drunk, too. He'd stay closer to her the next few days to watch for subdrop, but the slower she came down from the high, the less likely she'd have trouble. And if she did, they both knew what needed to be done—lots of cuddles, a little chocolate, and a few mind-blowing orgasms.

All doable.

"Sir?"

"Yeah, *bebé*. I'm here."

"That was incredible. I can't believe how fast I got there. I didn't think we'd make it with only fifteen."

"That's because you trusted me enough to let go, knowing you were safe. I'll always protect you, *querida*."

"I know you will." Her long pause made him wonder if she believed him. Then she glanced over at the window where this bedroom fantasy had taken shape. Her eyes opened wider when she saw that the curtains had never been opened. "Why, you—and here I thought I was displaying my naked body for all the neighborhood to see."

He chuckled. "I don't share what's mine. Oh, I might put you on display on occasion before my friends at the club, but they know you're off limits and wouldn't overstep. I have no clue about those horny teenage boys next door."

She smiled up at him. "Why don't we go to bed for the rest of the afternoon? I want you to feel as amazing as I do." She started to lift herself off his chest, but he held her tighter.

"No, *savita*. In this moment, nothing will satisfy me more than to sit here and hold you. Besides, we need to head to Dad and Karla's soon."

"I'm sorry I took so long to come down."

"Never apologize for allowing me to take you to subspace. It's one of this Dom's greatest rewards."

"Well, your amazing ability to put me into subspace makes you Captain Subspace in my book, Sir."

He chuckled as his mind conjured up an image of him in a ridiculous superhero costume with a cheesy pose. "Whatever you say, *bebé*."

They continued to snuggle another twenty minutes or so before he asked, "Should we check on the soup and start getting ready?"

She sighed. "I could sit here all night, but you're right." She pushed herself up to a seated position, and he helped her to her feet. "I'll get dressed."

When she assured him she wasn't lightheaded, he helped her to her feet, stared at her beautifully naked body, and counted himself one lucky bastard.

Chapter Four

"Guess who I'm going to be for Halloween, Grandpa?" her daughter asked at the noisy dinner table. Savannah's nerves had calmed immensely after this afternoon's session with Damián, but she was a bit unsettled after going into subspace. She couldn't wait to go home and cuddle some more. Subspace and aftercare made all the pain worthwhile.

Adam seemed to contemplate Mari's question as he chewed slowly on the green onion and cilantro toppings he'd put in his soup. He always treated the eight-year-old's questions with great respect and seriousness. Adam glanced at Savannah for help. She smiled back knowing the answer but not wanting to spoil the great reveal for Mari.

"Want a hint?" Mari asked.

Adam swallowed. "I might need one, hon. You have a wide variety of interests."

Mari smiled, taking his words as a compliment, as she should. "She's strong and brave. A warrior."

"Xena, warrior princess?"

"Who?"

"Never mind," Adam said. "I guess she was before your time. How about another hint?"

"She's a *Disney* princess."

"Jasmine?"

"Grandpa, be serious!" She rolled her eyes. "*Really* strong—and *super* brave."

He'd never guess. Savannah wondered how long Mari would string him along at this guessing game.

"I've got it!" Adam announced. "Merida from *Brave!*" He and Damián had taken Mari to see the movie soon after it released over the summer and Merida was all she talked about for weeks.

A good choice, but Mari shook her head. "No. I still like her a lot, though." She turned to Savannah and asked, "Can I learn archery sometime?"

"We'll talk about it later." Savannah smiled, feeling somewhat guilty. She hated saying no to her daughter's many interests, but between her work at Doctor Mac's clinic and the extracurricular activities her curious and enthusiastic daughter already pursued, archery might be more than Savannah could take on at the moment.

Damián patted her belly, but addressed Mari. "Maman has enough on her plate already, *princesa.*"

Fortunately, Mari flitted away from that notion almost as quickly as it occurred to her, and soon, she focused again on her adopted grandfather. Having Adam in her children's lives would enrich them in so many ways.

"But Merida wasn't disciplined enough. I want to be the bravest warrior ever—like you, Daddy, Tío Marc, and Tía Grant."

Adam's eyebrows rose briefly before he smiled. No doubt, he didn't count himself among the heroes, but everyone around him did. Savannah thought his eyes brightened a little, but it was hard to tell in the dim lighting.

Mari had been obsessed with heroes of all kinds lately, even naming Adam and Karla's puppy, Hero. No doubt Grant's private lessons had influenced Mari in a number of ways, too. She'd not only been teaching the girl martial arts, but, while babysitting after school, Grant and Mari had been watching age-appropriate movies depicting strong female heroines. Grant's choices were spot-on, even though she didn't have children of her own. Perhaps she had other nieces and nephews. The woman was so private no one really knew anything about her family.

Savannah wanted her daughter to be able to defend herself against any threat should the need ever arise. Marisol had come so close to being kidnapped by Lyle and her...and Gentry. Her appetite gone, Savannah wiped her mouth and set her napkin beside her half-empty bowl. "Adam, you might want to surrender on this one. I don't think you'll guess in a million years."

"Okay, I know when I'm licked. Tell me what you've decided on, punkin."

She gifted him with a triumphant smile and announced to everyone at the table, "Mulan!"

"Well, no wonder I couldn't guess. I haven't seen that movie yet," Adam confessed.

"Oh, it's very exciting!" Mari began. "When her father gets constrippted…" She looked toward Savannah for help with the word.

"Con*script*ed. Drafted might be an easier choice of words."

"Con-*script*ed," Mari corrected herself, never one to shy away from using a more complex word, "into the Chinese army, Mulan, his daughter, knows he won't be able to fight any more battles at his age."

Mari looked pointedly at Damián as if she'd do the same for her daddy, and Savannah thanked God his fighting days were over. He'd sacrificed enough. But her daughter's obsession with the Marine Corps and being a warrior had Savannah more than a little worried. The thought of watching her go off to war someday…

"So Mulan disguises herself as a boy—she even cuts off her super long hair—and takes her father's army papers and goes to fight for her country. She knows she could be killed by her own people if they ever find out, but she goes anyway."

"Did they find out she was a girl?" Adam asked, seemingly enthralled with the story already.

Mari sighed. "Yes, after she's wounded by a sword. But the officer in charge doesn't kill her. He makes her return home and leave the army, though. Tía Grant and I really didn't like that part at all."

The two men at the table who had served with Grant shared a smile. Damián shook his head. "No, I imagine Tía Grant didn't care for that one little bit."

Savannah didn't know a lot about Grant's history, but from conversations she'd overheard, there had been something similar in Grant's past in which she'd been sent home in the thick of things during a black-ops mission. The woman resented it to this day, almost two years later.

"But then—"

Adam held up his hand. "Hold on! Don't tell me anymore. I want to see it for myself. Sounds like a great movie. Let's watch it here after I buy a copy."

"I can bring my Mulan DVD for us, and we can have popcorn while we watch." Mari loved any excuse to hang out with her grandpa, Grammy Karla, and the triplets.

The baby inside Savannah chose that moment to attempt a back flip. "Oh!" The exclamation spilled out before she could stop it, and Savannah grinned before explaining. "Someone's gearing up for an active night, I think."

Damián placed his hand over her belly and held it there until the baby rolled again. "I can feel him, too!" This was one thing about pregnancy that never grew old.

"What makes you so sure it's a boy?" Karla asked. "I thought you weren't going to ask Doctor Palmer."

"We didn't. It's just a feeling I have." Savannah smiled at her friend. "But I'm relieved that there's no chance for a surprise like the one you and Adam received.

Karla giggled. "Count your blessings, but remember that it took a while for them to see the second baby—and they didn't see the third one until my C-section." Karla stifled a yawn.

"You must be in a perpetual state of exhaustion," Savannah said.

Karla smiled, her eyes missing that familiar spark. "Rori, once our Sleeping Beauty, hasn't been living up to her nickname lately, so Adam and I have been taking turns walking the floors with her. She likes me to sing to her—"

"My croaking just makes her cry louder," Adam chimed in with a smile.

Karla grinned back, but the dark circles under both their eyes told the story. "Probably colic. But Marisol was wonderful with her today, trying to teach her to crawl. She and Adam even gave me time to catch a little nap. I really appreciate that you made dinner, Savannah, giving me a little more down time. Thanks."

"No trouble at all. Glad I could help." Savannah glanced at Damián. "See what we have to look forward to."

He leaned over, kissed her cheek, and whispered, "Can't wait."

It pained her knowing how much Damián had missed out on from Mari's early years, so she didn't want him to miss a single moment with their second child. For the first few months, the bassinet would be in their bedroom. After that, despite being eight years older, Mari insisted that she be allowed to share a room with the baby for at least the next few years. The bonding that would take place in that room and beyond would be irreplaceable. Savannah would move the baby to another room if he or she was too much of a distraction and disturbed Mari's sleep, though.

Karla glanced at the babies scooting around in the multi-color, fenced-in play area in the corner of the dining room. Littermates Chiquita and Hero kept watch side by side, alert to the slightest distress among the babies. Adam and Karla had been taking turns keeping an eye on them, too, while trying to eat. "Let's just hope tonight won't be a repeat," Karla said. Her face lit up when she looked at the triplets, handful or not.

As if they knew they were being talked about, the triplets all began to coo and squeal for more attention. Karla had been finishing up feeding them when Damián and Savannah arrived in hopes that the grownups and Mari could enjoy their dinner with minimal interruption. Karla still nursed them several times a day, supplementing with formula when needed.

Savannah looked forward to enjoying that special time with her second baby. Breastfeeding was among the moments she treasured most with Mari when she was a newborn.

Unbidden thoughts of those first days, weeks, and months invaded her mind. Her breaths came in shallow bursts as she remembered looking over her shoulder in the hospital and refusing to let them put Mari in the nursery for fear those monsters would take her. Of being afraid to venture out even for Mass due to similar worries. With Gentry and Lyle in jail, would she have to concern herself with such matters this time?

Damián stroked her arm, momentarily banishing the monsters to the past. "You okay, *bebé?*"

Somebody's Perfect

No, Damián would make sure no one hurt any of them.

"Just a little indigestion." She smiled and stood. Needing a solid reminder that soon she'd have the trial behind her and would be holding her little one in her arms, she walked over to the play area to pick up Pax, who was making noise by banging together his wooden blocks. "Hello, big boy!" He latched onto her loosened hair and pulled hard. "My, you're so strong!"

Would Savannah and Damián have a boy this time? While she didn't have a preference for anything but a healthy baby, God willing, it would be nice to have one of each. She wasn't sure if they would try again, although she had to admit they hadn't really tried either time she'd gotten pregnant before.

Damián's arm wrapped around her back as he joined her and grabbed her hair to pull her head back until she met his gaze. He whispered, "Don't even think about cutting this hair into a *mommy cut*. I'll be happy to find ways to keep your hair away from tiny little fingers." Her stomach dropped, and she almost smiled at the excitement such a small Dom move could have on her. Maybe they'd both have a little fun tonight after all.

Without waiting for her response, he released her hair and began making silly noises at the baby. Savannah blinked back unexpected tears. Her emotions were on a rollercoaster ride.

Just a few more months. It seemed like a lifetime away, though, and so much could go wrong.

Don't think like that.

She needed a distraction. Perhaps throwing herself into making the holidays special for her family, starting with Halloween, would help to keep the ghosts of the past locked away so as not to cast a damper on anyone else around her.

"You look tired," Damián said so only she could hear. "Why don't we pack up and head home early tonight?"

She smiled and nodded. Adam was there in an instant to take Pax from her, so perhaps he hadn't spoken as quietly as Savannah thought. Or he and Adam had prearranged this early departure.

At the door fifteen minutes later, Savannah gave Karla a hug. "Sorry we can't stay longer."

"Don't be. I remember how tired you get at this stage."

Not to mention coming down off an amazing session with Damián. She couldn't wait to get Mari in bed and continue where they left off.

After one more hug and kiss for Karla and Adam, they were buckled up and driving toward home. While Mari babbled with Chiquita in the backseat, Savannah laid her head against the headrest and closed her eyes. "Why am I so tired?"

"Because you're almost six months pregnant." Damián knew it was more than that, but she appreciated that he didn't bring up the subject again. "Nap on the ride home. It's been a long day. I'll have you in bed in no time."

The mention of going to bed with him got her juices flowing. She'd rest now so she wouldn't be too tired tonight.

The sounds around her faded away as sleep welcomed her with open arms.

Suddenly, George Gentry's face bombarded her.

He stood in her bedroom, angry, pulling her kicking and screaming from under her bed where she'd sought sanctuary. Savannah tried to pry away his hand off her arm, but he was relentless.

"No! Don't touch me!"

"Stop teasing me, and maybe I'll leave you alone."

She continued to fight with everything she had as he carried her to his own bed. The place where he'd hurt Maman. No! Moments later, he ripped off her pajama bottoms and panties before laying himself on her. Naked. He fumbled to spread her legs.

Smothering. She couldn't breathe.

Escape! Go to your safe place!

Maman!

A helpless whimper awakened Savannah. She shook her head to rid herself of the flashback remnants and glanced over at Damián whose gaze remained on the road. Good. She hadn't screamed out anything he or Mari could hear. He turned to her briefly and smiled then reached across the console to hold her hand. "You okay?"

"Fine. Just dozed off." Her submissive nature warred with her reluctance to tell her Dom about this relapse. After so many months of being free from flashbacks and nightmares, today she'd simply had too much stirred up from the past. Savannah pulled her hand away and crossed her arms, rubbing some warmth into her upper arms.

"Cold?"

Frigid.

"A little," she answered.

He turned up the heat. "Gets cold a lot earlier in October here than in SoCal."

Oh, but San Diego County had its own brand of cold, the kind that seeped into your soul and never let go.

All too soon she'd have to return to the place that held so many horrific memories for her and face the past again. She'd be near Rancho Santa Fe and the house she'd been violated in so many times as a little girl. Near the hotel in La Jolla where she'd been humiliated and tortured countless times. While she wouldn't have to step foot on either of those properties, they would always reside in her psyche, just below the surface.

Her dinner threatened to come back up, and she gripped Damián's hand, hoping to draw from his strength to help her face those dark days ahead. She needed to show the jury what a monster George Gentry was. She needed to face him and crush him once and for all, much as Mulan did the Huns in Mari's movie.

Dear Lord, give me the steadfast strength of Damián and the fighting spirit of Mari to help me send that bastard away for the remainder of his despicable life.

Chapter Five

Damián listened as Marisol read them *Esperanza Rising* for at least the tenth time this month. He'd bought her the book because he wanted his daughter to know about the struggles of immigrants like her Orlando grandparents and great-grandparents who started out in America as migrant farm workers in the Thirties.

Having Marisol become fascinated by Esperanza's story pleased him greatly.

He glanced over Marisol's head at Savannah to find her staring into space. She'd been quieter than usual since they'd come back from Dad and Karla's. After her intense subspace experience this afternoon, was she experiencing subdrop?

As soon as Marisol wrapped up this story and he tucked her in bed, he and Savannah could have some time to cuddle and talk, maybe even finish what they'd started earlier. He'd had to fight a hard-on all night every time he pictured her during today's fantasy scene.

"Daddy, were your parents rich when they lived in Mexico, like Esperanza's?"

Pulled back to the present, he grinned down at her upturned face. "I wouldn't say rich. They were comfortable, though, before hard times came and they had to flee to California. But times were hard there, too. Everyone suffered during the Great Depression."

"I'm glad we have a house to live in and that you don't have to work in the fields. It would be hard to do with your leg."

His parents had spared him from a life like that by providing a stable home in Eden Gardens and everything they could for the two children who had lived—Rosa and him. "Yes, it would." Their lives had been easy compared to his parents' and grandparents'. And Savannah's.

"Listen, *mi muñequita*, it's time for you to go to bed. You have school in the morning." He took the book and laid it on the coffee table.

"Thanks for reading Esperanza's story to us again, sweetie." Savannah smiled at their daughter but still didn't seem to be completely present.

Twenty minutes later, with Marisol tucked in bed, he took Savannah by the hand and led her to their bedroom. "I think we have some unfinished business, *mi mariposa*."

He expected a little more enthusiasm from her, but she merely acknowledged him with a *mmm-hmm*. Time to find out what was going on. He continued past the bed to the aftercare chair. Her body grew stiffer when she sat on his lap, and she seemed to be trying to avoid his erection. "What's wrong, *savita?*"

"Nothing. Just tired, I guess."

He stroked her silky hair and pulled her head against his shoulder. "Do you feel like you're in subdrop?"

"Could be. I've rarely dropped, so I don't know for sure. Could be any number of reasons, but I'm feeling a little depressed tonight."

"Do you think it has to do with the trial?"

"Most likely. I'm not sure I'm ready for this."

"Try not to worry about it too much. We'll work to prepare you over the next two months."

"Not even two months."

"We'll have enough time. Don't you worry. You know I'll be there with you, too."

"I wish you could be with me when I testify."

He suspected that had her nervous. "Let me talk to Dad and see what he thinks will help to get you ready. But tonight, I want you to let me pamper you. How about I give you a massage and we just snuggle in bed?"

Her body relaxed for the first time all night. If she didn't want to have sex, didn't she know she could just say so? While he wanted her more each day, he didn't intend to force her to put out, which would make him no better than the assholes who'd used her body in the past.

They cuddled a few more minutes before he patted her thigh. "Okay, you can have the bathroom first. Then wait for me in bed."

She sat up, the muscles around her eyes relaxing for the first time since this afternoon. She smiled at him. "Thanks, Damián, for understanding that I'm not really up for anything more tonight."

"You know you can tell me when you don't feel like it. We don't have to have sex every night." Maybe he had gotten used to it for the past six months, but she had a lot going on right now.

Her teeth bit the corner of her lower lip. "I know. I'm sure I'd have gotten in the mood eventually, but...it seemed so daunting tonight. Thanks for understanding."

"I can't read your mind, *querida*. Talk to me about anything, whenever you need to."

She smiled and placed a peck on his cheek. "I promise I will."

He helped her up and watched her pad on bare feet into the master bathroom. He couldn't shake the feeling she was hiding something from him. Did it have to do with the upcoming trial, a resurgence of PTSD, or something not even on his radar?

Would he have to push harder to get Savannah to open up to him again? She'd kept so much inside when they first reunited but had made so much progress since then. Sadly, he knew how PTSD worked, too.

When she came out of the bathroom, he headed in there to take a cold shower.

Later, he massaged the tenseness from her shoulders and spooned against Savannah, hoping they could return to the way things had been before that fucking phone call from the DA.

*   *   *

His hands closed around her throat. Dizzy. Savannah tried to kick his weight off the baby but couldn't. The rapist had tied her hands to the bedposts. Useless.

"Please, don't hurt my baby!"

But the man relentlessly removed her panties. She pulled her legs up to her belly in an effort to protect the baby, but he twisted her body to her side and entered her from behind. Raw pain. Every inch of his penis abraded her vagina as he penetrated her.

Please, God, let the baby be okay!

At least in this position, the man's body wasn't pressing on the baby. Perhaps if she didn't struggle, he would finish quickly and get out of her home.

"You dirty little whore." Father!?! *How had he gotten out of jail? "Allowing that spic to plant his filthy seed inside you. I ought to cut it out of you and rid you of that bastard and its sperm donor once and for all."*

"No!!! Get out!" Savannah gasped for breath as she clawed at the air. When had he released her hands? His body pressed more tightly to hers.

"*Bebé*, wake up. You're having another nightmare."

How did Damián get in here? Didn't he know Father wanted him dead?

Perspiration chilled her face in the morning air as she blinked her eyes open and turned her head. Damián's face hovered above hers, his hand stroking her sweaty hair. Even though he wasn't touching her, she couldn't shake the feeling of being trapped. Wild-eyed, her gaze darted around the predawn bedroom, but she saw no one lurking in the darkness.

His hand stroked down her arm until he gently tugged her toward him, almost onto her back. So it had been *his* body—*his* erection—pressed against her backside that had triggered the scenario in the dream.

Had they had sex while she slept—without her consent—or was that part of the dream? She felt disconnected from her body—and from Damián, too, right now.

"Shh. It's over now. You're safe. I'm here." He continued with a litany of soothing euphemisms she wanted to believe but couldn't. This nightmare would never end.

Would she ever be safe from Gentry and the way he'd made her question even Damián's actions, who had never taken advantage of her, not even that first night in the penthouse? She doubted it. Not unless he was put away in a supermax prison ten stories underground, but men like him rarely served time in places like that.

"What was the dream about?"

Savannah met Damián's gaze once more. "I can't remember any details. Someone tried to harm our baby." While she wasn't being completely honest with him, she didn't want to disappoint him, either, by showing him what a bad mental place she was in right now. He'd worked so hard and had done such a great job at ridding her of the nightmares and flashbacks. It pained her to have him think she was reverting to old behaviors. He always told her how strong and brave she was. What if he saw what a coward she truly was inside? He respected and honored bravery in others above almost any other trait. Would he lose interest in her if she didn't live up to his standard?

Logically, she knew her years of abuse and neglect were a big reason for her insecurities, but tell that to her inner child who had learned never to trust anyone to be there for her.

He bent and gently kissed her lips then pulled back and smiled. "You have my word that no one will hurt you or anyone in my family ever again."

She wanted to believe him, but he and Adam had tried to outsmart Lyle and Gentry before, only to have their security breached when Savannah was kidnapped and Mari's safety compromised. They were dangerous, evil—even from behind bars. And soon Gentry would be let out of his cell every day and transported to his trial. Lyle would be there to testify, too, no doubt. Were either of them savvy enough to orchestrate an escape? It had been known to happen on the news, anyway. Bile rose in her throat at the thought of either of them being free again.

"I need to use the bathroom." She scooted to the edge of the bed and sat up, waiting for her equilibrium to steady as long as she dared before standing.

"Need any help?"

"No." She didn't want him to see her vomit, if she wasn't able to keep it down. "I'm fine. Just have to pee." Again, not a lie, but still not the whole truth. One of the tenets of their relationship was honesty, but until she came to grips with this assault to her psyche, she intended to deal with this herself.

Okay, not the smartest idea she'd ever had, but it was all she could come up with at the moment.

In the bathroom, she turned on the exhaust fan to drown out any sounds she might make and raised the toilet seat. But after a dry heave or two, she realized she wasn't going to throw up. She peed then went to the mirror to assess the damage. Dark circles under her eyes. More concealer would be needed today. She'd slept so little the past two nights. Thank God the weekend was here. She might be able to nap and catch up on her sleep. She also needed to finish Mari's costume for Halloween. Perhaps if she kept busy and skipped naps, she'd sleep better tonight. *Better* meaning without dreams.

But whenever she closed her eyes, the specter of Gentry waited in the darkness. Her vision blurred.

Why can't I have a normal life for me and my family?

Savannah blinked away the tears, trying not to sniffle or blow her nose and tip Damián off that she was crying. Again. After washing her face with cold water and drying it, she returned to the bedroom. She needed a distraction. While the thought of having sex after that dream was abhorrent, she needed to make it up to Damián for the half-truths she'd just told him.

Maybe if she offered to give him a blowjob, she'd relieve his stress and take her mind off the dream, too. They'd both end up satisfied.

Savannah crawled between the sheets and reached out to him. Still erect. "Whatcha doin', *bebé?*"

"What does it look like? I might not be up for sex this morning, but Chico certainly seems to be." She hadn't suffered a low sex drive since before they'd married. Was it just stress about the upcoming trial? She hoped so, because making love with Damián gave her a lot of pleasure. Usually. Right now, though, she'd suffice with giving him pleasure.

His eyes narrowed. "Chico?" She glanced away, and he stilled her hand. "Eyes."

With reluctance, unsure she could hide her feelings from him, she plastered a smile on her face and met his gaze. "I'm still half-asleep. I meant your cock. Please. Let me worship your cock, Sir."

He'd call her out again if she continued to slip back into old behaviors. A wordless diversion was necessary. Savannah resumed stroking his cock rhythmically, brushing her thumb against the notch until she felt precum on her hand. She swallowed down her initial revulsion. It had always been impossible for her to stay in the moment when she felt cum or precum on her hand, but she decided the best way to avoid that reaction was to use her mouth.

Getting onto all fours, she went down on his penis.

"Oh, yeah, *bebé*. So fucking good."

He took her head between his hands and guided it up and down on his rod. Interestingly, she didn't trigger with his hands doing that. She loved it when he took charge of her during their lovemaking. Perhaps because she relinquished control to someone she trusted.

Savannah opened her throat as he'd been training her to do. She gagged on the first few strokes, her eyes tearing up, but finally, he slid a few inches down her passage. She stopped moving and held him there until she had to pull back to breathe. While she hadn't perfected deep-throating him, she was able to take him deeper than she ever had before. With pleasing him her foremost goal, she could tell by his moans she'd accomplished that.

Heady stuff. She almost chuckled at the pun.

Her hand reached back and stroked his thighs, and he spread his legs wider to give her better access to his balls. She cupped and gently squeezed them as she bobbed her head up and down on him making slurpy noises that never sounded all that sexy to her.

"*¡Madre de Dios! Muy caliente.*"

But it must work for her man. She could hear the excitement in his voice. Pleasing him this way was one small thing she could do to maintain a sense of intimacy in their relationship. As he began to raise and lower his hips in time to the rhythm he'd set with his hands, he once again hit the back of her throat.

Savannah slowed her pace and relaxed her throat muscles, easing his penis down her throat as far as she dared. "*¡Ay, güey!* So good."

Guilty for making him wait made her keep him deep in her throat longer than she ever had before. She squeezed his balls, and his penis began to pulsate. "Don't stop, *bebé!*"

Tears poured from her eyes, ones she wouldn't have to explain away at least, and Savannah gave in to the fear and sorrow she'd been trying to hold at bay while Damián's hot cum spurted down her throat. As his climax abated, she pulled herself off him.

"Wow! That was incredible. I think you've mastered deep throating, *savita*."

He wiped some cum from the corner of her mouth. "Now, it's my turn. I want to eat your sweet pussy."

Blinking away the tears, she gave him a tremulous smile as he reached for the hand towel he kept on his nightstand. "No, I'm good." She scrubbed at any lingering cum on her hands then wiped her mouth and any errant tears away.

"You sure? It's been a while since you've—"

She pressed her fingers to his lips. "I'm fine."

Damián stared at her a long moment then tugged her down to his shoulder. She tried to pull away, not ready for closeness right now, but his hand on the side of her head forced her to stay there. His heartbeat slowly decreased its rapid pace.

After a few awkward moments, while she played idly with his nip, and he did the same with hers, he said, "Thank you for giving so much of yourself, *querida*. I wish you would let me touch you and give you an orgasm. It might help you relax. You've had one helluva week."

She shook her head. "Not tonight." Everything was too raw tonight. "Just hold me."

"Sure you're okay? That nightmare really seemed to rattle you."

"It's over now." God, she hoped it wouldn't return when she closed her eyes. She needed to convince him, though. "I just gave my man some awesome head and am now cuddling with him in bed. What more could a girl want?"

She couldn't understand how her libido had shut down so suddenly the other day or what to do to rekindle an interest in sex, but for now, she was content to be cocooned in his arms with some semblance of safety.

Chapter Six

Halloween arrived too quickly for Damián, because fewer than six fucking weeks remained until the trial. Savannah grew more distant and withdrawn by the day. The strong front she tried to put on didn't fool him for one minute. Whenever he asked her how she was doing, she'd give her old pat answer—*I'm fine*—while she was anything but.

That she refused to slow down at the clinic despite losing sleep to nightmares almost nightly now didn't help. Then she'd insisted on making Marisol's costume herself. Super Mom on steroids, but he needed to do something to make sure she was taking care of herself better.

He hadn't had a chance to talk with Dad at dinner last week or any time since. Maybe once they finished trick-or-treating tonight. They were headed to his house now, after hitting every house Marisol could find with a porch light on in their University Hills neighborhood.

Marisol sorted through her haul in the backseat while Savannah sat rigidly beside him with her head against the seat rest. Dad and Karla's would definitely be their last stop tonight. He and Savannah needed to have a talk. While he'd seen her smile a few times tonight watching Marisol strut around the neighborhood in costume, she did so less and less frequently in the last week.

Marisol was out of her seatbelt and halfway to the front door before Damián reached Savannah's door to help her out. They trailed their daughter up the winding sidewalk.

"Who's this?" Karla asked, opening the door before Marisol could knock and coming out onto the porch. Damián had given them a heads-up they were on their way. "Why, it's Mulan! All the way from China!" Karla executed a curtsy. "Your highness, please come in."

Marisol giggled. "It's me, Grammy Karla. Marisol!"

"Oh, my! I've never seen anyone look more like Mulan than the princess herself."

Karla asked Savannah and Damián, "Can you all come in for a little while?" She glanced up the driveway toward the street. "We don't get many people stopping by out here, and it's almost eight. Any stragglers can ring the bell if I don't hear them drive or walk up."

Savannah nodded, and Damián wrapped his arm around her waist with a pat to the baby for good measure. He tried not to think about all she'd have to endure in the coming months. Not just the trial, but going through labor and delivery, too.

Savannah's mind seemed to have been off the trial somewhat tonight, but Damián continued to worry about how best to prepare her to take the witness stand in front of that *cabrón* without being sucked back into her past.

Once everyone was inside, Dad wheeled the triplet stroller across the foyer. Dressed as three peas in a pod, the babies must have made the rounds in their neighborhood, too.

"Karla, those costumes are adorable," Savannah said. The smile erased the strain on her face, but he wasn't sure she was genuinely happy or just putting on a show. "Did you make them yourself?"

"Oh, Lord, no. But when I saw those peapods, I just couldn't resist."

The babies stared wide-eyed and in awe at Marisol before Kate let out an ear-piercing scream followed by wails from the others. "Hey, none of that!" Dad said. "Look! It's Marisol-Mulan, a brave hero to her people."

Unfazed by their reaction, Marisol pirouetted for them then remembered her role as Mulan and lifted her aluminum foil-covered sword high over her head. "I came to warn you! The Huns are here in the city!"

Dad shielded the babies with his body while peering through the glass storm door for unseen enemy combatants in the yard. Soon, Dad sighed theatrically, stood, and said to her, "Looks like you've frightened the Huns away, Mulan. I'm sure they've heard what a brave and mighty warrior you are."

Damián added, "And that's high praise coming from one of the bravest warriors of all."

Dad waved away his words, but Marisol stood a little taller before lowering her sword and nodding, always in awe of her grandpa and his heroism. Then the eight-year-old in her returned. She giggled as she set her purple pumpkin full of candy on the floor and knelt in front of the stroller, thrilled by the reactions of the triplets. Rori's eyes opened as wide as saucers, while Pax tried to grab her rope hair and pull it loose from its bun. That had been Dad's contribution to the costume, at Savannah's request. He'd fashioned it from a new batch of hemp he'd bought for rigging Karla at the club.

As if just remembering the primary reason for their visit, Marisol stood, picked up her plastic pumpkin, and held it out to Karla. "Trick or treat, Grammy Karla!"

Karla grabbed several hands full of goodies from her large half-filled bowl. Marisol would be bouncing off the walls for a month. When Marisol started to pull her pumpkin back, Karla added, "Wait! For protecting my home and family, Mulan," Karla said, "you deserve something extra."

Dad moved the stroller into the living room, followed by Karla and the Orlando trio. Inside, Karla picked up a large gift bag from the floor beside the door. Pink and purple tissue paper exploded from the opening. It looked more like a birthday present than a Halloween one, but Damián loved that Karla doted on his *muñequita* almost as much as Dad did.

Seconds later, she pulled out a black and white stuffed kitten and held it to her cheek, closing her eyes. "It looks just like Boots!"

"Sit down, Savannah." Karla motioned to her rocking chair. "I'm sure you're dead on your feet."

"Let me put on a pot of coffee," Dad said. "Savannah, would you like some herbal tea?"

"Sounds wonderful. It got quite chilly out there after the sun went down."

"And some hot cocoa for you, Marisol?" Dad asked.

"With marshmallows?"

"Mari, remember your manners," Savannah chided.

Chastened, she said, "Marshmallows, please, Grandpa, if you have some."

"No worries, hon. I know how my punkin likes her cocoa. We're always well-stocked." He turned to Damián. "Join me in the kitchen."

It wasn't a request. Damián followed Dad down the hallway toward the kitchen. Damián started the kettle while Dad pulled out a box of cocoa and a bag of marshmallows and retrieved several mugs. He glanced up. "Is Savannah doing okay? She looks a little…tired." Nothing much escaped Dad.

"She's worrying herself sick about the upcoming trial. We'll be heading to California in early December, *if* the doctor gives the go-ahead."

Damián's primary job was to keep her and the baby safe and protected. "How did Karla do on the trip out to our wedding when she was so pregnant?"

"If her doctor or I had known she was carrying triplets, we never would have let her go out there."

"I'm not sure she'd have given you a say."

A muscle clenched in his jaw. "She's headstrong, that's for sure. But if she thought there was any danger to her or the babies, she wouldn't have gone. I still hate to think what would have happened if she'd hemorrhaged in the desert on our trip the way she did here at home after the babies were born."

Damián closed his eyes a moment but couldn't shake the notion of something similar happening to Savannah.

"Aw, fuck, son. Don't listen to me. You have enough to worry about. Doc Palmer says that was a one in a million occurrence."

Damián nodded. "Believe me, you aren't making me think of any scenario I haven't already considered. Being an expectant father is worse than any mindfuck I could come up with."

"Hate to break it to you, but the worrying only gets worse after they're born."

He thought about the scare he'd had when he thought Gentry had kidnapped Marisol, too. "Tell me about it." Asking for Dad's help made him feel like a failure, but fixing this was more important than his ego.

"Listen, I wonder if you'd have time to talk later."

"I have time now. Shoot."

He raked the fingers of both hands through his hair until they butted into his suede hair tie, and he held on. "Dad, I'm out of ideas on how to prepare Savannah to face that POS Gentry on the stand without freezing or making herself sick. I thought maybe some BDSM techniques might help."

"That's more than a five-minute conversation," Dad said, pouring cocoa into a mug and adding the mini marshmallows. "I'll need to help Karla get the babies to bed within the next hour or so. And Savannah looks whipped. Why don't you stop by tomorrow for a late lunch? Say about one? Karla and the kids usually nap about then."

"Sounds good."

* * *

When Damián arrived during his lunch break from the shop, Dad held a finger over his lips. "Karla and the babies are napping." After he served Damián a quick bite and drink in the kitchen, Dad motioned him down the hallway toward his office.

Damián couldn't remember the last time he'd had one of these office talks—probably the one right after Dad's honeymoon when Damián had told him Savannah had shown up after all these years. This conversation was long overdue. Things had been going so well between him and Savannah until recently. He ought to be able to fix this himself, but his ideas about how to keep Savannah from shutting down any further had run dry.

Some fucking Dom and husband I am.

Time for him to grow a pair and accept help. Dad had helped him so many times before. Damián hoped he'd have the answers he needed for Savannah today. But how much did he want to admit to Dad about how distant the two of them had become sexually?

He rubbed the leather band on his wrist. During their last serious office sit-down, Dad had brought him this handmade gift from Sergeant Miller's oldest daughter, Tracy. Touching it grounded him in some weird way. He liked to think Sergeant's spirit came closer in the times he used it as a touchstone. Like today.

Dad took a seat behind his desk. "We'd better cut to the chase. They don't nap as long as they used to. Don't want to be interrupted, if we can help it."

"Yeah, I appreciate you taking the time for me. I'm worried about Savannah."

"Of course, you are. That's why I asked you to join me in the kitchen last night. Saved me the trouble of having to drag your ass in here. Good thing you finally asked for this talk." Dad leaned forward on his elbows and tented his fingers in front of his chin. "What's going on?"

Damián, comforted to know Dad would always have his six, explained how the trial date moving up had resulted in Savannah having nightmares again. That he didn't think she ate enough, and, most worrisome, she withdrew from him emotionally and...physically. He didn't say they weren't having sex anymore, but Dad probably guessed it. "I hate seeing all our hard work undone. She's shutting down again. I need some advice on how to keep her from pulling further away. Maybe some on how to train her to be ready for the trial, too, when she's going to have to face that POS from a few feet away. That's what's got her rattled the most."

"Can you blame her? You've given her space to deal with her fears, but that hasn't worked. You're going to have to find a way to make her deal with it."

"I have no doubt about that." He scrubbed his face. "I've never forced her sexually, but her innate service orientation sometimes has her forcing herself to try and please me, even when it's not what she wants to be doing. It's like she thinks I expect her to service me, but she won't let me reciprocate. How do I even reach her anymore?"

"Same way you did before. She's come a long way from that shell of a girl who showed up on your doorstep nearly a year ago. She responded to you because she trusted you to be open and honest with her."

"I thought that's what I've been doing."

"You've been loving, supportive, and worshipping the ground she walks on. Yeah, you have to be understanding of physical changes, what with her being pregnant, but you also have to be firm with her. It's what she needs most right now. She'll find her security in having you behaving consistently within the Dom/sub terms you two established in your relationship."

He thought about that a minute before responding. "Yeah, kinda like you were with me when I was showing signs of PTSD. BDSM helped me regain control when I was going through that shit, and it's helped Savannah with hers, too. But I've run out of techniques that help. I'm stumped." He gave a self-deprecating smile, hoping to lighten the mood. "In more ways than one."

Dad shook his head at the bad attempt at humor. "Fixing things is what you do best, son. Don't forget how far you've brought her since she witnessed Patti's cathartic whipping last winter."

But it wasn't enough, apparently, and time was running out. "I've tried everything in my tool chest—or toy bag, as the case may be."

"Savannah's a masochist, whether she self-identifies that way or not. She's used to you being able to take her to dark places and bringing her back even stronger."

"But with her pregnancy, I've been unable to play at the extreme level we did before."

"And the limitations will only increase in the coming months, until the doctor gives the all clear after the baby's born."

"That's too late."

"What have you tried so far?"

Damián mentioned his piss-poor attempts but withheld his suspicions about the night she'd deep-throated him. At the time, he'd thought those tears had been from her gag reflex. Looking back from where they were now, in effect, she'd raped herself on his dick. And he'd let her. Sure, he'd expected her to be honest with him about her feelings and didn't realize at the time she'd reverted to old behaviors. But a Dom was supposed to be observant. "Our last healthy scene was on the afternoon she learned the trial date. I managed to get her into subspace, but since then, *nada*."

Dad turned away a moment, intent on some spot across the room, before meeting his gaze again. "If your bomb isn't big enough, you drop a bigger fucking bomb."

What was he suggesting? "I can't strike her any harder in our scenes. What if I harm her or the baby?" He'd never be able to live with himself if he did that.

"I know that, dumbass. That's what mindfucks are for. You've pulled off some kickass ones with her. Come up with some way of making her believe she's being struck harder than she actually is, and you might push her to the place she needs to be." He let that sink in as Damián started to think about possible ways to play a mind game with Savannah when Dad added, "Hypnosis is your answer here. It helped you a few times in the past."

Dad had used every trick in the book during the first two years Damián had moved in with him after Balboa. And Savannah's therapist had encouraged them to use some of the induction techniques with her when she was in a bad place, so they'd certainly played around with it before. Just not for a kink scene.

"But what if I taint her testimony or cause Gentry's case to be thrown out of court?"

"Since when do the specifics of the trial come into your scenes? Your job as her Dom is to help her relax so she can reconnect with herself and with you. From what I can see and what you've told me, she's completely disconnected, and I can't blame her."

"Her therapist has been using hypnosis on her already. She even suggested we use some novice techniques at home anytime she's shutting down emotionally, but Savannah's good at hiding her feelings. She's done it all her life."

"That coping mechanism helped her survive a shitstorm of a life, but she didn't have a Dom back then to guide her, son. Don't let her go back there again."

"Some Dom I turned out to be for her."

Dad growled. "Cry me a river. So you aren't Jesus incarnate. Get over yourself. What else is stuck under your craw?"

He swallowed and met Dad's gaze. "When we've been intimate lately,

I don't think she's being honest with me about where she is mentally and physically. How do I trust her to stop when she needs to?"

"Sounds like both of you have some trust issues to work through. It's time for you to set a time to play at the club where you can both cut loose. Some public play might do you both good and might even help prepare her for being on the stand with all eyes on her."

"Sounds good, but she hasn't been interested anytime I've tried to play lately."

"Which one of you is the dominant in this relationship?"

"Point taken." He might have dropped the ball for a while, but Dad was right. Damián nodded.

"Your primary goal will be the mindfuck. Make her believe she's getting the level of pain she needs, and get her out of her head. Right now, her nerves are getting the best of her." He paused a moment. "What if we hold some kind of event at the club and surround her with people she knows and trusts—invite owners only and their subs?"

Damián thought a minute. The only event coming up was Thanksgiving, but that would be cutting it too close. He found himself rubbing the wristband when it came to him.

"My Alive Day is two weeks away. Marc's, too, so he'd probably bring Angelina. And Grant and Ryder were on that rooftop when the grenade went off, and you were up there soon after, too. It would be the perfect subterfuge to bring us all together to discuss it. Savannah would want to be there for me."

"Great idea, except that Ryder and Megan aren't in the lifestyle."

"Could they be kink curious or at least open-minded about it?"

Dad grunted. "Not something I intend to ask my baby sister."

"Marc hangs out with Ryder more than we do, since they live so close to each other. Maybe he can feel him out."

"I'll mention that to him when I call to tell him what we're planning. We can keep the kink stuff for after the Alive Day commemoration part of the evening. If Ryder and Megan aren't interested, they can shove off before the fun starts."

For the first time in a long time, Damián had a plan, which calmed his own insecurities. "Sounds good." Damián glanced down at the wristband before meeting Dad's gaze again.

"Now go plan your scene, son. And if you don't have her squawking like a chicken, I'll have you squawking while I tan your hide with your own bullwhip."

"Shit, Dad. Have a little faith." Suddenly, he made a decision. He might as well be up front about it all, while he had Dad's ear. "The last time we...were intimate... Well, after I thought about it a while, I think she did some things to please me rather than stop when she needed to. And, well, I was being a dick and not paying attention to her body language instead of just her...mouth..."

Dad glared at him.

"Yeah, I know. I told you I was a dick. And I've been reluctant to pursue anything with her since that night."

"Because you don't trust her to tell you no."

Damián thought about it a moment too long.

"I assumed as much. Catch-22. You want to be sure she's going to use her safeword before doing anything else BDSM related. But your own trust isn't going to return until you do a scene, and she uses her safeword."

The use of hypnosis might break down some barriers.

"Push her limits—but stay clear of known triggers," he warned. Dad sure was in paternal mode today. "Remind her ahead of time what you expect from her as your submissive and what the basic rules of BDSM are—safe, sane, and, most of all, consensual. She has the right to say no at any point *if* she uses her safeword. Bottom line, she has to agree to tell you any time you've gone too far or she can't handle it."

The possibilities for intense scenes were endless, and several scenarios played through his mind.

As if he could see the wheels turning in Damián's head, Dad chuckled. "I know you're going to give her a night to remember, son."

"I'll try something new that night so she won't be able to predict what's coming at her. We haven't played with wax before."

"Excellent choice."

"I'll have to run it by Doc Palmer to make sure she doesn't have any concerns, of course."

"I can tell you now to stay away from her belly, chest, and the arteries in her neck."

Damián nodded. He had two whole weeks to prepare.

Dad grew serious again. "Now that we have that sorted out, what would you like to do to commemorate your Alive Day? You know, this might be the first time we've gotten everyone together to talk about that day and definitely the first that will include Ryder. Long overdue."

Dad was right. *As usual.* While Damián and Marc had been given a lot of support because their injuries had been physical, Ryder and Grant probably harbored hidden wounds. Maybe even Dad, although his issues could stem from any number of conflicts he'd been involved in, military and civilian. He hadn't had an easy life.

They spent another twenty or thirty minutes discussing plans for the Alive Day before Damián said, "I really appreciate this, Dad. You put things into perspective for me."

"You know I'm always here for you. You're my family."

Something for which Damián would never be able to adequately express his gratitude. "Who did you go to when you were figuring out how to be a better Dom?"

"We all have our mentors. My buddy Jerry in LA was a big help."

Damián wouldn't ask if he still needed to go to someone for advice. Dad seemed to have it all together, at least as far as how to be a Dom. Like Damián, though, the man had his own demons to face.

As he left the house, he hoped he could make some breakthroughs with Savannah and give her back the inner strength to be completely honest with him. What was she afraid of? She had to know he'd never harm, leave, or abandon her.

Didn't she?

Chapter Seven

"I really appreciate you staying with the kids tonight, Cassie," Savannah said as she placed another plate in the dishwasher in Karla's kitchen.

"It is my pleasure. And with Teresa and Marisol here to help, I am sure we will have everything under control. You just go and have a good time."

Savannah tried to still the vultures of doom threatening to erupt in her stomach. She couldn't get out of spending this night at the Masters at Arms Club. She'd had an excuse not to go every time in the past few weeks when Damián had suggested they should, but she couldn't very well keep him away if the guys were planning some kind of cathartic session talking about Fallujah and its aftermath. Eight years ago today, Damián and Marc had nearly been killed. Their surviving needed to be celebrated.

But what if she suffered more flashbacks or triggers tonight in front of Damián? They came out of the blue these days, as if her mind had opened a door to make her face those horrific days from her past. Most of these memories wouldn't even be admissible in the trial, because the DA said she would only be able to focus on her mother's and John Grainger's murders and last spring's kidnapping. So why were flashbacks about that final year as Gentry's slave and her childhood abuse by him surfacing now? What good would it do to remember those times he'd never be charged with?

To ramp up her anticipation, Damián refused to tell her what they'd be doing together tonight as far as scening, although he did say he wanted to work on preparing her for the trial. Whatever that meant. He loved to mess with her mind. Her therapist had been talking with them about using hypnosis at home, and Damián had joined in a few sessions at counseling to learn more. He'd even gone on to be mentored by someone doing BDSM with hypnosis this past week. What did he have planned for her?

Anticipation, Damián called it. Unsure if she could get excited for him the way she used to, she just saw it as one more thing to dread.

Karla placed a detergent pod in the door's compartment and closed the dishwasher. "I'm so glad tonight came together so well on such short notice. I know it means a lot to Adam, and I'm sure everyone's going to get something out of it." She turned to Megan. "And we really appreciate that you and Ryder are joining us. Ryder was affected by that awful day, too."

"We wouldn't have missed it for anything," Megan said. "I think he's going to find healing tonight, too."

"I just hope it won't be too weird that we're dragging you two into a dungeon when you aren't into the lifestyle."

Megan glanced away, seemingly biting back a grin. Savannah remembered her first thoughts about BDSM—anything but positive.

"It's going to be interesting, but Ryder and I aren't prudes. Maybe we'll learn a thing or two, not that our love life needs any more spice."

Savannah experienced a pang of regret. Ryder and Megan had been married shortly before she had been, but because Savannah had let her past invade the bedroom, she'd placed a damper on the level of intimacy enjoyed with Damián. She hoped tonight would show Damián that she still found him desirable and wanted to rekindle that part of their relationship.

"So when Cassie assured me you wouldn't need me to babysit," Megan said, "since the kids will be asleep for the most part, I jumped at the chance. Mostly for Ryder, of course."

Karla turned to her Peruvian friend. "We're grateful to have you babysit, Cassie."

Cassie grinned. "I much prefer babysitting to what you all have planned. Besides, it would not be right going to a place like that without Luke." Her husband of a few months had stayed behind at his and

Ryder's ranch two hours west of Denver to tend to their horses, alpacas, and sundry pets.

"If not for being there for Marc tonight," Angelina said, "I'd be tempted to stay with you, Cassie, and spoil those adorable babies."

"Don't worry, Angelina," Savannah said. "Your day will come soon enough." She and Marc had been talking about a June wedding next year, although both seemed so busy she didn't know how much planning they'd actually done. Marc's EMT training and Angelina's new restaurant consumed most of their time.

"Thanks again for dinner, Angelina," Savannah said, stroking her belly when the baby kicked her. "You're a fabulous chef. I wish I could do more than operate a crock pot."

"You know I love to cook any chance I can. And it's been great doing so in here again." This had been Marc's house until he'd sold it to Adam and Karla just before the babies were born. Marc had later moved in with Angelina in Aspen Corners, near Breckenridge.

"I could watch you whipping up your dishes in here all day," Savannah said. "I learn new tricks every time."

"Come to my restaurant sometime," Angelina offered. "I reserve a table in the kitchen for my wannabe chefs where you can pick up even more ideas."

Cassie added, "Luke, Ryder, Megan, and I have been going there to eat once a week since it opened—sometimes in the regular dining room and sometimes in the kitchen. It would be even more fun to have the whole family together out there again."

Everyone in this group truly had bonded as one big happy family all because of those who had served in Iraq together. Damián had told her Luke had joined the fold when he'd done renovations on the Masters at Arms Club before it opened. With Adam and Grant's help, Megan had brought Ryder in as well. He'd isolated himself for too long out in the high desert of New Mexico. And now Luke and Ryder were in business together. Amazing how they all fit together.

Everyone had each other's backs no matter their differences of opinion on various issues. Not something one saw very much these days.

But Savannah hadn't gotten to know Marc and Angelina as well as the others. They rarely came to Denver. Tonight, however, a love of each other and a little bondage would strengthen their ties to each other. Not that she expected to be restrained herself. Her OB had cautioned them about unsafe play for the duration of her pregnancy.

"Just say the word, Angie, and we'll come to Breckenridge." Karla patted Savannah's belly. "But we'd better not wait too long. This one will be on travel restrictions soon."

Talk of travel threw a wet blanket over Savannah's mood again. "Actually, Doctor Palmer gave me the okay to fly to San Diego for the trial in three weeks, provided there are no complications between now and then. It's early enough in my third trimester that she doesn't anticipate any emergencies, but I'll have to be careful to remember to walk often, even during the short flight, and to drink lots of water, which will be fun on this bladder." She laughed without any humor.

Karla nodded her understanding. "At least flying should be more comfortable than all those hours in a car, the way Adam and I went out for your wedding. Especially if Damián is as bad as Adam and makes you stop and pee at every cactus." She smiled, shaking her head. "It's so nice not to have him freaking out over every breath I take anymore. Now he has to spread his worrying out over me and three babies."

Angelina put away the last of the remaining ingredients she'd used tonight, most of which she'd brought with her. "He's taken to those babies like a natural, considering he didn't have any experience with kids before."

Savannah couldn't agree more. "I could tell he'd be fine the first time I watched him outside playing with Mari in the snow when we moved into the club earlier this year. Adam loves you and your babies more than life itself, Karla."

Karla sighed. "Oh, I know how incredibly lucky I am. I just like to remind him every now and then that I'm capable of doing things for myself." Out of the blue, Karla wrapped an arm around Savannah and squeezed her tight. "I hate that you're having to deal with that asshole and the trial at a time like this, Savannah. You should be focused solely on your baby and your family right now."

Savannah felt the eyes of everyone in the room boring in on her and came so close to sharing with them what was going on in her head, but if she couldn't talk to Damián about it, she didn't feel right confiding with them.

"How are you holding up?" Karla asked.

Savannah shrugged. "I won't pretend it's not hard. I'll just be glad when it's over."

The other women expressed their empathy and support, although she feared she saw a little pity in their eyes as well.

Cassie, usually so quiet, spoke up then. "Savannah, simply tell your story. Justice will prevail, and he will at last be held accountable for the despicable things he did to you." She took a shaky breath. "And when you are on the stand, find a focal point that will help you avoid eye contact with him. Center yourself. Keep visualizing that moment when he will be found guilty and put away where he can never do harm to you again."

Cassie had brought her rapists to justice in Peru only a few months ago. She was probably the only person in this room who could understand what Savannah had been through. Overcome with intense emotion, Savannah blinked back tears as she crossed the room and embraced her for a long moment. "Thanks, Cassie. I hope I'm as strong as you have been."

"I am sure you will be even stronger. And Damián will give you additional strength as well. Let him take care of you. Pamper you. Love you."

Even more determined than ever to make tonight special with the man she loved, Savannah said, "I will."

"Group hug," Karla announced, and the other women joined them. Savannah felt the collective strength of the women in this circle of friends. She wouldn't be alone in this. When they broke up, several of the women, including Savannah, brushed away tears.

Karla set the dishwasher's dial and started it before turning to Cassie again. "We're going to be late. I think you know where everything is. You've been here often enough. Just make yourself at home, and if there's any emergency, text Grant. She's tending bar tonight, for old time's sake, and she'll be keeping her phone on and with her."

The Domme had been running the club ever since Adam turned it over to her this past spring when he moved his family into this house. Adam and Damián stepped in whenever needed because they were still co-owners, but Marc seemed to have removed himself from the club after moving two hours away to be closer to Angelina.

Savannah wondered if the two of them had found a dungeon in the Breckenridge area to play at. Damián's whip mentor, Gunnar Larson, had a private one near there. The whip master had invited Damián to visit a number of times over the summer, but they'd been too busy to go. Perhaps if they took Angelina up on her offer to dine at her restaurant, they could stay over at Cassie's or Megan's and check the place out. Not so much because Savannah wanted another place to play, but Gunnar intrigued her. She'd like to figure out what made him tick.

None of her business, though, whether Marc and Angelina played publicly or only in the bedroom these days. The strain she'd seen between them last winter and spring had disappeared, which was all that mattered. Their new log home was half-built in a secluded valley with great views of the mountains they said, somewhere near Cassie and Luke's. With the wedding supposedly a mere six months away and winter upon them, the house might not be ready in time. But they seemed happier than ever, despite the stress of their careers at the moment.

Tonight, these four couples would gather at the club for a chance to reminisce and enjoy a private play party. Damián had left before the table had been cleared, saying he needed to get their play station ready. Was he planning to have a public or private scene with her? They could very well be using one of the theme rooms they had frequented in the past.

The only question in her mind was how much clothing she'd be permitted to wear once she got there. Probably not much, based on how he'd asked her to dress—thong, wraparound skirt, tank top with bra insert, and his leather jacket. Last night, he'd asked Mari to paint each of Savannah's toenails in a rainbow of colors. Her little girl had enjoyed doing that, and had painted her own as well. Mari must think she had the coolest mom on the block.

If she only knew.

Chapter Eight

Damián had gone to the club early to set up their play area. Knowing she couldn't lie on her back anymore, he and Dad had come up with the perfect solution—a massage chair. Earlier this week, Grant had shown him what this bad boy could do. He grinned as he tucked the special disposable covering in place, because he intended to make his girl soaking wet later on when they played. Anything to make cleaning up the leather easier so they could move on to better things.

He straightened the implements he'd chosen on the tray near the chair and glanced toward the door. No sign of them yet. Grant was cutting limes at the bar, having promised to keep an eye on things tonight, serving double duty as bartender and dungeon monitor. She'd worry less about that latter role, knowing Damián and the others here tonight wouldn't be doing anything unsafe.

As a precaution, Damián had already assured Grant that he'd cleared everything with the obstetrician. Having never been pregnant herself, well as far as Damián knew, he didn't want Grant to question what he was doing or to freak out. Not that he could picture the calm, collected Grant freaking out about anything.

Even in Fallujah, Grant seemed to have had it all under control.

Damián, on the other hand, had struggled to maintain control for years, most especially on this of all days. Yeah, he'd put Fallujah behind him but understood the need to come together as survivors so that they didn't forget the losses his unit suffered, especially that of Sergeant Miller. And Ryder had suffered alone all these years, until Dad had sent him to check on Megan and a romance took shape. Tonight, they would celebrate the survival spirit of those who bonded in Iraq, and perhaps, they'd all find more healing tonight.

With everything at the ready, he sobered as his thoughts turned to his wife. Savannah probably had a bunch of days after years of torture and abuse where she felt like she could have died. But she had no single anniversary date to commemorate the amazing accomplishment of surviving the cruelty of the *cabrón* who had fathered her. Day in and day out from the age of eight, Savannah had endured a living nightmare. He needed to find a way to honor her perseverance, resilience, and strength. To have gone through all she had and still be able to escape that Christmas Eve, nineteen and pregnant. To have single-handedly protected their daughter from harm so many times over the years. And to have survived everything those bastards threw at her last March after the kidnapping—where the team had barely arrived in time before the *bastardo* killed her—*fuck yeah*, that deserved to be commemorated.

Laughter from the entryway alerted him that the gang had arrived. He draped a cloth over his station on the stage so as not to tip Savannah off yet as to what he had in mind.

Damián grinned as he crossed the great room to greet Savannah and the couples. But his gaze quickly zeroed in on his wife, who had removed her shoes but not his leather jacket. It looked so fucking hot on her with her red tank tee peeking out. He wrapped his arm around her waist in a blatantly possessive move, pulling her to his side and kissing her on the forehead. "I've missed you, *savita*."

Savannah giggled, a sound he'd missed hearing lately. "We've only been apart forty-five minutes."

"Way too long. Can I get you some water before we start?"

"That would be great." He'd stick to water, too.

A glance at the bar showed him that the other couples had already lined up and had Grant busy filling their orders. The Domme hadn't chosen to bring any of the male subs she usually played with tonight. The woman seemed to prefer being alone lately, as Damián had at one time. But he only hoped she'd find someone to complete her someday, like he'd found his Savannah.

Thinking it might be a good time to begin grounding Savannah for their scene later, he squared his shoulders in front of her, cupped her chin, and brought her gaze up to meet his. "You are the strongest woman I know, Savannah. Tonight, I'm going to challenge you, but I need to be able to trust that you will let me know when you've reached your limits or are too uncomfortable to continue."

Her breath hitched, telling him she was ready to surrender. "Yes, Sir." He streaked his blunt fingernails slowly up and down her arms, bringing more of her nerve endings to the surface. Goosebumps broke out along her flesh. He smiled. After weeks of being shut down, he hoped tonight would be a turning point for them both.

"Know that I am here to protect and guide you. I will always put your safety and best interests first. And you will always have your safewords, in case you need them. Tell me again what they are."

"Tamale for stop and guacamole to slow down."

"Excellent, *savita*. Now, expect to experience new sensations tonight. Some might make you uncomfortable, but they'll ultimately bring you to a deeper understanding of your power as my submissive and a greater sense of focus and control over circumstances around you."

Savannah bit the corner of her lower lip. Insecurity wasn't the response he wanted to see. But she bowed her head and said, "I'm ready, Sir."

He had his work cut out for him tonight. Taking her hand, he led her to where Karla and Angelina chatted. They zeroed in on her toenails, and Savannah explained Marisol had painted them at Damián's request. The splash of color would be perfect for what he had planned later.

Leaving them to chat, he went to the bar just as Marc guided Megan and Ryder toward the theme rooms on their first tour of the club before any scenes got underway back there.

"Two waters, please."

Grant smiled and handed him the chilled bottles. "All set for tonight, Damo?"

He nodded, but didn't know if she meant the Alive Day talk or the scenes he'd planned for him and Savannah. "As ready as I'll ever be."

She sobered. "How are you holding up today?"

He thought about it for a moment and made an interesting discovery. "That day seems like forever ago now. I've lost the bitterness and anger."

"Finding Savannah again was a big part of getting you to that place, too, I think."

Grant grinned and stared wistfully at Savannah, who was laughing at something Angelina said. "Savannah fits right in with the girls." Did Grant regret always hanging out with the guys rather than the girls? He'd never noticed.

Savannah's being a part of the extended family was something that made Damián even more proud of her, so he'd hold off dragging her away from them a little while longer.

Ten minutes later, Ryder, Megan, and Marc rejoined the group socializing at the bar. "No doubt Megan and I will find something to occupy our time here tonight. Nice club, by the way."

Dad's eyes narrowed as he seemed to contemplate Ryder's words. Apparently, Ryder and Megan were at least opened-minded about BDSM. Who knew? Maybe they'd become the newest members of the club, although the two-hour drive might keep them away more than big-brother Adam would.

Dad gestured toward the tables Grant and Damián had pushed together earlier. "Enough shooting the shit. We aren't here for the scuttlebutt. Let's get to the real gouge."

Damián appreciated Dad's cutting to the chase. He hoped talking about Fallujah would reduce his increasing tension about tonight's scene with Savannah.

He shifted his focus now to this time to reflect on the importance of this day, remember Sergeant Miller and his family's sacrifice, and maybe make more sense out of what had happened on that rooftop.

Grant had made sure everyone had something in hand to drink, so they each took a seat. When Savannah moved to take the seat next to him, he pulled her onto his lap. He wanted to feel her close to him for this.

"Hard to believe it's been eight years since we were in that shithole sandbox," Dad began, his hand idly stroking Karla's hand, which was joined with his on the tabletop. She looked at him, concern written on her face. What had he told her about Fallujah? For that matter, what did Angelina and Megan know? Savannah had heard some of it, what little Damián remembered anyway, but he'd been out of it mostly.

"I remember that day as if it were yesterday," Dad continued. "Sending Marc up to that rooftop after hearing the call for a corpsman. Not knowing for the longest time what had happened to my Marines was torture."

"Yeah," Marc chimed in. "When I got up there and saw the carnage, I didn't know at first how many Marines had been hit. Didn't take long to see I couldn't help Sergeant, though."

Damián waited for the images to bombard his mind again, but they didn't. Maybe he'd come to terms with that part finally.

"I was afraid I'd lose you, too, Damián," Marc said.

"I have to say, Doc, you hid your concern well. Hearing you tell me I was going to be okay gave me the assurance I would be. I have to admit, though, when I saw my foot dangling by skin and tendons, I had my doubts."

Savannah stiffened, and he had second thoughts about her hearing this. Hoping to put the focus back on Sergeant, he continued. "It all happened so fast. Sergeant and I were gabbing about stuff." He looked up at Savannah. "I was telling him about you, actually." Her eyes opened wide, since they'd only spent one day and night together by that point. "Then the grenade landed in front of us, and I just stared at it, frozen."

"We've gone over this before, son. You know that grenade exploded in a matter of seconds. There wasn't much anyone could have done to escape its blast."

Damián nodded. "Yeah, I know. Weird how your mind plays games with you."

Ryder, who had been quiet up to this point, cleared his throat. "Grant and I weren't close enough to do anything but watch and try to take care of you and Sergeant after the explosion. The guilt of losing a man who had a wife and kids back home ripped my guts out for a long time. Still does sometimes." Megan stroked his arm, ignoring the tears streaming down her face. "For a long time, all I could think was that it should have been me."

"Survivor guilt won't bring any of them back," Dad said. "Believe me, I know." A shadow passed over his face. Damián remembered the tattoo Dad had on his back naming the three men who had died on his watch, including Marc's brother. Dad would never forget any of them.

Hoping to lift the mood a little, Damián asked, "Any word from Mrs. Miller lately?" He fingered the wristband and almost thought he could smell Sergeant's cigarette in the room.

"Spoke with her this morning, as a matter of fact," Dad said. Of course, he would. He'd been faithful about keeping up with Mrs. Miller and her kids ever since Fallujah. "Said she started dating someone from her church a few months ago."

Some of the weight on Damián's shoulders lifted hearing that. "Glad to hear she's able to move on finally." He'd worried a lot about the Millers over the years but hadn't known what to do. He and Tracy Miller, Sergeant's oldest, had exchanged cards and notes ever since she'd given him that leather wristband she'd made.

"That's definitely a good sign that she's healing," Savannah added. "I can't imagine what she and those kids have been through." She stroked Damián's arm as if to remind herself he was here among the living.

"Karla and I plan to stop in again next time we head up to see our folks and Marge in Chicago."

"Are you going up for Thanksgiving?" Damián asked. Prior to last year, Dad usually stopped in to visit the Millers when driving to or from Minnesota where Marge, his first mother-in-law, used to live before moving in with Mrs. Gallagher in Chicago. The two women who had mothered Adam had really hit it off at Dad and Karla's wedding. And, even though East St. Louis was out of the way, he and Karla had visited on their way back from the Black Hills last December, too. Dad would never forsake the families of his three fallen Marines, but the Millers were special. The other two lost Marines had no kids.

"No, actually, with the babies being so small, we've decided to celebrate at home this year. You're all invited to our place, while we're talking about it. We have enough room to have a sit-down meal for a platoon in that place, so invite anyone you want. You guys can pitch in on the sides and desserts, but Karla wants to do the ham and stuff the bird this year."

"Angelina's given me some private lessons," Karla said. "I say, bring it, bird."

Everyone laughed, the tension in the room easing somewhat. Then Damián decided it was time to share his thoughts. He swallowed hard. So much for thinking he'd put it all behind him.

Chapter Nine

Savannah inhaled slowly, trying to hide her nervousness from Damián. Was she ready to hear more about that horrific day that had almost taken him from this world?

Damián's body tensed, and his arms pulled her closer seconds before he spoke. Savannah held her breath, her heart pounding as she waited to learn more about the man she loved.

"Breathe, *bebé*," he commanded before beginning his story. She let the air out in a whoosh and filled her lungs again. "In the first five or six years after Fallujah, I had mixed feelings about celebrating what I thought at the time was the worst day of my life." He swallowed, his Adam's apple bobbing before he picked up the bottle of water on the floor beside him to drink half of it before setting it down. "Those were some dark-ass days, especially the first five months. When the doctors at Balboa told me I was ready to go back out in the world, it scared the shit out of me." His arm tightened around her as if afraid she'd bolt. "I'm ashamed to say it now, but I planned my suicide for the day after I was released. Had my sidearm at Rosa's, although I never would have done it where she or the kids would have found my body. I'd planned on going down to Barrio Logan, a rough neighborhood in San Diego, where I'd have just become another of the twenty-two that day."

Savannah's heart beat so fast she almost couldn't catch a breath. He referred to the twenty-two veterans who took their lives daily in the States. While he'd told her there'd been a point where he hadn't wanted to go on, she hadn't heard him speak about the details and how close he'd come to putting his plan into motion before. Suicide using a firearm rarely failed.

Savannah shuddered at the image of his bloody young body dead from a self-inflicted gunshot wound. She didn't want to intrude on his story, but needing even more physical contact, she leaned her forehead against his ear and whispered, "I'm so glad you didn't."

He drew her closer. "Me, too, *bebé.*"

She stroked the nape of his neck, much as she would comfort Mari when her daughter was upset.

Damián drew a ragged breath, patting her thigh as if to reassure *her*. "Then Doc and Top marched into my hospital room at Balboa and busted my balls but good." He grinned, expelling his breath and some of the tension ebbed from his shoulders. Savannah had never heard him express these feelings before. "I owe you guys for my still being here."

"No man left behind," Adam said. "That responsibility doesn't end on the battlefield for a Marine."

"Glad you had Adam and Doc there when you needed them, Damo" Ryder said quietly. Savannah glanced his way and saw the haunted look in his eyes. Had he, too, almost become a statistic? Two veterans who'd nearly become casualties after the fact from one incident. No wonder the number of suicides among veterans was so out of control.

Damián nodded. "I'll have to be honest with you guys, though. I don't remember much about my actual Alive Day. One minute, I'm talking shit with Sergeant on that roof. Next thing I remember, I'm waking up in a hospital in Germany. Nothing in between, except for what I've seen in nightmares and flashbacks."

"Would it help you if the others who were there shared what they remember?" Adam asked him.

"I was okay with doing this today, given that I don't remember a lot about the explosions and their aftermath. But you guys weren't unconscious for most of it, so no pressure on anyone to share. I know it had to be a shitstorm for you guys."

That he was concerned about them made her love him a little more, if that was even possible.

The other three men and Grant looked at one another. When no one spoke, Ryder cleared his throat. "Thanks, man, but I need to get this out."

He grew silent again as Megan stroked his thigh, which seemed to give him the courage he needed. "I'd never watched anyone die in front of my eyes before." He swallowed hard and cleared his throat. "Grant and I were like you and Sergeant, Damo, just shooting the breeze. When you screamed *grenade*, we barely had time to look up before both your bodies flew into the air and landed on each other."

"Damo, you saved our lives or at the very least kept us from being severely injured," Grant added, her leg beginning to shake uncontrollably with barely contained emotion. "Grateful doesn't begin to express how I feel. I don't know what demons you had to fight to choose life over death, but I'm damned glad you're here with us tonight. You'll always be a hero in my book."

"Sergeant's the hero," Damián countered.

She smiled at him, shaking her head because it was probably the response she expected. "When we pulled Sergeant off of you so Doc could assess your condition, I'll admit I wasn't sure you'd make it."

"That makes two of us," Ryder said.

Grant glanced down at her shaking knee, her face becoming ashen as the images of that day likely bombarded her. Savannah wished she had someone here tonight to give her a hug, but knew the tough Marine wouldn't have accepted comfort from anyone.

She seemingly willed the trembling to stop and whispered, "It was clear right away that we'd lost Sergeant." Once again, she met Damián's gaze. "But you were conscious. I don't think you were aware of the severity of your injuries yet."

"I've had flashbacks where I can see my bloody boot lying cockeyed and the pool of what I thought at first was Sergeant's blood until I saw it pouring from where my foot used to be attached to my leg."

Dear God. And Savannah thought *her* flashbacks were bad. How did he deal with such horrific ones? Had he experienced any while with her? She knew she shouldn't interrupt, but the need to know took precedence. "How often do you still have flashbacks, Sir?"

He grabbed and pulled her hair until she was forced to meet his gaze and then gave her an enigmatic smile. She held her breath as she waited for his response. "Not very often. I'm only triggered by a noise or the smell of blood. Or when I'm emotionally spent and not sleeping well. But I haven't had one in a long time. Actually, you were there for the last one."

"The night Mari and I moved in with Adam and Karla?"

He nodded.

Yes, she remembered that night so well. Her inability to wake him from his nightmare flashback had scared her to death, and she'd left for fear he might hurt Mari or her or both. "Promise me you'll let me know if they return?"

He stared at her a long moment. "Will you promise me the same, *savita?*"

Her heart thumped. Was he aware that she hadn't been sharing her own flashbacks with him? She'd told herself she was protecting him from the ugliness, but if he were going through a similar time, she'd want to know so she could help him. She needed to come clean with him, but the club and this gathering weren't the place to remedy what she should have done over a month ago.

"Yes, Sir. I will." *Just as soon as we get home.* She'd kept him out of the loop too long. Having his own experience with PTSD, he might be able to help with hers.

"Deal then, *querida*, and we'll talk more about this later." His focus returned to their circle of friends. "Sorry. That was too important to put off."

Yes, he totally knows. So why hadn't he called her on it? Maybe he wanted to give her every opportunity to come forward on her own. Or perhaps he'd planned something for tonight that would have pushed the issue to the forefront.

Did he intend to punish her for her dishonesty? She blinked away the sting in her eyes. She'd never wanted to disappoint him, but she'd totally messed this up.

Marc turned toward Damián. "I'll tell you the truth, when I first saw you lying there, I expected you to bleed out before I could apply a tourniquet. I couldn't really do anything to help Sergeant by the time I made it to the rooftop, but I refused to let you be the first Marine I'd lost despite my best efforts. You were in pretty rough shape."

Ryder added, "Doc kept telling you that you were going to be fine, but I figured he was just trained to say that to help the dying stay calm. Grant and I had to fight to keep your head and shoulders down so you couldn't see the extent of your injury."

"Yeah," Marc said. "I tried to keep you from going into shock. Of course, with all that blood loss, you did anyway."

Adam, who hadn't said much other than to guide the conversation, spoke up next. "Doc, if not for you, he probably would have died." Then he turned to Damián. "I'll never forget them bringing you down on a stretcher. You were knocking at death's door for sure. Then when Doc didn't come down behind you…" His focus returned to Marc. "Thought maybe you were upset about losing Miller and was afraid you wouldn't be thinking about protecting yourself from further attacks up there. Had no clue you'd been injured, too, until Grant and I cleared the stairs and saw you lying there, unconscious."

"Neither did I." He shrugged and glanced away. "My injury wasn't nearly as bad as Damián's. I never really commemorated my own Alive Day, until tonight."

"I'd have lost you both if not for the medical treatment you administered to Damián on that roof, Doc, and the treatment received from the doctors and nurses in the field hospital and later at Landstuhl."

Angelina placed a kiss on his cheek. She, too, wasn't trying to hide her tears.

"The thing that stands out most in my mind about that time," Marc continued, "was you figuring out I was Gino's brother when you came to see me in the field hospital. Learning more about how my brother died— a hero's death—and seeing what being a hero meant, with Damián and Sergeant and all the others in the unit, helped me begin to put the past to rest. Then having my parents show up in Germany, well, that was a shock."

"You know how much they love you," Angelina said.

"I do now. I was kind of a jerk back then."

She shook her head and smiled. "No comment."

The room fell silent as perhaps those who had lived through that fateful day reminisced in private. Damián hadn't finished sharing, though.

"I didn't want what happened that day to determine the rest of my life. I wanted to get control back in my hands. This…"—he pointed at his prosthesis—"wasn't going to determine my destiny." He paused and looked around the room, not just at the people but the club itself. "When you asked me to be a part of this crazy idea to start a sex club, which is what I thought of it as at first, I had nothing to lose. Why not join in? It would be a good distraction." He sobered. "But this place and this lifestyle played a big part in helping me regain a sense of control."

He paused a moment to finish his bottle of water before continuing. "I was one of the lucky ones. I stared down death and beat the fuck out of it. Just before that grenade exploded, I was talking with Sergeant about this woman." He stroked Savannah's cheek, and she closed her eyes and leaned into his hand. "About how much I regretted that she wasn't going to be a part of my life. But then I got a second chance with her, too, thanks in part to this place and you guys.

"November 15, 2004 used to be one of my darkest days. Then Savannah was abducted March 19, and Marisol nearly was, too. I'd never felt more helpless, much more so than in the aftermath of Fallujah."

Tears streamed down her cheeks now, too, and she rested her head on his shoulder as they caressed each other. "That was nothing compared to what you all went through."

"Hear me out, *bebé*." He turned to the men and women in the circle. "Not to take anything away from anyone who served, but PTSD isn't limited to veterans," Damián said. "And come March 21, the anniversary of the day Savannah was rescued at that cabin, I want you all to join me in commemorating her first official Alive Day. Her strength, resilience, and survivor instinct need to be saluted, too."

Self-conscious of everyone's gazes on her, several of them nodding their agreement with Damián, she said, "Today is about the warrior heroes in this room. You all went into combat, nearly got the crap knocked out of you, saw unspeakable things, and still returned home as heroes and survivors. I'm so proud to know each and every one of you."

Damián caged her chin and forced her to look into his eyes. "Accept the fact that you nearly lost your life that day, *querida,* and probably came close on other days in your young life as well. This will be an important step for you in putting the past behind you."

By dredging it up again?

But those who had shared their memories tonight seemed to be finding some peace with the event that changed so many of their lives. Each handled the memories from that day differently. Adam still didn't talk about his own feelings but did help others to open up. Grant remained completely buttoned up, while Ryder still seemed close to the edge but moving in the right direction. Marc appeared to be almost guilty calling this his Alive Day when he came home with all his body parts intact.

And Damián, who lost his foot that day, seemed to have mostly let it go. Of course, he remembered but didn't let that moment in time rule his life. He mostly functioned with no real issues because of his sense of purpose and hope.

Tonight, Damián opened up about things she'd never heard him speak of before. But his mood and body language had lightened up as the discussion progressed. The man amazed her, but she had to admit he often had insights that she didn't concerning herself. It was so much easier to see someone else's situation more clearly than one's own.

But this still wasn't the time or place to discuss what happened to her.

"We will talk later," Savannah whispered. She sounded like she was giving Mari a *we'll see*, but this night wasn't about her, and she couldn't help but feel embarrassed to have her trials compared to theirs.

To herself, though, she tried to see where she was on the spectrum.

Damián and these vets would always be her rock. They gave her hope that perhaps someday she would find her own strength and courage to overcome the horrors of her past. Right now, though, Savannah was anything but strong. Look at how she'd cowered for weeks over her upcoming trial testimony.

Damián was right about one thing, though. If he and his team—Adam, Grant, and Marc—hadn't arrived in time, there was no doubt in her mind that Gentry would have killed her when he'd finished torturing her.

She owed her very life and happiness to the people in this room. Damián most of all, because he'd brought her into this family of choice.

Chapter Ten

The group wrapped up their intense session with some claps on the back and a few man-hugs. Another Alive Day almost over. He hadn't planned on telling everyone about his near suicide attempt—especially not Savannah—but it just came out. Of course, Dad and Marc knew, and he'd told Angelina once when he wanted her to know Marc had helped save his life a second time—by calling Dad to Balboa the day before his release from rehab.

After he'd confided in Angelina where he'd been at that dark time in his life, she'd admitted to similar thoughts. Her promise to tell him whenever she had a flashback was a step in the right direction for them both. Talking about his anxieties and fears could make Savannah more comfortable about doing the same. *Mierda*, he needed to remind her he wasn't looking for perfection, because he wasn't perfect, either. Being human meant they'd make mistakes. The important thing was to learn from them. Time for him to man up and admit his own shortcomings more often if it meant providing her with a deeper level of trust. If she was afraid of looking vulnerable and imperfect, this might be a huge step in her healing if he helped alleviate some of her fears.

Despite Savannah's discomfort about her proposed Alive Day, Damián was determined to give his wife her own commemoration next spring. If he had to do it, then she damned well did, too. Although he had to admit it had been his choice to do this tonight.

Damián hadn't just blurted it out, either. He'd thought about suggesting it all week, but had chosen to bring it up tonight so he could cast the spotlight on her to see how she handled it. Uncomfortable to the extreme. He only had from now until she took the witness stand in three or four weeks to condition her to face the monster from her past and remove her fears.

He couldn't wait to move on to the next part of the evening. Luckily, talk soon turned to that very topic, lifting everyone's moods, judging by the laughter in the room. Grant reminded the two guests of some of the rules then added, "Ryder and Megan, you're welcome to watch anything going on in the great room or any area where you're invited to do so. Please remember to remain silent unless asked to speak so as not to pull anyone out of their scene."

Perfect segue. "You're welcome to watch the scenes Savannah and I will be doing in here." While she didn't say anything, he felt Savannah tense beside him. She needed this.

Ryder nodded, without consulting with Megan, and said, "We'd like that."

After the club owners and their subs headed to the theme rooms they'd reserved for the evening, Damián took Savannah's hand and led her to the stage area. Karla would be playing with Dad tonight rather than singing, so he and Grant had agreed that the stage would be the best place for Damián to do two of the scenes he'd planned for Savannah.

Her gaze fell and lingered on the massage chair he'd obscured with a large tarp, which he could later move to the floor to keep things from getting too messy. True to her discipline, she didn't ask what was under it.

Good girl.

He turned on the Nine Inch Nails CD he'd chosen to set the mood and tempo and parted her jacket to reveal breasts tightly encased in a red tank tee, leaving little to the imagination. Savannah's gaze flitted to the others in the room, as if suddenly shy. This would be the first time they'd done such an intense scene in front of others since the Princess Slut one. Among Damián's ongoing goals for Savannah was getting her to view her body as the masterpiece it was, but he would have to ease her into it.

"Eyes, *savita.*"

He read concern and perhaps some embarrassment in them but hoped to banish any negative thoughts by getting this scene into full swing as quickly as possible.

"Remove the jacket, *savita*."

She spread it open farther and let it slide off her shoulders and down her arms to the floor. He picked it up and placed it on a nearby table. Respect the Harley emblem.

"Now the skirt." He waved his fingers in the direction of the garment.

With trembling fingers but no hesitation, she released the bow at her side, and the gauzy material puddled in a cloud at her feet. She lowered her gaze to the floor, her trust and submission greatly pleasing to Damián.

"You always make me proud to accept your submission, *savita*." He stepped in front of her to take in her sexy body in a slow, sweeping gaze. "So beautiful." A blush tinged her cheeks, whether from his compliment or because her body was exposed in front of others, he wasn't sure. The tank tee and thong hid little from the imagination, especially his, because he'd memorized every inch of her.

Closing the gap between them, he stroked his hands over her belly before bending to place a kiss on the top of her baby bump. Damián whispered to the baby that this would be a good time for a nap. She needed no further distractions. "Daddy will take good care of Mommy over the next couple of hours, Baby Orlando."

She giggled at his half-silly remark. Yeah, as if he had control of their baby now any more than he would after he or she was born. But he'd reduced some of the tension she'd been feeling.

Damián stood straighter to walk around behind her and pulled her against his erection to let her know how much simply looking at her excited him. It had been way too long since they'd been intimate. He placed a protective hand under her belly as he nuzzled her neck.

Sucking her earlobe between his teeth, he tugged, eliciting a breathy rasp. Releasing it sooner than he wished, he whispered so only she could hear, "I can't wait to fuck you later."

Instead of leaning into his body with a sigh as she used to at such a declaration, she stiffened. *Well, fuck.* Would he be able to reignite the flame inside her tonight? She used to enjoy having sex with him, but the closer they came to the trial starting, the more she regressed. He hoped to get them back to a place where they could enjoy sex again. A night of fun

BDSM ought to help him achieve that.

"Present yourself for me, *savita*."

Damián put some space between them to watch as she moved into one of the first positions he'd taught her. Clasping her elbows at the small of her back, her breasts jutted forward, making him harder. She planted her feet shoulder width apart. As always, her presentation was flawless, and he was lost for a moment in her beauty.

"Very nice, *bebé*."

She smiled but didn't relax her stance. Savannah's gaze zeroed in on the seating area in the great room. That confirmed for Damián that she was still far too preoccupied with who might be watching rather than paying enough attention to her Dom at the moment.

Well, he grinned, *game on.* Tonight was all about commanding her attention, and he had a lot to accomplish, so he'd better get started. He walked around behind her, preparing to rock her world.

* * *

Damián stood behind her, but she felt the heat of his gaze on her backside. He'd laid out whatever implements he must plan to use tonight on a table covered by a cloth, but her attention went straight to the large piece of equipment hidden by the tarp in the center of the stage. What did he have in mind for her tonight? Would she at least be allowed to wear her thong, even though it hid next to nothing?

When they'd first arrived at the club, she'd thought the room a bit warm, but stripped bare now, she realized her embarrassment and nervousness only made her hotter.

Savannah avoided looking in Megan and Ryder's direction. In the past, Damián had played publicly with her in various degrees of undress, but not when she'd been six months pregnant and with two friends in the room who were new to BDSM and the club. That factor made it difficult for her to concentrate.

But she reminded herself that Damián found her body beautiful and sexy no matter what, so she pushed away any insecurities or cares about what anyone else might think. If he wanted to show her off to others, then she'd be the most attentive submissive in the club to make her Dom proud. While Angelina and Karla enjoyed being bratty with their Doms, who seemed to love it despite token protests, Savannah preferred to let Damián guide and dominate her without interference. After being controlled by men for so much of her life, that didn't make sense. But those men hadn't treated her with the respect and adoration Damián did.

Realization hit her like a lightning bolt. She'd known for a long time that the primary difference in her relationship with Damián and those other men was that she'd made the choice to surrender her control to Damián. He'd never taken anything she hadn't wanted to give him. Yes, he'd sometimes pushed her harder and sooner than she was ready, but he would stop if she couldn't take whatever it was he was doing.

If she used her safeword, which she still had an aversion to doing.

Mindful that she was supposed to be focusing on her Dom and her body's response to his commands and actions, she waited patiently as he came close again. Savannah took a deep breath. Would she be staying here on the stage or moving to another apparatus for whatever he had planned?

"We're going to do some impact play first."

Thank God. She craved a cathartic whipping, even though she knew Damián wouldn't give her the intensity she needed until after the baby was born. Still, she'd gladly take whatever he would dish out.

His use of the word *first* made it sound as if he planned something more later tonight. Oh, how she needed this time with him.

"I want everyone to see that pretty ass of yours turn red for me, so we're going to move this over to the center post."

Leave it to Damián to know what his good girl needed most. She smiled, audience or not, and without making eye contact with the Wilsons or Mistress Grant, she let him guide her across the floor. She didn't care now that all she wore was a skimpy thong that hid nothing but her mound and the skintight tank tee.

After placing the padded wrist cuffs on her, he hooked them to the post above her head, while keeping her feet planted flat on the floor so as not to strain her legs, always thoughtful of her comfort level. He slapped her bare butt a couple of times with his hand to bring the blood to the surface, alerting her he might be less gentle tonight.

Sweet Baby Jesus, am I ever ready for this.

Damián circled her body and the post, letting his fingernails graze lightly over the skin across her shoulders and down her back, raising gooseflesh throughout her upper body. Her nipples bunched, eagerly awaiting the kiss of whatever implement he chose to use. The slight abrasion from the wooden post would intensify once the impact session got under way. Was he going to use the whip? She hadn't noticed whether the tables and chairs had been moved away to give him ample room. Or could he be planning to use a four-foot whip instead of the eight-foot one he preferred when she wasn't carrying his baby?

His nails raked over her butt cheeks. *Oh dear Lord.* She grew wet, wanting him to touch her more intimately there. It had been so long since she'd been filled with such desire. Getting out of her head for a while helped.

"I've been anticipating this for more than a week, *savita*," he whispered in her ear.

Me, too.

He cupped her chin and turned her face toward his, bending to kiss her lips. His hand lowered her jaw as his tongue plunged inside her mouth. He stole her breath, and her heart rate ramped up. He ended the kiss way too soon, releasing her and moving to stand behind her, grabbing her butt cheeks and grinding his leather-covered erection against her crack to let her know she turned him on. She couldn't contain the moan of desire that escaped.

His fingernails left a trail of gooseflesh up and down her arms, leaving butterflies erupting in her stomach as her chest grew tighter with anticipation. The baby chose that moment to attempt a somersault, which was becoming more difficult for her little one as Savannah's pregnancy advanced but apparently not impossible.

The rasp of his fingernails continued their trek, moving to her breasts and belly. He returned to her side and bent down to place a kiss on her belly before his gentle hand caressed her abdomen as if to comfort the baby or perhaps to lull him or her to sleep again while they played. Staring down at the top of Damián's head, she waited for him to glance her way or show his hand and clue her in as to what he had in mind. Then she realized he had a bullwhip coiled on the belt loop of his leathers. How had she missed seeing that before?

So this *would* be a whip session. She grinned.

He seemed to be in no hurry, though, as he continued to touch her from her scalp to the backs of her legs and everywhere in between. Savannah wished he would hurry before everyone came out of the theme rooms to join them, although the clock on the wall told her it had only been about fifteen minutes since they'd broken into their separate areas. Most of them would want to play for a couple of hours before having to return home to their responsibilities.

Curiosity got the best of her, and she dared to glance toward Megan and Ryder. Megan sat curled in his lap, his arms around her as they watched with rapt attention. A flush crept up Megan's neck and into her friend's face when her gaze met Savannah's. If Megan thought *she* was embarrassed…

Slap!

Damián's hand smacking against her butt brought Savannah's focus back to her Dom.

"Where should your eyes and focus be, *querida?*" She stared into his brown eyes, breathing deeply, feeling ashamed that he'd caught her lapse in attention. Rather than appear disappointed, though, he merely grinned. There was something a little devious about that smile, as if she'd played right into his hands.

"I see we are going to need to do something about that." His words only served to ramp up both her anxiety and her anticipation. "I'm going to count backwards from twenty, *savita.*" Hypnosis? While they'd been playing around with it at home this past week, she thought it was more to help take her mind off the trial and other worries. Had he been trying to see if she was a good candidate for it? She could have told him she was, having been through hypnotherapy on multiple occasions. But never in the middle of a BDSM scene.

Without another word, he began to induce her. She knew no one could put a person in trance without their consent, but she was more than willing. "Twenty, nineteen, eighteen, seventeen…" With each number, the strain and tension flowed out of her body. While still aware of her surroundings, the sights and sounds in the room became muted and she became hyperaware of her Dom's eyes, his voice, his touch. "…two, one."

"Deep, cleansing breath. On the exhale, release any remaining tension."

She relaxed even more after doing as he'd instructed. He spent what seemed like another ten or fifteen minutes taking her deeper into trance. When she felt as if she couldn't get any more relaxed without falling asleep, he continued.

"When I touch or stroke your arm, you will pull out of trance immediately. You will remember everything that happens while under hypnosis." She always did the same with her therapist, recalling everything that was said, what she thought, and every other aspect of her time in trance. The clink of a glass from the bar area jolted her momentarily. She thought she smelled candles. She needed to shut those extraneous matters out and focus on Damián and his commands. She took a deep breath and released it, relaxing even further.

Damián took a deep, cleansing breath of his own. Was he nervous? Should *she* be? "Now, let's begin, *savita*."

I trust him to do me no harm.

"Whenever I—and only I—tap you on the forehead, you will go deeper into trance and feel the impact of whatever implement I'm using twice as hard as the time before. With each tap, any place I touch you with my hand or any of my toys will also be that many times more sensitive than before. Are you ready?"

"Yes, Sir." *More than ever.*

"Now, we're going to try something new." The whip certainly wasn't new, although it had been a while. So what did he have in mind?

"Close your eyes and lean against the post to stabilize yourself."

She took her position and waited.

Tap.

She relaxed into the wood. Waiting.

Crack!

The whip cracked in the air. She jumped before realizing that had just been for show, probably for the Wilsons' benefit, because she hadn't felt the sting of the whip.

But the next hiss of the bullwhip had the leather impacting against her butt with a significant sting. Nothing she couldn't handle, but definitely more sting than he'd given her in recent months. Two more landed on various places on her butt, and she relished each delicious bite of the leather.

Tap.

Hiss.

Crack!

The air whooshed out of her lungs as this strike made contact across both butt cheeks. *Dear God!* He was using more force now. What would the next one be like? She didn't have time to dwell on it before the whip struck in the same place the last one had hit, or near enough.

"Oh!" She couldn't keep the surprise to herself and gasped before trying to prepare for the next. How many would there be? Had he said? She gripped the chain her wrist cuffs had been attached to and waited. *Crack!* The slicing pain of the whip reverberated to her core, followed quickly by another. She writhed as the pain registered in her brain. These were comparable to the lashes he'd given her last spring when he hadn't held back due to her pregnancy.

There was a slight lull, and she wondered when and where the next lash would land. She didn't have to wait long. He tapped her forehead once. The next lash cut into one of her most tender areas, where her butt met her thighs.

Jesus, Mary, and Joseph!

He was moving into Patti's pain levels now. Savannah didn't consider herself a hardcore masochist like Victor's slave did, even though she was a bit of a pain slut. She wasn't sure she could take another blow like that but didn't want to safeword and disappoint Damián after he'd planned this special session for them.

Toughen up, buttercup.

With pain like that, there would have to be marks. Savannah so loved seeing the marks Damián put on her in their early days together and couldn't wait to see these. She tried to catch her breath, waiting, but soon the heat of Damián's body warmed her back, and the brush of his leathers abraded the tender skin of her butt even more. She held her breath, waiting to see what he intended to do next. He cupped both of her breasts before squeezing her nipples.

"Ack!" Had his hypnotic suggestion intensified the sensation there, too? They hadn't been this sensitive in over a month.

His teeth captured her earlobe and bit down. Hard. Her knees buckled, but he caught her, his arm like a band around her torso between her breasts and baby bump, lessening the strain on her arms.

"How are you doing, *bebé?*"

"Fine."

"Only fine? Perhaps I need to start over."

"No! I mean, that was intense, and I'm loving it…"

He chuckled. "Then you'd like me to continue?"

She nibbled her lower lip. "Will it hurt twice as much as the last ones?"

"Would you like it to?"

No. Yes. "I'm not sure."

"You know your stop and slow-down words. Use them if you need to."

The heat of his body left her, and she heard the distinctive swoosh of the cat o' nine. He'd never used one on her before, but she'd watched him use it on Patti. Her body stiffened, awaiting impact. She'd expected the falls to land on her back, but instead, they slashed across her butt and thighs in the same places the whip had already made raw.

"Shit!" The word came out unexpectedly. Damián's only response was a chuckle, the rat bastard. Another slash, and she refused to give him the satisfaction of knowing he had her on the edge of falling apart. Then pain became pleasure. She'd crossed that fine line somewhere between the second and third blows of a cat o' nine tails. The next slash of the tails robbed her of breath and any remaining thought.

He touched her forearm, bringing her out of trance in an instant. Disoriented at first, she blinked a few times. She hadn't used her slowdown or safeword. While proud of herself for not giving in, she realized she probably should have at one point. Her response to this whipping had brought back memories of how she fought letting Gentry or Lyle know they'd hurt her. But this was Damián. And she loved when he dished out pain. He would have been disappointed if she hadn't been able to take it. She could have taken even more to please him. She knew he needed to release some of his own pent-up frustrations and did so by throwing a whip.

They hardly came to the club anymore. And sex at home had been absent for nearly the past month. Was he even interested in her anymore?

Her answer came immediately.

Grinding his pelvis against her sore backside, he ignited flames inside her as long-overdue desire licked at her body. She rubbed her butt against him, wanting him to remove the thong and bury himself deep inside her. But he wouldn't do that in the club, not in the public area with an audience, anyway. At least, he never had before.

The throbbing in her core derailed her. When he nudged her thighs open with his knee, sawing the top of his thigh against her mostly exposed sex, she almost exploded then and there. In retrospect, she was glad she hadn't stopped the scene. As always, Damián found a way to give her what she needed.

As if she wasn't already about to come, his free hand pushed aside the triangular strip of mesh cloth on the front of her thong, and he ran his finger between her lower lips.

"Oh! That feels so good!"

She hadn't expected him to home in on her sex so quickly but opened her legs wider to better accommodate him. Every place he touched was on fire.

"My good girl is so wet for her Dom." His husky words only made her wetter.

Trying to regain her wits, she responded for his ears only, "Only for you, Sir."

"Do you want to come, *savita?*"

"Oh, yes, Sir! Please!"

He chuckled before stepping away and extricating his body from hers. "I think you've been on your feet long enough."

No! He wasn't going to let her come? Savannah couldn't keep her moan of frustration inside, which only elicited another chuckle from Damián. Apparently, he was in a sadistic mood tonight. Nothing more than she deserved after she'd been shut down for so long and uninterested in sex.

But her husband wasn't vindictive or punitive. He understood she sometimes had her dark days, just more so lately than she had been having those thoughts.

He massaged her arms and shoulders after unhooking the leather cuffs from the chains and her head lolled back as she gave into his ministrations. When he removed the cuffs from her wrists and set them aside, he took her arm and turned her toward the stage again. She glanced around, still a little disoriented, and saw that the tables and chairs were way too close to the center post for him to have been able to throw the whip.

"How did you have enough room to inflict that much pain?"

He kissed her forehead. "It was mostly in your imagination, responding to the suggestions I made as I put you in trance."

If there had been a mirror, she'd so have glanced at her butt to see the stripes he'd placed there, but something told her she wouldn't find any because the intensity had all been in her mind. What the ever-loving—

She caught a grin on Ryder's face before her gaze met Damián's again. "Impossible. I know what I felt."

He unhooked the coiled bullwhip from his belt loop, unfurled it, and tapped her butt with it. "That's about how hard I struck you with my whip."

No way!

"What about with the cat? I almost screamed *guacamole* at one point to slow down. Just the *sound* of the cat-o-nine freaks me out, but when it slashed my bare butt and thighs, I didn't think I could continue."

"The only difference in intensity was inside your mind. I told you to expect it to grow harder each time, and it did—but only in your head."

"Unbelievable. I thought this whipping had nothing on the first time I saw you whip Patti—and you were barely touching me."

Damián grew serious. "There's something I want you to tell me. If you were at or beyond your limits with the cat, why didn't you use your slowdown word or your safeword?" When she didn't respond, he continued. "If you weren't under hypnosis and those strikes had actually been at full strength, I could have inflicted bodily harm to you. That's not acceptable, Savannah. I need to be able to trust you to tell me where you are if I don't see it myself. Now, explain yourself."

She lowered her head to stare at his chest, no longer able to make eye contact. The heat of shame crept up her neck and into her cheeks.

"*Bebé?* I asked you a question." He cupped her chin and forced her to meet his gaze. "Tell me."

"I...didn't...want to...disappoint you."

"What makes you think I'd be disappointed? This is a safety issue, Savannah." He wasn't using one of the nicknames he gave her while scening.

She picked at the skin around her fingernail. "But I'd already been sexually distant the last month. I felt I owed it to you to at least be willing to play tonight any way you wanted to. It's your Alive Day." That sounded pathetic even to her ears, but she couldn't stop there. "When you stopped before giving me an orgasm, I realized I was right. I accept that you'd want to deprive me of what I've withheld from you lately."

She ventured a glance at his face. Something she couldn't quite identify flashed in his eyes then smoldered under the surface. "You don't owe me sex, Savannah. Servicing me when you want to is something I find fucking hot, but servicing me when you know it's hurting you should never happen." Damian gave her a look that clearly told her he knew about the deep-throat incident she'd thought she'd hidden so well. "Looking back, I realized what happened, although I was less than observant when your mouth was on my dick. I'm sorry for that, but please promise me you won't ever force yourself again."

Even though she was a master at hiding her feelings and faking it, at some point she'd have expected him to see through her façade and notice her misery. But he was her Dom, not some all-knowing demigod.

Before she could respond, he reinforced his words with, "Even if it's as simple as you aren't in the mood or have too much going on—which you most definitely do right now—don't you think I can understand and accept that? How can you expect me to trust you if you won't let me know when I've gone too far? I'd never forgive myself if I'd hurt you, Savannah, but I can't read your mind. It fucking pains me to think you'd believe I'd punish you for saying no to something or having an emotional response to doing it."

In not using her safeword, she'd actually caused him to be profoundly disappointed in her, the very thing she wanted to avoid. Tears stung her eyes. "I'm…" She swallowed past the lump in her throat. "I'm sorry, Sir." While lying about and hiding her emotions had served her well in the past as a coping mechanism, she could see that it wouldn't work in a healthy relationship.

"We can't play again unless you promise me you won't withhold something like this from me in the future. *¿Comprendes?*"

She nodded her head vigorously. "Yes, Sir. I've learned my lesson. I promise to let you know when I'm nearing my limits, and I need you to point it out anytime you think I'm hiding my emotions. It can take up to six weeks to correct or change a behavior, so I might not be aware I'm doing it at first. But I assure you I won't put myself in a dark place again with my misguided sense of what a wife and submissive should be doing to please her man." She gave him a lopsided grin. "I do have a tendency to want to please people, especially you."

"That's your submissive nature and when your heart's in it, I want nothing more than having you serve my needs, just as I find great pleasure in doing the same as your Dom. But I'm holding you to this promise, *savita.*" His Dom stare sent flutters through her stomach. "And the repercussions next time will be severe, including depriving you of all scening and orgasms for an extended period of time so you won't forget yourself again."

"Thank you for loving me and for protecting me, even from myself sometimes. I am honored to be your submissive and your wife." They leaned toward each other as if drawn by a magnet, and the kiss they shared was so tender tears welled up behind her eyelids. After the kiss ended, she unabashedly brushed them away. He smiled as he brushed a stray one off her cheek.

While her actions—and inactions—had jeopardized any hope of achieving the orgasm she so desperately needed tonight, she wanted to share one more thing. "Sir?"

"*Sí, savita?*"

"That scene under hypnosis was incredibly hot. For the first time in a long time, I was on the verge of exploding. After a month of not even wanting to be touched, much less have an orgasm, it felt so good to get that close again. Thank you for your persistence. I hope we can try that again—soon."

His smile brought enormous comfort to her. "Who said this scene is over?"

That was it? He'd already forgiven her? She loved how he didn't bear a grudge or hold onto disappointment or anger but simply explained where he was coming from and how they could move forward.

She needed to be more like Damián and let go of her hatred and fears. He'd certainly had reason to hate Julio, the insurgents who blew away his foot, and Lyle and Gentry for what they'd done to them both. But he didn't allow them to consume him or make him into some cowering, bitter creature.

He took her hand. "Come. Time for a test ride."

As they approached the stage, she asked, "I hope that means what I think it does."

Damián chuckled but didn't say anything more.

Chapter Eleven

Savannah's focus turned to the stage area as he led her back there. Once again, she wondered what could possibly be under the blue tarp and whether it was meant for her.

Without leaving her to ponder much longer, he lifted the tarp away to reveal a padded chair with another covering on it in the middle of Karla's stage.

"Dad and I just bought this earlier this week for the club. You'll be the first submissive to try it out."

A massage chair? The bigger the boy, the bigger the toy, with Doms being some of the most impatient to try them out on their submissives and bottoms.

Savannah had never sat in one before, although she'd seen one in her OB's office building lobby. She actually was honored to be the first. As one of the newcomers to the club, she often felt like a novice with everything. Besides, after the stress she'd been under the past few weeks, not to mention how tightly coiled her nerves were at the moment, the idea of a massage sounded like heaven.

While she'd prefer he take care of her need for an orgasm first, she knew not to ask or push for one. He'd let her come when he was ready.

After readjusting the protective covering, he helped her into the seat. "Lean your head back and relax your entire body into the chair. ¿Comprendes?"

"Yes, Sir." Sinking back against it, the leather squeaking, she found the chair even more comfortable than expected, so much so that she could have fallen asleep in it.

Damián shook out the tarp, laid it on the floor, and slid it underneath the chair to the base. Between the chair's covering and the tarp, she wondered what kind of mess he expected her to make. What did Damián have in mind? Perhaps something more than a simple massage.

His body blocked the view of her from their audience, well, except for Mistress Grant, but she was busy wiping down the center post. Damián must have asked her ahead of time to help him with that so he could keep the flow of his multi-faceted scene going.

Her comfort was short-lived when Damián spread her knees apart as he positioned her legs into the calf massagers. Self-conscious of her nearly naked pussy, she must have resisted him a little.

"Open wider for me, *mi mariposa.*" It wasn't a request.

Savannah forced herself to relax her thighs and let him minister to her the way he wanted, the imagery of a butterfly spreading its wings flitting through her mind.

"I know you would keep your hands where I place them, but I think you might enjoy the feeling of helplessness these restraints will give." Without waiting for her response, as if it would matter, he secured her arms to the horizontal hand and arm massagers using a fancy Shibari tie he'd probably learned from Adam.

When he stepped away, she saw Megan and Ryder in front of her again and tried to ground herself with her breathing. The stage lights shone brightly upon her, making the rest of the room too dark to make out the figures of those present. She remained hyperaware of being watched. In her therapy sessions, she'd been taught to lightly stroke her wedding band with her thumb. In these restraints, she could still manage that and did so.

Don't be embarrassed.

Trust him.

So what if he liked to show off her body a little bit. She smiled. While no exhibitionist by any means, she found herself stressing less about who watched and more about what Damián had in mind.

After tying her arms where he wanted them, he walked out of sight behind her. She couldn't see him from this position but heard the rustling of something. What could he possibly need other than the remote?

As if on cue, the massagers in the back of the chair began to roll up and down her spine. She hadn't expected it to feel like an actual massage, but moaned as she let the machine work its magic, giving in to the sensations fully.

Again, she became aware that he'd left her exposed for all in the room to see, but she kept her gaze down, refusing to look in Megan and Ryder's direction. Still, her cheeks flamed with embarrassment.

My Dom thinks I'm beautiful, even this pregnant. That's all that matters.

With the edge wearing off her need to come, she decided to give herself over to her Dom wholeheartedly.

Damián came into her field of vision again to stand between her and the Wilsons carrying a small tube and squeezing a cream or liquid into his hand. Lube? But she still wore her thong. He warmed the liquid between his palms. Savannah kept her eyes downcast, submitting to him as she awaited his instructions or gestures, but she felt his gaze warming her insides as well.

He surprised her by kneeling at the foot of the chair and gently massaging the warmed oil into her feet, ankles, and shins. Her skin tingled, whether from the massage or moisturizing oil or the friction of his hands on her skin. Excitement bubbled up inside her again. Was he planning a full-body massage in addition to what the chair could do? Her apprehensions about the rest of the evening ebbed away.

"So soft. Silky." She didn't know if he meant the oil or her legs but decided it was the latter. While he loved her breasts, he was also a leg man.

"Thank you, Sir." Keeping her skin moisturized at Denver's elevation wasn't easy, but she appreciated that her efforts had been noticed. No doubt the oil would help in that regard, too.

He applied more of the herbal-smelling oil to his hands and began working up to her knees and thighs. Her breathing grew shallower as he ignited another fire in her core the closer he came to her pussy. He teased her as his hands moved closer to her mound and then moved away, over and over again.

Please, Sir! Don't make me wait any longer!

But she remembered her discipline and merely let him continue his torturous ministrations. She closed her eyes and tried to control her breathing. Suddenly, the chair began massaging her scalp. Nothing better than a scalp massage. Between his hands on her legs and the stimulation at the back of her head, she nearly came on the spot.

You don't have permission to come.

Damián's words from her training days came back to her. In some ways, she felt like they were starting over. In others, they'd taken an enormous leap forward in their dynamic tonight.

Still, she groaned her frustration as he continued to tease her by slowly massaging oil into her inner thighs, coming ever so close to her almost-bare pussy then retreating again. Suddenly, her arms and calves were being squeezed by the pads of the chair, holding her in place. An image of something she didn't recognize pulled her out of the scene. Something white and shiny was all she remembered from the flashback. Panic. Her desire to have an orgasm warred with a need to tell Damián she was freaking out.

Instead, she took a deep breath and tried to rationalize her reaction. She'd been in arm restraints plenty of times, all the way back to the beginning of her Top/bottom relationship with Damián. Why were they making her lose it now?

But her breathing became more rapid and shallow as the chair squeezed her arms and legs again. Perspiration broke out on her forehead, causing her to shiver even though she wasn't cold.

"*Savita*, are you okay?"

Tell him.

"I'm fine, Sir."

No! Be honest!

"Where are you?"

"In the club's great room." She couldn't have said where she'd been in that momentary flashback anyway. It had been too quick.

If she used her slowdown word, would that mean he wouldn't allow her to come? *God, I need release.* But the third time the massage chair's pads inflated, she couldn't stand it anymore. She needed to be released from this chair.

"Guacamole, Sir!" She needed to slow this down.

Damián stood and moved immediately to her side. "What's going on, *bebé?*"

"I don't know, Sir. I was in the zone and loving the massage you were giving me. Then the chair started squeezing my arms and legs, and I saw a flash of white that caused me to break out in a sweat."

"White?"

"That's the only thing I saw. Just a bunch of shiny, white something or other."

He picked up the remote and pushed a couple of buttons. The pressure of the pads on her arms and legs ceased immediately. "Deep breaths." He took a towel and wiped the sweat from her forehead, staring into her eyes as if assessing her condition. "Better?"

"Much. Thank you, Sir."

He tucked the towel into the waistband of his leathers and leaned in front of her face so that only she could hear. "Thank you for using your slowdown word, *querida.* I know that wasn't easy for you, but I had no way of knowing that the squeezing of your arms and legs would be a trigger until you told me."

"I didn't know, either, until it happened."

"Now that we can both trust each other to be honest, would you like to continue with this scene if I stop the massage chair from squeezing your arms and legs?"

She smiled. "Very much, Sir. That's when I first became uncomfortable. Until then, I was loving what you were doing."

"*Bueno.* But no one said anything about the goal tonight being to make you comfortable, *savita.*"

Her excitement left her breathless.

"Ready to continue?"

"Yes, Sir." She beamed at him, happy that he hadn't taken everything away because she'd used her slowdown word. Once they zeroed in on the element that freaked her out, he just eliminated it from his scene and was ready to move on.

With a devilish grin, Damián pulled out a pocketknife, opened it, and slipped the back side of it against her skin and under the string of her thong—first the left side then the right. So much for the sexy thong she'd bought for him. He yanked the scrap of material between her thighs and tugged the triangle away. The string at the back slid between her ass cheeks, creating yet another layer of sexual arousal. He tossed the thong on the floor.

He walked behind her again and returned carrying a shiny, hot-pink ball about the size of one used in billiards. He playfully tossed it between his hands, coating it with the massage oil as much as teasing her with the possibilities of what he had planned. No way was that going to fit into her vagina, even if she was about to pass a small bowling ball through there come January.

Leaning on the arm of the chair, he bent down and kissed her, slow and deep, as he wedged the ball between the juncture of her thighs and pussy. It fit snuggly, but he pressed it against her clit as if to ensure it was in the perfect spot, then stood up, and walked away.

"Ready to ride, *bebé?*"

Ride what? The ball? Or the chair?

The back and seat of the chair pulsated to life, now firing on all cylinders. Her eyes rolled back as she gave in to the bombardment of sensations, unable to focus on any particular spot until the ball started pulsating between her legs, becoming the center of her universe.

"Oh!"

Her tiny bundle of nerves, which had been on the brink of orgasm since the whipping, sent jolts of electricity down her legs, up to her breasts, and all over her body.

Her breaths came out in hissing little pants, much as if she were practicing her Lamaze childbirth breathing. If he'd turned off the machine right now, she'd have come out of the chair, ropes or not, and demanded he finish her off.

As if she wasn't being stimulated enough, Damián took a bullet vibe and ran it lightly over her left nipple. Overload! By the time he reached the right one, she was a goner.

"Please, Sir, permission to come!"

"Not yet."

She groaned. Her pussy ached, feeling empty and desperately needing to be filled by his cock. But Damián wouldn't make love to her with an audience. At least, he'd never done so before. She couldn't wait to get him home but hoped he'd give her something now. She desperately needed to get off.

Apparently in no hurry whatsoever, he bent down and took her other nipple between his lips. His teeth bit down on it. Hard. She arched her back out of the chair toward him. She couldn't hold out much longer under this barrage of sensations. Her body began shaking with her effort to stave off the orgasm more than from the pulsing of the chair and vibes. Sweat broke out on her upper lip.

"Come for me the first time, *savita*."

Did that mean there would be more? *God, I hope so.*

He pulled the ball-shaped vibrator off her clit then pressed it against her bundle of nerves again. Back and forth, he played with her as waves of pleasure coursed through her body from her head to her legs. The pressure kept building until she could no longer hold back. Mewling cries of joy and ecstasy filled the room—and probably could be heard down the hallway in the theme rooms, too—but she didn't care. Wave after wave of euphoria flowed through her. She didn't want the ride to end, but all too soon, she came back to earth. The vibrating ball was gone and the chair was once again on a gentle setting. She took several breaths as Damián gave her another deep kiss.

"Sir?" she asked when she stopped to breathe.

"*¿Sí, querida?*"

"I think I know what you can get me for Christmas."

He chuckled deep in his chest. "I'll have a talk with Santa about whether you've been naughty or nice."

"I'm going to guess you prefer naughty."

He chuckled. "You know it." He stood. "Now, relax for me again, *bebé.*"

She felt like a wet noodle after her earth-shattering orgasm. How much more relaxed could she be? She hadn't realized how stressed she was until she'd sunk into this chair.

"We aren't finished."

"We aren't?" The Dom stare he gave her was worthy of the best, and she cast her eyes downward again. "I'm ready, Sir."

When he went to work removing the ropes from her arms, she wondered what he had in mind next. The chair's vibrations ceased as he went behind her to ready whatever else he had in mind. She became aware of Ryder and Megan again, having totally shut them out for the last part of that scene. She blocked them from her mind again, not wanting to ruin what had been an incredible scene so far.

What more did Damián have in store for her? She hadn't heard what he had planned, but so loved when he surprised her. She'd come a long way.

Suddenly, the smell of something burning assaulted her nose. Fireplay? No, she definitely smelled candle wax. Savannah smiled. She'd seen Marc and Angelina playing with wax in the club before, but it would be a first for her and Damián. This should be fun. Unless he'd simply lit candles to set the mood.

But Damián returned carrying two candles—one pink and one black. Two of her favorite colors. Would they sting? Burn? Turn her on? Freak her out—in a bad way? She held her breath in anticipation.

"I want you to hold perfectly still, *bebé*."

"Yes, Sir."

He held the pink candle about fifteen inches above her left ankle and let the first bead descend onto her pale skin. Savannah gasped but maintained her position. While hot upon impact, the heat quickly dissipated as the wax trailed over her ankle until it cooled and set. Not too bad. While she hadn't been able to gauge the impact of the first drop, now she was ready. He held the other candle about eighteen inches above the same spot. The first droplet of black wax landed beside the pink, directly on her skin. "Oh!" This time she jumped a little but quickly moved back into position. The black was hotter than the pink one and didn't cool as quickly, either.

Seeing the two colors intermingling around her ankle reminded Savannah of her and Damián coming together, white-hot passion—a little pain mixed with a lot of pleasure. Is that why he chose those colors?

Holding the candles over her other ankle, the black one once again higher than the pink, he tipped them and the wax hit her ankle at almost the same time. He'd definitely been practicing. But then, he'd always been able to hit his marks.

When they splattered against her skin, she moaned, but the pain was less this time. Perhaps she'd mentally prepared herself better for it. Forever wanting to keep her off guard, though, he started flicking the candles at her much like Father Martine might sprinkle holy water, splashing wax onto her feet, ankles, and shins.

"Oh, God!" She jumped, raising her foot several inches into the air, which only brought her leg closer to him at the exact wrong moment. As the next drop of molten black wax dripped onto her skin, she squealed. "Oh dear Lord!" Apparently, he'd positioned the black one higher so that it could cool more before striking her tender skin, but she'd negated the distance by moving.

"Sorry about that, *bebé*, but hold still. I don't want to hurt you."

Remembering to remain focused and in control, she willed herself to stay within the confines of the chair. In rapid succession, he let the black and pink candles alternately drop wax onto one ankle and shin until he'd nearly covered it before alternating between the two candles, each splat dropping to a beat of the throbbing music.

"Sir?"

"Yes, *savita?*"

"I would love to have a photo of the wax, if that's okay."

"Certainly. Let's wait until it's finished."

As he continued to splatter her with the pink and black wax, all thoughts drifted away. Mesmerized, she watched the colors intermingle and become one with her skin. With most of the wax concentrated on her ankles, it felt as if he were fashioning wax cuffs on her. As the wax thickened, her body lightened to where she almost floated away.

Damián stopped abruptly, blew out the candles, and withdrew behind the chair again. Pulled out of her semi-trance, she flexed her feet, but the hard wax wouldn't allow for much movement. She admired the patterns.

He returned with two white candles in hand. Apparently, her artiste wasn't finished with her yet. Good. A giggle of anticipation bubbled up inside her. She was enjoying this. So many new ways to play tonight.

The flames on the two candles burned brightly. Would they burn hot like the black one or milder even than the pink? He waited until they'd built up some melted wax near the flames before using movements like someone playing maracas might do.

The white flecks splattered on her shins and over the black and pink ankle "cuffs." The room began to fade away as more white wax splashed onto her feet this time. Savannah's heart pounded. She tried to fill her lungs with air. In strobe-like effect, her mind flashed between the droplets of wax and shiny gobs of sticky, wet semen. She swallowed hard to keep the bile down. Just like before when the chair squeezed her arms, all she could see was white, only now she realized it was a dress. Her arms and legs began trembling as more droplets fell on her legs. She could no longer tell if she saw wax or cum at this point. Her grasp on reality loosened, and sweat broke out on her forehead and upper lip.

Her gaze went to the many pairs of legs surrounding her. Men in suits. She didn't remember a time where she'd been with more than two men at once, but there had to be half a dozen here. She refused to glance up at them, but clearly, they were jacking off onto her feet—and the most beautiful dress she'd ever seen.

Oh, God. I'm going to be sick.

Chapter Twelve

Damián grinned seeing and hearing how much Savannah loved the kiss of the wax. This would definitely be something they'd do again, during and after her pregnancy. While he'd had to limit his palette to her lower legs and feet during her pregnancy, one day he'd paint her breasts and belly, too.

Wanting Ryder and Megan to see what he was doing, Damián moved to stand beside Savannah while continuing to flick wax from the white, lowest temperature candles he'd be using tonight. The micro burner's butane flame on the table behind her burned hot and ready for more, much like he did. His new toy made it easier for him to change colors rapidly without striking matches. He planned on having candle wax flying fast and furious for the next five minutes or so, after seeing how she took so well to wax play.

While the pink and black candles he'd burned earlier symbolized the two of them, these white ones epitomized Savannah's sweet innocence. He came in closer, knowing these wouldn't hurt as much as the black one had. He'd underestimated how hot that one would be at first.

Standing at the base of her feet, he dripped the wax onto the make-shift cuffs he'd made around her ankles, smiling. Damián continued to focus on the dripping wax. Savannah's toes curled away from him. Wanting to see the pleasure on her face, he glanced up but noticed she had a white-knuckled grip on the armrests. Her body was ramrod straight as her gaze remained glued on the dripping wax. The expression on her face was filled with nothing short of horror.

The fuck?

What happened to her giggle just a few minutes ago? He uprighted both candles. Flashback? Had someone tortured her with wax, too? *Dios*, was anything safe for them to do? Right now, he needed to bring her back. "Savannah, where are you?"

She didn't respond or acknowledge his presence in any way but kept looking at the wax. He glanced at the splatters of white against the pink and black, too, but didn't see any patterns or anything that might trigger her.

He definitely needed to do a safety check on her. Damián hurried behind her to ditch the extinguished candles then knelt beside her.

She blinked but didn't meet his gaze. "Please, stop." Her plaintive voice ripped his heart out. She kept staring down at the wax on her ankles and feet. *Mierda*. What the fuck was wrong?

Once again, he turned toward her feet and ankles. And then he saw what she must see. *Aw, fuck*. Cum.

Madre de Dios.

He grabbed a towel and tossed it over her legs and ankles before caging her chin and turning her to face him. "Savannah, eyes."

She resisted his hand for a moment then blinked and looked at him. Her eyes seemed glazed and unseeing. She tried to look back at her feet, revulsion in her eyes.

"Tamale!" she screamed, pulling her feet toward her as she tented her knees. She'd never used her safeword to stop before, so this trigger must be a bad one.

"Savannah, tell me where you are." She didn't respond. "You're safe here with me. No one can hurt you. Tell me what happened." He turned her face toward his.

She blinked again, her eyes seeming to focus on his. "I don't know," she whispered, her voice trembling. At least she was speaking to him. A shudder rippled through her.

"You're safe now, *bebé*. Let's get you out of this chair." He stood, grabbed the medical scissors, and cut the ropes binding her to the chair. He then took her by the hand, helping her to her feet. Megan handed him one of the aftercare blankets from the basket nearby, and he wrapped it around her. Savannah winced when she tried to take a step. Damián couldn't carry her to the aftercare loveseat with any assurance he wouldn't drop her. He turned to Ryder, hating that he couldn't carry his own girl when she needed him, but her safety was more important than his pride. "Ryder, can you carry her over there for me?" He pointed toward the loveseat near the stage.

"Sure thing."

Damián turned Savannah's face to his. "*Savita*, Ryder's going to bring you to me. Then we'll have our aftercare time and talk about what just happened."

Savannah nodded numbly but didn't let go of Damián's hand even after Ryder lifted her. She kept her gaze on Damián's face as Ryder carried her, staring up at him with those big blue eyes that were no longer as happy and expressive as they had been a few minutes ago. Seeing such pain in them nearly gutted him.

Damián sat down to receive the precious bundle. With Savannah resting on his lap, Damián centered his attention on her. He pulled the blanket tighter around her and pressed her cheek to his shoulder, saying comforting things he hoped would ease her stress level so they could discuss what had happened. While rubbing the back of her head, he played the scene over in his head but found no answers.

Remembering Savannah wanted photos of the pink and black ankle cuffs—and hoping they could help bring back the sense of enjoyment she'd had to that point in the scene—Damián turned to Megan and whispered, "I need you to peel off the white wax, Megan." Megan nodded.

The massage oil he'd applied before should make it easier to remove the first layers of wax that were attached directly to her skin, but he wasn't sure how tightly the white wax would adhere to the colored splatters.

Ryder stepped forward and placed a folded aftercare blanket on the floor near Savannah's feet for Megan to kneel on, ever attentive to his own wife's needs. Megan went to work on her task, gently peeling the wax away. Thank God the two of them were here.

After several minutes, when Savannah's breathing seemed to be steadier, Damián smoothed the hair away from her face before saying, "I'm so proud of you, *savita*."

Her body stiffened. Didn't she believe his words? He'd never lied to her. "What was that thought, *querida?*"

She nibbled on her lower lip before responding. "I stopped your scene. I'm sorry, Sir."

"It was *our* scene, and you only stopped because you were triggered or had a major problem with what I was doing. That's how this is supposed to work. You use your safeword when you're having a problem with a scene. As your Dom, I wouldn't want to continue a scene that was doing more harm than good."

"I don't know what happened. I loved the wax play at first." As if feeling Megan's hands for the first time, she sat up and looked down. "Don't take it all off. I want pictures." She met Damián's gaze. "If that's okay, Sir."

He was happy to hear he'd done the right thing there at least. He nodded. "I asked Megan to remove only the white wax. Then we'll get you some photos." He pulled her toward his body again, needing contact with her as much as he possibly could. "Now, close your eyes while Megan takes care of that for us."

"Sir?"

"Yes, *querida?*"

"I don't know what happened," Savannah whispered.

Join the club.

"I loved the pink and black wax. The cuffs were freaking awesome. But the white…it took me back to a scene when I was younger, but I didn't recognize it or anyone there."

So she hadn't seen Lyle or her father? Who else had abused her? Too many men to count, thanks to those *cabrones*. His heart rate kicked up before he forced himself to regain control of his emotions. 'If you can't control yourself, you can't control others," Gunnar Larson, his whipmaster mentor, had told him countless times during his training.

"Can you remember anything yet?"

She stopped breathing a moment then whispered, "I was wearing the most beautiful dress. Formal. Princess-like."

"Like a prom dress?"

"Yeah, but I never went to a prom or fancy dance."

"Some other special occasion? Maybe a wedding?"

"Never. Ours was the first I remember attending."

"Anything else stand out?" He wanted to get her to talk about it before the memory faded into her subconscious again.

"It's just flashes of scenes in a kaleidoscope. There were half a dozen men standing around me in a semi-circle." She swallowed, and her hand began to tremble.

"What were they doing?"

"Jacking off onto...onto my feet and my dress."

Jesús. No wonder she triggered. He rubbed her arm through the blanket to try and bring some warmth back into her body and to give himself time to figure out what to say or do to make it better.

"I don't recall any time when I was with that many men at once."

"Recognize any of them?"

"No. I didn't see any faces. Only penises and...semen."

Not unlike when witnesses in armed robberies report seeing nothing but the handgun pointed at them.

"I was on the ground or a bed or somehow below them." She shuddered.

"Only in a physical sense, *bebé*. You were never beneath them in any other way. Those men were scum." He reined in his anger before projecting it to her.

"I thought I'd dredged up all the bad things that had ever happened to me in all the work you and I have done and with my therapist. Where did this come from?"

"Triggers can come out of nowhere. You saw the white wax, it looked like cum dropping onto you, and your mind flashed back to that time."

"But why can't I remember the circumstances of the event?"

"If it's something you need to remember, you will. Maybe your mind isn't ready to deal yet with whatever happened back then."

Megan sat back on her heels slowly as if to give them privacy. Ryder had knelt beside her, rubbing her back in the uncomfortable position.

Damián glanced down at Savannah's feet; he saw that she'd managed to remove all of the white wax.

"Megan did a fantastic job, Savannah, if you want to look." He hoped this was the right thing to do so soon.

Savannah seemed cautious at first, then sat up, and held out both her feet. The wax cuffs remained intact, pink and black. He held his breath, waiting to see what her reaction would be.

"Would you mind taking a few pictures, Megan?" she asked.

"I'd love to." Ryder helped his wife to her feet, and she went to where she'd been sitting earlier to get her phone or camera. Savannah seemed to perk up as she sat up and looked down at her feet again. No sign of the past trauma, she smiled. "I have to say I love playing with wax, Sir. Just not with white candles."

"Trust me. I plan to get rid of the rest of the white ones for whenever we do wax play again."

She extended her feet again for the photos, and Megan said she'd text the images to them both and delete them from her phone. Megan and Ryder excused themselves to go to the bar and talk to Grant. Savannah relaxed into Damián's arms again. Everything was under control again, thanks to some help from their friends. He hoped the episode with Savannah wouldn't scare them away from the lifestyle.

"I was afraid I'd disappointed you." Savannah sounded fragile again, and he lowered her head from his shoulder into the crook of his arm until she stared up at him. "The only way you could disappoint me, *querida*, would be by letting me do something that you couldn't handle without telling me to stop. I had no idea the problem was so big until you said *tamale*." While he was beginning to see she was in distress, he hadn't acted quickly enough. "The important thing is that you used your safeword to protect yourself when you needed to. That gives me enormous relief and confidence that you will do so again if you need to."

She smiled. "Thanks for taking such good care of me, Sir. I never doubted you'd listen to me, if I ever used it, but your quick response kept me from sinking any further into that awful nightmare."

A sob tore from her, and Damián pulled her back up against him, resting his head on the top of her head as he held her tighter. "I have you, *bebé*. You're safe. No one can hurt you ever again."

"You make me believe that," she said with a sniffle.

Dios, he hoped he could always protect her from harm. There was so much evil in the world. She'd suffered through enough of it by the time she'd turned eight. And yet tonight he'd been the one to cause her harm, even if unintentionally.

Damián would have to pay better attention to her from now on. They still had a trial by fire to get through in a month or so. He vowed he wouldn't leave her side or let her down for a minute.

* * *

Savannah wished she had a clue what was going on the night after that phenomenal visit to the Masters at Arms Club. All day long, she felt as if an enormous weight had been lifted off her shoulders. When Damián called from the shop this morning to tell her he had a special night planned—just the two of them—she'd been anticipating this evening ever since.

Karla and Adam agreed to keep Marisol, although Savannah had spent a few hours with her after school since she'd been away from home last night, too. Intuition told her this would be no ordinary night. Judging by the lengths he went to with his attire, she was certain.

Sitting across from him at dinner, she admired how well Damián wore the black linen shirt with piping on both front panels. On the left side over his heart, she'd had two tiny iridescent blue butterflies hand-embroidered, one larger than the other, to signify them and their emergence into a new phase in their lives as a married couple. She'd chosen it for him for Father's Day and had cried when he'd told her he and Rosa had given their dad one on his last Father's Day. Knowing Damián's taste, Savannah hadn't gone with the more elaborate ones. But he seemed happy with the gift just the same, even though this was the first time he'd worn the long-sleeved shirt, because his body tended to run more hot than cold.

But on this snowy November night, he looked incredibly handsome—*no, sexy as hell*—in it. She'd known he would, with the tight cuffs and button-up collar, but had no idea what the overall effect would be on her libido.

As if she'd needed any visual stimulation after last night. She'd been horny all day, because he had insisted they go to bed and sleep last night after her meltdown.

But she'd bounced back incredibly fast, feeling a sense of empowerment that using her safeword had taken her from the trigger scene and into Damián's arms and safety so quickly.

She nearly giggled. *Dear Lord, it felt good to be feeling amorous again.*

Wet and breathless, she finished her second virgin margarita and smiled across the table at him as he settled the bill. He didn't seem to notice the signals she thought she'd been sending him. Couldn't he tell how much she wanted to make love tonight?

In fact, he seemed nervous and preoccupied, blowing out puffs of air periodically and adjusting his collar as if it choked him. Halfway through the meal, he undid the top button. He seemed even more nervous than on their wedding day. She believed him when he said he wasn't upset with her for calling a halt to their scene last night. So what was it?

"Is everything okay at the shop?"

"Yeah. Great, actually. Two old bikes came in for custom restorations. One's a '60s classic. I told the guys I'd be working on that one myself the next few months. Between those and regular maintenance customers like to do during the winter when they can't ride as much, we'll be busy through spring."

Savannah bit back her smile. She'd arranged to have his team work on restoring the classic bike he seemed so excited about. It was as close to the one he'd had to sell when she'd gotten him fired from the hotel as she could find. While she could afford to buy him one that had already been restored, she knew half the joy for Damián was to do the work himself. But if she'd told them the bike would be for him, he wouldn't have allotted the time to work on his own bike while he had customers waiting. So she and his top mechanic had devised this plan. The restored bike would be a birthday surprise for him in February. She'd have had the baby by then, too. Savannah couldn't wait to ride on that Harley with him.

She still planned to pay for the work he'd be putting in on the classic. The shop was doing well. Damián had little interest in financial matters at home or in his business, so he'd hired an accountant, but she didn't want Damián to find anything amiss when they went over the year-end books for taxes.

So what else could he be worried about? Her? While she'd let the trial consume too much of her life the past few weeks, with a disastrous effect on their love life, last night had remedied that to a great extent. And tonight would be wonderful, too. She intended to make love with Damián after they got home. If only he could be a little more relaxed and at least pretend he was having fun.

She dabbed the sides of her mouth with her napkin. "I'm having a good time. Thanks for planning this date. Dinner was out of this world." She reached across the table to cover his hand and met his gaze once more. "I'm looking forward to getting home, not that I want to rush anything."

"I do. Want to rush things, that is." He smiled as he put his debit card and receipt in his wallet and stood, coming around the table to help her up from her chair.

Twenty minutes later, they walked into their house. Chiquita and Boots lay curled up together on the sofa. Chiquita lifted her head to make sure everything was okay then resumed her nap without any concerns.

The dog had been alerting on Savannah's stress for weeks now. Even Chiquita could tell that the crisis was over, at least as far as Savannah's stress level. She and Damián would continue to prepare her for the trial, setting up daily relaxation exercises for reinforcement along with her twice-a-week appointments with her therapist until the time came to go to California.

Don't let the trial put a damper on tonight.

"We'll be spending the next part of our evening in here. I need to set up some things, so wait for me in the bedroom until I come for you."

What on earth was more important than going to the bedroom to-gether—now? But she didn't express her dismay in the delay. Damián loved surprising her and taking charge—and she loved letting him.

"Would you like me to change into something else?"

His smoldering gaze caressed every curve and valley of her body, inch by inch, before meeting hers again. His smile said it all. "You're dressed just the way I asked. Fucking perfect, just the way you are."

He'd had the new dress delivered this morning from a boutique in a trendy part of downtown Denver. No doubt one of the girls had helped him find it, perhaps even Karla, who had given her an enigmatic smile when she'd dropped off Mari earlier this evening. She certainly couldn't picture Damián going shopping for women's apparel in a fancy dress shop. Herself, either. Clothing was functional to her. She rarely, if ever, purchased anything pricy for herself but did so for Mari on special occasions.

The dress box had included a note in Damián's handwriting with instructions on what to wear tonight. And what to leave off, including her bra and panties. She'd worn a garter belt with silk stockings that was decidedly unsexy tucked under her belly, but that's what he'd asked for. She'd also been told not wear any jewelry other than her wedding band and very little makeup, not that she ever wore much more than eyeshadow and mascara. Tonight, she'd opted for just the eyeshadow. Her toes were still done in a rainbow of colors from two nights ago.

Now that they were home, he seemed less nervous at least. She gave him a peck on the cheek and headed up the stairs.

"Journal about last night while you're waiting," he called after her.

She'd already begun a journal entry about it this morning but would take this opportunity to refine and finish it. "Yes, Sir."

While he could read her journals as her Dom, he'd never done so. Sometimes, he would ask her to share what she'd written, if willing, but he seemed to not want to cross the boundary into invading that personal space. He'd told her, perhaps rightly, that he feared if he read them she'd likely modify her feelings to what she assumed he wanted to hear.

While Savannah tried to be open with him verbally, she'd lapsed confiding her true feelings during the last few weeks. Now she regretted that, because if she'd been open, perhaps they could have worked on her anxiety and fears in a constructive way.

She made a vow not to hide her worries or negative emotions from him ever again. He was her Dom and part of what he'd promised to do was shoulder her burdens for or with her.

Savannah was on the third page of today's journaling her feelings about that last two days when Damián appeared at the doorway. "Ready for the next part of our special night?"

She smiled. "Absolutely." He crossed the room to help her out of their aftercare chair, which happened to be the most comfortable piece of furniture in their bedroom for curling up and writing.

He held her hand as they exited the room, and she noticed the flickering of candles bouncing off the walls in the hall and stairway, coming from the living room. Her heart warmed to think of the planning and preparation that had gone into tonight, but she gasped when she reached the top of the stairs and looked down at what must have been a hundred candles of various sizes and colors arranged three or four deep, forming a horseshoe.

"Damián, what a romantic you are." Savannah leaned toward him to place a kiss on his lips, but he took her upper arms and pushed her away with firm but gentle hands.

He smiled then drew a deep breath and sobered. "I've been planning this for a while now. After last night, I knew the time had come."

She cocked her head and wrinkled her brow, but he merely took her hand and led her down the stairs into the opening until she and her white dress were bathed in the warm glow of candlelight. Her heart beat rapidly. Had he done all this to set the tone for making love? Unlikely. He said he'd been planning this for a while. Seemed to be more than an ordinary date night with benefits. Something was up.

Chapter Thirteen

Damián moved to stand in front of her and took both of her hands in his. He was often serious but nothing like this.

"Savannah, last May, you knelt before me in our beach cave and gifted me with your beautiful submission."

"And I meant every word I said, although I still have a lot to learn about what that entails, as you might have noticed last night."

He shook his head, a hint of a smile. "It's a journey, but what we experienced at the club was a turning point. You trusted me enough to use your safeword, which, in turn, allowed me to trust you even more."

"I should have known I could trust you—"

He placed a finger over her lips. "Trust is earned. I am honored that you reached a place where you could do so. I know this is often done more formally surrounded by others in the lifestyle, but I didn't want to wait to schedule another night at the club. Besides, I wanted to be sure of your answer before putting myself out there in front of others."

She started to have an inkling of what this was about but wasn't sure she was worthy yet. Not after the way she lapsed this Fall. But he seemed to be battling some insecurities of his own about where he stood with her.

Savannah's heart thumped so hard surely he could hear. They were about to cross an important threshold in both their marriage and their D/s dynamic. But what if she let him down again?

"I welcome my role as your one and only man and ask you if you are willing to accept my protection and guidance as we go through the rest of our lives together as Dominant and submissive."

"Sir, I…are you sure I'm ready? In the past month or so, I've withdrawn emotionally, lied to you while trying to hide my deepest feelings, and regressed in so many ways."

Again, Damián halted her words, growing more serious. "Savannah, I'm not expecting perfection. We spoke about this last night on the way home from the club. You admitted how detrimental such behavior is to your well-being and to our relationship. And you've agreed that you have no intention of going down that path again. I believed you last night, and I trust you in the future to be honest with me."

"I'm so ashamed of my behavior. But I also know how lost I am without you by my side helping me through those dark places."

He cupped her face and leaned forward to kiss her before pulling away but keeping his hands in place. "Recognizing that and remembering how it feels is huge. We're a team, *savita*. We've both been to hell and back, but now we need each other." He swallowed. "You pledged your heart and your eternal love to me when we married, but..." He let go of her and bent down to pick up a square, flat box from the coffee table but didn't open it immediately. "Tonight I will ask even more of you. I want you to wear a symbol that our D/s relationship is unbreakable. That we accept each other, flaws and all, and intend to spend the rest of our lives going deeper into the lifestyle together. I will grow as your Dominant, and you into your role as my submissive."

Her jaw dropped as tears pricked the backs of her eyelids. Early on, she'd wondered about being collared, after Karla told her about her own private collaring during their honeymoon. But she hadn't given it another thought, assuming that she was far from ready given her myriad of mistakes.

"But I still have so much to learn. Are you sure?"

He smiled, relaxing his shoulders. "Yes, *savita*, I have never been more sure of anything. If this were any other thing we were discussing, I might remind you to trust your Dom's judgment, but I can't strong-arm or coerce you into this decision. It has to be one you're ready for. And if you aren't ready tonight, we will revisit this again sometime in the future."

No pressure. My decision. The sense of empowerment those thoughts gave her was earth-shattering.

Before she could give him an answer, he continued. "Over the past six months, we've discussed every aspect of what we want our D/s relationship to be. You've explored anything I've asked you to without complaint or hesitance but with total trust that I would do you no harm and that exploring the lifestyle might actually provide more healing. I will never demand perfection or excellence, *bebé*. I only demand that you do your best and that you come to me whenever anything is bothering you rather than suffer alone in silence. Open, honest communication will always be my greatest protocol."

"Sir, you must know I will always do whatever you ask of me. I want to please you above all else. And I've seen what happens when communication breaks down. I was afraid you saw me as perfect—and I never wanted to disappoint you—but by hiding things from you, I did that very thing." She blinked away the sting in her eyes, and he brushed a tear off her cheek with his thumb.

"Does this mean that you are ready to wear my collar, *savita*?"

More tears spilled as she nodded. "Yes, Sir. I would be honored to wear your collar."

He opened the lid of the box and lifted a platinum-colored collar from the cotton batting, letting the empty box fall to the floor. "This isn't a sign that you have perfected all there is to know about submission any more than it means I am suddenly the perfect Dominant who will never make a mistake. We're both human with a lot of baggage. But this I know—as we continue to explore this lifestyle together, the bond between us will grow deeper every day."

Too choked up to speak, she merely smiled. The circle of delicately etched metal had a pink sapphire in the front that would rest in the hollow of her throat. She dashed away the remaining tears from her eyes and noticed there was a tiny butterfly etched on either side of the gemstone.

"Savannah, will you accept this collar as a token of my love, discipline, guidance, and protection?"

She blinked, staring at the beautiful collar, and more tears spilled down her cheeks. Looking up at Damián, she detected a flash of uncertainty before realizing she hadn't said yes. "Sir, if I wasn't so pregnant, this would be the part where I would sink to my knees, bow my head, and pledge my undying loyalty and submission." She did the latter two. "I am yours, Sir Damián, and I will proudly wear your collar as long as I live."

His eyes lit up with more than the reflection of the many candles in the room. Then he grew serious again. "You are not to remove my collar except under a doctor's orders or if I grant you permission. It is much more than a pretty necklace."

"I have no desire to ever remove it, Sir." She reached up to place her hand over it.

"And while wearing my collar, you will at all times remember our protocols. In addition to communication, that includes that you remember how beautiful you are, how worthy you are, and that you have honored and gifted me and only me with your precious surrender."

Pride swelled her chest. "I look forward to deepening our Dominant/submissive relationship in the months and years to come, Sir."

She remembered the first time she'd called him that, back in the beach cave on the day this baby was conceived.

'One day, in a secluded cave by the peaceful sea, the princess had come full circle. She willingly submitted her body and mind fully to her noble knight. But not her heart.'

She looked up at him, and he blinked at her.

'Because she'd surrendered her heart to him, long, long ago.'

He leaned forward and placed a kiss on her cheek. Had he been lost in that memory, too? She smiled, lifting her hair so he could place the collar around her neck. The cool metal soon warmed to her skin as the clasp gave a quiet snick. She wondered if he had a key for it or if the lock was merely symbolic.

Damián took a step back and looked searchingly into her eyes. "Savannah, by accepting my collar, you've shown me you have the ultimate trust in my ability to fulfill my role as your Dominant and to work together with me to build and strengthen our married D/s life together. And if I fuck up, you have my permission to call me on it rather than keep it to yourself."

Nothing would change her mind about submitting and surrendering herself to this man, no matter how much time they had together. She grinned. "I have never lacked confidence in your abilities, Sir. Only mine."

"Confidence, like trust, increases with time." Before she could say anything more, he added, "I know you have a lot going on right now, but remember this above all. With my collar resting at the base of your neck, you will find a grounding talisman with you at all times. Touching it will be the same as touching me. This collar is an extension of me and will be your rock when scared or simply needing to reconnect with me from afar. Know that, when wearing this collar, you will never be alone."

Damián wrapped his arms around her and drew her closer, bending to place a kiss on her collar first before homing in on her lips. He tugged at her hair as he tilted her head back and deepened their kiss.

A sense of peace and well-being she hadn't felt in weeks enveloped her. How their dynamic would change from this point forward, she couldn't say. One thing she did know, though. While this collar came with great responsibility on both their parts, she would gladly spend the rest of her life giving him her undying submission and striving to make him even more proud of her.

* * *

Mine.

As he deepened the kiss, Damián marveled at the sense of purpose and responsibility that washed over him seeing Savannah wearing his collar. He hadn't expected it would move him to his core.

While she'd been his wife for months, something about this moment changed everything for him. They had just cemented their relationship on even more solid ground.

Grounded. That was the word for it.

He held her tighter as he continued to explore her sweet mouth, tasting of lime, fruit, and Savannah.

My collared submissive.

He'd always taken his responsibilities as her Dom, teacher, and protector seriously, but just as placing a wedding band on her finger had taken their commitment to a deeper level, so did this collar.

Pulling away, he cupped her cheeks and smiled. Her eyes burned with an inner fire he'd missed seeing there these past few weeks. No matter what adversity might line their path, they could tackle anything together as long as they stayed committed to one another in their marriage and in their D/s dynamic.

Nothing could tear them apart. The two of them were two strong and determined survivors.

He took her in his arms again and placed another kiss on her lips before trailing several more down her neck to the hollow where it met her shoulder. She gasped at the sensation. So sweet. He could taste her all night, but he craved a closeness they hadn't experienced in a while.

When they separated, she smiled. Before he could formulate a word, she said, "I need you inside me, Sir."

His cock jerked against his crotch. Apparently, he wasn't the only one needing that intimacy. While he'd planned a slow seduction tonight, he wasn't sure how long he could wait to bury himself inside her again if she kept saying things like that.

"Let's blow out these candles and go to bed where I can worship my submissive's body properly."

Within five minutes, they'd extinguished all but one flame—the internal one that had been ignited more than eight years ago in their beach cave and had burned strong and bright ever since. Circumstances had threatened to blow out that flame many times, but it continued to smolder under the surface until they found each other again each time and rekindled their passion.

He couldn't bear the thought of being away from her for more than a few hours.

"Follow me, *querida*." He took her hand and led her to the staircase where he motioned for her to precede him. He wished he could carry her, but was afraid of what a misstep might do to her and the baby. Instead, he contented himself to ascend behind her in case she lost her balance. In the bedroom, he pulled the comforter and sheet back, turning toward her just as she presented him with her back. She held up her hair in a silent request to unzip her.

As he drew closer, her essence swirled around him, arousing him even more. He bent to place a kiss on the clasp on the collar, capturing a bit of her silky skin above and below before trailing his lips up the column of her neck to her earlobe. Taking it between his teeth, he nibbled, first gently then harder.

Her moan further ignited his passion. He made quick work of removing the dress, which had served its purpose. His own clothes followed, and he ground his erection against her backside, bare except for her garter belt. His hands cupped her breasts as he pressed her up against the edge of the mattress, careful there was ample room to keep the baby bump off it.

Slow down, man.

He didn't want to rush things or this would end before it started. His hands roamed over her satiny body, starting at her shoulders, moving down her arms, and encircling her waist to cradle their baby within the womb. The garter belt framed her ass perfectly.

"Sir?"

"*Sí, bebé?*" He'd never grow tired of hearing her call him Sir.

"Permission to take charge?"

What the—? His dick surged against her ass, game to find out what she had in mind. He remembered a similar time in the past after she'd made a major breakthrough and suddenly felt empowered enough to take the lead—as far as he'd let her, anyway. "I'm all yours, *querida.*"

"Lie on the bed on your back. Sir," she added, as an afterthought.

He chuckled but did as she instructed. His erection grew harder still as she crawled onto the bed to join him. When she straddled his hips, he nearly lost it.

His gaze lowered to her brown nipples when Savannah leaned forward, grabbing onto the headboard. Her seductive smile stirred his passions to the boiling point.

"Lick them."

He didn't need to be told twice as he took one plump nipple into his mouth, while his hand squeezed the other. Whatever had gotten into her, he liked it. He'd been overly cautious making love with her in the past few months. Clearly, she was ready for more.

"Are you ready, Sir, for the ride of your life?"

"If I were any more ready, I'd be done."

Her self-confident laugh made him more than anxious to get started. Raising her hips, she released one of her hands to reach between their bodies.

Damián halted her with his own hand. "Both hands on the head-board, *bebé*. I don't want you to lose your balance." Taking his dick in hand, he rubbed the head between her folds to lubricate his dick with pussy juice but found she needed no help in that department. So wet. And waiting.

Taking her by the left hip to indicate she should lift up, he positioned himself at her opening and smiled.

She bobbed up and down a few times making sure his dick was coated before finally seating him fully. Home. Being inside her gave him a wonderful sense of belonging he found nowhere else. She flexed her pussy muscles, and he nearly came undone.

"Thanks for helping me do my Kegels, Sir."

"Anytime. Now, let's go for that ride."

Not comfortable simply lying there while she did all the work, he placed his hands on the sides of her belly to help lift the baby's weight in the rhythm she set. At first, her lower body did all the moving, but then Savannah leaned down and offered him her breasts. He took one ripe nipple into his mouth and bit down. Her pussy responded by clenching his dick. She did love having her nipples stimulated. And he loved being the one to do it.

When her pace increased, he knew she was ready to come. Hell, so was he. It had been too long. Not content to simply lie there, he lifted his hips in counter measure to her coming down over his dick, grinding against her as he buried himself deeper.

"Oh!" Her eyes opened wider in surprise. Yeah, she liked that, too.

He lowered his hands to just above her hips and helped set a new rhythm before slipping his hand under her belly and down to her clit. The swollen bud was hard against his finger. He stroked her with the same pace as he rammed himself inside her. Soon she was mewling and panting, her plump breasts bouncing above his mouth and harder to catch.

"Come for me, *savita*."

"I...want...you..."—with each pounding of his dick, she got a word out—"to come, too."

"Don't worry about me. I'll be right behind you." Well, under her, too.

She squeezed her eyes shut as he stroked her clit faster. "Oh, Sir... Yes, Damián! There!" She said something incoherent, and his dick throbbed with his own impending release.

"Come with me, *bebé*!"

And they exploded together, Savannah screaming and he grunting to completion.

After cleaning up, he pulled Savannah into the spoon of his body and kissed her neck and collar. "That was incredible. I'm going to enjoy revisiting this position again. Soon."

"I don't know what came over me. I like being on top—but still want you to be *my* Top in this relationship."

He chuckled. "No worries there, *savita*." He grew serious, leaning his forehead against the back of her head. "I'll always be your Dom." He took a deep breath. "And as I vowed last night and a hundred other times, I'll do everything in my power to protect you, Savannah."

Chapter Fourteen

Savannah awoke Thanksgiving morning to the scent of roasting turkey and sage and momentarily forgot where she was. Damián lay behind her, his hand protectively holding her belly while he slept. A quick glance at the empty air mattress told her Mari was already up and gone.

Karla had convinced them to stay at their place Thanksgiving Eve, but part of the deal was that Savannah would be helping in the kitchen. Sitting up as quickly as she could these days, she ran her fingers through her hair to unflatten it. Damián stirred.

"Come back here, *savita*."

"I can't." Could she still say no to Sir? Well, she could try. After all, they weren't in a scene and had never been high protocol. "I promised Karla I'd make the mashed potatoes. Smells like she has the turkey well on its way to being done."

He glanced at the alarm clock on the nightstand. "We aren't eating until two or three. Plenty of time." He propped his head onto the palm of his hand, the dragon tattoo on his pec and upper arm begging to be stroked. Or kissed.

So tempting.

No. Her hand went to the band around her neck, but he hadn't said anything earlier about her obeying everyday commands. "I'm tempted to join you, truly I am, but I need to peel about fifteen pounds of spuds to have enough for the crowd she's expecting. And I promised Karla to help with anything else she needs, but I've spent half the morning in bed."

He trailed a fingertip down her arm, making her flesh rise in his wake. "You needed your sleep."

Don't distract me, Sir. "What I need is to see what Mari's up to, although I'm sure she's keeping an eagle eye on those babies." Her daughter would be such a help to her when their new baby came.

But her need to please Damián warred with her prior commitment to Karla. Perhaps if she got his permission. "Is it okay if I go downstairs now…Sir?"

He grinned. Her use of *Sir* outside of a scene must have pleased him greatly. She'd have to remember to use it more often.

"I suppose the reward will be worth it. We'll have time to ourselves tonight when we go home. Go."

She leaned down to give him a kiss, but before he could pull her into his embrace, she stood and crossed the room to her overnight bag. After slipping a cranberry-colored, form-fitting cotton sweater over her head—Damián insisted she not hide the baby under tents, as he called traditional maternity clothes—and pulling on a pair of stretchy maternity jeans, she waved goodbye just as he sat up on the edge of the mattress to make an effort at getting out of bed, too.

Using his Dom voice, he said, "Savannah."

She stopped in her tracks with her hand on the doorknob and turned. "Yes, Sir?"

"Don't be on your feet too long. I'll be down to check on you after my shower."

She smiled and relaxed. "I promise I won't." He always made sure she took good care of herself and the baby.

In the kitchen, she found Adam seated at the table holding his little girls—one on each thigh—while Mari chased after Pax, crawling and giggling as he made a beeline toward the dining room with her daughter in hot pursuit. Their laughter was infectious.

"My, so much energy this morning!" Savannah said, laughing. "Where can I bottle some of that? I feel like such a slacker."

Karla set the baster on the spoon rest as she turned to greet Savannah. Her hair had been pulled into a clip at the back of her head, accenting her rosy cheeks, no doubt red from standing in front of the recently opened oven door. "Nonsense. But if you figure out where to get some of their energy, sell me a few quarts, please. I'm a little low, too."

"Kitten, don't overdo," Adam said, using his Dom voice, "or I'll make sure you stay put for a while with some strategically placed rope." Apparently, both Adam and Damián were in Dom mode today. Well, situation normal.

Karla gave him a smoldering look, and Savannah felt the passion burning between them. "I hope you'll do that anyway, Sir, after the babies go to bed."

Savannah cleared her throat as if to remind them they weren't alone. The uncovered roasting pan sat on top of the stove, the turkey not yet brown. The sight and smell took her back to Thanksgiving as a child when Maman prepared a feast—a mixture of American and French favorites—usually for the two of them. Sometimes Gentry joined them, but her sharpest memories were of Maman laughing as they wrapped their pinkies around the wishbone and pulled. Somehow, Savannah managed to come away with the longest part the two times she could recall.

Savannah wished Maman was still here. Blinking away the tears, she said, "That smells divine, Karla. What time did you put it in?"

"Angelina said between six and seven would be plenty of time to allow it to rest before carving. I managed to make the seven o'clock mark—with Adam's help. Should have chopped the onions and celery last night. But what do I know?" she asked with an unapologetic shrug.

"It will be fine, hon," Adam chimed in, while making a face at Rori who grabbed onto his chin and pried open his mouth.

Karla laughed. "You won't even eat it, Adam, so your vote doesn't count."

"Like hell I won't. You made it this year, so I'll be having some, especially given how you've been stressing out about it for the past week."

Karla ignored his comment, becoming serious as she surveyed the kitchen then picked up the baster as if just remembering what she was doing before Savannah had come in. Her having so much to do made Savannah feel even guiltier about sleeping in.

"It's just so important that everything be perfect on the first Thanksgiving meal I've ever pulled together," she said, as she squirted turkey drippings over the bird's skin. "And with Mom and Daddy arriving any minute from Chicago, I want to show them I can do this."

Savannah hadn't noticed Karla's parents being anything but loving and supportive and wondered why she would think otherwise. "Mom's bringing nine or ten pies in their SUV, thank goodness, which is why they chose to drive down instead of fly. I don't think I could have tackled pies, too." Karla set the baster on the spoon rest again and replaced the lid on the roasting pan.

That seemed to be Adam's signal to set the girls on the floor. He watched them crawl off, gurgling as they made a beeline to their brother and Mari, who had returned from their foray into the dining room. Adam stood. "Looks like you're ready for me to put that bird back in the oven, Kitten."

"It's all yours. I can't believe how heavy the roasting pan is with a twenty-three pound bird inside. Good thing I have a big, strapping Marine on duty." Karla gave him a kiss on the cheek before turning toward Savannah. "I appreciate having your help, too, Savannah. It takes a village."

Savannah crossed the room to give Karla a hug. "Don't worry about a thing. You have everything under control. But I truly am sorry I slept so long."

"Oh, sweetie, you're seven months pregnant. You needed it. Besides, Marisol's been a great distraction for the kids, so you helped just by staying over last night. I'm just glad you were able to sleep in with all the noise around here."

"I assure you, we didn't hear a thing." Putting some distance between them, she added, "I'll just wash my hands and start peeling potatoes."

"Now that's something I have some expertise doing, too," Adam said.

With the turkey roasting again, Karla began cutting up broccoli for her fabulous casserole. After washing and rinsing the potatoes, Savannah split the pile between her and Adam, and the two of them worked in companionable silence seated at the table.

Karla bubbled with excitement, sharing stories about two special Thanksgivings she'd spent with Adam—one as a teenager and again last year. From what Savannah could fathom, Thanksgiving held special meaning for them. And this year, their table would be filled with nineteen family members, including the three newest additions who couldn't eat solid foods yet. Their loss.

The remaining guests should be arriving soon. In addition to Karla's parents and Rosa's family, the Wilsons and Dentons were driving in together from Fairchance and bringing Adam's mother and brother, Patrick, with them. Adam's former mother-in-law, Marge, had opted to go on a cruise with her sister this month to help the woman deal with her grief over the loss of her son this past July. Marge would be missed as she fit right in with everyone.

Cassie was baking her mouth-watering amaranth bread, and Ryder made a traditional black bean salad from the pueblo he'd lived on. The ethnic diversity of their extended family had expanded everyone's cultural horizons tremendously. Rosa and Mrs. Gallagher had rounded out the meal with candied yams and baked apples, respectively. There would be so much food—and love—in this house today, and Savannah was so happy she and Mari would be a part of it.

Marc and Angelina would be hosting her mother and brothers for a private dinner at her restaurant in Breck, but Savannah, Damián, and Mari would see Marc at least on Saturday at his parents' resort in Aspen where Rosa's kids and Mari were going to take more ski lessons. Damián sounded as though he might attempt to learn as well, which surprised Savannah. He'd asked her to come along but not to say anything to Mari yet. He so hated to appear incapable of doing something in his daughter's eyes, but Savannah had all the confidence in the world in his ability to master anything he set out to do.

The only other person missing today would be Mistress Grant, who had turned down Adam's invitation saying she'd be out of town on assignment. The secretive woman didn't allow anyone to get too close to knowing her or what made her tick. But she'd always tried to make time for Mari, taking a special interest in teaching the little girl how to protect herself even against much larger foes. That put Savannah's mind at ease a little bit. If anything ever had happened to Mari—or her baby or Damián—Savannah didn't know what she'd do.

Shaking off those negative thoughts, she cut her last potato into the stock pot. "Want me to split the rest of yours?" she asked Adam.

"Nah. Maybe see what else Kitten needs."

Standing, she crossed to the island. "Okay, what's next?"

Karla surveyed the area and picked up a brick of Velveeta. "Could you cut this into one-inch cubes for the casseroles?"

"I think I can handle that." She'd barely sat down again at the table beside Adam when she looked up as Damián walked into the room, his wet hair pulled back in a ponytail. Her heart still skipped a beat every time she saw his handsome face. He approached her and bent to place a kiss on Savannah's cheek. "Did you eat breakfast, *savita*?"

"I'll get something in a minute, but I don't want to spoil my dinner."

Her husband's low growl told her she wasn't pleasing him at the moment. "That's hours away," he pointed out.

"It's my fault," Karla interjected. "I'm a slave driver. Both of you, help yourself to some pumpkin bread on the counter. Savannah, I can work on the cheese."

"No, that's okay. I can eat and work at the same time." Savannah felt a strong need to continue doing something mindless to keep her thoughts away from the upcoming trial.

Damián microwaved two pieces of bread, slathered both with soft butter, and brought them over on a single plate, setting it beside her before scooting a chair closer to join her. He broke off a piece of one and held it up to her mouth. "Open."

Rolling her eyes, she did as he instructed, knowing it would be futile to refuse. She kissed his fingertips before he removed them and smiled like the dutiful submissive she tried to be. After chewing and swallowing, she peeled the foil away from the cheese. "Mmm. Karla, this bread's delicious."

Mari came over to wrap her arm around Savannah's back. "I helped make it last night, Maman."

"Well, then, I'll need the recipe so you and I can make more at home."

"You've got it," Karla said. "It's super easy. I used a box mix." She shrugged unapologetically and smiled.

Damián kissed Mari on the top of her head. "What has my *princesa* been up to this morning?"

"I played with the babies. I taught them how to crawl faster."

"I'm sure Karla and Dad will love you for that."

"We love our Marisol no matter what," Adam said.

When the doorbell rang, Karla dried her hands on a dishtowel and patted her hair. "That must be Mom and Daddy. She texted about an hour ago with their arrival time. Excuse me, I'll be right back."

When Savannah had first met Karla, she'd envied her for having the persona of a young, naive girl. Savannah had felt old since she was eight. But after having three babies, nearly dying afterward, and working on the first tracks of an album she planned to market as an indie vocalist next year, Karla had proven that she could handle anything life tossed at her. Such a strong woman.

Adam was the one who worried her more. While he put up a solid front, Savannah caught moments where a haunted expression crossed his face as he looked at Karla or the babies. The "what would I do without them?" look held a touch of "I don't deserve them" that confused Savannah. No one had earned the right to happiness more than this man who always put everyone ahead of himself his entire life.

Survivor's guilt? What had given him such feelings? So much of his past was a mystery to Savannah. She wondered if Damián knew his adopted dad's story.

The sound of Rosa's voice made Damián's face light with joy. He loved his family and must be so pleased to have everyone together today.

Like Savannah, Rosa had survived horrible abuse, as had her daughter, Teresa. But day in and day out, Rosa relaxed more and brightened the days of all around her as she seamlessly managed the clinic.

A quick glance at the others in the kitchen doorway showed Teresa and her little brother, José.

But look who else had decided to join them!

Chapter Fifteen

Damián had been worried about Rosa spending her first Thanksgiving in Denver alone after she'd rejected repeated invitations, but she'd finally agreed to come yesterday. She usually preferred to stay invisible and in the background, telling him she sometimes felt she was a burden or in the way. *That would be the day.*

Damián wondered what changed her mind. *Madre de Dios!* Standing behind Rosa and her kids, he saw Doctor McKenzie. Had the good doctor had anything to do with the change of plans?

Damián stood and crossed the room to hug Rosa and kiss her cheek. "Good to see you, sis."

"I hope we are not imposing."

"You're family," Karla said, beaming at her. "How can you impose on family? And Doctor Mac, consider yourself family, too!"

Damián extended his hand to shake the doctor's. "Doctor McKenzie."

"Please call me Mac. I don't intend to be dispensing medical advice today, unless there's an emergency like a tryptophan coma or something."

"Come in." Damián gestured them into the kitchen. "I think you know everyone except maybe Adam Montague."

Dad shook his hand. "I can't thank you enough for all you've done for Savannah and Damián's family. From what I've heard, Rosa loves working at your clinic."

"Rosa's one of the best managers I've ever hired. She runs the place so efficiently I can't imagine how I got by without her. Can you, Savannah?"

"Absolutely not, even though I've only been there a few months longer than Rosa has."

Damián owed the good doctor a huge debt of gratitude for all he'd done for his family—from hiring Savannah and Rosa to helping out the night Savannah arrived from SoCal last December, beaten and injured by Lyle, to when Doctor Mac made sure Marc had the medical supplies he'd need during the raid to rescue Savannah from Gentry.

The doctor smiled down at Rosa who gifted him with a shy smile. "You're too kind, Robert." When had he become *Robert?* And was Rosa blushing? Damián glanced from her to the tall man beside her and wondered if something was going on between them other than a professional relationship. He hoped so. Rosa needed someone like him— an honorable man, patient and gentle to the extreme. Doctor Mac would never abuse her or her kids.

"Uncle Damo," Teresa said, placing a kiss on his cheek, "I have to talk with you when you have a minute."

Worried at first by her serious tone, Damián searched her face, but sunshine seemed to pour from her eyes. Curiosity got the best of him. "I'm just in the way here. Let's go talk now." Before they went into the living room, he ruffled José's hair. "What's my nephew up to?"

"Just school and stuff." He didn't sound too happy about it, either.

"Well, why don't you and Marisol go play a while before dinner?"

"Let's play Mulan!" Marisol shouted.

"I wanna be Spiderman." The two negotiated what they'd play as they left the room and walked toward the stairway to head upstairs to the playroom.

"No, Pax!" Karla excused herself to chase after her son down the hall.

"I'd better go corral the girls, too," Adam said, "so Kitten can finish getting dinner ready."

"How can we help?" Rosa asked.

"I'm not the one giving the orders on this ship today, but I need to finish up those potatoes. How'd you like to keep an eye on the triplets?"

"I'd love to!" Rosa said. She'd always loved babies.

"Follow me." He led them down the hall toward the living room.

"Come on, Teresa. Let's find ourselves a quiet room to talk."

"Feel free to use my office," Dad called after them. Damián nodded.

As Dad found seats for Rosa and Doctor Mac—er, Mac—Damián and Teresa made their way to the office at the back of the house. He couldn't wait to hear what was up. Teresa had made great strides in healing from the trauma of what Julio had done to her a year ago. Savannah's counseling in Solana Beach and at the clinic here had helped, but Teresa's rape experience would never go away.

Savannah still suffered from flashbacks and triggers and probably would to some extent for the rest of her life. At least Damián could help Savannah find ways to minimize and control hers better through their Dominant/submissive lifestyle. But Teresa only had Savannah and her family's support to overcome hers.

Rather than sit behind the desk, Damián took one of the two seats in front of it, and they rearranged them to face one another.

Teresa drew a deep breath, still seeming too somber. "Uncle Damo, I need your advice." She glanced down at her hands, which she twisted in her lap, before meeting his gaze again. "About a boy."

Damián smiled. He'd hoped this day would come where she'd put her trust in a boy again, but she hadn't seemed interested—until now. "Tell me about him."

"He's in my music class at school and recently signed up for the same vocal trainer that I use." Ever since Teresa had met Karla, she'd wanted to be a singer, too. "He's super shy, but I think he might like me."

"Why wouldn't he? You're a nice *chica*."

"No, I mean like, really *like* me. The way boys like normal girls."

"Who says you aren't normal?"

"Well, you know I'm different from the other girls at my school." She glanced down again, realized her knee was bouncing, and pressed her hand on her thigh to forcefully stop the nervous response.

"Here's what *I* know. You're smart and kind. You love to sing, and you bring a lot of joy to your family and those around you."

She glanced back up and smiled at him. "Thanks, Uncle Damo. But you're my uncle. I don't know if that's how non-relatives see me. Except for Jonathan. He's different with me than with the other girls."

Damián tamped down the overprotective dad mode—or tried to. "What's he saying or doing to make you think he's interested?"

"Well, he always tries to sit next to me in music."

Ah, that kind of thing. Damián relaxed somewhat.

"And sometimes we sit together in the cafeteria." She glanced away again. "That's where he asked me on Tuesday if I'd like to go see a movie with him tomorrow night."

Go on a date? Was she ready? Taking a play from Savannah's bag of psychology tricks, he asked, "How do you feel about that?"

"Well, we've been getting to know each other for nearly three months." Her knee began bouncing again.

Sharing classroom space was no comparison to sitting side by side in a darkened movie theater with a guy she hardly knew. Damián wanted to meet and size up the boy first, but Teresa wasn't asking him for permission to go out with Jonathan. What exactly *did* she need from Damián?

Teresa bit her upper lip, avoiding his gaze. "I don't know what to talk with him about other than music."

Damián had no clue what young people talked about on dates. Maybe Rosa could help out here.

"Have you told your *mamá* about him?"

She shook her head. "Mamá hates all boys, except for you, José, and Doctor Mac," she corrected with a smile. "She doesn't know how to relate to guys any more than I do."

That Teresa, who'd suffered trauma at the hands of the same man Rosa had, was in a place where she was ready to move on was a testament to the ability of the young to put the past behind them. He did want her to find happiness when she grew up and to have a family someday, which meant eventually she'd have to go on a date with a guy. She'd turned seventeen in September, so she was plenty old enough to date.

Then he thought back to when he was seventeen and what he'd been doing with teenage girls in Solana Beach, and that only convinced him that she was too young to go out on dates. But if she didn't take these first steps, would she have an aversion to men her entire life? Still, while he worried it might be too soon, it warmed his heart that she was ready to lose some of her fear of the opposite sex.

He remembered she'd asked him a question before his mind had taken off down that path.

"What do you talk about in school?"

"Music mostly."

"Obviously, that's something the two of you have in common. It shouldn't be so different when you're out on a date. There won't be much talking in a movie theatre, anyway." *But he'd better keep his hands off her.*

"He wants to take me out for Mexican after the movie."

Damián's first meal with Savannah was at a cantina. Right *after* they'd had sex, both of them nineteen. Mierda*, I'm not ready for this girl to grow up and start dating.*

"Would you like me to meet him and have a little talk with him when he comes to pick you up?" If he got a bad vibe from the kid, he'd kick his ass right out of Rosa's house.

Teresa laughed. "I don't think he'd survive having you grill him. And when word got out, I'd probably never get another boy to ask me out—ever."

"Who said anything about grilling? Just want to ask him some questions. Get to know him a little."

She rolled her eyes but continued to smile. "I'm seventeen, Uncle Damo. And thanks to my self-defense classes, I can take care of myself, if necessary."

True. He'd made sure she could fight off anyone who threatened her physically. Time to let her stand on her own. Hell, she'd be heading off to college in nine months, and he sure wouldn't be able to screen her dates there.

"Then why don't you tell me more about him now so I don't have to give him the third degree?"

"Well, he's well-liked by other students, both boys and girls. He does better than I do at math, but I score better on music exams. And he ran for and won a seat on the Student Council."

"Sounds like a good kid." So what advice should he give her that would keep her safe? "Okay, when you go out, trust your instincts. If something doesn't feel right, listen to your intuition. You'll have your cell phone. Call me, and I'll come and get you."

"I appreciate that, Uncle Damo, but I don't think we'll have any problems like that. Getting him to talk might be the most awkward part."

Bueno. "Just don't get all hung up on getting him to like you. The purpose of a first date is for you to get to know each other better and for you to see if he likes you for who you really are. Don't fall into a trap pretending to be who you think he wants you to be."

"What if…"—she glanced down—"…he wants to kiss me?"

Fuck. Maybe he wasn't as shy as Teresa made him out to be. "How would you feel about that?" Savannah would be proud of him for remaining this calm outwardly.

"Kinda strange. I don't know him well enough that way—yet."

Good girl.

"You'll know when you're ready to kiss or be kissed by someone you genuinely like."

She bit her lower lip, serious again. "You don't think he'd do anything to…hurt me, do you?" Her concerns weren't unfounded, but he didn't want her to go through life being overly fearful, either.

"He'll answer to me if he does. Set your boundaries. Be clear about them. Don't let him disrespect you or push you past the boundaries you set. If he tries to force you into doing anything you don't want to do after you tell him no, knee him in the balls."

Teresa's eyes opened wider before she met his gaze. "Promise me you won't threaten to kick him in the…teeth if you meet him eventually?"

Damián grinned. "Who, me?" He drew his brows together. Was there something she was leaving out? "Why wouldn't I like him?"

She rolled her eyes. "Because you're a Marine—and a daddy." She smiled indulgently. "But I value your judgment. You're the only father figure I have."

"You know I'll treat your dates the same way I will Marisol's, when it's time for her to date."

Like threatening to roast the boy's nuts over my welding torch if he disrespects or hurts her in any way.

"That's why I think it's best that I do this on my own, but I still wanted your advice. And I'll make sure Jonathan knows what will happen if he ignores my boundaries. That he'll have to answer to you." Her beaming smile told him she wasn't concerned. "I hope he doesn't run before the movie starts, but I'll feel safer having him know I'm under someone's protection. Just in case."

"You know you always will have me and our extended family looking out for you."

"Now, I just need one more thing."

"Name it."

"Could you help Mamá understand why I want to go out with him?"

Ah, this conversation might be more about that than getting Damián's dating advice. "You can talk to your *mamá* about anything. You know that."

"Not about boys."

He shook his head. "I don't want you to keep anything from her. Talk to her tonight. I can take her aside after dinner to prepare her, if you'd like, but I want you to talk to her just like you're talking to me. She might need some reassurance that you'll be safe, though. That he's a good boy and someone you consider a friend at this point, but who you want to get to know better."

"Maybe if you were with me she'd be calmer about it."

"Done. After dinner, the three of us can talk."

"I'd like that." She launched herself into his arms and placed a kiss on his cheek. "I love you, Uncle Damo. I'm so glad we moved closer to you. It was scary being in California and so far away from you after…"

He regretted that he hadn't been able to protect her when it counted most, but he could only start here and do his best from now on. He pulled away, cupped her cheek, and brushed her face with his thumb. "Love you, too, *princesa.*"

Teresa's resilience and strong spirit did his heart good. He hoped she'd always take healthy precautions but not hold back on living her life to the fullest. Her confidence would grow in time, and someday, he hoped she'd live life without worrying about what dangers lurked in every corner. Cautious and prepared, sure, just as he encouraged Savannah to be. But not living in fear anymore.

He wanted that for both of them, more than anything else.

Chapter Sixteen

Damián wouldn't even let Savannah carry the bowl of mashed potatoes to the buffet in the dining room, so she picked up one of the pies instead. She had to admit she was feeling tired, and her back had been aching for the past two hours, so she didn't fight him for the honors.

After setting the bowl down, he turned to Savannah, wrapping an arm around her back. "You okay, *bebé*?"

Of course, nothing got by Damián. She forced a smile. "I've probably done more than I should at this point. My back is aching."

"Okay, you're going to take a nap after dinner."

"After stuffing ourselves on all this food, I think everyone here will want to do the same."

When they returned to the now-vacant kitchen to get the remaining two pies, she tried to knead the knots out of her lower back.

"Hands on the counter and bend over."

Her eyes grew wide at the unexpected order, but the no-nonsense stare he gave her told her to do as he said. When she'd assumed the position, most of the pressure on her back disappeared immediately. Then his hands wrapped around her sides, and his thumbs pressed hard against the lumbar muscles, exactly where she hurt the most.

"Oh dear Lord, that feels incredible."

"Why didn't you say you were in pain earlier?"

She nibbled on her lower lip. "It wasn't severe." *Yet.* "Minor discomfort at most. I'm used to it."

"It's my responsibility to make sure you remember to take care of yourself while you're busy taking care of others. Don't go that long again without asking for help—or some relief."

He continued to rub her lower back until she moaned then gave her a quick slap on the butt.

She smiled, pleased that he wasn't angry with her, only concerned. Standing upright and turning toward him, she placed a kiss on his lips. "Thank you, Sir, for taking such good care of me."

He wrapped his arms around her, staring into her eyes. "You mean everything to me, Savannah. I worry about you."

"I know. I promise not to give you another thing to fret about. Now, let's go enjoy that fabulous meal with everyone."

Seated at the table, Savannah stroked her belly when the baby became active again. She shifted on the chair cushion several times trying to find a comfortable spot while also trying to keep up with the conversations going on around her.

"You okay?" Damián whispered in her ear.

"The baby's doing calisthenics on my bladder, but otherwise, I'm fine."

Rosa sat across the table from Doctor Mac who was on Savannah's left side. She caught Rosa casting longing glances his way a couple of times during dinner as well as earlier in the kitchen. Why hadn't she noticed an attraction growing between her and the doctor before? While one-sided at best, Rosa did seem to be a little infatuated with him, which surprised Savannah. Unfortunately, the dedicated, workaholic doctor didn't seem to have a flirtatious bone in his body. He took everything so seriously, and his only priority in life was providing the best affordable healthcare to those in the community who didn't have access to insurance or couldn't afford their copay responsibilities.

Day in and day out, Rosa came into the clinic and went about running the administrative duties of his practice, but Savannah had had no clue she harbored other-than-professional feelings for her boss.

Rosa had been dealt a cruel hand in her marriage. Thankfully, her ex wouldn't see freedom for twenty to forty years, depending on how generous the parole boards in California were.

Would Savannah have to live in fear of the day Gentry was released from prison? Would he even get that far in the justice system or would he find a way to beat the rap? First, he'd need to be found guilty. Then, based on how sentencing went, she'd have to sweat it out every seven years after he became eligible for parole. She couldn't fathom living under that man's ominous shadow again, not knowing when he might show up and disrupt her life again.

To deflect attention, she seized the moment to share what she was most thankful for. Months ago, Damián had had her start a gratitude journal to record her thoughts on what she appreciated about each and every day. She'd come to appreciate so many things, big and small. "I want to jump on the bandwagon and say how much I appreciate Damián and all of you for welcoming Mari and me into your arms wholeheartedly less than a year ago when we arrived here with nowhere else to go." She couldn't believe that had only been weeks before last Christmas. How her life had changed for the better since then.

Damián spoke next. "I am most thankful for my beautiful wife and daughter—and the little one coming in two months." He leaned over to kiss her on the cheek and patted her belly, eliciting a kick from the baby.

In turn, everyone at the table took the opportunity to express his or her gratitude, with Adam and everyone thanking Karla for hosting such a wonderful dinner and for all the prep work that had gone into it.

"And I am grateful to Angelina for the cooking lessons and to those who helped prepare it for us all to enjoy. Oh, and that I didn't burn anything," Karla said, followed by laughter at both tables.

From the head of one of the tables, Adam's mother said, "Karla, I'll never be able to thank you and your friend Grant enough for reuniting me with my son after too many years apart." Her eyes grew bright with unshed tears.

Teresa cleared her throat and caught her lower lip between her teeth before saying, "I'm grateful that Mamá moved us to Denver, far away from…" Her voice drifted off, and José added his agreement before Teresa turned her head and smiled toward Damián. "And that I have an awesome uncle who's the best dad I've ever known."

"And the best brother ever," Rosa added shyly.

"I'm thankful for another great dad, Adam, who not only brought our daughter happiness but also gave us three precious grandbabies," Jenny said.

Carl raised his glass of cranberry juice. "I'll second that!"

"And I," began Patrick at the next table over, "thank Adam for sending Ryder to my sister when he thought she might be in danger. I've never seen her so happy."

"Without Megan," Ryder said, "I don't like to think about where I'd be today." He leaned over, and a smiling Megan met his kiss.

Luke, sitting beside Cassie at the same table, added, "And, Megan and Ryder, by taking care of my rescue horses, you two sure made it easy for me to keep my girl all to myself up on that mountain with her alpacas."

Cassie's cheeks grew ruddy as she grinned back at him.

So much love and happiness, just as Savannah had anticipated today. When it seemed everyone had taken a turn, Mari, seated next to her grandpa, raised her juice glass. Her face seemed uncharacteristically solemn as she looked from Savannah to Damián. "I just want to say…thank you, Maman, for finding my daddy. Now I have a great big family, and pretty soon, I'm going to be a big sister, not just an auntie."

Savannah's heart ached for all the years Mari and Damián had lost, but she wouldn't wallow in regrets. They had the rest of their lives together, and that's all that counted.

"Oh, and I'm thankful I'm going to go skiing at Uncle Marc's mountain Saturday!"

Damián shifted in his seat, and Savannah couldn't hide her smile. If anyone could get Damián out there, it would be Mari—who had been begging him to learn to ski ever since Marc gave Mari and Savannah their first lessons last December. And Savannah would be looking on from the same observation area Damián and Angelina had watched them from a year ago.

If he didn't dote on his daughter, Damián might have found an excuse to get out of Saturday's lesson. While Savannah still wasn't sure how he'd manage with his prosthesis, Marc had assured him he had a friend joining them who would outfit him and give him pointers on navigating the slopes like a pro.

Damián had come such a long way in not letting his missing foot keep him from losing out on life, but he still didn't like to appear vulnerable or weak in front of Mari or Savannah. Not that he didn't enjoy making Savannah a little uncomfortable in front of others at the club. She smiled. Maybe it was time to get *him* out of *his* comfort zone.

If only he realized Mari adored the ground he walked on—or in this case, skied on. Nothing would ever change that.

"You aren't eating, *querida*."

"I know, but I think I need a nap more than anything else right now."

When she started to rise and pick up her plate to begin clearing the table, Damián took it from her just as Adam announced, "You ladies go relax in the living room. Since you did most of the cooking, it's our turn to clean up."

Karla stood and began unstrapping Pax from his high chair while Cassie and Jenny each took one of the baby girls. "Let's play Quiddler," Karla suggested.

Fatigue overcame Savannah. "If you'll all excuse me, I hear a comfy bed telling me it's time to take a nap."

"Oh, I understand completely," Karla said. "Go on up. We'll try to keep the noise level down."

"Believe me, I could sleep through an earthquake right now."

She parted company with them in the foyer and started up the stairs. The nagging lower back pain had returned. She probably needed to do more exercise to strengthen her abs. She'd ask Doctor Palmer about that at her next appointment.

Once in the guest room, she stretched out slowly, placing a pillow between her knees, which alleviated the worst of the backache. Everything else faded away as soon as she closed her eyes.

* * *

When Adam told each of the guys to grab a beer so they could go watch football, Damián excused himself to check on Savannah. American football wasn't his sport anyway, and he needed to be sober to drive his girls home tonight. As he passed the living room door, he glanced inside and saw that Marisol, José, and Teresa were in the fenced indoor play area, each playing with one of the babies, while the other ladies huddled around a large, round card table laughing over the cards Megan had played.

Climbing the stairs as quickly as he could manage, he entered the guest room, closing the door behind him. Savannah lay on the opposite side of the bed with her back to him, so he removed his boots, clothes, and prosthesis and crawled onto the mattress to spoon against her back, wrapping his arm around her to cup her breast.

"Mmm," she said, pressing her ass against his groin. "You better hurry before my husband catches us."

He chuckled. "Oh, *bebé*, if I came up here to make love to you, I'd take it nice and slow. But I'd rather wait until we go home tonight." He stroked her arm through her sleeve. "How are you feeling? You admitted being uncomfortable at dinner."

She rolled toward him slightly but remained on her side. "The baby's been bouncing off my uterine walls today. Maybe I overdid it."

His hand stilled. "Should we get you checked out? Is there any danger to you or the baby?"

"It's normal practice contractions, I think. Worse than I had with Mari, but I'm not bleeding and can still smile through them, so I don't think we need to worry."

The mention of the possibility of her bleeding made his own blood run cold. "Just the same, I'm going to ask Doctor Mac to come up and check on you." He was sitting on the edge of the bed, putting his prosthesis on in seconds.

"I don't want to bother him on his day off. He works so hard. Honestly, I think the problem is that I haven't been exercising enough. I miss my pole-dancing classes."

He chuckled, glancing down at her. "You don't know how hot it makes me picturing you on a stripper pole. Real sorry I missed out on seeing you working out on one. Maybe after the baby, Doctor Palmer will okay your using one to help get back in shape. I could install a pole in the house."

"I don't want to turn our only spare bedroom into a dance studio or workout room. We don't have as much room as Adam and Karla do. But I'll talk with the doctor, and if she's okay with it, I might look into taking some sort of postpartum exercise class."

"Now, hang tight." He put on his jeans and stood while donning his shirt. "I'll be right back with the doctor."

"Really, Damián. This is normal."

"I want a professional opinion."

Twenty minutes later, Doctor Mac proclaimed her as having Braxton-Hicks contractions and cautioned her not to overdo it, to monitor her blood pressure, and to head straight to the emergency department if she noticed any bleeding, hypertension, or the contractions became regular and more intense.

"Savannah, I also want you to relax more," the doc said. "If that means cutting back on your hours at the clinic, it's more important that you stay healthy and carry this pregnancy to term, especially with all you have going on right now."

Damián couldn't agree more. "Any suggestions on ways to reduce stress, Doc?"

"Walking, reading, meditating, having massages or even sex, as long as your OB approves."

Savannah met Damián's gaze and smiled. "I have a wonderful massage therapist on call day and night who offers fringe benefits."

He hadn't realized he'd been giving her exactly what the doctor ordered. He grinned back. "Anytime, *bebé.*"

To Damián, the doctor said, "Whatever makes her slow down and take better care of herself is the right stuff. Trust your instincts."

"I promise you both that I'll take it easier and try to worry less. But please don't cut my hours just yet, Mac. I have so many clients who need me."

Damián sobered, growling deep in his throat.

To appease him, she suggested setting timers to remind her to relax once an hour between clients. Mac made her agree to reschedule any appointment if overly fatigued or stressed.

At least Damián could rest assured she'd be in good hands if anything happened while she was at the clinic. He'd keep a better watch on things at home by rescheduling his shop hours to coincide more with her work schedule. He'd also make sure Mari knew what to do in case of a crisis, without worrying his daughter unnecessarily.

After the doctor left, Damián joined her in bed again. He lowered his face, kissing her collar and nuzzling her neck above the top of her shirt.

She moaned and whispered, "What are you doing?"

"If you have to ask, then I'm doing it wrong."

"Shouldn't we wait until we're home?"

"I didn't say how far I planned to take this, but…"—he nibbled on her earlobe, tugging at the stud earring with his teeth—"I have doctor's orders to help you relax. And besides, I need a nibble or two to tide me over."

Her hand reached between their bodies, and she stroked his hard-on. "You're sure we have to wait 'til tonight?"

"Anticipation is good for us both." And yet, he couldn't keep his hands off her—cupping her full breasts, pinching her nipples, and making her hiss.

"Sadist."

"At your service, *savita*. Although I've been curbing those tendencies for a while now."

Savannah had no clue what being with a real sadist would be like, but she liked to tease him about his role as the club's sadist service top. While her tolerance for pain was increasing, he didn't consider her a masochist, either.

Before things got out of hand and he didn't want to stop, he sighed. "Did you nap when you came up here?"

"A little bit."

"Do you want to sleep more?"

"Not really." She sighed. "I suppose we should return to the crowd downstairs."

"Probably."

With a boost from him, she sat up and gave herself a moment to adjust to the new position. He sat on the mattress beside her.

"Damián, did you see the way Rosa looked at Mac?"

"Yeah." He still couldn't believe it.

"Do you think something's going on—or is she just lusting from afar?"

"Rosa doesn't lust. Hell, she swore off men when Julio went to jail the first time."

"Well, mark my words, but there's definitely a spark of interest on her part. Of course, Mac can be pretty oblivious about anything except his practice and his patients."

"You're a hopeless romantic, *bebé*. Maybe we were just imagining things, now that I think about it."

"I'm just saying," she said in a singsong voice before standing up and slipping into her shoes.

"Ready to go back down?"

She nodded, taking his hand, and they walked down the staircase together.

Chapter Seventeen

Damián tried to balance his weight on the blade while Evander, Marc's friend, showed him how to wield the ski poles. Thank goodness Marisol, José, and Teresa were off with Marc again and not watching Damián painstakingly try to maintain his balance on this white shit. For two days, he'd struggled to get it. Today, he'd insisted that Savannah stay with Angelina at the restaurant back in Breckenridge where she, Megan, and Cassie were having a cooking lesson in Angelina's kitchen. While her back pain had eased up some, there was no reason to have her up here shivering her cute little ass off watching him make a fool of himself.

But watching Evander getting around like a ski pro with an above-the-knee amputation had Damián determined to at least cruise down the bunny slope before the end of the weekend. Marisol wanted to see him ski. He couldn't deny her such a heartfelt wish.

Damián dug the poles into the packed snow and propelled himself forward, only to feel his good leg slipping out from underneath him. *Bam!* Before he knew it, he was sitting on his ass in this cold, wet shit. Again.

"Here, man. Let me give you a hand," Evander said, helping him back to his feet.

"Maybe skiing isn't in my genes."

Evander gave a hearty laugh. "You think we have snowy peaks in Jamaica? It's all in your attitude, Damo. Look at our Olympic bobsled team. Now grow a pair, and get back on your feet."

Damián wouldn't be outdone by this Caribbean vagabond who had somehow landed in Crested Butte a year ago teaching amputees how to ski. Marc's sister, Carmella, had invited Evander to the D'Alessio resort to provide weekly ski lessons to those with physical disabilities.

Evander had agreed to work with Damián this weekend, and Damián was determined to succeed if it killed him.

Damián's goal wasn't to descend the treacherous black diamond runs here in Aspen any more than he planned to compete in the Paralympics or Invictus Games. He only wanted to stay upright long enough to show Marisol he could do anything he set his mind to—and so could she. He adjusted his grip on the poles as he glanced at the daunting bunny slope ahead.

"We're going about this all wrong," Evander said, shaking his head vehemently as he waved his hands in front of him like a baseball umpire calling a player safe at home plate. "When are you going to trust me and take off that prosthesis?"

"Haven't I fallen on my ass enough today?"

Evander howled with laughter. "Hell, no, man! The day's still young."

"Thanks for the vote of confidence." The man's eternal optimism was beginning to grate on Damián.

"Aw, I'm just pulling your leg." He chuckled at the irony. "Now, if you're ready to quit trying to ski like a two-legged man and do it my way, we can get somewhere."

Damián sighed. He hated making concessions to his physical limitations, especially publicly, but based on the last hour or so, he wasn't going to get anywhere like this. "Fine. What did you have in mind?"

"Lose the prosthesis. I'll be right back."

Damián hopped back to the bench a few yards away and plopped down. Marisol wouldn't want to leave for at least five or six more hours, so he might as well keep trying.

When Evander returned, he carried two contraptions that looked like forearm crutches with mini skis on the ends. "These are outriggers, similar to the ones Hawaiians attach to their canoes. But you're going to use them to give you the balance you need to get around on the slopes on one leg. Close your eyes."

Damián stowed his prosthesis in his seabag and did as instructed, despite his uneasiness at trusting someone he barely knew.

"Now, visualize yourself zipping down the slope shifting your weight from one leg to the other until you have a good rhythm going."

Even though he only had one leg now, Damián decided to humor his ski instructor. He mentally shifted his body from side to side, leaning on the outriggers. He conjured up the feel of snow hitting his face as he imagined himself racing down the slope with Marisol watching and cheering him on.

"Okay, now let's get out there and put that visualization into practice."

'Mind over matter.' How many times had he heard that? Countless physical therapists had told him that's all he had to do to give himself the freedom to live outside the box. He realized it was the same dark, isolated box he'd locked himself into before Savannah had come back into his life.

"Find your center of gravity."

He leaned forward a little. Nope. He caught himself with the outrigger then tilted his body slightly to the side and waited for Evander to adjust the height of the right outrigger.

"Try that."

He leaned in again. "Better."

"Ready for the snow?"

Ready as I'll ever be. "Sure."

"Okay, watch how I use this pair of outriggers, and then you do the same."

Damián watched Evander ski away with exaggerated slowness, trying to make it look easy, no doubt. *I can do that.* He needed to master something to show Marisol the importance of not giving in or giving up. No, he just needed to try to achieve that goal. Damián set his ski and outriggers in motion. His sense of balance was much improved with the outriggers compared to when he'd tried to ski on his blade with flimsy ski poles.

A sense of achievement welled up inside him. Maybe he'd get the hang of this after all.

An hour later, about the time he'd agreed to meet up with Marc and the kids, Damián tried to tamp down his nervousness. He hadn't fallen since he'd decided to do it Evander's way with outriggers, so why would he fall now?

Because his daughter was watching.

Don't fuck this up.

He spotted the four of them on the intermediate slope and wished he'd told them to rendezvous on the bunny slope. But he hadn't wanted to look like a total wuss.

Drawing a slow, deep breath, he set the outriggers and propelled himself toward them.

"Daddy! You're skiing! I knew you could do it!" Seeing a joy-filled Marisol clapping and bouncing up and down in support of him made pride well up inside his chest as he sped toward her.

"Thanks, *muñequita!*" He picked up speed and tried to stop, but forgot what to do in all his excitement.

"Way to go, Uncle Damo!" Teresa shouted seconds before she and Marisol opened their eyes wide as he hurtled toward them. Marc lifted Marisol into his arms to pull her out of harm's way just as Teresa scooted José to the side in the nick of time before his brain finally engaged and Damián brought himself to a sudden stop.

A giggling Marisol came rushing over to him and wrapped her tiny arms as far as she could around his waist. "Don't worry, Daddy. You'll get better with practice. I'll help."

Having Marisol see him as being able to accomplish something important to her only made him want to try harder to overcome his fear of failing before her. "Don't worry. I'm going to get the hang of this, and pretty soon. We'll be skiing together every season now." And next season, Savannah could join them and, eventually, so would their baby.

Marc joined them, clapping him on the back of his jacket. "Not bad for your first weekend on the slopes, man."

"I want one of those, too," José said, pointing to the outrigger.

No, you don't.

"You're wicked on that thing, Uncle Damo," Teresa said.

"A real *duppy conqueror,*" Evander said when he caught up. The Bob Marley song about overcoming adversity would be playing in his head the rest of the day. "I told you you could overcome anything you put your mind to, man."

Damián spent the rest of the afternoon skiing with Marisol after sending Marc off to the lodge to hang out with his brother and sister. The days where Marc would have avoided the time spent at the lodge had passed. He seemed much more at peace now that he was with Angelina again and training for a new career as an EMT. There was no better corpsman in the Navy; he'd saved Damián's life at risk to his own.

"Race you down the hill, Daddy!" Marisol announced, breaking into his thoughts as she set off down the intermediate slope. He wasn't so much giving her a head start as just watching her slice and swerve down the hill like a pro. Not wanting to be too lame, he set off after her. With his weight and the smoothness of the outriggers, he made a decent showing at the bottom.

"I won!" she shouted, beaming up at him.

No, princesa. *Today, I'm the winner.*

Chapter Eighteen

Savannah's chest tightened as she walked into the courtroom on the first Wednesday in December. She'd waited for and worried about this moment for months, and now the time had come. Before moving two steps inside the room, her gaze went straight to where the District Attorney said the defendant would sit, but the table was vacant. Still, her mouth became dry as her throat constricted. Thank God she had Damián here with her. She didn't think she could face the monster alone. Already the breakfast Damián insisted she eat threatened to come back up at the thought of being in the same room with Gentry again.

The judge wasn't on the bench yet, either. They'd come early enough that Savannah could compose herself before everyone took their places. The DA had wanted her here today to hear motions and watch jury selection, primarily to acclimate her to the courtroom setting. No doubt, the attorney for the People wanted to ensure Savannah could overcome her nerves and prove she would be able to maintain her composure in front of the bastard who'd fathered her when the time came for her to testify.

I can do this. I will do this. For you, Maman.

"Deep breath, *savita.*"

She took a deep, cleansing breath, visualizing her nervousness and fear leaving her body on the exhale, then smiled at Damián and squeezed his hand.

Before Savannah would have the chance to tell her story, the DA intended to call the forensic anthropologist and medical examiner to testify about the remains found buried in the rose garden for nearly twenty years. Maman's and John Grainger's bodies had been there all along, right outside her front door. She shuddered. Damián leaned toward her, squeezing her waist as he pulled her into his heat. "Cold, *querida?*"

She shook her head and forced a smile to her lips so as not to have him worry. "It's just nerves." Visitors were instructed to sit anywhere on the right-hand side of the gallery, so he guided her to the row of padded seats directly behind the district attorney's table before motioning for her to sit down first.

The earliest the DA expected Savannah to testify would be Monday, assuming she handled the proceedings well today and tomorrow and didn't lose her shit when George Gentry walked into the room. The DA had threatened to eject her, Damián, or both of them if they caused any distracting drama, especially in front of the jury or the judge.

Savannah wanted desperately to hear the expert witnesses and others give their testimonies before and after her own, though. She would be here for her mother and John, no matter how uncomfortable she became. She had every intention of remaining calm. No one would be escorting her out of this courtroom against her will.

Of course, Savannah had schooled herself decades ago in how to shut down emotionally. Damián had been working to undo that survival mechanism which left her body detached from her feelings. He'd worked on helping her stay in the moment while, at the same time, acknowledging her feelings. She needed to be able to focus without being pulled back into the terrifying, degrading experiences in her past. Her former and modified behaviors would be at war with one another for the duration of this trial.

Her gaze remained riveted on the chair where Gentry would be sitting. She tried to visualize him to diminish the initial shock of seeing him again. She'd worked so hard to block his image out of her mind since her kidnapping, but found that impossible to do.

Damián reassuringly squeezed her waist again. They'd already talked about her doing whatever it took to get through the next couple of weeks in this courtroom, or however long this trial might take. The sense of foreboding she'd felt over the impending trial had nearly made her sick these past two months. All too soon, she'd come face to face once again with her worst nightmare.

The chair at the defense table held her gaze captive much like the man who would occupy it had for ten long years.

"Breathe, *savita*." He touched her shoulder, signaling her to relax. She did as instructed—and took another breath besides—but the tightness in her chest didn't ease up. "Eyes."

Savannah blinked rapidly, somewhat dazed as she clawed her way back from her fears. Damián cupped her chin and turned her face toward him. "I. *Said*. 'Eyes.'"

Meeting his gaze brought her a small sense of stability again. Hard to believe he'd been back in her life barely a year. She'd been reminded of that two days earlier when Adam and Karla had celebrated their first wedding anniversary. The night of their wedding, Savannah and Marisol had arrived on Damián's doorstep while fleeing Gentry and Lyle. Damián had slowly become her rock since then.

She placed her hand on her growing belly and rubbed it to center herself. They had so much to look forward to, once they put this trial behind them and closed this final chapter to her horrific childhood once and for all.

Savannah had chosen a wardrobe of loose-fitting clothing today, not wanting to accentuate her pregnancy in, she supposed, an effort to protect her baby from Gentry's glares. She couldn't hide being almost eight months pregnant, though. By late next month, they'd have a new baby. Their fairytale, as well as their family, would be complete—unless and until more babies followed this one.

"You're stronger than he'll ever be, Savannah. You've got this. But you won't go through the trial alone. I'll be beside you for the entire thing."

Her husband, Dom, protector, and closest friend wouldn't let anything or anyone hurt her, not even that bastard Gentry or his accomplice, Lyle. But she also would need to take care of Damián so he wouldn't lose his shit, either. He hated Gentry, too, and she didn't want him to do anything to jeopardize the outcome. She definitely didn't want Damián thrown into jail for contempt of court—or worse.

"Promise me you won't let him get to you, either, Sir."

He grinned. "Who, me?"

She cocked her head and narrowed her eyes, not the least bit assured. Gentry would be under heavy guard. Surely Damián could see that any physical or verbal outburst on his part would only hurt their case. After all, hadn't he been working with her through various grounding techniques to not lose *her* cool?

Savannah knew the worst battles here would be fought on the psychological level, though. Gentry had spent decades twisting her mind into a distorted reality, leaving almost as many mental scars as he'd caused physical ones.

To reassure Damián, she said, "I feel nothing but rage toward the man who claims paternity of me. But he can't hurt me ever again." Perhaps if she said the words enough, she'd internalize them, too.

"No, he can't, *bebé*. He'd have to go through me first."

"And me next."

They both looked up to find Adam standing in the aisle beside Damián wearing his uniform with his cover tucked under his arm. She hadn't expected to see him until next week.

"What are you doing here?" she asked. "Did Karla come, too?" A quick glance behind him and toward the doors showed no sign of her.

"No, she's in Denver. Megan and Cassie are staying with her, Marisol, and the triplets until I get back. And Marc, Ryder, and Luke will be taking turns spending the nights there, too." Always overprotective. She loved it.

Savannah's eyes stung at how this family of choice rallied around one another at times like these. Marisol had mentioned last night that Megan was there when Savannah called her to say goodnight, but she hadn't mentioned that her grandpa was gone.

She stood, closed the gap between them, and wrapped her arms around him, resting her face on his chest. "I didn't want to take you away from Karla and the babies any sooner than when you were to testify next week."

"You didn't, hon." Pulling away, he grinned and gave her a wink. Suddenly, Adam became serious. "But she and I agreed that I need to be here with you two for as long as it takes so that your one and only focus will be on this trial and taking care of each other. Besides, I plan on flying back at oh-dark-thirty Saturday to surprise her. Then I'll catch the red-eye back Sunday night."

"Dad,"—Damián cleared his throat, standing directly behind her— "I'm glad you're here, too." Savannah realized he'd be as much a support for Damián as for her. "We have a two-bedroom suite at the Camp Pendleton lodge, if you'd like to stay with us." The base had a number of rooms and suites reserved for honorably discharged and retired Marines, she'd discovered.

He nodded, thanked Damián, and gave her husband an expression she couldn't quite read before Adam met her gaze again. "The DA wants me to testify early in the trial about what happened in the cabin when we rescued you."

"Yeah, I'm sure she thought you'd make a more rational witness than I would," Damián said, not seeming upset that he hadn't been chosen to do so. Adam would remain calm and controlled under cross-examination. And his uniform, with all his ribbons and badges, would give him an instantaneous air of respectability and authority.

Still, she hated pulling Adam away from Karla and their babies for what might be a week or more spent sitting in the hallway waiting to be called in to testify, because he wouldn't be allowed in the courtroom while others were testifying before him. The DA had considered Marc but ultimately decided Adam would be best.

Of course, Savannah wouldn't be banished from the proceedings. Being the only living victim of the capital crimes Gentry had been charged with, California's Marsy's Law and its Victims' Bill of Rights permitted her to remain present throughout the trial.

Stretching up on tiptoe, she placed a kiss on Adam's cheek and whispered, "I can't tell you how much this means to me, Adam."

Giving her a gentle hug, he said, "I'll keep telling you this until you believe me, Savannah—you're family. Kitten and I both feel the same way. And family is there for each other. Always. No matter what."

Pulling away again, she smiled at him through trembling lips, so touched that he would come all this way to be here for her and to testify. Time and again, he'd shown she was like a daughter to him. He'd treated her like a member of his family since the night he'd taken her and Mari in when they'd left Damián's apartment, long before she'd married Damián.

Actually, Adam was more of a father to her than Gentry had ever been. Was Adam upset that she didn't call him "Dad," especially after she'd called him that once when he'd given her away at her wedding? Would she ever be able to use the honorific title given the aftermath from years of abuse by the man on trial here? Perhaps not. But Adam didn't seem hurt or annoyed in any way that she continued to call him by his given name.

"Thanks, Dad," Damián said, clapping him on the shoulder. He had no qualms calling Adam 'Dad,' but his own father had been a good man, from what Savannah had heard from Damián and Rosa. "You don't know how much this means to us."

"Hell, you didn't think I'd miss watching Savannah take that POS down, did you? The DA said my testimony would precede yours, so I should be allowed in here." Adam smiled at her then asked, "So how are you holding up, hon? I know you've waited an awful long time to get justice."

Drawing herself up to her full warrior height, she squared her shoulders and smiled back, albeit with a sense of false bravado. She wanted them to be proud of her. "Trust me, when I'm finished with him, he won't want to mess with any of us again." Having these two men here gave her the courage she needed. She'd never want to disappoint either of them.

"Finish the job for us, hon."

She wrinkled her brow and tilted her head at Adam's words. Last night, lying in bed in their suite, Damián had alluded to some sort of retribution he and Adam had delivered following her rescue from the high desert cabin near Bear Mountain, but he hadn't provided any details. That suited her just fine; she didn't need or want to know. All that mattered was that they, Grant, and Marc had rescued her before Gentry could do any lasting damage. They'd been there for her afterward, too, taking care of her following the ordeal until she could get to the hospital. Adam and Damián had stayed with her for all or most of her care in the days and weeks that followed until she'd completely healed. Physically, at least.

All that seemed like a lifetime ago.

Now she belonged to Damián—body, heart, and soul. Her hand stroked her collar as a talisman of hope and security.

Damián placed a protective arm around Savannah's back, his hand toying with the loose hairs at the nape of her neck, sending a delicious thrill through her body. "Let's sit so you can rest your legs a while," he murmured.

No sooner had she positioned herself in the chair between the two men, Adam closest to the aisle, than a door at the opposite end of the room opened and the monster who still haunted her dreams so many nights walked into the room. Gentry's gaze homed in on her immediately. She gasped with the impact. The charged energy arcing between them sucked all the air out of the room. He sneered at her.

Damián made a fist, relaxed his hand, and then made another fist, scaring her a little. He struggled for control of his emotions as much as she did.

"Breathe, *querida.*" He leaned forward to break the visual hold Gentry had on her, and she blinked several times before focusing on Damián's face.

She couldn't do as Damián said. Her lungs were paralyzed.

I can't do this. I can't face him again.

Their baby kicked or elbowed her, jarring Savannah out of her fear-filled retreat. She needed to remember to breathe without reminders and to keep her body from becoming so tense she blocked the baby's oxygen levels. Although putting Gentry behind bars would make life safer for everyone she loved and achieving justice for her mother and John Grainger had been Savannah's utmost goal for months, nothing could ever be worth risking her baby's health.

"You're okay, *bebé.*"

She nodded. "That bastard is nothing but my sperm donor. He can't hurt me." She hadn't realized she'd spoken aloud until Damián stroked her cheek and agreed with her. The words came out like a mantra, probably because she'd repeated them so often these past few months.

Lifting her gaze toward her husband, she smiled. "You've shown me how a loving father behaves with his daughter, each and every day."

He placed a kiss on her lips, grounding her in the present. Savannah turned away and sat up straighter, steeling herself for what was to come while avoiding Gentry's gaze. She started to stroke her belly then forced her hand to still. If he didn't already know she was pregnant, she didn't want to telegraph the fact. Seated where she was, he couldn't see the baby bump. Had his goons informed him of such, though? After losing her mother's fortune, could he still wield immense power over former employees, court officials, and the police? Somehow, he'd managed to get this trial moved up by at least a year. Was the judge in his pocket?

She prayed not. But what if they didn't get a conviction? That bastard had never been held accountable for any evil thing he'd ever done. Why should she hope that would change?

Was her sperm donor's gaze on her? She could imagine the seething hatred streaming from the eyes of the beast, much as it had when he spoke about Mari while torturing her at the cabin.

Don't give him the satisfaction of acknowledging his presence.

Her lungs contracted, and she forced herself to keep breathing steadily and to not let the monster see his effect on her.

"Don't let him intimidate you, hon," Adam said.

Too late. She was way beyond intimidated; she was scared to death. She'd try to keep from showing that but could feel her fear oozing from every pore.

"Gee, he doesn't look too happy to see me," Damián said with a grin. She could well imagine why after the intense hatred Gentry had expressed toward Damián the night he'd brought her home after rescuing her from the abusive clients in the hotel's penthouse. Gentry loathed Damián with a passion and must have wished his gaze alone could strike down her man in this very courtroom.

Could Gentry get to either of them?

When Savannah's hands began to shake, Damián wrapped his larger one over both of hers and squeezed, as if commanding them to stop. And they did. "You're safe, *querida*," Damián whispered. She allowed herself to relax a little bit.

Clearly, neither of the two men beside her was going to give up any control or power to Gentry. She wanted to show Adam and Damián she could be as strong as they thought her to be, but it had taken all the courage she could muster to simply walk inside this room.

Savannah nodded to them both, pulled her left hand back, and squeezed Damián's forearm. After taking a deep breath, she almost allowed her gaze to stray toward the defendant's table.

"Eyes on the judge's bench, Savannah," Adam said in his Dom voice. "Don't make eye contact with that shithead. Keep your focus on the judge or the DA."

While the judge hadn't arrived yet, she shifted her gaze to the DA. Savannah breathed in and out slowly, less fearful than she'd been moments ago.

When the judge entered the courtroom, the bailiff instructed everyone to stand and brought the court to order. Adam whispered that was his cue to vamoose and left the courtroom.

Here we go. Will justice at last be mine?

Chapter Nineteen

The arduous jury selection process took until late Thursday morning. Damián's mind was numb by the time he heard the judge announce the lunch break. "Court will reconvene at one-thirty this afternoon."

Damián glared at Gentry's back as he was led out of the court in his fancy gray business suit. Would the jurors be fooled into thinking he was an upstanding businessman and worthy citizen of the county given what he wore?

If only he'd killed him when he had the chance. After rescuing Savannah last March, he'd come fucking close.

As retribution for what Gentry had done to Savannah—from the brand to her labia and rapes and assaults too numerous to count—he and Dad *had* inflicted a special kind of torture on the bastard by applying electrodes made from a wire coat hanger to the old man's shriveled junk. Frankly, they were surprised Gentry hadn't filed charges of assault and battery against them. Damián smiled, remembering the car battery they'd used. Dad had exacted the most damage, saying he didn't want Damián to have nightmares about it for years to come. Not that he was so certain Dad wasn't haunted by it a little, though. Something sure had been bothering Dad ever since they'd done the interrogation scene with Marc. The only nightmares that haunted Damian's sleep featured images of Savannah strapped down to the ottoman in that cabin, bloodied and crying as they rescued her from that fucking animal.

What if Gentry realized he had nothing left to lose after the district attorney threw the book at him with so many counts of murder, attempted murder, kidnapping, and more? Would he go after Damián or Dad in retribution?

Savannah squeezed his arm. "You okay?"

Hell, he was supposed to be here to support *her*, not the other way around. *Fuck that shit*, as Dad would say. He leaned over and kissed her on the cheek. "I'm fine, *bebé*. How're you holding up?"

"Nervous. Exhausted. But also anxious to get up there and tell my story."

His hand moved to the small of her back. She visibly relaxed as the courtroom cleared out. "You're going to do great. That sick bastard won't know what hit him."

"I just..."—she nibbled her lower lip—"wish I didn't *have* to face him."

"Me, too, but you're ready for this, *querida*. Remember your breathing. And ground yourself by touching your wedding ring or your collar whenever you need to calm yourself while on the stand."

She nodded.

"Let's go grab some grub while we can," Dad said from behind Savannah. He must have come inside after seeing court had adjourned. "My treat."

"Sounds good," Damián said. "Thanks, Dad." He needed to get Savannah away from the courthouse for a while. To breathe and eat in order to keep up her strength.

After a quick lunch at a nearby café, they returned to the courtroom a few minutes early and waited in the hall with Dad for the courtroom doors to reopen. Savannah had gone quiet again at lunch, picking at her fingers until one was bloodied, an old habit he thought he'd cured her of doing.

Moving to stand behind her, he massaged her shoulders, digging his thumbs into two knots on either side that were as big as golf balls. She moaned, her head lolling backward.

He couldn't help but worry about the effect her testifying would have on her and the baby. Stress was a killer. He needed to keep her relaxed, strong, and healthy the next few days.

Savannah had said she only wanted to spend quiet time with him this weekend. So he'd already made some plans that would help take her mind off the trial however briefly.

Just before one-thirty, they said goodbye to Dad, who would wait in the hallway, and returned to their seats. He was fucking pissed that Savannah had to sit this close to that *cabrón* all this time to only watch and listen to a shitload of fucking *nothing*.

Patience, Damo.

When the judge called the district attorney forward late in the afternoon to begin her opening statement, Savannah tensed and began picking at her fingers again. He placed his hand at the nape of her neck and tapped the clasp of the collar. She stopped the nervous behavior instantly and leaned back against his hand but kept her gaze riveted to the DA, who turned to face the jury.

Had he prepared her enough for this? Surely he had. She was a fierce warrior woman about to meet her most brutal foe on a level playing field for the first time ever. Savannah would no longer be the victim. This time, she would walk away the vic*tor*. Damián had helped her visualize that moment over and over. Feeling her settle into his touch and regain her focus a few moments ago told him she was ready. If he stayed zeroed in on her and her needs, he could help her get through this ordeal relatively unscathed.

"Good afternoon, ladies and gentlemen of the jury, and thank you for your attention to the evidence you will hear during this trial. My name is Elizabeth Sullivan, and I represent the People in the case before you." Standing in front of the jury and between the two counsel tables and the judge's bench, she directed everyone's attention to a screen on the wall opposite the jury box. Images of Savannah's mother and the man he'd seen in newspaper reports identified as John Grainger were projected.

"This is Elise Pannier Gentry. Loving mother. Active in her church and community." She paused as a photo of Savannah and her mother replaced the first one. *Dios*, Savannah looked so young, so innocent. "After a day at the beach with her young daughter twenty years ago, Elise went home to find a violently jealous husband. He savagely strangled her in her bed. Her body was then unceremoniously buried under her rose garden at the home the defendant lived in until her remains were found this past March." She gave them a few moments to reflect on her image before continuing.

A good-looking man's photo came up next. "And this is John Grainger. Businessman. Community leader. Beloved son and brother. And Elise's hero, who planned to help Elise and little Savannah escape from their abusive home." Another dramatic pause. The photos were a good touch, putting faces to the victims who couldn't be here. "Mr. Grainger was killed execution style by a gunshot to the back of the head."

Without warning, John Grainger's photo changed to one showing forensic teams exhuming bones from a rose garden. Savannah gasped, and he whispered as forcefully as he could without disrupting court, "Eyes." When she didn't follow through, he added, "Not a suggestion, *savita*."

Slowly, she dragged her gaze away from the photo and met his gaze. Her eyes were bright with unshed tears. They didn't speak further, so as not to let the DA or judge overhear them, but he mouthed the words, *"I am…"* He hoped his words would set off in Savannah's head the mantra they had worked on for weeks now.

She gave him a wavering smile as a single tear tracked down her cheek. He could almost hear her speaking the words:

I am strong.

I can't be beaten.

I will tell my story.

Savannah drew a deep breath, let it out, and returned her attention to what was unfolding at the front of the room. The internalized mantra seemed to give her renewed strength. On the screen, the previous image had been replaced by a close-up of a human skull, the back of it shattered as if by a gunshot wound. It disappeared in a flash as the DA clicked a remote and once again faced the jury. At least it hadn't been her mother's skull.

"And this is Savannah Orlando, daughter of the defendant." A photo of Savannah in the hospital bed last March showed her face bruised and bloodied with dark circles under her eyes. "Kidnapped from her residence in Denver under orders from the defendant and brought back to the defendant's home in San Diego County, she was then taken against her will by the defendant to his remote cabin in San Bernardino County where she was brutally assaulted and battered by him for nearly twenty-four hours last March."

Savannah had almost lost her life at the hands of that sadistic bastard.

After another dramatic pause, she continued. "During the course of this trial, the People will present evidence showing beyond a reasonable doubt that the man you see seated here, George Albert Gentry,"—she pointed at the defense table—"is guilty of viciously ending the lives of two people—his wife, Elise, and her friend Mr. Grainger. Savannah is the only surviving witness to her mother's murder and will tell you her story shortly."

The eyes of the jury scanned the room, each of them eventually settling on Savannah after recognizing her from the police photo. She tilted her chin up in proud defiance. While Damián admired the hell out of Savannah's courage, the DA's scowl said she wasn't happy. Apparently, victims are supposed to be meek and cowering. Well, not his Savannah.

Soon enough, Sullivan drew the jury's attention back to her.

Damián stroked Savannah's forearm, and she relaxed a little. *Dios*, he'd be glad when her testimony was behind her, although she'd insisted on being here as all of the evidence was presented, before and after she took the witness stand.

The DA continued. "In the coming days, the People also will present the medical examiner's expert testimony along with that of a forensic anthropologist. Together, their testimony will establish how and approximately when the victims died."

Again, Savannah's body stiffened. The DA had made the right call to have her in the courtroom today, desensitizing her to the massive amount of gruesome, detailed evidence that would be presented during the trial. He almost thought the opening statement was as much intended to prepare Savannah as it was to begin to sway jurors to vote Gentry guilty of every crime he'd been accused of.

Savannah's strong resolve would be no match for Gentry. She'd have her day in court—literally—and would grab the bastard by the throat, figuratively, and take him down at last. Savannah would finish exacting the justice he and Dad began, making certain the bastard never breathed free air the rest of his life.

Damián became lost in his own thoughts and missed the DA's final words, but when the judge asked if Mr. Abbott, the defense attorney, was ready, Damián's attention turned to Gentry. Abbott stood to begin his opening statement. Seizing his opportunity, Gentry boldly faced Savannah and mouthed the words, "I will win." Savannah squeezed his hand tighter than a pair of locking pliers. Apparently, he'd gotten her attention, too.

"Where are your eyes supposed to be, *savita?*" he whispered. She took a deep breath and blew it out slowly, only slightly loosening her grip. "I will keep an eye on Gentry for you."

"Thank you, Sir."

The defense attorney's voice droned on far too long as he attempted to paint a picture of George Gentry as an upstanding citizen who contributed greatly to his community and society in general. No resemblance whatsoever to the creature Damián knew and detested. Gentry seemed to have a savvy lawyer. Did he have cash reserves after the court awarded Savannah the monies from her mother's will and trust? Or did Gentry have rich friends he duped into paying for his defense?

Damián's gaze shifted to the jury once again. The guy on the far end seemed to be nodding off. *What the…?* It was fucking day one of the trial. Didn't he know what an important job he'd been called upon to do here? Or was he merely bored, too, by the defense attorney's attempts to sway their opinion and had already made up his mind? Maybe he'd perk up when actual evidence was presented and the witnesses gave their testimony.

Would that begin today? Tomorrow? The defense attorney continued to tout Gentry's supposed virtues. At this rate, the experts might not be heard until tomorrow.

Would the jury see through all this bullshit and give the bastard the verdict and sentence he deserved? Why the hell hadn't he finished him off when he'd had the chance?

Savannah placed her cool hand over his fist and squeezed, calming him instantly. Damián gave her a reassuring smile before remembering back to that cabin, Gentry blubbering and cowering from him and Dad while they wired his junk for the branding that had been long overdue. He and Dad had talked about it over the summer, and neither of them regretted what they'd done. Both Gentry and Lyle deserved that and much worse.

Still, Damián worried more about Dad testifying and Gentry recognizing him from what they'd done. He held no illusions that Gentry already knew Damián was there. He hadn't hidden that fact at all. While Dad had remained masked at that point, he'd definitely spoken to Gentry at the beginning of the rescue. What if Gentry recognized his voice and noted his size, putting two and two together? The last thing Damián had wanted was to involve Dad, but he'd been overruled.

When he noticed Savannah clenching her own fist at her side, he tucked her cold hand inside his until her skin grew warm again. Her body became less rigid. Good thing he was here. She needed him, and like most Doms, he welcomed being needed.

He hoped the outcome of the trial would be what they'd been dreaming of for months. Then they could get on with their lives, go back to Denver, and focus on the baby and Marisol.

How long before they called on her to testify? In some ways, Damián wanted to get her testimony over with so Savannah wouldn't have to lose another night's sleep. In others, he wanted more time with her to work on her grounding techniques. Tonight, they'd find more ways to help her hold up under the strain of being on the stand. He wouldn't be able to convey grounding reminders to her in the moment, or they might taint the jury as to whether she was being coached.

Would that be enough to get her through this?

Hell, yeah, it would. She was the strongest, most courageous person he knew. All Savannah had to do was believe in herself and tell her story.

Chapter Twenty

Savannah fought back the tears on Friday as she was bombarded with piece after piece of gut-wrenching evidence. Her stomach knotted at times as she listened to the testimony of the medical examiner and forensic expert and saw the graphic photos shown to the jury. When juxtaposed with the images in her head from that night, tears streamed down her cheeks. Her breathing grew shallow.

Damián rested his hand over hers, drawing her back to the present. She looked down and saw he'd been trying to keep her from picking at her fingers again. The ones on her right hand were practically raw. She'd put some Band-Aids on them for Monday's session to keep from doing further damage.

He squeezed her hand reassuringly, and she flipped hers over to take hold of his as if he were her lifeline. Because he was.

Savannah had hoped to begin her own testimony after lunch, but the DA still questioned the forensics expert at two o'clock.

Based on the physical remains, the expert had no doubt that her mother had been strangled because the hyoid bone had been broken. Unfortunately, they couldn't say who strangled her. Savannah hoped that her account of that night would lead jurors to conclude that it had been Gentry, though.

On cross-examination, the defense tried to discredit the experts, but he couldn't refute any of the evidence.

Once she'd laid the foundation for the murder charges, the DA turned her attention to Savannah's kidnapping at Gentry's and Lyle's hands.

With a deputy from San Bernardino County on the stand, the DA showed photos on the screen of Savannah's wounds sustained during the aftermath of the kidnapping while at Gentry's cabin. Because she'd survived this attack with very little memory, the images seemed disconnected from what she remembered. She shivered, and Damián made a fist. He'd seen what had been done to her before, and it was no easier for him to see the images, either. Savannah placed her chilled hand over his fist, lightly stroking his warmer skin with her thumb. Damián had nearly lost her again to Gentry's cruelty, but he didn't have the blessing of being unconscious for much of it. Most likely, he hadn't blocked out any of it the way she had.

She sighed. Today had proven to be a long day for them both.

The defense stood to ask some procedural questions of the deputy during cross-examination, and then the deputy was dismissed from the stand. With barely a pause, the DA stood and said, "The People call Adam Montague to the stand."

The door at the back of the courtroom opened and closed, and Adam marched up the center aisle to the swinging gate, his back ramrod straight and head held high. After he was quickly sworn in, he proceeded to walk in front of the jury to the witness stand. Several female jurors smiled as he passed. There was something about that panty-dropping uniform. Savannah loved seeing Damián in his, although it was a rare occasion.

Adam was asked by the DA to state his rank. "U.S. Marine Corps Master Sergeant, Retired, ma'am."

They were playing his military service to the hilt. Adam told her the other day that the DA had asked him to wear his uniform. Anything that gave him instantaneous credibility with the jury was fine with Savannah.

"Where did you serve and for how long?"

"Camp Pendleton after boot camp and for just over twenty-five years."

All too quickly, her mind was brought back to the matter at hand when Adam was asked questions about how he knew Savannah Orlando and what he'd found when a group of retired Marines rescued her from Gentry's cabin.

"What did you observe when you and your team found her?"

"Savannah was stretched out naked over an ottoman where her arms and legs had been restrained. Gentry stood over her holding a flogger with metal studs. Her back was covered with raw, bleeding stripes. Blood dripped from the studs on the flogger in the defendant's hand."

Once again, one of the photos taken at the hospital of her injuries was projected and the DA directed Adam's attention to it. Looking more closely this time, she saw that the photo displayed Savannah's bloodied back from shoulders to just above the crack of her ass. Bruises had begun to show over her kidneys where she'd been kicked by Lyle during the kidnapping.

"Does this photo fairly and accurately represent the injuries you saw on Savannah's body that day, Master Sergeant?"

"Yes, although by the point those were taken, she'd been cleaned up at the hospital in San Bernardino. We didn't take any pictures of her right after the rescue mission."

"Master Sergeant Montague, how did you know where to look for Mrs. Orlando?"

"We knew there was a threat against her and had placed a tracking device in a necklace she wore."

"And was she wearing that necklace when you found her?"

"No. It had been removed at the defendant's home in Rancho Santa Fe."

"How did you know to go from there to the cabin?"

"Lyle Gibson told us where he'd taken her."

"Objection. Hearsay," Abbott said.

"Your Honor, Mr. Gibson will be an upcoming witness and can corroborate this at that time."

"Sustained. You can ask Mr. Gibson about his direct involvement."

"Please tell the court how you located Savannah in such a remote location."

"Mr. Gibson's phone had the coordinates for the cabin, and he provided them to us."

"After you located Mr. Gentry and the now Mrs. Orlando at the cabin, what did you do?"

"My team and I took charge and got her away from him as quickly as possible."

"Who joined you to make up your team?"

"Two other Marines and a Navy Corpsman who had served with me while in the Corps, none of us active duty."

"Why didn't you let the authorities handle the case?"

Adam took a deep breath, turning toward Gentry before answering. "Because we knew what he was capable of—and no disrespect to law enforcement," he added after returning his attention to Sullivan, "we thought we could handle things more efficiently ourselves. Considering that we achieved our mission, I'd say we made the right decision."

Indeed, they had.

During cross-examination, Savannah held her breath. So far, the defense had tried to discredit every expert who had come to the stand. There was no telling what would stick with the jurors, if anything. Perhaps the cumulative effect would leave enough doubt for them to let that bastard go scot-free.

Abbott buttoned his suit coat as he approached the podium. Savannah held her breath.

"When you arrived, Master Sergeant Montague, did you confront the defendant physically?"

"Yes. We needed to get Gentry away from Savannah as quickly as possible and subdue him so that we could administer medical aid and get her out of the situation pronto."

"What type of force did you use?"

"The riveted flogger was shot out of his hand, and he was thrown up against a wall. Then I took over watching the prisoner while Savannah's injuries were tended to."

"So the defendant was shot by one of your team members?"

"No. Not then, anyway. The flogger was shot from his hand by my finest marksman without leaving a scratch."

Savannah had been so out of it she hadn't known how the rescue had gone down. Hearing about their heroics only made her more proud of them all.

"Did you receive training in interrogation and torture techniques, Master Sergeant Montague?"

"All recon Marines go through SERE training, sir."

"SERE?"

"Survival, Evasion, Resistance, and Escape training school."

"And during this training, you were taught ways in which to torture prisoners and combatants?"

"We were taught ways to withstand torture in the event we were ever captured by combatants," Adam clarified.

"And did you use any of those tactics on the defendant during the raid?"

"No, sir," he answered without hesitation.

Abbott's eyes opened wider. Did he know something she didn't? More likely, Gentry had made something up.

"You didn't threaten the defendant verbally or physically beyond that initial encounter when you entered the cabin?"

"Oh, yes, sir. That we did. We didn't use SERE tactics on him, though."

Abbott sighed. "Would you tell the court in what way you did threaten the defendant?"

Adam glanced briefly at Damián, who stiffened beside her. Then his gaze returned to the defense attorney. "First, I threw him across the room to another wall to get him away from Savannah and my team. Then I shoved him to the floor when he didn't take the hint where I wanted him to be." Several people chuckled at his description, but she wasn't sure if they were in the gallery or on the jury.

"Anything else?"

"I told him to shut the fuck up." Adam glanced at the judge. "Pardon my language, but that's a direct quote for the record." The judge nodded, seeming to bite back a grin himself. Adam returned his attention to Abbott. "And when he called his daughter a filthy whore, I punched him in the mouth."

More laughter erupted in the courtroom, but Abbott didn't give it time to build before trying to drown it out. "Any other altercations between the defendant and you or your team members?"

"Yes, sir. When Gentry pulled out a .22, another team member shot the gun out of his hand. *That* time, we drew blood, but not before Gentry's bullet lodged into the leg of the man who is now Savannah's husband, a Marine who'd already lost his foot in Iraq."

Savannah glanced at the jury and noticed a couple of people glaring at Gentry for shooting an already wounded veteran. Perhaps Adam was winning over the hearts and minds of some of the jury, but it was too early to tell.

As if the defense attorney had seen that reaction, too, he hastened to say, "No further questions, Your Honor." When the DA indicated there would be no redirect, both attorneys released Adam, and he was excused by the judge.

The judge advised him that he could remain in the courtroom for the remainder of the trial, if he wished. Savannah was surprised that Gentry would allow his attorney to let Adam stay in here where he could serve as support for her. But what more could Adam possibly testify about?

She and Damián scooted over to make room for Adam, and she squeezed his hand in a silent thank you. Shortly after four, the DA asked to continue with her next witness Monday morning. The judge adjourned court.

Would it be her turn next?

Savannah turned to give Adam a big hug. "Thank you for being there for me—back then and again today."

"I wouldn't be anywhere else, hon. Either time."

When she separated from him, Damián wrapped an arm around her and pulled her to his side. She realized they had two whole days off. Two days to worry about giving her testimony or, better yet, to find diversions. While Adam planned to fly home tomorrow to see Karla and the babies, she and Damián would be staying out here for the duration. She wasn't supposed to be on a plane any more than necessary and only in an emergency.

Savannah suggested, "Why don't we go to dinner?"

"Listen, kids, hope you don't mind me skipping out on you, but I've got an appointment to meet up with someone from a local contracting operation."

Contracting? Adam was planning to hire a builder?

"What's up?" Damián asked.

"I'm thinking of starting up a VIP and personal security business in Denver next year."

Oh, *that* kind of contracting. Was he hurting for money? Savannah would have to talk with Karla later. Adam would be too proud to tell her about any financial difficulties, but she had the means to help their extended family and didn't see any reason not to put the offer out there.

"I had no idea you wanted to do something like that," Damián said, seeming a little more interested than Savannah liked. She preferred he spend his time at his Harley shop—and with her and Mari.

"Three babies in diapers all needing college funds is enough to drag any man out of retirement. Derek Reed's picking me up at five-fifteen in front of the courthouse and said he'd get me back to Pendleton tonight."

Ah, normal financial worries then.

As they walked out of the courtroom toward the exit, she said, "You know, Adam, you can count on us to help any way we can. My financial adviser says I need to find some creative ways to invest Maman's money, so if you need venture capital, just say the word."

Adam grinned. "I might take you up on that, Savannah, but only if I know I can make a go of this and that you'll see a return on your investment."

"Adam, you of all people will succeed at anything you try." They paused on the sidewalk outside the courthouse. "After all, I've heard nothing but praise from the guys and Grant about the way you ran your Marine unit. And they tell me you did most of the work getting the Masters at Arms going. There's no doubt in my mind you'll be equally successful at this, if you put your mind to it."

"Appreciate the vote of confidence. We'll talk more back in Denver, after I find out how much I'll need as seed money in addition to my savings."

"What do you know about Reed's organization?" Damián asked,

always protective of his substitute dad.

"He and I have a mutual friend, Jerry Patterson, who runs the club in LA that I modeled the Masters at Arms after. I think you might remember the place, Damián." Adam gave him a teasing grin.

Damián's gaze shifted quickly to Savannah as if to see her reaction before returning to Adam. "Yeah. Marc took me there once...just before we deployed."

No doubt, they'd gone there to relieve some understandable anxiety before going off to war. That they'd visited such a place as active-duty Marines surprised her. Didn't they have a code of ethics they were supposed to adhere to? Whatever, Savannah couldn't fault him for going because she hadn't been a part of his life at the time. She squeezed his hand to let him know she didn't care about his past adventures in the BDSM world. He was her Dom now.

"Anyway, Jerry used to do contract and security work in Southern California, so I asked him for a referral. Reed's a retired SEAL master chief, which means I already know I can respect the hell out of him and trust he'll be a straight shooter. From our phone call last week, sounds like Reed's operation is a little more all-encompassing than what I plan to take on. Like Gunnar's Forseti Group, AdEPT takes on missions and clients in hot spots all over the world."

"Karla would kill you if you left her home that long with three babies," Damián pointed out.

He'd beaten Savannah to stating the obvious. Besides, if anything happened to Adam, what would Karla do?

"Nobody has to tell me that shit's a younger man's game. I'm only interested in the personal, VIP, and event security arms of this type of organization. I'll mostly be a desk jockey, not someone out in the field again. But before I jump into anything, I'd like to see what all such an operation might entail."

"Did you talk with Gunnar?"

Adam laughed. "He's way out of my league. I'll be small potatoes in comparison. Local shit only."

"Smart thinking," Damián said with a nod. "You'll let me know if I can do anything to help?"

"Roger that."

Damián glanced at Savannah and winked, which totally confused her. He'd better not be volunteering his services as a security guard or worse anytime soon. They had a baby on the way, and she didn't want him getting hurt doing anything dangerous.

Damián brought her attention back to the conversation. "I guess we'll see you tonight. Will you need a lift to the airport in the morning?"

"No. You sleep in. I'll be catching a ride with someone I found on the base message boards who has a flight out at about the same time. Nobody else needs to be up at four o'clock to head to the airport."

"Well, if that falls through, we're right across the hall." Damián smiled at her. "Now, Savannah and I are going to have dinner at a favorite place of mine and Rosa's in Solana Beach."

Even though it didn't sound as though a sunset was in her immediate future, her spirits lifted as worries about Adam's plans flew out the window. She wanted to know more about Damián's youth here in SoCal. What better way to find out than to spend time in his old neighborhood?

She gave Adam a peck on his stubbled cheek, took Damián's hand, and said goodbye as they walked to where they'd parked the car. What else did Damián have in store for her this weekend? She'd been so consumed by the court proceedings and anticipation about giving her testimony that she'd only made arrangements to have Sunday dinner with Anita. Whatever, she'd make the most of her downtime and try to leave the trial behind them until Monday morning.

Hours later, her stomach full of the most delicious Mexicali soup she'd ever had and an enchilada reminiscent of their first meal together, Savannah lay wrapped safely in Damián's arms by ten o'clock, quickly lapsing into a deep sleep. Contrary to what she'd expected, the demons didn't dare torment her tonight. Perhaps Damián kept them at bay.

Chapter Twenty-One

T he weekend sped by, but it had been relaxing all the same. Damián had surprised her with a spa afternoon Saturday, and she'd experienced the most incredible massage she'd ever indulged in—other than the one at the club on Damián's Alive Day. Perhaps she ought to make that a regular thing when they returned to Denver. He'd followed that up with a romantic dinner at sunset on the pier at San Clemente.

On Sunday, they'd slept in and made love when they first awoke, although she'd been too uptight to climax. That was happening a lot lately. Too much stress.

After Mass at San Miguel's, the church where they'd been married, they went to Anita's house as planned for dinner. She served a delicious Southern California meal of fish tacos, grilled vegetables, and Spanish rice. Anita had wanted to attend the trial to be there for Savannah, but Savannah vetoed that. She had intentionally shielded the woman who had taken her in all those years ago and cared for her during her first pregnancy from the ugly details. Anita already knew enough to make any normal person sick.

Savannah had forgotten what a great cook Anita was but mostly enjoyed catching up with her about her grandkids, the church, and life in SoCal. She didn't miss a lot about San Diego but did miss Anita and the people at San Miguel's.

After dinner, they'd walked on the beach and watched the sun set before driving to the airport to pick up Adam. This week, Adam chose to rent his own small unit at the lodge, saying he needed more room, but she suspected he wanted to give them time to themselves. Since she and Damián had a suite, the three would still hang out together there in the evenings and mornings, making their time out here feel a little more like home—as best they could.

When she awoke at three Monday morning to go to the bathroom, she thought she and Damián might make love again so she brushed her teeth. But when she returned to her beloved's side, he was fast asleep again. When the alarm went off at six-thirty, she groaned before remembering that today she might be called to the stand to testify against Gentry. *Bring it!*

"We'd better get ready!" she said, tossing the sheet and coverlet off, but Damián pulled her back toward him and she relented easily, facing him.

"First things first, *bebé.*" With a hand to the back of her head, he pulled her mouth to his and kissed her senseless. His tongue tangled with hers as if he'd never kissed her before. Unfortunately, the way she was stretched out caused a stitch in her side and an urge to pee. She groaned and pulled away. "Sorry. I have to go to the bathroom again."

"You and your bladder." He grinned.

"Blame your kid for the interruption, not me."

He patted her belly and helped her to a sitting position on the edge of the mattress. "I forgive you both." She grinned at him over her shoulder. "*¡Ándale! Ándale, querida!*"

"I'm hurrying as fast as I can." Both of them were anxious to get this over, no doubt.

"*Bueno.* I'll text Dad that we'll be ready to eat in thirty."

"Sounds good." She'd cooked breakfast for her and Damián this weekend, and this morning, Adam would join them. Cooking helped take her mind off the trial.

Damián got up from the other side of the bed and reached for his prosthesis. "Okay, I'll start the coffee."

By the time Adam arrived, she'd prepared scrambled eggs, bacon, cinnamon rolls, and the thing she needed most this morning—herbal tea. She wished she could have caffeine but would settle for the soothing brew.

Adam regaled them with stories about the antics of the triplets, who were crawling in earnest now. Savannah's hand went to her belly. She couldn't believe she'd be experiencing some of the same in eight or nine months when their baby was crawling and getting into everything. She couldn't wait.

After breakfast, the three left for Vista, arriving ten minutes before the trial was set to commence. Having Adam and Damián seated on either side felt incredibly right.

Safe.

Protected.

Loved.

She took her seat moments before court came back in session and waited for Lyle to be called to the stand. Savannah's heart skipped a few beats. While she knew the rat-bastard had turned state's evidence and would be testifying against his former employer and partner, Savannah still wasn't ready to face her other nemesis so soon.

The tremors began in Savannah's legs then moved into her arms and torso. Damián's finger brushed the back of her neck, bared again because she'd piled her hair in a bun high on the back of her head. Gentry had preferred her hair down. She would do nothing to give the twisted monster any satisfaction or reasons to fantasize about her.

Her breakfast threatened to come back up. A knot formed in the pit of her stomach, and she swallowed hard, waiting for her first glimpse of Lyle since her kidnapping. He'd been Gentry's lackey for as long as she could remember and had tortured her—body and mind—for a solid year after her sperm donor had grown tired of her when she turned eighteen. She hadn't seen Lyle since her kidnapping. Memories of the many times he'd inflicted extreme pain on her left her quaking in fear.

Damián tapped her collar, his presence reassuring her again that she was safe and to stay in the present.

You can't hurt me anymore, she said repeatedly, hoping she'd believe it at some point. Unfortunately, in exchange for putting his partner in crime away, Lyle could be released sooner than she'd like.

Don't think about that eventuality now.

If sitting through his testimony meant moving her closer to putting

Gentry behind bars for life, she could deal with whatever he had to say. As long as Lyle stayed away from her and her family for the rest of their lives, that is.

She'd watched for Lyle to enter the courtroom the way she had, from behind her. Instead, he was led in from the side door Gentry came through each morning. Of course. He was already serving his sentence of twenty to life. Lyle wore an orange jumpsuit, his wrists and ankles shackled. Too bad Gentry hadn't been forced to appear in court dressed like the criminal he was instead of in a fresh Armani suit each day.

Lyle shuffled across the well to the witness stand. How did he like being restrained against *his* will the way he'd done to her so many times?

Again, Damián's touch at the nape of her neck broke into her thoughts, bringing her back to the present. *Feel, but don't get mired in the past.* Her shivering lessened slightly as she pulled herself together to keep Gentry and Lyle from seeing any outward signs of weakness or hints on her face of the terror she felt.

She glanced at Gentry; his expression toward Lyle took her by surprise. He seethed, glaring at Lyle with pure hatred. Until now, she'd only seen that much vehemence exhibited by him toward Damián and her. Apparently, he wasn't looking forward to Lyle's testimony any more than she was, which gave her hope that Lyle might damage his innocent façade. What did Lyle have on Gentry that made him so angry? Or was he simply upset that the man he'd trusted with his secrets and who was all up in his business had dared to squeal on him?

After taking the oath to tell the truth, Lyle sat down. Would he be truthful? Could he be? She didn't consider him the most moral or ethical person she'd ever known, by any stretch of the imagination. He'd associated with Gentry, after all. *Lie down with dogs and wake up with fleas.*

Savannah already had to pee in the worst way, but nothing would pry her out of this seat to miss a single second of her former handler's testimony. The two men stared each other down until, suddenly, Lyle's head turned and his gaze bore into her.

The air was sucked from the room, and everything faded but the intense, silent exchange between the two of them. She stared back into the face of evil. While Gentry authorized everything that had been done to her, Lyle had taken sadistic pleasure in carrying out those orders and making sure she was humiliated and tortured to the limits of her tolerance—no, far beyond that point, time and time again.

His face was blank—expressionless—almost as if there was no recognition. His eyes were sunken, lifeless. Prison life wasn't agreeing with him. *Good.* He deserved to feel like the caged animal he'd tried to make her into. An ounce of justice had been served. Now to get the pound.

She'd never been able to read Lyle, other than to assume he'd deliver the worst punishment Gentry had allowed him to dish out. Neither Lyle nor Gentry confided in her, not that she'd wanted to know ahead of time what sick acts they had planned. They simply told her what to do, and she did it for fear of the horrendous consequences.

Had he admitted to any of that in his plea deal? Probably nothing more than the kidnapping charges for taking her across state lines. She wouldn't be given the opportunity of receiving justice for what they'd done to her all those years ago up until she'd run away at nineteen. The DA wanted to focus on the charges easier to prove with existing evidence. But if Lyle could help put the mastermind behind bars for life, she'd be satisfied with that.

"Breathe, *savita.*"

Damián's whisper broke through her tunnel vision and reminded her to take care of herself and the baby.

The district attorney stood at the podium, looking down at her notes. Savannah's chest grew tight again, prompting her to take another breath.

After some preliminary questions, Sullivan dove in. "Mr. Gibson, please tell the court what your relationship was with the defendant, George Gentry."

"He started out as my business mentor right after I earned my MBA, twenty-three years ago. Then, two years later, we became partners."

Twenty-three years ago. She hadn't realized he had worked for the man that long.

"To what do you attribute your rapid success in Gentry's organization?"

Lyle stared at Gentry a moment and then said, "I helped him hide the bodies."

Was he speaking literally or figuratively? Her mother had been killed twenty-one years ago. Her heart began to pound loudly, making it difficult for her to hear the DA's next question. Could he know anything about her mother's death?

Savannah began hyperventilating and cupped her hands over her mouth and nose to breathe into them. Damián stroked her back, whispering soothing words in her ear as he helped her recenter herself.

"Please tell the court what you mean by hiding the bodies, Mr. Gibson," the DA asked.

"On the night he murdered his wife—"

"Objection!" Abbott shouted. "Lacks foundation."

"Sustained."

"Mr. Gibson, please tell the court what you mean by hiding the bodies."

Lyle puffed himself up. "On the night his wife died, I got a call from George at about ten o'clock telling me to come to the residence because he needed help disposing of something. When I showed up, I found him with Mrs. Gentry, who *appeared* to be strangled to death on the bed." He glanced at the defense attorney as if to dare him to object again.

Savannah's cheeks grew wet with unchecked tears. To hear Maman talked about like so much trash to be taken out and disposed of hurt her heart. No one should be treated that way, much less her mother. Her *dead* mother.

"After discussing the situation with him, I went to the garden shed, took out a spade, and dug a hole six-foot long by five-foot deep under the rose bushes."

A sob ripped from her throat as she pictured the scene, and Damián tightened his arm around her back. "You can do this, Savannah," he whispered.

By sheer will, Savannah kept herself from making another audible outburst. She wanted the jurors' attention to stay on the man describing the nightmarish events as if it were just another business meeting with

Gentry.

"I knew what he wanted the hole dug for, so—"

"Objection. Speculation."

"Sustained," said the judge.

"What did you think this hole would be used for?" the DA rephrased.

Lyle smirked at Gentry. "I dug it with the assumption it would be used as a grave—and it was."

"Objection."

"Your Honor," Sullivan said patiently, "the People have established the facts that two bodies were found buried in the location Mr. Gibson is speaking of."

"Overruled."

Lyle's voice was devoid of emotional reaction, as if describing a typical day at the office. How could anyone follow such despicable orders without a shred of moral decency?

"Soon after I'd finished digging the hole, the defendant carried down her body wrapped in a sheet, and we placed it in the grave."

"What made you think there was a body inside the sheet?"

"He carried the bundle over his shoulder, and I saw two bare feet dangling out the bottom of the sheet."

"Did Mr. Gentry tell you whose body was wrapped in the sheet?"

"No, ma'am. But I assumed it was hers, since I'd just seen her lying on the bed, lifeless."

"What happened next?"

"We put the wrapped body in the hole. I'd only dropped a couple shovels full of dirt on top of it when a car drove into the circular drive. A man was behind the wheel of the Volvo. I remember wondering at the time how this *other man*," he emphasized the words while staring at Gentry, "got through the locked gate, because I had definitely secured it behind me. *Someone* must have given him the access code."

"Objection. Speculation."

"Overruled."

"Did you recognize the man?"

"Never saw him before in my life."

He took a deep breath before adding with little or no emotion. "Immediately after he got out of his sedan, he demanded to know where Elise and Savannah were. One look at what I was doing, and I guess he figured out where one or both of them were."

"Objection! Speculation."

"Sustained."

"What did he do next?"

"The man called George a murderer—loud and clear—and before I knew what was happening, George pulled out a handgun and pointed it dead center at the man's chest." He glanced at the DA with an out-of-place grin. "Pardon the pun." Then his expression grew matter-of-fact again and moved back in Gentry's direction. "I dropped the spade and backed out of the line of fire. This wasn't included in my 'other duties as assigned.' I had no intention of getting shot."

Yes, Lyle would only think about himself. That's all he'd ever done.

"George ordered the man to interlace his fingers behind his head and to kneel at the foot of the grave I'd just dug. The man refused, and George shot him in the knee then ordered me to drag him over to the grave and to toss him in. I did so quickly, because I was afraid he'd fire off the next round at me. The man writhed in pain, but when he looked inside the hole, he screamed Elise's name and half-fell, half-jumped inside. He'd started pulling the sheet away when George shot him a second time in the back of the head."

More tears flowed for John, the gentle man she'd met only once, but who had been so kind to her and her mother. He'd been their only hope of escaping to a new life, and they'd both lost their lives in the bargain. Savannah's shoulders shook as she cried silently as Damián gently rubbed her back and whispered, "I'm so sorry, *querida*. Are you sure you're okay to stay?"

Afraid he might make her leave, she dashed the tears off her cheeks to face him and hissed, "Yes!" Nothing could tear her from this room, not even her Dom. She'd better pull herself together. Now.

Chapter Twenty-Two

Lyle was the only known witness to Grainger's murder and to the burial of her mother's remains. Savannah needed to know what had happened, to have the blanks filled in for her. Surely his testimony coupled with hers later on, as well as all the experts who'd already testified, would result in justice for her mother and John, at long last.

Thank God Lyle had corroborated that he and Gentry had buried a body without calling for medical help, a coroner, or law enforcement, which in and of itself showed guilt. And the DNA evidence had proven that the bodies were those of Maman and John.

The judge called for a fifteen-minute recess. Perhaps he'd noticed her emotional state. She wasted no time escaping. "I need to use the restroom," she whispered to Damián. He helped her to her feet and held onto her elbow as they left the courtroom together. He stayed at her side to the ladies' room door. "I'll just be a minute." She forced a smile for him, hoping he wouldn't worry about her. *Fat chance.*

After relieving herself, she stood next to an older woman washing her hands at the sink.

"Honey, I hope you don't mind." When Savannah made eye contact in the mirror, the stranger said, "My husband and I bought your...family's house this past summer after..." Her voice trailed off, and she glanced away when Savannah reached for a paper towel. "I'll admit I was curious about what he'd been accused of doing and just had to come up here for the trial." The woman shrugged unapologetically.

Another nosy person here for all the salacious details, no doubt. How anyone would want to purchase a house where two brutal murders had taken place and then attend the trial to get the disgusting details was beyond Savannah's comprehension. She'd wanted to be rid of her mother's family home as quickly as possible. The multi-million-dollar property had sold at a fraction of what it was worth, apparently to this woman, but all Savannah could think was *good riddance.*

"It breaks my heart to watch you having to listen to these awful things, especially in your condition," the fifty-something woman said. Savannah hadn't been aware she was being ogled by other people in the gallery.

"Thank you," Savannah said dismissively, drying her numb hands with a paper towel.

"He's a sick bastard, from what I've heard so far."

Oh, honey, you don't know a tenth of what he's done. Wait until she heard what had happened to Savannah growing up, if they were able to reveal that during the rebuttal portion.

Not wanting to talk about it with a stranger, Savannah nodded, anxious to get back to Damián. Addressing the stylishly dressed woman with a smile, she said, "I appreciate your concern," before starting toward the door.

She'd almost made her escape when the woman halted her by saying, "I also wanted to bring you this."

Savannah turned to face the woman who held out an object wrapped in white tissue. For the briefest of moments, her mind flashed to what her mother's body must have looked like in its makeshift shroud. As if the woman realized belatedly what the bundle looked like, she quickly unwrapped it. "I'm so sorry! This…this is what I wanted to bring to you. I'm sure it must have been yours."

In her hand was Savannah's Christmas Barbie—the last one Maman had given her. Its blonde hair was no longer shiny and smooth. Smudges marked its face. And the dress had tears in it.

Savannah's heart grew full to almost bursting with the sudden connection she felt with Maman. Despite having been through a lot, too, the doll was the most beautiful one Savannah had ever seen. "Where on earth did you find her?" she asked, reverently reaching out to accept the precious gift.

"In a bedroom closet. There was a secret compartment against the back wall."

When Savannah heard her father's footsteps in the hallway, she pried open the tiny door and shoved her Barbie inside. He had long ago threatened to burn the doll if she didn't stop "playing" with it when he was in the room with her. The doll had been her lifeline from the turmoil her life had devolved into. She'd received it when she was seven—her last Christmas with Maman. For several months, Savannah had kept the Barbie doll away from her father, who seemed unaware of her hiding place. She only pulled the doll out when she was missing Maman especially hard.

Like today. Her father had promised...more like threatened...Savannah that he would be doing something special with her tonight during their alone time. She didn't want him to come into her room again or anywhere near her, but all too soon, the bedroom door creaked open.

"Savannah. Daddy's here. I have a special surprise for you."

"Honey, are you okay?" The woman's cool hand covered and gently squeezed Savannah's forearm.

Savannah blinked and found herself hugging the doll to her chest as tears streamed from her eyes. That had been the first time he'd put his penis inside her. She'd needed Maman to comfort her that night. Needed the Barbie, the last physical connection she had with Maman. But she'd had neither.

She hadn't thought about the doll again for the next half-dozen years or more. By then, she'd assumed Gentry had found and destroyed it. Until today. It was as if her Barbie had come back from the dead.

She shivered at the analogy. If only Maman could do the same.

"I'm so sorry. I thought it would bring back some happy memories for you. Given the wear and tear, she most definitely was loved by someone. I washed her dress and cleaned her up as much as I could before bringing her to you."

Savannah forced a smile. "Yes, she's very special to me. This was the last Christmas present my mother gave me. I always wondered what had happened to her. I haven't seen her since I was...eight." She nearly said raped the first time. Savannah knew she was rambling but couldn't help it. "I'd completely forgotten about that secret storage place when I cleaned out the few things I wanted to keep before we sold the house."

Not only had this been a gift from Maman, but the doll also resembled her mother. Same hair. Same eyes. Savannah held the doll in front of her and stared into the Christmas Barbie's sparkling blue eyes then wrinkled her brow.

"That's not right," Savannah said.

"I'm sorry? It's not your doll?"

Afraid the woman would take the doll back, Savannah took a step back and pulled the Barbie closer, continuing to stare into its eyes. "She's supposed to have brown eyes." *Maman's eyes were brown.* "In my mind, at least, she always had Maman's eyes, not blue ones."

The woman leaned over to take a closer look at the doll's face. "It looks like the original color to me. Perhaps you just remembered it wrong."

She couldn't imagine how such a vivid memory would be so far off. Had she needed that connection with Maman so strongly during those dark days that she'd seen Maman's face in the doll she treasured over all else? Had that memory glitch helped her feel protected by Maman when Gentry had molested and raped her? Most likely.

"Funny how the mind can play tricks on you," Savannah said then smiled up at the perfectly coiffed woman. "Thank you for bringing her back to me. I'll share her with my daughter when I get back to Colorado."

"Speaking of getting back, I'm sure the recess is almost over, so we'd better return to our seats."

Savannah squared her shoulders, and the other woman held the door open for her. A worried Damián waited there. He quirked his brow when he saw her clutching the Barbie doll close to her chest.

She smiled. "I'll explain later."

"Everything's okay?"

She nodded. "Let's go back in."

They made their way back down the hallway to the courtroom. Savannah found peace and comfort holding onto her doll, as if it were a talisman or once again the personification of her mother. But how had she been so wrong about her memory of the doll's eye color? And did that mean any of the testimony she would give during the trial would be erroneous as well?

Still, sitting through the rest of Lyle's testimony, her thoughts were a jumbled mess, and she found herself wishing it would be over for the day so she could simply cuddle with Damián.

Lyle's testimony and cross-examination took the rest of the day. She'd managed to hold up under the pressure of being in the same room with Lyle again.

Because it was so close to five o'clock, the judge adjourned until the following morning. Savannah said goodbye to the woman seated behind her who had given back her doll, just as the DA came up to the three of them.

"Savannah, excuse me," the DA said, "but could we meet briefly in the back?"

"Absolutely!" Dread seeped into her body as she wondered what was up.

In a conference room, Sullivan said she merely wanted to prepare her again for the defense to cross-examine Savannah after the DA finished with her line of questioning. She anticipated this would most likely happen tomorrow.

Her body felt hot and cold at the same time, and Damián wrapped an arm around her.

"Remember the things I told you before," she said. "Take your time to answer each question. If you don't understand the question, ask Mr. Abbott to repeat it. Don't answer anything you don't know the answer to. It's okay to simply answer that you don't know or can't recall." The barrage of reminders became overwhelming but continued to come. "But only answer the question asked, preferably with nothing more than a yes or no. You want to give as little detail as required to answer each of his questions. Don't provide explanations or unnecessary details. If the questioning becomes too distressing," the DA continued, "you can ask the judge if you can take a short break to regroup."

"*Querida*, that's good advice. Anytime you need to go outside for a breather, do it. I'll be here in the courtroom with you. Make eye contact with me if it helps to ground you."

"Actually, it's probably best that she not do that, Mr. Orlando. We don't want the jurors to think that you're coaching her responses."

Damián growled low in his throat. Savannah reached out to hold his hand. "It's okay. If I need you, I'll ask for a break, and we can get away from prying eyes. In the meantime, I will use the grounding techniques you and my therapist have taught me to get through this."

While she wished the worst was already behind her, knowing Damián would be here for her made all the difference. She could face anything that evil man spewed at her as long as Damián's comforting arms were a short distance away.

"Speak clearly," the DA continued. "And, above all, don't forget to keep breathing."

Savannah smiled at Damián. "Don't worry. I have been taught by the best how to maintain focus and not get mired down in memories of the past." To Damián, she said, "You prepared me to have the confidence to tell my story, remember?"

"And you've been an excellent student," he said with a grin.

The DA asked if she had any questions. When Savannah shook her head, the attorney excused herself, saying she needed to prepare for the morning's session.

"You aren't going to give that bastard any satisfaction," Damián said.

Adam added, "Stay focused. Say as little as possible. Gentry will blow his cool if Abbott can't get the responses he wants out of you, and that will give the jury another nail for his coffin."

Savannah nodded, and after being bombarded with a few more pieces of advice, she zoned out.

"Eyes, *savita*."

Numb and a bit overwhelmed, she turned her gaze to Damián, who cupped her cheeks.

"You've got this, *bebé*. Remember to breathe. Find something to ground yourself that isn't me." He grinned. "And tell your story. Even if you don't look at me, touch your wedding band or your collar and know that I'm there with you, cheering you on."

She nodded. At least she knew he wouldn't be far away. "Thank you, Sir." He lowered his face to hers for a sweet kiss. She licked her lips when he pulled away, savoring his taste.

"Let's get out of here so you can have a little break before tomorrow morning," Adam said.

And, with one strong Marine on either side of her, she left the courthouse, palms sweating and heart racing as she clutched the doll to her chest. She couldn't believe how quickly her protectors whisked her away.

On the drive to Oceanside, she explained about the doll and how much it had meant to her when she'd been a little girl. She almost mentioned her revelation about how her memory had failed her. However, she didn't want them to question whether she'd be telling the truth and nothing but the truth. But she'd certainly tell her story the way she remembered it.

The three of them enjoyed dinner on the pier, Adam recounting how much the town had changed since he was first stationed here as a young Marine in the nineties. She could barely imagine the debauchery that must have gone on here with so many Marines frequenting the establishments in town. Today, it was a beautiful tourist spot.

She wished she could be one of those tourists. If only she didn't have to return to the Vista courthouse in the morning.

Don't let Gentry see your fear.

Easier said than done.

Chapter Twenty-Three

B efore court began on Tuesday morning, the DA came up to Savannah in the gallery and told her she would be the next witness. Damián and Adam spent the next few minutes shoring up her nerves, but all too soon, she heard Sullivan speak the words she'd longed for and dreaded at the same time: "The People call Savannah Orlando to the stand."

Savannah's throat closed up in a panic. How would she ever get the words out to tell her story if she couldn't even swallow? Any courage she'd gathered flitted out the window.

This would be her chance to put her mother's murderer behind bars forever. Then a frisson of trepidation coursed through her. She couldn't mess this up.

"Savannah?" the DA's assistant prompted in a whisper.

"Breathe, *savita*. You've got this." Damián squeezed her arm as he helped Savannah to her feet.

Drawing strength from Damián, she took a deep breath, held her head high, and walked toward the bar. Gentry's gaze stabbed at her belly. It wasn't the first time he must have seen she was pregnant, but she gave in to the urge to place her hand across her abdomen to protect her baby from his vile stare. She could hear him calling her a dirty slut and a filthy whore, but this baby, like Marisol, had been conceived in love.

He can't hurt your baby or you.

She'd been instructed to stop at the thigh-high swinging door to await instruction from the bailiff, seated near the defense table. She refused to glance at or acknowledge the existence of the monster seated next to him as the bailiff came toward her and guided her in front of the jury box and to the witness stand. The court clerk asked her to raise her right hand, and Savannah swore to tell the truth—*at long last*—and nothing but the truth. She then entered the witness stand. A bit of her courage returned as she took another deep breath and faced the DA.

Maman, I need you now more than ever. Without a blatant sign, though, she wouldn't be sure Maman had heard her plea. Her chest tight, she forced air into her lungs.

I will tell my story.

Good thing Gentry couldn't see the fingers of her right hand. All four were covered with Band-Aids. Every now and then, she automatically tried to pick at one only to find she couldn't reach the skin.

After asking some preliminary questions to establish who she was and what she did for a living, the DA zeroed in on the reason they were here. "Mrs. Orlando, how do you know the defendant?" The DA pointed toward Gentry, but Savannah refused to look at him.

"George Gentry, the defendant, is my biological father." Bile rose in her throat. Even giving him that much of a connection to her made her sick to her stomach, but she had to be truthful in order to be considered a credible witness.

"Please tell the court about that last day you spent with your mother." Clearly, the DA wanted to give her more time to compose herself before getting into the details of the murders.

Relief washed over her. Savannah took a deep breath to steady her nerves. "We went to the cave at Thousand Steps Beach for a picnic. It was a favorite spot for my mother and me." She glanced at Damián— thinking about the two special times they'd spent there, too—before returning her attention to the prosecutor. "Only this time was different."

"How so?"

"She met a man there that day."

"How old were you?"

"Eight." Her life as she knew it had ended that night. Tears welled and threatened to spill, but she was brought back to the present by the DA's next question.

"What do you remember about this man who joined you and your mother at the beach?"

"His name was John."

"John who?"

"Grainger. I only learned his last name earlier this year after his re-mains were found buried on my mother's property." She refused to say it was that bastard's property. He might have controlled it during the years since her mother's murder, but the courts had quickly awarded most of his assets to her once her mother's will had been taken into consideration.

"Tell us what you remember about John."

Savannah smiled as she pictured his movie-star handsome face, the ocean breeze lifting the hair off his forehead. At the time, she'd been reticent with him, but in retrospect, she could see he had been an honorable man.

"He was kind to me the short time I spent with him—and he made Maman smile." She hadn't smiled like that in a very long time.

"Who is Maman?" Sullivan asked.

"My mother, Elise Pannier Gentry. She was of French descent and preferred that I call her Maman." She had Mari call her Maman as well. Pulling herself back from her thoughts, she added, "I could tell by the way she smiled and looked at John that Maman trusted him, which put me a little more at ease."

"Objection. Speculation."

"Sustained."

Gentry made a sound, and she looked up to see him snarling at her before his attorney whispered something to him, and he schooled his emotions.

His response to her memories about Maman's potential new love gave Savannah the courage to continue. He hated the thought that Elise and Savannah would look to other men as their protectors and partners. Turning her focus to the DA again, she waited for the next question. Would she ask for Savannah's opinion about what type of relationship Maman and John had?

"What was your impression of Mr. Grainger?" she asked.

"After only knowing him a few hours, I wanted to go away with them, even if it meant my mother and I would have to give up living in our big house, and I'd have to leave my toys behind. Maman said I could bring my cat. All I wanted was to be with Maman and Whiskers." Her voice broke remembering her beloved pet, another casualty of Gentry's evilness.

"How did you feel about moving away from your father?"

"Objection. Irrelevant."

"Sustained."

The DA nodded. "Describe your relationship with your father."

"We weren't close." *Ever.* "He had little time for me—in those days—so I just wanted to be wherever my mother was." But all too soon, she'd learned there were worse things than having a father who ignored her. "I knew I wouldn't be happy in that house without her." The monster who had fathered her had overshadowed every aspect of her life in the mansion once Maman's light had been extinguished.

"What happened after you left the beach that day?"

She realized she'd become sucked into the past again. "Maman and I returned from the beach early that evening. She told me to pack a bag with only the things I must have in our new home. She told me to go to bed early that night, in case Father came home early." *She must have been worried I wouldn't have been able to keep her secret.* "Maman said she'd come and get me when John arrived for us."

"And did she come to your room that night?"

Savannah shook her head, her eyes stinging with sadness and regret.

"Please respond verbally for the record, Mrs. Orlando," the judge advised.

"No, she didn't."

"But something did wake you? What was that?"

"The sounds of Maman screaming at Father." She detested calling him that, as if he'd ever earned that title, but the DA had advised her to use the word for the benefit of the jurors.

"Objection. Speculation as to who her mother was screaming at."

"Sustained. Strike 'at Father' from the record."

"Do you know who your mother was yelling at?" the DA asked.

Savannah glanced at the defense attorney, expecting another objection, but when none came, she answered, "Yes. She called him by his name, George, repeatedly."

"What happened after you awoke to your mother's screaming that night?"

"Maman shouted, 'You can't stop me, George. I've put up with your abuse long enough.'" Savannah forced the words from her constricted throat as the memories came flooding back. *Feel, but don't get mired in the past.*

She touched her wedding ring, remembering where she was. "Maman yelled that she was leaving him and taking me with her. Then I heard a slap."

The DA asked, "What happened next?"

"Right after the slapping sound, Maman screamed in pain. Then I heard him call her a filthy whore." She drew a deep breath to keep herself from sinking into her past association with that phrase. "I didn't know what that meant at the time but knew it wasn't nice by the way he said it."

"What did you do?"

Her throat closed at the memory. "I went to find her." *To make him stop being so ugly to her.*

"Please speak more loudly, Mrs. Orlando," the judge admonished.

Savannah cleared her throat and repeated her words with more force then added, "I thought I could help her, so I slipped out of bed and snuck down the hallway. Afraid that someone was attacking my mother, I opened the bedroom door and looked inside. A man was on top of Maman. It sounded as though she was having difficulty speaking. As if she was being choked."

"Objection. Opinion."

The DA paused and nodded when the objection was overruled then said, "You said it sounded like she was choking. What else do you remember?"

Savannah swallowed hard, the scared little girl inside her reliving that frightening moment. "My father…had his hands around Maman's throat."

"Where were they in the room?"

"Both were on the bed, my mother on her back with my father straddling her waist." Flashes of that horrific night threatened to overcome her ability to speak, but she forced the emotions back down in order to focus on telling what she had seen. *This is all in the past. Feel the emotions, but don't go back there.*

She reached up to touch the warm metal of her collar. There wasn't anything she could do to change what happened that night other than to make Gentry pay for his crimes. He couldn't harm Savannah—not physically, at least. "His hands were around her throat. He was strangling my mother."

Savannah drew a slow, deep breath, providing another chance to ground herself in the present.

Think of it like a movie in your head, not something you actually witnessed.

"Your father was strangling your mother," the DA repeated. "What did you do?" The patient Sullivan was determined to keep her focused and to get these details into the record. Savannah appreciated her diligence—for Maman and for John—even if it was hell for her.

With a shaking hand, Savannah picked up one of the small bottles of drinking water that had been provided for witnesses, opened it, and took a sip to ease her dry mouth and give her another moment to compose herself. Then she set it down and continued.

"Father's hands were around Maman's neck. She was making gurgling noises. She couldn't breathe." As if she were the one being strangled, she swallowed hard to keep her throat from constricting. *I can't lose my shit now.*

With Damián's instructions going through her head, she touched her collar again and searched for a focal point.

The decorative pin the DA wore on her lapel caught her eye—an iridescent blue butterfly with black on the edges of its wings. It reminded her of the pair she'd seen at the beach cave the last time she'd been there with Damián. Was Maman sending her a sign that she was here with her? Even if only a coincidence, the pin gave Savannah the courage to continue.

"Maman's legs were kicking in the air over the edge of the mattress, but she couldn't get him off of her. He was too heavy, too strong. Her face was turning red, and her eyes nearly bulged from their sockets." The words came out in a rush now, along with the memories. "Maman sputtered and gasped for air." Savannah's heart beat faster as the panic her mother must have felt threatened to erupt inside her.

"What did you do?" the DA repeated, bringing her back to the courtroom.

"I ran across the room to the other side of the bed so I could face him, and I begged him to stop because Maman couldn't breathe. But he wouldn't let go of her. There was blood on his hands from where Maman had tried to claw his hands off her." Savannah had just painted Maman's fingernails a pretty shade of pink in the cave that morning.

"And what did Mr. Gentry say?"

"Nothing. He just kept squeezing her throat. He looked so angry. His face was red, too. Maman's fingers kept trying to break his hold. She fought so hard." Savannah blinked away the tears, not wanting to break down or show weakness. She needed to stay strong and finish telling what happened that night.

"Take your time, Mrs. Orlando. I know this has to be difficult for you."

But necessary. I can't let Maman down again.

Chapter Twenty-Four

"I climbed onto the bed and pushed against his side, but he didn't seem to notice me at all. I pounded on his arm." Her tiny hands were so inconsequential. "Finally, he released one hand long enough to swat me away." Like a pesky fly. "I landed in a heap on the floor, hitting my head. When I regained my senses, I stood and turned toward the bed. Maman's legs had stopped kicking. Stopped moving altogether. Her hands lay limp at her sides. Her body was very still." *Deathly still. Dead.* But she would let the jury draw that conclusion on their own to avoid another objection from Gentry's attorney for testifying about something she wasn't an expert on.

Her shaking hand went to her collar, the warm metal calming her instantly. Wetness cooled on her cheeks. She ignored the tears, hoping they wouldn't be noticed by the jurors or DA, who would be upset with her for becoming emotional, but it was so hard to talk about her mother's murder without doing so.

"What was your father doing at this point?"

"His hands maintained a chokehold on Maman's neck. I don't know how long he did so, but after what seemed like forever, he let go, got off the bed, and staggered a bit. I climbed back up on the bed and begged Maman to wake up. Her eyes were open, but I knew she wasn't awake at all. She was lifeless."

Savannah heard a sniffle from one of the jurors but tried to keep herself focused. She couldn't leave any important detail out. This was for Maman.

The DA held out a box of tissues to her, and Savannah plucked two to wipe away her tears, assuming it was okay to shed tears under the circumstances. "What happened next?"

"My father told me to return to my room. That he would come and tuck me in later. He had never tucked me in before, so it surprised me." She shuddered, remembering what would happen later that night and many nights to come.

"And did you go to your room?"

"Not right away. I kept trying to wake up Maman. When I begged Father to call the doctor, he yanked me off of her, grabbed me by the upper arms, and shook me viciously several inches off the floor. So hard that my teeth rattled against each other. His eyes were even scarier than before."

"Was he saying anything at this time?"

She nodded, at last facing down the monster who had haunted her nightmares, narrowing her eyes at him. She relayed his words just the way she remembered them, vivid ever since that mental block had lifted while she was being tortured by him last March.

"He told me, 'You're just like her, you dirty slut.'" Someone in the jury box gasped, but words like "dirty slut" no longer held any power over her, thanks to Damián. Suddenly, she felt Damián's warm gaze washing over her. She couldn't face him for much-needed comfort for fear the jury would misconstrue her actions and think he was coaching her. But his presence gave her the strength to continue.

"Father yelled, 'I told you to go to your room. You will do as *I* say from now on. No more being coddled by your sorry mother.' And then the most ominous words of all. 'I'll take care of *you* later.'"

An ache tore at her heart as she added in a near whisper, "That's the last time I saw my mother."

A juror now sobbed openly, but Savannah tamped down her own emotions. She needed to stay strong. For Maman. For John.

"What happened next?" the DA prompted.

"I ran to my room." Although she now knew there was nothing she could have done to save Maman that night, she wished things had come out differently. Perhaps if John had come to get them sooner or if they hadn't returned to the house after the beach at all…

Don't go there. Tell your story as it happened.

"I was afraid of Father now, so I hid under my bed." Realizing she was feeding the twisted bastard the words he thrived on—admitting her fears out loud—she lifted her chin in defiance and hazarded a quick glance his way. He sneered at her, as if daring her to continue telling the truth about what happened.

Never again would she be silenced by him.

Savannah turned back to the DA. "He wanted my mother out of the way to get to me. He knew she'd have protected me from him."

"Objection. Speculation."

"Sustained. Mrs. Orlando," the judge admonished, "please limit your responses to the facts as you witnessed them and wait until you've been asked a question." To the jury, he added, "The jury will ignore Mrs. Orlando's last statements."

Unable to help herself, she added, "I was an innocent eight-year-old—at least until *he* came to my room later that night." She stared at Gentry, daring him to deny what she'd said, even though she knew he couldn't speak and she'd gone beyond what she was supposed to say.

A juror made a gasping sound. At least they were engaged and listening. She'd been warned by the DA not to bring up the incidents of molestation and rape for fear of causing a mistrial by tainting the jury, but Savannah hoped they'd all figure out what really happened, even if they weren't supposed to draw their own conclusions.

"Objection, Your Honor. There was no question asked."

"Sustained." The judge addressed the court reporter. "Please strike Mrs. Orlando's last statement from the record."

The DA cleared her throat, looking pointedly at Savannah to urge her not to try that again and to bring her back on track. "How long did you hide under the bed?"

Savannah swallowed hard, remembering that scared little girl cowering in fear in her hiding place. She'd wished Whiskers had been with her and wondered where the cat had gone that night, but didn't cats sense death and trauma and hide from it? Instead, she'd clung to the Barbie doll Maman had given her the previous Christmas. The one she'd recently been reunited with.

"I'm not sure how long I was under there, but it was pitch dark when Father came into my room, calling out to me." *Breathe in. Breathe out.* "I could only see his shoes. They were caked with mud. I'd never seen Father's wingtips anything but shiny before." She'd let them draw their own conclusions since they'd heard the evidence about where her mother's and John Grainger's remains had been found.

"I didn't make a sound," she continued. "I didn't want him to know where I was hiding—but he found me anyway." Savannah's throat closed off. Okay, perhaps she did still harbor some fear when it came to Gentry.

"What did your father do next?"

Drawing a ragged breath, she answered, "He pulled me out from under the bed."

Out of the corner of her eye, she saw Adam shove Damián back into his seat before he could make a scene going after Gentry.

Savannah made eye contact with Damián and touched her collar, her signal to let him know she was okay. After months of working with Damián, she'd internalized the truth—she wasn't a whore and never had been.

I'm Damián's good girl.

Damián gave her an almost imperceptible nod as his body relaxed against the back of the chair.

After a brief recess, the DA shifted gears to asking about the kidnapping last March.

"Lyle Gibson and another man broke into my apartment in Denver. I was alone with my seven-year-old daughter. I managed to hide her in a duffel bag in the closet before one of them placed a smelly rag over my nose and mouth, and I blacked out."

"Objection."

"Overruled. Continue, Ms. Sullivan."

In subsequent questioning, Savannah described the kidnapping much as one might a movie, as much as she could remember. She quickly moved ahead to how she only remembered regaining consciousness strapped to an ottoman in the remote cabin at Gentry's compound in San

Bernardino County.

"I thought he was going to kill me—and still believe that was his ultimate intention."

"Objection. Speculation. Move to strike."

"Sustained." The judge asked the court reporter to remove her remark from the record.

Savannah rubbed her wedding band to ground herself without letting the abuse of the past overwhelm her again.

She went on to talk about her mental and physical anguish before and during the rescue and then waking up in the hospital. As if Sullivan knew the only thing she could say beyond that point had already been detailed by a medical expert, she said, "No further questions, Your Honor."

The judge called for a lunch recess. Damián forced her to eat, but she couldn't remember an hour later what had been on her plate. When they returned to the courtroom, she sat and waited to be recalled to the stand to face the defense attorney's cross-examination. This was the part she'd been dreading the most, because she couldn't predict what would be asked of her.

On the stand again, she realized her focal point was gone, so her gaze zeroed in on Damián. As if he'd said the words aloud, she heard these words in his voice, "You can do this."

Gentry's attorney stood, buttoning his suit coat as he walked to the podium. Her heart pounded so loudly she was afraid she wouldn't be able to hear the questions. The DA hoped the defense would slip up and open a door for them to pursue a line of questioning about all the horrible things Gentry had done to her, but until that happened, the DA merely wanted her to come across as a sympathetic witness to the jurors. Hopefully, she'd succeed at that, if not already then under the defense's scrutiny.

"No questions, Your Honor."

That was it? Hopes that the defense would slip up and open up the opportunity for her to really tell her story were dashed. Apparently, the bastard had hired a savvy attorney.

"You're excused, Mrs. Orlando," the judge said.

She stood and made her way on shaky legs toward the gallery. Gentry's gaze was fixed on her belly as if wishing to cause her bodily harm. She put a protective hand over their baby, as if to shield him or her from the monster's gaze, and picked up her pace.

Damián stood to welcome her with open arms and a quick hug before guiding her right out of the courtroom. He whispered that Adam would stay behind to let them know what they might have missed. But Damián had seen she needed to get away.

In the hallway, he turned to her. "You did great, *bebé*. How are you feeling?"

"Exhausted. Exhilarated. Glad that part's over, and dreading what's to come."

He wrapped his arms around her, and she basked in his heartwarming, protective embrace. "I'm so proud of you, *querida*. You're the strongest person I've ever met."

She didn't feel particularly strong, although she'd done the best she could do. And yet, it was a hollow victory.

Damián kept one arm around her lower back as he propelled her down the hallway to the ladies' room. "I'll wait for you here."

Gentry wouldn't go down without a fight. The defense would present the rest of its case now. How could Gentry be defended for all the reprehensible things he'd done?

When she came out of the restroom, Damián smiled at her. He took her hand, and they returned to the courtroom to find Abbott and Gentry having a heated discussion about something. The judge was nowhere to be seen. At their questioning glances, Adam told them, "I'm not sure what's up, but they called for a fifteen-minute recess."

Adam leaned over and kissed her on the cheek, whispering, "You did an incredible job, hon."

The remainder of the afternoon was spent with Abbott calling in three witnesses to describe Gentry's behavior on the Saturday the murders took place. All had been in negotiations with him on a business deal that afternoon. No one recalled him being distracted or upset. They'd clinched their deal, shared an early dinner, and had gone their separate ways.

Hearing their perceptions of George Gentry the acute businessman didn't surprise her. He had always projected himself in the best light possible, and business always came first. Savannah knew the murders had not been premeditated. So what this testimony could do to exonerate Gentry's actions that night, she couldn't see.

But one of the three men kept staring her way several times, making her squirm in her seat. Was he one of the men who had abused her during her year as a sex slave? She'd blocked out all but the last few of those clients.

Savannah nearly ran from the room to vomit several times during the man's testimony and leaned closer to Damián for comfort.

"You okay, *bebé?*"

She nodded numbly as she processed today's events so far. How could the jury learn anything about what happened behind closed doors in that house and at his hotel unless she was given a chance to tell her story? Of course, he wasn't charged with those crimes.

But the window on her being able to tell about them had slammed shut. The defense attorney hadn't asked the questions that would have allowed her to tell the full story about this monster.

She anticipated a conviction was likely, given they couldn't refute the testimony of two eyewitnesses and the damning forensic evidence that, in her opinion, removed reasonable doubt. But she had so fantasized about facing Gentry down and telling the world what this truly despicable man had done to try and ruin her and any chance she had at a normal, happy life.

Damián's love had thwarted him in that respect.

After the witness completed his testimony, the judge adjourned court until tomorrow morning. His gavel pounded, making her jump, and everyone around them rose to their feet at the bailiff's order. Damián helped her to her feet. She nearly sagged against him when he pulled her into his arms. "It's almost over, *bebé.*"

Tears sprang to her eyes as her hopes for true and complete justice slowly withered away.

"Let's get out of here," Adam said when she failed to make a move to leave.

Savannah nodded, bending to pick up her purse before being led out between her two protectors. She'd have to content herself with knowing Gentry would pay with his freedom for murdering Maman and John and for his part in her kidnapping, unlawful imprisonment, attempted murder, and abuse earlier this year. That would have to be enough to satisfy her.

That and knowing he truly didn't beat her, because she *had* found happiness, first with Marisol and now with Damián and their new baby. She held her head a little higher as they descended the steps and headed to their SUV. In the end, Gentry hadn't gained anything at all, and she had everything she ever wanted.

Chapter Twenty-Five

The next morning, she took her usual seat behind the DA's table only to find Gentry and Abbott arguing quietly at the defense table before the judge entered the court. Were their options running out? Desperation setting in? Was Gentry trying to take control of the case and his attorney in the eleventh hour? He'd never been good about allowing anyone else to have power over him, apparently not even his defense attorney who was trying to keep him out of prison.

"Do you have any other witnesses to call, Mr. Abbott?" the judge prompted.

Abbott glanced at Gentry who jerked his forehead toward the judge, as if egging him on to do Gentry's bidding.

"Permission for counsel to approach the bench," Abbott said, barely containing his reluctance.

When the judge beckoned the two attorneys forward, the prosecutor and defense attorney crossed the well to stand before the judge. Their voices were too low for her to make out anything, but the discussion went on for five or six minutes, leaving Savannah to wonder what was happening. Surely he wasn't throwing in the towel and changing his plea to guilty.

Finally, the judge announced, "The defense attorney has requested a short recess to consult with his client." He pounded his gavel, and the DA motioned for Savannah to wait for her as she returned to her table to load up her briefcase.

"Let's talk outside," Sullivan said as she approached them and led them to a small conference room. Seated around the table, she turned to the three and said, "The defendant wants to take the stand to testify on his own behalf—against his attorney's counsel, of course. It's a foolish decision on Gentry's part, but Abbott's been unable to dissuade him. The judge wants him to try again privately, but I have a hunch that Abbott thinks he's going to commit a fraud against the court."

"A fraud?" Savannah asked.

Sullivan nodded. "I suspect Abbott thinks Gentry will lie on the stand."

Well, that was a given, as far as Savannah's experience with Gentry was concerned.

"When we reconvene, before the jury returns, I'm sure Abbott will first try to withdraw from the case due to a conflict of interest. You won't hear that conversation in front of the court, but this judge won't take lightly throwing a trial this far in. If he doesn't accept Abbott's reason—or more likely his refusal to provide one—he'll deny the request. Then Abbott will be forced to do his client's bidding. If you hear Mr. Abbott say that the defendant is going to 'testify in the narrative,' then my hunch is right."

Savannah tilted her head in confusion at yet more legal jargon.

Sullivan continued. "To testify in the narrative, Gentry would take the stand and tell his story without being questioned directly by his attorney, who does not want to be a party to the fraud. Mr. Abbott might ask introductory questions then let Gentry go in whatever direction he wishes from there. For all intents and purposes, this type of testimony is a clear indication to a judge and anyone familiar with the law that Abbott doesn't expect Gentry to tell the truth. Of course, I will object when I see where this was going, and Abbott will ask to approach the bench. If I were the defense attorney, I would tell the court that it was my only recourse because I'd been prohibited from withdrawing from the case and was proceeding in the only way possible. Defense attorney ethics only require that he provide a vigorous defense, not be a party to a fraud."

How any ethical attorney could represent that scum was beyond her, but she supposed he had a legal right to some kind of defense under the Constitution and state law.

"The jury, which won't be privy to all of this wrangling," Sullivan said, "will ultimately decide who's telling the truth."

"So Gentry's going to be allowed to get on the stand under oath and spout a bunch of lies, and there's nothing you can do about it?" Savannah asked. The thought of listening to Gentry twisting reality into some wonderful fairy tale made Savannah's stomach turn. A narcissist like Gentry would definitely puff himself up by telling a pack of lies.

What a travesty of justice.

"On the contrary." Then Sullivan smiled, confusing Savannah even more. "This is nothing short of a win for us, Savannah. I'm not sure what specifically Mr. Abbott anticipates Gentry will lie about, but that's where you'll come in."

"Me?"

She nodded. "The judge will allow me to call any witnesses who can rebut what Gentry has lied about in order to set the record straight. At the very least, I would call you to the stand and question you about specifics of his narrative that you can refute."

"Savannah would have to go back on the stand?" Damián asked, pulling her closer in a protective gesture.

"Yes, but…" Sullivan continued to smile as she shifted her gaze back to Savannah, "…this would give us the opportunity we've been waiting for. If your father brings up anything about his relationship with you that contradicts your knowledge and recollections, I'll call you back to the stand."

Savannah remained silent a moment, trying to digest what all this meant. "You mean I'll be able to tell the jury about every despicable thing he's done to me since I was eight, not just what he's been charged with?"

"Yes, as long as he brings up incidents or makes false statements. But keep in mind that the defense can cross-examine you on anything you say. Prepare yourself for having Mr. Abbott question everything you choose to reveal."

Afraid to get her hopes up, Savannah nodded. The trial had been relatively easy for her up to this point. Not pleasant, but nothing she hadn't been able to handle. Facing down the monster who'd raised her and recounting the horrific things he'd done to her would open her up to a lot more pain. But, just as in BDSM, sometimes pain was needed for catharsis.

Hearing Gentry take an oath to tell the truth and then lie through his teeth wasn't something she wanted to witness. But she'd go back in there anyway. Each day brought them closer to the end of this nightmare.

Savannah's head was spinning as she tried to make sense of all this, but Sullivan said, "Go get some lunch. Enjoy your break then be back here about fifteen minutes early with any questions you might have. Savannah, I'll give you a notepad to jot down any lies you catch him in. I'm sure there will be numerous ones, and I don't want you to forget any of them. I'll get you back on the stand as soon as possible, but most likely, it won't be until tomorrow. I'll use your notes to help form my list of questions." She squeezed Savannah's forearm. "Relax, Savannah. We've got him on the run. This trial is almost over. Soon, justice will be yours."

Savannah nodded as the DA walked away at a brisk pace. Why couldn't she lose the feeling that Gentry still had some nasty tricks up his sleeve?

* * *

Damián could tell by the way Savannah's body became even more tense after Sullivan left the room that she was on edge. He pulled her into the crook of his arm. After initially resisting him, she settled in with a sigh. Damián hoped she'd take the opportunity to at least rest her eyes for a minute. She needed all the down time she could get.

But all too soon, she sat up and asked them, "What do you think he'll say?"

"A pack of lies," Damián said. "I'm glad his attorney can see through his bullshit."

"I have a sinking feeling that this isn't going to go as well as Sullivan hopes it will."

Dad leaned forward over the table. "I don't want to hear any stinkin' thinkin'. You have one more small hurdle to get over, then you're going to get to stare him down and let the world know what he did to you."

"This is the chance you've been waiting for to tell your story, *querida*."

"I know, but I'm scared." Her voice sounded small.

He wasn't the least bit worried that, once she took the stand, she'd knock them over with the truth. She was just tired, and he couldn't blame her. They'd been in the courtroom over a week now. The trial and her pregnancy were taking a lot out of her. With any luck, they'd get out of California before another week passed.

"We'll be there cheering you on from the gallery," Dad said, squeezing her shoulder at the same time he leaned closer to whisper, "But one thing you don't have to worry about is that shithead—pardon my language, but that's what he is—getting anywhere near you or your family ever again. I'll even put security details on each of you around the clock once my agency is set up."

After the kidnapping, they'd learned not to underestimate Gentry's reach. But if he and Lyle were incarcerated, he hoped the threat would disappear, too.

"Thanks, Adam." Her voice cracked, and he squeezed her hand.

"It'll be over soon, *bebé*." Damián wasn't certain he wanted to listen to the horrific details of Savannah's life, but he intended to remain strong for her. He wove his fingers between hers and squeezed. They would get through this—together.

"I'll do my best." She didn't convince him that she was certain, though.

But all too soon, they were headed back to the courtroom where they took their seats again near the prosecutor's table. With just a few minutes to go, Sullivan returned and asked if they had any further questions. The three assured her they didn't. The DA equipped Savannah with pad and pen before settling in at her table to prepare for this circus.

Gentry and his attorney returned soon after as well, hardly speaking to or looking at each other. When the judge reentered the courtroom, Abbott asked to approach the bench again, and both attorneys went forward. This time, their chat ended much more quickly. Sullivan returned to her table and motioned for Savannah to come forward. Damián helped her to her feet and remained close as the DA told them what she'd expected was about to happen.

Great. Damián had mixed feelings about having Savannah go through this, but in the end, this could be the catharsis and empowerment she needed.

When the attorneys returned to their tables and the jury was seated, the judge addressed the defense attorney. "Mr. Abbott, are you ready to proceed?"

"Yes, Your Honor. The defense calls George Albert Gentry to the stand."

Gentry was guided forward by one of the armed deputies. After he lied to the clerk about promising to tell the truth, the *cabrón* took the stand. Immediately, his gaze zeroed in on Savannah, who gasped at the intensity of the hatred spewing from his eyes. Damián reached for her hand and squeezed it.

"Mr. Gentry," Abbott said, "you've heard the testimony in the court during these proceedings and have indicated that you'd like to tell your side of the story. Please go ahead."

"Thank you."

After Abbott took his seat at the defense table, all eyes turned expectantly to Gentry. He thanked the judge and his attorney for the opportunity to tell his story. Savannah's entire body became rigid just hearing Gentry's voice. Damián realized it was the first time she'd probably heard him speak since the kidnapping and rescue.

Dios, would this nightmare ever end for his precious Savannah?

Once again, Damián wished he'd killed the bastard when he'd had the chance. Then this nightmare would have been over for Savannah.

Gentry launched immediately into a rambling spiel about what a loving husband and father he was, which took up the rest of the morning session. After a break for lunch, he resumed the stand to continue.

"If it pleases the court, now I would like to tell what really happened on the evening of the twenty-first of July 1992."

* * *

Savannah sat rigidly as she waited for Gentry to start spewing his venom. The baby attempted a somersault, which wasn't possible at this stage of her pregnancy. Savannah shifted to a more comfortable position and drew several deep breaths, wishing she could stand up and walk around to calm the baby. She stroked her belly in an attempt to relax them both.

Gentry launched immediately into a preposterous scenario, saying Lyle had been the one to shoot Grainger when the latter man had attempted to break into the Gentry home. Clearly, he grasped at straws. He would blame everyone else in an attempt to clear his name. Every now and then, he glanced toward the jury box as if to gauge how well they were eating up his lies.

This went on for at least half an hour. Then Gentry's gaze bore into her again, robbing her of several breaths before Damián tapped her collar and she regained her composure. Savannah held her head higher and waited for whatever would come out of his mouth next.

If he thought he could reduce her to silence or tears the way he'd done so many times in the past, he'd be sorely disappointed. She would never be that frightened little girl again.

After a long, tense moment, Gentry continued, this time going on and on about how his wife ran around with other men, the last of which was Grainger. How she didn't take care of her husband or daughter the way a wife and mother should. How Savannah had been neglected.

Some jurors might have drawn the conclusion that Maman was sleeping with Grainger, but Savannah would never know. She couldn't blame her, though, if she had. Her life had been hell with Gentry. Savannah just hadn't been aware of how bad it was, because Maman always shielded her from the ugliness in their household.

Was he casting enough doubt to sway any jury members? She tried to read their expressions, but they were playing it close to the vest. All eyes were riveted in Gentry's direction, though.

Savannah listened to him rant for the better part of an hour as he cited examples of what he was saying and continued to twist the truth just enough that it would be difficult to prove otherwise. She jotted a few notes, if he said something she could solidly refute.

Then, suddenly, he started in on Savannah, and her pen began flying across the page.

"My daughter has always been the most important person in my life." *Oh, you aren't really going there, are you?* "I tried to do my best to provide her with everything she could possibly want or need. Like on her sixth birthday."

She remembered the party around the pool with her friends from first grade. She wouldn't give him credit for this event in any way. He'd barely shown up before it was over. Maman had asked her what theme she wanted, and she'd asked for a Disney Princess one.

"When she told me she wanted to do a Disney Princess theme, I got on the phone to hire former cast members from Disneyland—at great expense, I might add—to come dressed as Aurora, Cinderella, and Ariel."

She smiled as she remembered the joy she'd felt that day as Maman rushed around making sure everyone had a good time, especially Savannah. Maman knew those were her favorite princesses.

"I see by Savannah's smile that she remembers what a good time we had together that day, too."

Rudely brought back from her pleasant memory, she cast a glance at the jurors who were staring at her, some of them smiling. She narrowed her gaze at Gentry then remembered the pad and paper and jotted down a note to tell Sullivan why she'd been smiling just now. He painted a picture of himself as father of the year when he was anything but. Maman had been her only parent present at that party. Gentry couldn't be bothered.

"If it were up to me, Savannah would have never been punished. She was such a pleasant, happy child. But her mother"—Gentry's mouth drew into a thin, tight line as his eyes narrowed—"was a firm disciplinarian who often spanked and sometimes even beat the child."

Another lie! Damián stroked her nape to center her again as she scribbled on the notepad so as not to fall behind. Gentry was rarely home to notice or care that she was being raised to be a responsible, well-behaved child. His portraying Maman as abusive was as far from the truth as one could get. She scribbled another note. The DA had been right to arm her with paper and pen to keep track of all the lies.

"It broke my heart when Savannah would run to me when I came home to tell me that her mother had spanked her hard enough to make her cry."

Savannah only remembered one such spanking, although she'd never sought comfort from Gentry. He'd always scared her. That day, she'd lied to Maman about borrowing an heirloom brooch of hers and losing it while playing. Ironically, the brooch had been excavated from near where the human remains had been found, and Savannah had since had it cleaned and placed in her jewelry box along with other treasures that once belonged to Maman.

Realizing what he was trying to do, she made a note to explain to the jury that she had deserved to be punished any time Maman had deemed it necessary. Maman was never cruel in her discipline—and nothing she'd done out of love came close to being as awful as what Gentry had done to her later.

"I'm sure Savannah could tell the court about other times when her mother abused her."

Abused? What on earth was he talking about? Maman *never* abused her. She flipped to a new page and made another note.

"It's understandable that she would block out those traumatic images of her beloved mother abusing her. She put Elise on a pedestal after she disappeared, pretending she was nothing short of Joan of Arc."

Even when he'd told her Maman had deserted her, deep down she hadn't believed him.

"I would venture to say that not only was Savannah being abused by her mother, but also by that...by my wife's lover, John Grainger." Gentry's composure almost cracked before he caught himself.

"Did Grainger ever lay a hand on you, Savannah?" Gentry asked her.

"Objection, Your Honor," the DA said. "The witness is merely to provide his narrative, not speak to others in the court."

"Sustained."

Savannah made a note to clear the blot Gentry had tried to place on John's character when she took the stand again. John had been a perfect gentleman the one time he'd been with Savannah.

John Grainger actually treated me in a fatherly way for the brief time he could.

Unfortunately, beginning that very night, Gentry would notice her in ways far from fatherly.

"We lived in one of the most prestigious homes in the exclusive Rancho Santa Fe area. I worked long hours building a lucrative business so that I could provide for Savannah and Elise. I hired some of the best tutors for Savannah's private lessons beginning the year she entered third grade."

Because he wanted to control who I might file a complaint of child abuse with, since that was the year he began molesting me.

"Even though Savannah was as ungrateful as that fil—her mother—I never neglected Savannah or shirked my parental responsibilities to her."

No doubt he'd almost let slip the words *filthy whore*, two of his favorite terms for both Maman and Savannah. She couldn't wait for him to show them the vile human being he really was.

Gentry turned to the jurors. "I'm sure some of you have children who can be less than appreciative of all you do for them, too." Several of them nodded.

Great. He was trying to play on their sympathies and commiserate about their children.

"Objection," Sullivan said. "Witness should not address the jurors directly."

"Sustained."

Red splotches rose in Gentry's pasty cheeks. He wasn't used to being thwarted. "I never quit trying to show Savannah my love," he continued, as if he hadn't been admonished. His gaze returned to hers. "Take the night Savannah turned eighteen, for instance. I could have turned her out in the world to make it on her own. Instead, I pulled out all the stops to give her a party at my hotel that she'd never forget."

Her eighteenth birthday party? She had no memory of any such thing. Flashes of white came before her eyes in a strobe-like effect. She'd seen that during the wax play scene and then had been triggered. She blinked a few times, trying to remember details from that night, but nothing came to her. What on earth had happened at that party that was so horrific she'd blocked it out?

"She'd worn a white chiffon formal gown and Elise's white opera gloves."

Maman's? She hadn't known they'd been hers.

The room suddenly closed in around her, and she began breathing rapidly. How much more would she have to listen to?

Damián and Adam both grounded her again with gentle touches and soothing whispers.

Soon, she could hear Gentry's sniveling voice again going on about some make-believe party. While she didn't remember any party, her life changed drastically after that birthday. From then on, Gentry began to pimp out her body, up until she ran away.

"I special ordered that ball gown for her. It was studded with thousands of tiny diamonds." He continued to reminisce about this birthday, while she was lost in fractured memories she couldn't quite conjure up.

Savannah glanced at several of the women on the jury who wore smiles, no doubt with visions of her in a formal princess gown dancing through their heads.

It didn't really happen like that.

Or did it? Was that evening buried in a self-protective fog because something happened that was so terrible her psyche couldn't handle it? Were those flashes and her trigger related to the events at that party?

Until that birthday, what Gentry had done to her had been her own private shame. She'd never let a soul know what her incestuous father was doing. As a child, she'd been locked away from anyone but her tutors, and Father's threats of what would happen to her if she told them what was going on scared her into silence. Then he'd become her pimp, making her existence known in a perverted way as his sex slave.

Damián brought her back to the present with a sharp thump on her collar. Could he tell she'd been sucked into the past, or was he periodically reminding her to stay in the moment with random touches and taps?

Focused again, she jotted down more notes for later, her hand trembling with each scribbled word.

"And after you blew out the candles on your cake, I still remember placing a diamond tiara on your head and crowning you my princess."

Flashes of what might be the party he described crossed her mind's eye, but were gone before she could process them. Was her mind filling in the images based on his words, or was she actually remembering something?

His simpering tone made her cringe inside. When Damián placed his hands over hers, she realized she'd been picking at the skin around her fingernails again. How had she forgotten to replace the Band-Aids? She quickly reached into her purse to pull out some tissues to stop the bleeding.

Princess Slut.

Savannah thought of Damián and how he'd made her feel special using that endearment. Gentry had only made her his slut, but to her Dom, she was a Princess Slut.

"I also was the lucky man who had the first dance with you that night." *No, if this party was real, you must have forced me to dance with you.* She imagined his clammy, hot breath on her bare shoulder, his hard penis pressing against her abdomen through the layers of lace and chiffon of the dress, and his fingers pinching her arm when she didn't look up at him as adoringly as he demanded.

Wait! How did she fill in those blanks unless they truly had danced at an eighteenth birthday party? A sick feeling settled in the pit of her stomach. What on earth had happened back then?

"I've always treated my little girl like a princess."

Lies! Everything he said was a lie.

"Do you need some water, *querida?*" Damián's voice came to her as if from down a long tunnel. She nodded, but Adam was the one to stand and go in search of water. Damián stayed with her, his arm around her back, repeating her mantra and reminding her she was strong and would soon be able to tell the true story. But there were too many gaps in her memory for her to talk about that night.

When Adam returned with a small bottle of water, another flash of memory bombarded her. Lyle handed her a glass of punch the night of that party. But she didn't remember anything that followed—except in brief snatches here and there.

Did he drug me?

Chapter Twenty-Six

G entry grinned evilly at her then pulled out an eight-by-ten photo and held it out to the bailiff to present in the overhead.

The DA stood. "Objection. Procedure. Permission to approach the court."

Abbott and Sullivan both went forward and examined the photo, said a few words to the judge, nodded, and returned to their tables. "Objection withdrawn, Your Honor."

"Exhibit is accepted. Bailiff, you may publish the photo."

As if aware of the hold he still had on her, Gentry grinned while Savannah turned her gaze to where the photo would be projected. Her heart racing, she waited, having no clue what it might depict. Then it came up and she stared in horror at a young Savannah standing next to Gentry. She truly looked like the Cinderella princess Gentry had described at her eighteenth birthday party.

Her heart began racing, and her palms became sweaty. Something awful happened to her wearing that dress, because it was the same white dress she'd seen herself wearing when she'd been triggered during the wax play scene. Was that on her eighteenth birthday, the way he'd described it? Did that really happen?

She studied the photo more, looking for answers. Her hair had been piled high on her head similar to the Disney princess's updo. Tendrils curled around the sides of her neck, leading the eye down to the princess cut gown with its form-fitted bodice and billowy skirt. There was a smile on her face. Had he forced her to smile like that? But it seemed genuine. Had she actually been happy that night?

No, her sketchy flashes of memories of her wearing that dress didn't mesh with Gentry's glowing narrative. Bile rose in her throat. There were so many holes in her memory. What if she couldn't remember what had happened and the jury was left with only this image?

Were her flashbacks actually from that night or one of the many other nights where she'd been turned over to Gentry's associates?

Did it matter? She had enough stories to tell that would refute the glowing picture he tried to paint of his fathering skills.

But she hadn't dreamed up those flashbacks. Men surrounding her. Penises in hand. While her memory was unclear, something awful had happened to her the night that photo was taken. Her stomach began to churn again.

Without waiting for the judge to call a recess, she edged in front of Adam and ran from the courtroom. She'd made it halfway to the bathroom when she heard Damián telling her he was right behind her. Inside the stall, she lifted the seat, bent over, and lost her lunch. The sound of someone entering the bathroom sent her into dry heaves. After a few minutes with no more vomiting or gagging, she reached for a wad of tissue and wiped her mouth. She wished she had her purse so she could suck on a mint to get rid of the nasty taste.

Oh, God. How was she going to go back in there and face the courtroom after having such a meltdown? She'd remained poised throughout this ordeal, right up until Gentry made her question what was real and what was made up.

"*Querida*, are you okay?"

Damián? He'd followed her into the ladies' room? Knowing he was so near lifted her spirits a little, and she flushed and left the stall to be wrapped immediately in his arms and held like the cherished princess she was to him.

"Shh. It's okay, *bebé*. The truth's going to come out when you get your turn to set the record straight."

She pulled away and looked up at him. "But I can't remember everything. How can I refute what he's saying if I don't remember what happened that night?"

"That was only one night of many. So what if he gave you a party to celebrate your eighteenth birthday? That doesn't negate all the times he raped and tortured you, *savita*. Nothing has changed because of one silly photo."

She hoped he was right but didn't know what to think anymore. "Let me freshen up before we go back." She turned to the sink to cup water in her hands to rinse out her mouth when Damián's body heat infused her. "I grabbed your purse. Maybe you have some mints or something in there."

She stood, her eyes lighting on the bag. "Oh, thank you!" She gave him a peck on the cheek. "You're my hero."

He chuckled just when the door opened. A woman stepped inside, looked at the two of them, and then blushed. "Sorry. I'll come back." She left quickly.

"I think you'd better wait outside before you get arrested for being a perv or something," she teased.

"I'll be waiting right outside for you."

She scooped up water from the faucet and swirled it in her mouth before popping a mint and staring at herself in the mirror. Dark circles under her eyes spoke to her lack of sleep recently. But now, the whites of her eyes were bloodshot from throwing up. Upon closer inspection, she realized her eyes looked dead, lacking all emotion. This wouldn't do. She needed to go back in there the warrior princess Damián expected her to be. The warrior she knew herself to be, she corrected.

I am strong.

I can't be beaten.

I will tell my story.

Standing tall, squaring her shoulders, she marched out of the bathroom. Damián's appreciative smile fueled her courage before she noticed Adam standing next to him.

"The judge called a recess at the DA's request, so you haven't missed anything." He glanced at his watch." We have another five minutes before they plan to reconvene."

Together, they walked leisurely back into the courtroom, Savannah between her protectors. Sullivan gave her a worried glance when she entered then motioned for her to come forward. After conferring with her over the bar and assuring her she was okay now, Savannah took her seat and waited for the judge to return. When court reconvened, Gentry took the stand again.

Abbott cleared his throat, "Mr. Gentry, please continue."

"That night, my daughter changed. Suddenly, she couldn't get enough of men."

Savannah's eyes opened wide. *Surely you aren't going there.*

"She danced with just about every one of my business clients and allowed them to paw all over her, one even ripping her dress."

Apparently, you are.

"I had to throw the beautiful gown away after that night. By night's end, it was filled with semen from my nymphomaniac daughter's sick liaisons in a closed off section of the ballroom. Apparently, she and my business partner, Lyle Gibson, had entered into a contract agreeing that she'd offer her body in exchange for money to my potential business clients. It started that night. I had no idea what those two were up to."

You filthy whore. The unspoken words reminded her of the vile accusations Lyle and Gentry had repeatedly made about her.

No! She hadn't willingly given herself to them. And he'd been the one to sign the contract—not Lyle, who only served as her handler and enforcer. She made a note on the pad. They'd both taken what they wanted against her will. She had signed that damned contract under duress and with coercion, fearing what would happen if she'd disobeyed either of them.

A buzzing in her ears drowned out whatever he said afterward. Glimpses of a ruined dress flashed before her eyes. Her stomach roiled again as the smell of semen clinging to her bodice and exposed skin assailed her nostrils.

"Soon you'll be able to tell what really happened, *querida.*" Damián's whispered words drew her back to the present. "No one will believe that old goat after you tell your story."

"The next thing I know, my daughter is propositioning *my* business associates in the penthouse of my very own hotel. I couldn't believe it when I watched the videos from that night."

He'd filmed her that night, too? Had he gotten off watching that video?

Savannah wanted to scream but didn't want to anger the judge. Instead, she gulped air into her lungs and tried not to hyperventilate as she imagined her father masturbating to videos of her being assaulted and degraded that night and so many nights afterward.

Damián stroked the back of her neck, and she almost melted against him. Thank God he was here to keep her grounded in the present.

"My once sweet and innocent daughter was lost to me. I wanted to have nothing more to do with her, but I was still her father. I thought I could show her that she didn't have to turn tricks to make it in this world. And yet I couldn't very well turn her out onto the streets, so she continued to live in my mansion where I at least could make sure she was fed and clothed and didn't go down a path of drug use on top of prostitution."

A need to vomit again threatened to send her back to the bathroom, but she refused to show him any sign that he was getting through to her.

"Of course, I did have to have interventions from time to time, hoping to get her to turn her life around. And to think, her mother must have seen this in her from an early age. No wonder she'd tried to beat the evil out of the child all those times."

Savannah's eyes narrowed. What on earth was he talking about? Was he merely trying to justify killing Maman by painting her as abusive? Would any juror believe his side of the story?

"Elise was half-crazed the night she died, bragging that she'd found someone else to keep her and wouldn't need my money any longer."

His money? It was always Maman's money keeping *him* in a lavish lifestyle. Savannah jotted down more notes.

"Elise threatened to kidnap my child and run away. I had to stop her. I had to try and protect my innocent daughter."

That's not what happened at all!

"And now my daughter's memory has been twisted by that Mexican sitting next to her who has her brainwashed."

Damián's arm tightened around her back. How could the judge and DA expect her to sit here quietly while Gentry told such blatant lies about her, her mother, and now her husband? A twinge in her back alerted her that she'd tensed up, and she tried to draw a breath, but her lungs remained too constricted.

Say one more thing, you fucking bastard, and I will make sure the world knows the truth about you.

Normally, Savannah didn't use such language, even when speaking to herself, but he wasn't going to come after Damián without making her royally pissed. She took another deep breath to compose herself and jotted down more notes. Then she waited for her turn.

Gentry sneered at her, as if he thought he could beat her.

I can't be beaten.

Never again.

"Orlando was a bus boy in my restaurant and took it upon himself to drag her from the penthouse one morning, thinking she was being abused by some of her johns. He did who knows what with her before returning her to my house that night. She wound up getting pregnant, either by him or someone else she was with."

Another lie. Savannah blinked at his audacity, trying to figure out what any of this had to do with the case. What else was he going to twist around before he finished? She made another note to set the record straight.

Soon, she could tell them what really happened, as much as she could remember, anyway.

Savannah wouldn't let him sully what she had with Damián. She leaned toward her husband and kissed him on the cheek. "If I haven't told you lately, thank you for rescuing me that day."

"*De nada.*" He grinned at her. How the two of them could share such a moment in the midst of this was a testament to how secure she felt with him by her side. A peaceful calm overcame her, empowered by Damián's love.

Savannah turned back to Gentry, whose face had turned a mottled red as his gaze shot bullets toward them. Ineffective compared to the ones he'd used to take John Grainger's life that night.

You will never win.

"All I've ever done is try to protect my daughter." His voice cracked.

Oh, please. No crocodile tears on top of all the lies and drama.

"If that makes me guilty of something, then so be it." He turned to the judge. "That is all I have to say."

"Would the People care to cross-examine the defendant at this time?" the judge asked.

"Yes, Your Honor, but given the late hour, the People request an adjournment until tomorrow morning."

The judge checked the clock on the wall. It was after four. "Request granted. This court is adjourned until nine in the morning." He banged the gavel.

The District Attorney smiled reassuringly at Savannah and came over to ask if she might spend the rest of the hour discussing where Gentry had lied to better target her cross-examination as well as her questioning of Savannah during the more structured rebuttal.

"Of course." Savannah picked up her purse and tucked the notebook under her arm. "Thank you for the notebook. I'm not sure I'd have remembered every lie he told, given the emotions of the day."

Gentry had presented them with every opportunity the DA and Savannah had hoped for. At last, she'd soon be able to tell her complete story. While her childhood abuse and rapes weren't part of the trial initially, Gentry had opened the door to introduce that part of her life with him.

So why was her heart racing and her hands all sweaty? Because she wasn't sure she could remember the things her mind had blocked out all these years.

Pressing her fingers into her lower back, which had been aching all day, she wished she could crawl into bed and snuggle with Damián until the trial was over. If the guys asked to go out to eat tonight, she'd request they drop her off first or pick up some burgers and call it an early night.

They opted for the latter, but she barely noticed the taste of the burger, even though it had come from one of her favorite places to take Mari for comfort food when they'd lived out here. Her body felt lethargic, and she went to bed almost immediately after eating, letting the world fade away.

For a few hours, anyway.

Chapter Twenty-Seven

Damián never wanted to kill anyone so much in his life. What they'd put Savannah through in that courtroom today should have brought on new charges against Gentry.

After the DA had discussed the things she could testify about, Sullivan had encouraged Damián to take her back to the lodge so she could rest up for tomorrow. They'd picked up carryout on the way, because no way was he letting her go to bed without eating.

By seven o'clock, she lay curled on her side, arm and hand wrapped protectively around the baby bump. Even in sleep, she thought about the baby. Not wanting to disturb her rest, he just sat in the chair watching over her.

Tomorrow was going to take another toll on her, but soon it would be over, and they could go home to Marisol. He missed his little girl so much. Talking on the phone and doing video chats didn't cut it. He needed to wrap her in his arms and hug her until she squirmed.

Every time Damián thought about what Gentry had done to Savannah, starting when she was about Marisol's age, the blood boiled inside him. Why didn't he castrate that monster when he'd had the chance?

Savannah moaned in her sleep, and he quickly shucked off his clothes to join her. He whispered soothing words to her, a mixture of Spanish and English, while stroking her hair away from her forehead. She relaxed, remaining asleep.

He closed his eyes for a moment, glad one more hellacious day was over.

"No," Savannah moaned. "Don't touch me. You promised."

Damián awoke again in an instant, searching the barely lit room for who had invaded their suite, but soon realized she was dreaming. The alarm clock showed it was only nine-twenty-three.

"Shh, *bebé*. You're okay." His fingers pressed the worry lines from her forehead. "I'm here. Nobody's going to hurt you." *Never again.*

Savannah didn't open her eyes but relaxed into sleep again. She had to be totally exhausted. Who could blame her? Even the strongest warrior needed to rest now and then.

When her face contorted again as if in the throes of a nightmare, Damián shook her awake. He couldn't stand to see her hurting, even if the pain was all in the past.

She blinked a few times and zeroed in on him. "Damián? Did I wake you?"

"I was watching you sleep. You seemed upset." *To put it mildly.*

Savannah wrinkled her brow, glancing away. Then a look of horror crossed her face. She met his gaze once more. "The party. That night. He *lied* to me."

He didn't have to ask who she was talking about and assumed she was talking about her eighteenth birthday. It must still be fresh in her mind from Gentry's testimony in court this afternoon.

"What did you remember?"

Again, she scrunched up her pretty face. "That's just it. I got little snatches of memory, but nothing solid enough to know what happened. But I'm absolutely certain that he promised me something and broke it."

"You said that while you slept, too. Then you swatted the air and yelled at someone not to touch you."

She seemed to try and pull up the memory but shook her head. "I can't remember. It's so frustrating. That night is such a blank. Of course, I'm sure it didn't happen the fairy-tale way Gentry described it. I need to set the record straight in court tomorrow, but I can't if I don't remember the details."

He stroked his hand up and down her arm, trying to provide comfort. It frustrated him all to hell that he couldn't help her by providing her the answers she needed.

"Oh!" She reached for her belly, rubbing it in circular motions.

Damián's heart jumped into his throat as he sat up in bed. "What's wrong?"

"Just more Braxton-Hicks contractions. Practice for the big day."

"Are you sure?"

She smiled. "Absolutely. I've been having them off and on since Thanksgiving."

When he pressed his hand against her belly, it was rock-hard.

"Maybe my nightmare triggered something. I'm not sure I can go right back to sleep."

Both of them were wide awake now. He didn't want her to stay up worrying about something she couldn't do anything about. If she couldn't remember the dream, then she needed to let it go.

"Why don't I get you a glass of warm milk or a cup of tea to calm your nerves?"

She tossed the sheet and summer blanket off and sat up. "I'll help."

In the kitchen, he put the kettle on while she chose a chamomile tea bag from the tin. Soon after, they sat down in the breakfast nook. A bottled water sat in front of him; he'd decided coffee might keep him up. He talked her into having a slice of apple mountain berry pie that they'd been eating since their weekend visit to the Julian Pie Company. He made sure she ate the bigger share, though. She liked sweets more than he did.

She remained quiet, blowing on and sipping the hot tea, deep in thought as she savored the pie. Then her eyes opened wide, and she set her fork down.

"I need to have a hypnotic regression!"

*   *   *

"What? Now?"

"Yes!" Savannah couldn't understand how they hadn't thought of it sooner. "It would be the perfect way for me to go back to that party and find out what really happened. I need to know what happened that night before I take the stand tomorrow."

"My expertise with hypnosis is solely BDSM, nothing this serious."

"Let me see if I can get in touch with the hypnotherapist from the clinic I worked at in Solana Beach. I know it's late, but maybe she'll be willing to help. She was appalled to find out what had happened to me as a child."

Time was running out. She knew that the way Gentry had portrayed that night couldn't possibly be what had really happened. She was never a nymphomaniac or sex addict.

After obtaining Michelle Patterson's number from Anita, Savannah called to explain what she needed. Michelle only asked that they arrange for someone to meet her at the Pendleton gate and bring her to the suite at the lodge.

"I'll call Dad and see if he can meet her at the main gate and get her on base."

An hour and twenty minutes later, Damián met Michelle and Adam at the suite door. She suggested that Dad videotape the session in case there was an appeal. Savannah had weighed the chance she was taking, but this didn't relate to the charges Gentry faced in court. For her own peace of mind, Savannah needed to know what really happened that night.

Michelle asked, "Where would you be most comfortable—lying on the sofa or the bed?"

Savannah glanced across the room to the sofa. "Let's do it in here."

"Let me get you a light blanket in case you get cold," Damián offered before heading to the bedroom.

Savannah rearranged pillows on the sofa while Adam tested his phone video for the best spot to record. When Damián returned, she stretched out on her side and placed the blanket over her.

Michelle sat in a chair beside the sofa, asking about Savannah's past experiences with hypnosis. She told her about her therapist and Damián's past efforts without going into why Damián was hypnotizing her. Damián, seated at the other end of the sofa, shared his "go deeper" and "come out of trance" commands with her.

"We'll keep the same touch to the arm as a signal to come out of trance immediately. You will retain everything you remember while in trance. But if I see you're in distress, I'll touch your hand, and you will recenter yourself by taking a slow, deep breath." After explaining that a regression induction took many more steps than she'd experienced before, Michelle soon had Savannah deep into trance and guided her back to her eighteenth birthday.

"What's going on around you, Savannah?" Michelle asked.

"It looks like a…coming-out party. I'm dressed in a beautiful white princess gown, like the one Maman wore to her first cotillion when she made her debut to Charleston society." She furrowed her brows. "It's all happening so quickly. My father places a tiara on my head. We pose for a photo, and Father whispers he has no interest in my body anymore. I smile for the photographer.

"Move forward to the next significant happening."

"We sign a contract saying that I am free of him."

Best birthday present ever.

Her smile faded. "He's making me dance with him. I'm not comfortable having him hold me like this, but if it means I'll be free of him at last afterward, it's worth it." She moaned, and her heart began to race. "He lied about having no interest in me, because I can feel his erection against my belly."

When her breathing became rapid and shallow, Michelle tapped her hand. "Deep breath, then let it out, and we will continue," Michelle instructed in a melodious voice.

"I plead a headache, hoping to be sent home early, but Father tells his business partner, Mr. Gibson, to bring me some aspirin and a cup of punch. Mr. Gibson makes me uncomfortable, too. He leers at me as if ready to stake his own claim on my body."

"What happens next?"

"He shakes out two tablets into my hand and hands me the punch. I try not to touch him. After swallowing the pills, I hand the empty cup back to Mr. Gibson. Father asks if I'd like to lie down, but I say no. I want to go home, but that isn't an option he offers."

"Move forward to the next significant thing."

"I notice there aren't any women at the party. Even the servers are males. Strange, but I don't really have my own friends who could have been invited." She paused a moment. "I become a little flushed and go out on the balcony to get some fresh air. My palms are sweating, and I begin having trouble catching my breath. A weird sense of euphoria hits while I lean against the railing. "I suddenly feel like I'm high or something."

"What did the pills you took look like?" Michelle asked.

"Round, white tablets. An E on one side. Mr. Gibson held an Excedrin bottle, so I assumed they were aspirins."

"Then what happened?"

"Someone comes up behind me and places his hands around my waist, pulling me against him. I wrench myself away and turn around. He tells me my father sent him to check on me, so he must be one of his associates. He attacks me again. I struggle to get away. But he's all hands, clawing at my breasts, pinching my nipples through my dress. I push him away and stumble backward into someone else who holds me by my arms while the first man takes my jaw and pries my mouth open. He…forces his tongue inside my mouth." Tears wet her cheeks as she fought to fill her lungs.

A tap to her hand pulled her out enough to drag air into her lungs. Savannah relaxed, distancing herself from the emotions of that moment.

"Let's move on to the next significant thing that happened," Michelle suggested.

"My skin is on fire. Excruciating pain burns my face, arms, wherever I'm being touched. My heart is racing; I'm afraid it will explode from my chest. I rub my clammy hands on the skirt of the princess dress. I hope I'm not leaving any marks. This is the most beautiful dress I've ever worn.

"Something weird happens next. I start getting…turned on by the way these men are touching me. I grope the crotch of the one in front of me and kiss him back. I don't even know who this man is! Why am I behaving like this?

"A familiar voice from behind me shouts, 'Release her,' and they do. I fall against the balcony railing, gasping for air, and turn to find Father standing in the doorway, sneering at me."

'Inside, you dirty little whore.'

"He is angry. Says some ugly things."

"What things?" she prompted.

"He calls me a dirty little whore." Her mouth becomes suddenly dry. "I haven't seen him this angry at me since I was little. I'm more afraid of him than ever. My entire body shakes, so I do as he says. Mr. Gibson is waiting inside the doors and yanks me by the arm across the room and through accordion doors into another area of the ballroom I'm not familiar with."

"What happens there?"

She swallowed hard. "The room is filled with men. It looks like all the people I had seen at the party earlier. Maybe even some of the servers. They're all leering at me. Mr. Gibson pulls some papers out of his pocket and waves them at me, saying that I've agreed to service them—*all* of them—and anyone else he and Father say I should." Her brow wrinkled in confusion. "He's holding the contract I signed earlier." *That contract wasn't meant to free me at all. Why didn't I read it? Of course, what other options do I have? I can't escape Father. Now he plans to hand me over to other men. I still have no control over my life or my body.*

"I turn to run away, but several of them surround me and block my exit. They force me onto a table...no, wait. It's a slant board. They must have brought it in here just for this. They tip me at an angle with my head lower then my feet at first, making me dizzy. All I can see are the men standing around me. Some unzip themselves." Her heart pounded harder as her throat closed up. "I fear they are all going to take turns raping me. They pinch my skin, my nipples, my privates. God, the pain! Every part of my body is hypersensitive."

"What do you think was the reason for that?"

"Maybe that wasn't aspirin I took but some kind of drug."

"What happened to you while on the table?"

"I think I blacked out for a little while." Or had she merely blocked that part out? "When I come to, I'm still on the board and several men are ejaculating onto me and my dress." Her chest, face, and feet were wet with cum, and her stomach roiled. "I'm going to be sick."

Michelle tapped her hand. "Pull away from the emotional power of the scene, and tell me what's happening as if you're a fly on the ceiling."

Savannah took a breath and viewed the scene from above. "Shimmers of light from the sparkling crystals on the dress are juxtaposed with the flecks of shiny puddles where their semen lands on my body. The bodice of the dress has been ripped open, leaving me naked above the waist. And there are red stripes across my chest where a flogger or single tail must have been used while I was unconscious."

Savannah tried to block the image, but it only came through more vividly. Her breathing became labored. She wanted to escape the room.

From her right came Michelle's voice. "When I bring you out of trance, you'll remember every detail of what you saw during this session and will be able to tell your story when you're on the stand tomorrow as if watching a movie."

She felt a swipe down her arm. Savannah opened her eyes and blinked a few times. Even though the room wasn't brightly lit, it took a moment for her eyes to seek out Damián's. Adam and Damián came into focus. Her husband's jaw was clenched so tightly she was afraid he was about to ram his fist through a wall.

Then he smiled, and her body sank into the sofa. "Welcome back, *querida*."

"You don't know how happy I am to be here with you and not in that dark place anymore."

"I hate what that bastard put you through."

Unable to speak past the knot in her throat, she nodded. After a moment, she said, "There are still some fuzzy areas. I might never remember those. But I have enough detail to refute the lies Gentry told on the stand today."

"That's all that matters," Michelle said, standing. "You stay there, Savannah." Turning to Adam, she added, "I think I can find myself off the base okay."

"It's late. I'll make sure you get home safely."

"Michelle, I appreciate you coming out to do this tonight on such short notice."

She shrugged. "I'm a night owl. No problem at all."

"You've helped me immeasurably. I owe you one."

"Just try and stay calm during your testimony and deliver another healthy baby. That's all I want from you."

After Michelle and Adam said their goodnights and goodbyes, Damián helped Savannah to sit up before seating himself beside her and pulling her into his arms. "I'm so sorry you had to go through all that, *bebé*. Both a decade ago and tonight."

A flash of memory from the regression invades her consciousness again. "Oh God. I recognize the first man who groped me on the balcony. He testified on Gentry's behalf." She fought the urge to vomit.

"Where are you, Savannah?"

She drew a ragged breath. "Here with you, Sir."

"All that suffering happened in the past."

She nodded. "Gentry, Lyle, and those men can never hurt me again."

"That's my good girl. Stay in the present."

She nodded. "Best of all, I'm going to go into that courtroom tomorrow and send Gentry away for the rest of his life." That needed to be her sole focus tomorrow.

"Yes, you are, my warrior princess."

Damián held her in his arms again after they went to bed, as if to help keep the nightmares at bay—and it worked.

Chapter Twenty-Eight

The next morning, Savannah's chest burned as she forced air into her lungs. The pounding between her temples and throbbing in her lower back didn't bode well for her giving her rebuttal this morning after Gentry was cross-examined by the DA. But the sooner she got this out of the way, the sooner she could go back to Denver and put this all behind her for all time.

Once again, the three of them entered the courtroom before the jury or judge had taken their seats, a little earlier than usual. The DA hadn't arrived yet, either, but the defense attorney was already seated next to Gentry.

Despite her best effort to avoid eye contact, her gaze was inevitably drawn to the two men at that table. As if connected telepathically, Gentry turned in her direction, a self-satisfied smirk on his face before his gaze strayed briefly to the entrance behind her.

Flashes of the many times she'd seen that expression in the past, usually the precursor to a severe punishment or new degradation of some sort, robbed her of any bravado she might have mustered this morning.

Something's wrong. He's up to no good.

Damián took her by the elbow to keep her moving toward their seats. She hadn't even realized she'd stopped in the middle of the aisle. Adam preceded them into the row behind where they had been sitting yesterday. The room was fuller today than it had been before; this trial was attracting a great deal of public interest. More strangers she'd have to speak in front of. People had such prurient interests.

But Damián had prepared her to be exposed in front of both strangers and Gentry when she told this story. Soon, she could tell all the lurid details of what had been her hellish life under this man's evil sovereignty. At least she'd be clothed, unlike her practice sessions with Damián. The corner of her mouth quirked upward, and she relaxed a little.

Damián leaned forward to place himself between her and Gentry, breaking off eye contact between them. Without his telling her to do so, she tilted her head back and met Damián's gaze.

"Remember your mantra, Savannah?"

She responded, "I am strong." *Thanks to you.* "I can't be beaten." *Never again.* "I will tell my story." *At last.*

He smiled. "That's my good girl."

I am Damián's good girl.

She basked in the warmth of his approving smile, flashing back to the moment where he had claimed her horrific brand as his own. She'd trusted him then. She would trust him now. He would stay beside her today and throughout her rebuttal as she faced down the greatest evil in her life and told her story.

"Ready, *bebé?*"

Pulling her shoulders back, she nodded. Shifting her focus to the witness stand where she soon would be seated again, she repeated her mantra over and over as she mentally prepared herself. She couldn't wait to set the record straight about the monster who had terrorized her since she was eight—the man who had also killed her mother and John Grainger.

He needed to pay for those crimes most of all, but that testimony had already been presented. Today was all about reclaiming her power and not letting him perpetuate any more lies about her.

But when Damián sat back in his seat, Savannah once again felt the intensity of Gentry's stare boring into her. She ignored him as best she could, but sweat broke out on her palms. Why didn't he leave her alone? Even now, he tried to torment her. Why couldn't he see that, for once, *she* had the upper hand? That his reign of intimidation was over?

The doors opened at the back of the courtroom, and out of the corner of her eye, she saw Gentry's chair swivel around. Unable to ignore him any longer, she watched as a hateful grin lit his face.

What now?

"Mr. Damián Orlando?" a deep voice asked.

Savannah, Adam, and Damián turned simultaneously toward the aisle to see a tall man standing there dressed in a khaki uniform with a sheriff's badge on his left breast.

"Yes, sir," Damián answered.

He then addressed Adam. "Adam Montague?"

The deputy used the *Romeo and Juliet* pronunciation ending in -*gu* rather than -*tag*, which Adam corrected when he responded. "Yes, I'm Adam Montague. How can we help you?"

"You're both under arrest."

Savannah gasped. For what? This couldn't be happening. They didn't even live out here anymore. How could they have committed a crime? They'd barely left her side.

Savannah tried to focus on the officers, but her gaze was inexorably drawn in Gentry's direction. He sat grinning at her, evil oozing from every pore, and mouthed the words, "I told you—I will win."

He was responsible for this. Well, who else would get away with filing bogus charges and having a judge follow through?

"Now, if you gentlemen will come with us." Adam's being in uniform might have garnered more respect than they might otherwise been afforded.

Her heart pounded harder, bringing back her headache. What would happen to them behind bars?

No! This can't be happening!

The three of them stood, Damián helping Savannah to her feet and Adam moving around them to get closer to the deputy.

"Under arrest for what, deputy?" Adam asked in a low voice.

"Step outside, sir," the deputy repeated, "and we can go into more detail."

Before doing as ordered, Adam turned to Gentry and made a crackling, sizzling sound. Savannah caught a glimpse of the old man as all color drained from his face. Fear. No, absolute terror. The former master sergeant's height and demeanor had intimidated her when she'd first met him, but Gentry looked as if he'd seen a ghost from the bowels of hell. Why would Gentry be so afraid of Adam? He didn't even know him!

Adam must have sensed that Gentry was behind these arrests, too.

Wait! Did this have to do with what Damián had alluded to their first night back in San Diego, before the trial began? She leaned toward Damián and whispered, "What's this about?" She couldn't ask what they did to him, or she'd be admitting their possible guilt.

Without answering, Damián turned away to be led out of the courtroom with Adam and another deputy falling into line. She followed, hastily trying to keep up. In the hallway, the deputy who had spoken to them in the courtroom pulled from his pocket two folded legal-looking documents. "These are the warrants for your arrests."

Without giving them a chance to look at them, they handed the papers to Savannah and ordered both men to turn around. Savannah nearly lost it as she watched first her husband then Adam being handcuffed, just before they were patted down and had their rights read to them. The surreal words were lost in a barrage of silent screams inside her head.

"My wife will need the keys to our rental," Damián told the deputies.

"And we might as well give her our phones and wallets for safekeeping," Adam added.

How could they remain so calm at a time like this?

The deputy nodded. One removed the wallet and phone from Adam's pockets while the other retrieved the same, as well as the rental key, from Damián's. The key fob was warm in her hand. Damián's body heat. She clutched it to her chest.

It was only when she went to put everything in her purse that she glanced down at the top warrant in her hands.

"Assault and battery," she read aloud. "And terroristic threatening?" *What the—*

"Mind telling us who we're supposed to have assaulted or threatened?" Adam asked. She noticed the ruddiness in his neck, so perhaps he wasn't taking this as calmly as she thought. Why was he putting on a facade for the deputies—or was it for her? Something told her he wouldn't be able to charm his way out of this. Whatever *this* was.

"A complaint was filed against you both yesterday afternoon, and the judge issued warrants for us to pick you up and return you to San Bernardino County. Now, if you'll come with us…"

Damián muttered under his breath, "That sonofa—"

Savannah turned to her husband. "Damián?"

"Gentry's behind this, I'm sure. He's just trying to rattle you, *bebé*, by getting us out of the courtroom before you tell your story."

Well, Gentry was doing a masterful job of it. She clasped her hands together to keep them from visibly shaking in front of Damián. But how could she go back in there alone? How could her safety net be yanked out from under her today of all days?

"Could I please have a moment with my wife, deputy?"

After taking in her swollen belly and obvious distress, he relented with a sigh. "One minute." They didn't move from where they stood near him, though, giving them no privacy.

Damián said, "Eyes." She dreaded the moment he'd be taken away from her but met his gaze as if her last lifeline was being ripped away. "Listen to me. We're going to have to go deal with this shit. We'll get back to you as soon as we make bail, but we have to face it. That won't happen before you have to take the stand this morning."

"No, Damián! You can't leave me here alone! I can't face that monster without you!"

Damián growled. "Yes, you can, and you *will*." The fierceness in his tone bore through her fear. "You're the strongest person I know, Savannah Orlando. You already testified about what happened to your mother and what he did to you last March. Just tell the rest of your story. Tell the story. Remember the details that came out last night. Block him out. Don't get bogged down in the emotions of the past. Stay focused only on the story of what happened to you. Find a focal point. Use your touchstones. You're a warrior headed into battle, and nothing will piss him off more than knowing he can no longer rattle or manipulate you."

"Mr. Orlando, let's go."

The deputy took his upper arm, but before he could pull Damián away, he said, "Take a deep breath, *savita*. Now."

Savannah glanced at Adam before Damián demanded, "Eyes." With only slight reluctance, she brought her gaze back to her husband's. Her Dom. "Deep. Breath."

Though shaky, she managed to pull in enough air to appease him, even though her chest was too tight to breathe deeply. In a moment of false bravado, to keep him from worrying, she tilted up her chin. "I'll be okay, Sir. I'll remember everything you've taught me."

She didn't feel particularly strong or capable at the moment but didn't want him to think about anything except his own predicament right now. "Do whatever they tell you to, Damián," she admonished. To Adam, she said, "Keep him safe." Thank God Adam, in his uniform, would be with him. Damián might not be treated as unfairly as he might have been if alone. She hoped they would be kept together. "And I don't want either of you to wind up with any other charges before I can post bail."

"Yes, ma'am," Adam said with a grin. How could he find this the least bit amusing? "Don't worry about us, hon. You go back in there and show him what Savannah Orlando's made of."

She tugged on Adam's sleeve until he leaned down, and she kissed him on the cheek before turning to Damián. "I love you. I'll make you proud, Sir." Her throat closed on the last word, but her voice didn't crack.

His gaze bore into her soul. Then he smiled. "You already have, *querida*."

She brushed his lips with hers before the two men she'd counted on to be here during the greatest test of her life were led away.

She called after him, "Whatever false charges he's had filed against you will be thrown out, I'm sure. And I'll get to you as soon as I'm finished here." They'd retreated several yards before she realized she didn't know where they were going. "Wait! Deputy, where are you taking them?"

"San Bernardino County Central Detention Center," he called over his shoulder.

She'd been rescued from Gentry's cabin in that county. Had something happened after she'd been airlifted out that would convince a judge to issue a warrant on charges of assault and battery? Damián had been shot during the rescue. What could he possibly have done to Gentry while wounded?

And how was she going to get through today's rebuttal without her two solid rocks, her protectors, in the room with her? She blinked away the tears. Her hands tingled before she had the wherewithal to take a few slow, deep breaths to keep herself from hyperventilating and tried to regain control.

Could she walk back into that room alone? The door swung open, and she turned as the DA came up to her. "Is everything okay, Savannah? What was that all about? We don't need any drama or distractions today."

"I'm sorry. It's over now." She hadn't seen the DA enter the courtroom before the arrests, but at least the judge and jury hadn't witnessed this disaster.

The DA glanced around, as if expecting to find Damián and Adam, then focused on Savannah again. "Will you be ready for me to call you this morning for rebuttal after my cross-examination of Gentry?"

Savannah nodded.

Rather than crumble in despair, Savannah followed Sullivan back into the courtroom. Her gaze zeroed in on the bastard who'd done this and so much worse to her. She hoped her face exuded the hatred she'd harbored for him since the night he'd first molested her twenty years ago. Her glare would wither a stronger man, and the smirk that had been on his face when she first came back inside slowly waned.

This beast had stolen her innocence and her childhood and had loomed large and ominous in her nightmares ever since.

I am *strong.*

I can't *be beaten.*

In strobe-like effect, Gentry's image alternated between the younger, more vibrant man from her childhood and the old man who sat here today. For the first time since she'd escaped Gentry's house that Christmas Eve nine years ago, scared and pregnant, she was able to put the beast into realistic context. The man seated in front of her today was but a shell of that specter. He'd lost weight. His skin was sallow, almost pasty, and his hair white. Funny how being incarcerated could put a crimp in his golfing activities, ability to dye his hair, and visits to the tanning booth. He wasn't the strong and invincible man she remembered.

I will *tell my story.*

Back straight, shoulders set, she returned to her seat knowing she wasn't really alone. Her hand went to her collar, and she surrounded herself in the glow of Damián's love, training, and encouragement. She felt the warmth of Adam's paternal love and support. It was as if both men still sat right here on either side of her.

Gentry was about to discover that his years of abusing and torturing her, whether directly or by allowing others access to her body, had only made her the most formidable opponent he would ever face in this lifetime. He'd honed her into the warrior who would singlehandedly take him down. This morning, she would continue to tell her entire story, sparing no details.

Gentry would be forced to listen to her telling what happened in her voice. He'd hear her describe the unspeakable horrors he'd perpetrated on her and, if he didn't know it already, would discover how much she despised him.

If there was any justice to be had, when this trial went to the jury and judge, he'd be found guilty and receive the harshest sentence possible. With any luck, that would be one or more life sentences with no possibility of parole, and he would never experience freedom again. A small price to pay for all he'd stolen from her.

He might have thought removing her safety net would paralyze her, but the anger seething beneath the surface now would be what she needed to bring him down.

Savannah took several slow, deep breaths and prepared for the triumph to come.

I will not be beaten.

*   *   *

"You okay?" Dad asked as they sat together in the back of the deputies' SUV. The walls were closing in on him, and he couldn't help but flash back to the time he'd been hauled off to juvie after punching the crap out of Julio for beating Rosa.

"It's Savannah I'm worried about. What if she—"

"Savannah can do this. If you ask me, our being arrested is only going to increase her resolve to put that shithead away for life. That woman's tough as nails. Maybe without us being there to prop her up, she'll surprise you."

"Fuck, I know she's strong. She and I worked hard for months to prepare her for when she'd have to face that *maldito bastardo* alone on the stand. But we both expected me to be in the room to welcome her down from the witness stand with open arms. She'll have no one now."

"She knows you'll be with her in spirit. I overheard her repeating her mantra this morning. You've done all you can. Speaking of spirits, maybe say a prayer that her mom will be with her in our absence. Hell, I'll even ask Joni to be there for her in my absence. I've learned to never underestimate the power of having a loved one helping out from the other side."

Damián nodded. He'd sensed Mamá's presence over the years, and Savannah had confided that she believed her mother had visited her at the Thousand Steps Beach cave last May. Perhaps John Grainger, too. He sent up a silent plea for one or all of them to join her today, if they weren't there already.

He needed to talk about something else, or he'd go insane.

"So you're going ahead with the VIP security firm, Dad?" Damián asked, trying to focus on something else momentarily. The driver deputy glanced in the rear-view mirror, looking back and forth between the two of them as if trying to figure out their relationship. Good thing they were being careful about what they talked about. Damián knew how it was when he'd been incarcerated in juvie. Even the walls had eyes and ears.

"It looks like it. But before I decide on anything, I want to talk it over with Duncan Wilde, a Marine who runs a security agency based in Denver. His primary mission is to hire disabled vets. So I want to make sure I won't be unwanted competition for his Lost and Found Investigative Services. I respect the hell out of them and their work."

Dad rubbed the back of his neck. "And then there's Karla, who might be a tougher sell." He laughed. "But I think as long as I promise not to take on the tougher, hands-on cases, all I have to do is prove that this is the best way for us to send our kids to college. My pension sure as hell isn't going to cut it. And her indie music recordings aren't going to sell well until she's able to go on tour."

Maybe he should talk with Savannah about putting some of their newfound wealth in a college fund for the triplets, especially in case anything ever happened where Adam and Karla weren't able to pay for their college tuitions. Damián had worried about money since he was a kid, but that had changed when she'd inherited tens of millions from her mother. They chose not to live lavishly. However, providing for the best education for the next generation in the family wasn't a luxury item.

"Dad, if anything happens, Savannah and I will make sure everyone's taken care of."

Adam squeezed his shoulder. "I appreciate knowing that. Takes away a lot of stress. But as long as I'm able to provide for my family, I will."

Having exhausted this conversation, Damián nodded and leaned over to whisper, "Do you think these charges will stick?"

"Gentry's reputation will be mud after Savannah's finished with him."

If only Dad hadn't insisted on joining him in giving that bastard what he had coming. Then, at least, Dad would still be with Savannah. Damned sloppy on Damián's part. Should have taken out the trash himself.

Long stretches of desolate, scrubby, desert-like landscape whizzed by the tinted window as they sped toward San Bernardino, every mile taking him farther away from his precious *savita*.

Gentry might think he had the upper hand now, but he wasn't going to win the game. No jury could listen to Savannah's story and not be moved to convict his ass and send him straight to hell.

He hoped they'd be out of jail in time to see that happen. He wanted some satisfaction, too.

"Sorry I dragged you out here," Damián said.

"I'd like to see the day when you start telling me what to do," Adam said. "I chose to be in that courtroom."

Damián grinned. "Okay, but Karla's going to be furious when she finds out we got arrested." As far as he knew, Dad hadn't told her about what had happened last March during the aftermath of the raid.

He laughed. "When she hears, she'll probably think I went after Gentry and tried to tear him apart limb from limb in the courtroom—not that she'd blame me for doing so." Adam stared out the window a moment.

Damián grinned as he remembered the sound of Gentry's screams. While they hadn't delivered total justice, no doubt a pedophile like Gentry would get what was coming to him once he made it into the state prison system and out of the North County jail.

But his levity was short-lived. That bastard was in the room with Savannah, who now had to face him all alone.

Damn it. He should be back there with her!

Chapter Twenty-Nine

When Gentry returned to the stand, the DA asked him several innocuous things before launching into a methodical line of questioning intended to give Gentry enough rope to hang himself.

"I wanted to do something special for my daughter on her eighteenth birthday to show her how much I loved her. I pulled out all the stops," he boasted.

"You even spent a lot of money to buy her a special dress because you wanted her to look beautiful," the DA continued.

"Her dress was covered in tiny diamonds. It looked exquisite on her. Nothing was too good for my darling princess."

Savannah cringed at the word she now only associated with Damián and her daughter.

The next questions came rapid-fire. Gentry's response of *yes* sounded repeatedly.

You invited guests? Many guests? Important people? Powerful people? All of them male? Powerful men? Men who had money? Did you consider all of them your friends? All there at your invitation?

And then she started bringing out the questions he had to answer in the negative.

You did not invite any of their wives or daughters? Their girlfriends? None of Savannah's friends? No one she asked you to invite?

"She'd been tutored at home since the age of eight and had no friends, except for some business acquaintances of mine."

"No family? No friends? Doesn't that seem like an unusual guest list for a young girl's birthday?"

Gentry squirmed in his seat before settling down again. "She was going to go into business with me, so it was the right time for her to be introduced to some of the people she'd be working with."

"What was her title in your company, Mr. Gentry?"

His face grew red as he searched for some bogus title to give her, knowing full well she'd been nothing more than his slave to be handed over to his business clients and associates in hopes of making him more money with better deals.

He pulled the collar of his shirt away from his neck. "She was in new client acquisitions."

"Clerk? Associate? Manager?"

"What difference does it make what her title was?" Gentry asked testily.

"If the Court were to subpoena your accountant to produce payroll records from the year after your daughter turned eighteen, would her name be on them?"

Gentry narrowed his eyes at the DA and remained silent until prompted to answer the question by the judge. "No. She was paid in other ways."

"Savannah Gentry worked for your company for more than a year, and yet she is not listed on any payroll records for your company?"

Now he turned his venom on Savannah. Her heart nearly pounded out of her chest at the betrayal she read in his eyes. Sullivan had him cornered.

"Let's talk about how you cared for your daughter. The night of her eighteenth birthday, you said you found her in compromising positions with your partner and numerous male business associates." The DA asked the next two questions, both eliciting a *no* from Gentry. *Were you angry that your partner would betray your trust? Were you mad at those men for taking advantage of your precious daughter?* "Was Lyle still your partner or in your employ after that party?"

"Yes, until his arrest earlier this year."

"Until then, you trusted him to care for your daughter when she was in your hotel's penthouse?"

"Perhaps wrongly so, in retrospect, but yes."

The only thing that Gentry regretted about his handling of her was that Lyle had allowed Damián to take her away from the penthouse for that one perfect day at the beach cave.

"Did you or Mr. Gibson ever call security or the police on the men in the penthouse with Savannah at the hotel you owned?"

Gentry spit out, "Of course not. She met with them willingly."

"Did you monitor who came and went from that penthouse while she was there with your clients?"

"I put Lyle Gibson in charge of handling these meetings. He was always close by to keep an eye on things."

On *her*. Never the men. They could do whatever they wished to her, and he wouldn't intervene.

"So you gave your partner permission to handle these *meetings* with your daughter for years. Did you talk with Mr. Gibson on a daily basis?"

"Every weekday and sometimes weekends."

"About business?"

"Yes."

"About Savannah?"

"Not that often."

"You didn't regularly discuss Savannah's performance?"

"That was an HR matter."

Savannah had never met anyone from his human resources department in her life.

"You never told him to use her to further your business dealings?"

"Of course I did. Her job was to solidify deals with my clients, whom I knew better than Lyle did."

"Did you ever give him orders about what he should allow these clients to do to her?"

"If I thought she had something to offer to ensure the deal would happen, then yes, I discussed with Lyle what talents, er, *skills* would guarantee success."

"Did you ever order Mr. Gibson to use your daughter's body to cement business dealings with these clients?"

He glanced toward the jury box before narrowing his eyes on Savannah. "If Savannah chose to use her sexual assets to close deals, that was of her own doing." A chill crept down her spine.

"Savannah met with your business clients in the hotel penthouse?"

"It's a suite that included a receiving area with a desk and chairs. Much more economical than procuring other office space. My headquarters were filled to capacity."

"Did she meet with them willingly?"

Gentry loosened his tie and unbuttoned the top button of his shirt. A sheen of sweat dotted his forehead. The DA was literally making him sweat. This was going much better than Savannah had imagined.

"She signed a contract with my company agreeing to these responsibilities."

"Do you have a copy of this contract?"

"No. It was destroyed years ago, after she left my employ."

"Mr. Gentry, your hotel had the best security money could buy. To keep her safe. To keep her secure. And yet you allowed hotel security to show men—both familiar and unfamiliar to them, including some businessmen visiting from other countries or states—into the secluded penthouse where your daughter had been brought to await them?"

"I told you. It's where she conducted business."

Savannah swallowed, blinking away the tears at the memory of that scared, lonely girl who'd been so horribly used and abused by her father, Lyle, and the countless stream of men. How had she survived? Truthfully, she almost hadn't, if not for Damián.

"Was Savannah ever recorded in the penthouse by surveillance cameras?"

"Of course. It was added insurance that she wasn't being forced to do anything she didn't want to do. No one saw those videos except me."

"Do you still have those surveillance videos?"

His gaze bore into Savannah. "No. They were stolen when my hard drive was taken."

Up to this point, the DA hadn't wanted to bring those into court physically, but would she change her mind now that they had been brought up in testimony? Blood whooshed through her ears at the thought.

"And you never caused her bodily harm or condoned others to do so to Savannah during that year she worked for you?"

"Of course not! I loved and cherished my daughter. I provided her with everything she could want or need. A lavish home. Designer clothing. All the food she could eat. I still would if she hadn't abandoned me to become a slut for that spic she ran off with!"

Someone on the jury gasped. He'd lost his cool, forgetting the image of a respectable businessman he exuded in his expensive suit. This had to be a plus for when she gave her rebuttal, too. Sullivan was carefully closing the net that would catch the monster in all his lies.

"Let's talk about that, sir. You just said she ran off with a spic. By spic, do you mean Damián Orlando, Savannah's husband? The man who served his country honorably, lost his foot in an explosion in Iraq, and was medically discharged from the Marine Corps? That's the man you called a spic?"

"Who else? Savannah is under his control." Gentry pointed toward Savannah; everyone's focus shifted to her. "He has some kind of unhealthy power over her. Why else would she go running to his shabby dump in Colorado a year ago to shack up with him? You see how grotesquely pregnant she is with his latest brat. Yeah, he knocked her up and left her with the first bastard kid when he kidnapped her from my hotel. No wonder she had to marry him this time."

Savannah didn't flinch at his ugly accusations. *You will get to have your say next.* She rubbed her wedding band over and over, hoping to find some sense of calm. Thank God Damián wasn't here. She doubted he would care about the racial slur so much as being accused of abandoning her when he had actually tried to contact her after that day at the beach only to have Gentry intercept his notes.

"You never laid hands on her in anger? You never touched her sexually? You never raped her?"

"I spoiled my daughter, gave her everything she wanted. She loved me and showered me with affection in return."

"By sharing her bed with you?"

Gentry leaned menacingly in Sullivan's direction as if he wanted to come off the witness stand and strangle her. "Savannah and I shared a beautiful and special relationship that you couldn't possibly understand." His demeanor as a successful businessman in his expensive Italian suit was slowly being whittled away—and she hadn't even given her rebuttal yet.

Sullivan let those words hang in the air for a pregnant pause before saying, "No further questions, Your Honor." The DA took her seat. It would be Savannah's turn next, well, unless the defense asked any questions. Sullivan didn't expect Abbott to do so, and he didn't. Gentry's admissions had left him little room for damage control. Abbott would just want to uphold his reputation and ethics at this stage.

Savannah's heart jumped into her throat as Gentry stepped down, never taking his creepy, penetrating gaze off her as he walked to his seat at the defense table.

All too quickly, the judge asked Sullivan if she wished to call any rebuttal witnesses. She stood and said, "The People call Savannah Orlando to the stand."

Savannah walked forward to take her seat on the stand. Having already been sworn in, she was merely reminded of her oath, rather than having to take it over. With a sense of false bravado, she held her head higher, avoiding any glances toward Gentry's table.

Would she succeed in swaying the opinions of the jurors who might believe Gentry's narrative of lies from yesterday? She certainly hoped so.

Once seated, the DA wasted no time. "Mrs. Orlando, how would you characterize your father's relationship toward you?"

Finally, her chance to negate the lies he'd recently spun, as well as the charade that he'd perpetrated since she was eight.

"Evil. Abusive. Controlling."

"Please cite examples for why you see him that way."

"From the age of eight—the night I found him choking my mother on their bed—until I turned eighteen, he sexually molested or raped me almost daily."

A jury member gasped.

Oh, sweetheart, you haven't heard the half of it.

"Objection," said Mr. Abbott. "Permission to approach the bench, Your Honor."

Savannah overheard some of what the DA said about the defendant having opened the door with his narrative. She'd told Savannah earlier to expect this objection to be overruled, because Gentry had portrayed himself as being an exemplary father—until the point where he'd driven a tank through the door. By telling her side of the story in her rebuttal, she would finish tearing down the walls.

"Objection overruled." *As predicted.*

The attorneys returned to their places, and the DA continued. "We've heard your testimony under oath about what you witnessed happening to your mother that July night. I know this is difficult, Mrs. Orlando, but can you describe to the court what happened later that evening?"

"Yes." She swallowed, her throat suddenly dry. "I'd hidden under my bed for hours. Then my father came into my bedroom and…touched me in places he shouldn't have."

"Can you be more specific?"

"He touched my breasts and genitalia. Put his finger inside my…vagina." She almost said *pussy* but didn't think the jury would approve of her using such a vulgar term, even if her Dom preferred the term in private.

"Did he rape you?"

"No. Not that night, anyway."

"When was the first time you were raped by your father?"

Savannah wished she could call him *the defendant*, too, but didn't want to sanitize the fact that her own father did these things to his eight-year-old daughter. "A few months after Maman disappeared. I was eight." She clasped her hands together, her thumb stroking her wedding band as she tried to ground herself without going back to that night emotionally. She failed miserably, overwhelmed by images of his hands on her young body, of him forcing his huge penis inside her, of her relentless screams echoing through the room and hours of sobbing long after he'd left her.

Don't get sucked into the emotions of the past.

Damián's post-hypnotic suggestion helped calm her. She'd been much more exposed and vulnerable the night at the club on his Alive Day than she was here, albeit that night she'd been among friends, unlike today. She didn't even have Damián and Adam here for support today.

She also hadn't had Gentry's angry gaze boring into her like she did now.

Thankfully, Damián's words helped her recenter herself. As always, he'd known just what to do to prepare her for this ordeal, even if it hadn't gone as they'd planned. Savannah took a cleansing breath.

The DA asked the bailiff to republish the photo Gentry had introduced earlier and bring it to Savannah while she told the clerk the exhibit number for the record. Savannah needed no reminder. It was the "Cinderella Savannah" photo from her eighteenth birthday party standing next to the arrogant, beaming Gentry. Only this time, she noticed she was holding the rolled-up contract like a scroll or a diploma.

"Please tell the court if this is you in the photo and what the occasion was."

"Yes, that's me. I was with my father at my eighteenth birthday party, which was held at his hotel in La Jolla. We're in the ballroom overlooking the ocean." Peace and tranquility was just outside the windows of that room, only she was subjected to unspeakable acts within.

"You're smiling in the photo. Why is that?"

"Because moments before I had signed the contract I'm holding in which my father told me he was freeing me from him sexually." Another gasp from someone in the room broke into her thoughts.

"And did the rape and abuse stop?"

"Father did stop raping me, yes. But the contract wasn't as he'd described it to me when I signed. I learned later that very night, in fact, that he'd merely intended to turn me over to his business associates to let them use my body for everything they desired short of sexual penetration, in exchange for them giving my father more advantageous business deals. Later, when I was informed about what I'd signed, I realized I'd been duped."

"No one told you that such a contract could not have been upheld in any court of law in the state of California and probably anywhere else? That you didn't have to honor it?"

"No. Not until much later, after I gained my freedom, did I realize that." Would the jury penalize her for her naïveté and ignorance? "Please keep in mind I had just turned eighteen. And the decade before that had been spent having everything about my life controlled by this man. I knew nothing about what a normal father-daughter relationship looked like, much less what was or wasn't legal. I only knew what my father told me and what he did to me if I didn't obey."

"Who else signed the contract?"

"Only my father. He signed right after me." She didn't want to remember what ensued afterward, the first night in which she'd been abused by his business acquaintances.

"Not Lyle Gibson?"

"No. Only my father. But Mr. Gibson was there that night. He became my handler and made sure I kept up my contractual promises for the next year."

After the hypnosis session last night, she could now say with certainty that he hadn't signed because she'd pictured the contract perfectly. She wished the DA's office had been able to find that signed contract on the damned hard drive, instead of an unsigned copy. Perhaps the signed one no longer existed. Surely Gentry wouldn't be stupid enough to keep such evidence around all these years. After all, it wasn't for anyone's eyes but hers and Gentry's. He'd simply needed to convince a broken, terrified Savannah that he owned her—body, mind, and soul. And he succeeded—until Damián Orlando came along in the restaurant that day.

The DA nodded, glancing at her legal pad. "Please tell the court what happened after the contract had been signed—after this photo was taken."

"My father made me dance with him to celebrate." She shuddered, remembering how closely he'd held her. "A short time later, I went outside for some air, and that's when I learned that the contract wouldn't grant me my freedom in any way. Instead, it indentured me as my father's property to be used and abused by anyone he chose to allow access to me." She paused and, for the first time today, forced herself to look closely at the man who had done this to her. "That was the first night my father let other men use my body for sexual purposes."

"These men used you in what way?"

She swallowed down bile as the images from her hypnotic regression threatened to overwhelm her again.

Breathe.

Stay in the moment.

Feel, but don't get sucked into the past.

She touched the warm metal of her collar, and released some of her tension. "They drugged me and tied me down on one of the tables in the ballroom." Remembering the night at the Masters at Arms Club when she'd freaked out in the massage chair, everything suddenly became clear. The white of the dress and the semen. Being restrained while lying down must have been a trigger because of the reclining tilt of the chair. She'd flashed back to the night of her eighteenth birthday. As if this had ever been about giving her a special party or to release her from him.

"Mrs. Orlando?" the DA prompted.

Blinking back to the present, she continued. "Several men, including my father and one of the witnesses who testified for the defense earlier, took turns ejaculating on me and on that beautiful dress."

The defendant. *He was never a father to me.*

Last night, with Michelle's help, she'd remembered more about that party and now knew what had happened to the beautiful gown after the men had ripped the bodice and covered her breasts and the skirt with their semen. Gentry had made her wear it home, although he'd covered her breasts in his suitcoat so that the hotel staff wouldn't suspect what had happened that night on the premises. The moment she was alone at home, she'd ripped the rest of it to shreds, never wanting to see it again. Had Gentry retrieved it and kept it as some disgustingly twisted trophy? Did he have someone clean the gauzy skirt and cut the diamonds off? She couldn't picture him throwing away that much money.

"What other acts were done to you that night? Take your time, Mrs. Orlando."

Savannah knew the DA was trying to help her set the record straight, and no one wanted to spell out what monstrous things Gentry had done to her, but Savannah also wanted this to be over.

Reminding herself she still had a story to tell, she composed herself.

I will not be beaten.

Chapter Thirty

Savannah described what she recalled, most of it only coming back as a result of last night's session. After fifteen or twenty minutes, the DA seemed satisfied that they'd gone into enough detail.

"Were any consequences laid out for what would happen to you if you failed to sign the contract?"

She shuddered. This she'd remembered all along, without the benefit of hypnosis. "My father told me that he would sell me to a street pimp in San Francisco." She almost laughed at thinking this was her greatest fear at the age of eighteen. So naive.

"How long did you have to endure the terms of this contract?"

"While there was no end date on the contract, I had to endure this treatment for a little more than a year, until I was able to escape from my father's house."

"Tell us a little about what that year involved."

"As I said, Lyle Gibson enforced my father's contract," she added. Lyle certainly was no innocent bystander in what had been done to her during that time. "He made the arrangements for my body to be used by the men Father told him he wanted to make business deals with. Mr. Gibson then videotaped those sessions for Father to watch later."

"Please tell the court if there were any consequences for not following through with the requests made by your father and his clients over the course of that year?"

"Mr. Gibson would remind me every time I was to meet with clients what my father would do if I messed up and lost them both money. The threat of being sold as a sex slave was always foremost among their threats."

"What are some of the other tactics used to gain your acquiescence?"

"I would be locked in my room, although that was actually a reprieve for me. Still, at those times, my father would withhold food from me."

"Did your father follow through on any other specific threats?"

"Yes. With the help of Mr. Gibson, he would beat me if I didn't perform to his expectations. Those beatings escalated in severity throughout that year."

"Do any of these beatings stand out in your memory?"

"All of them do, but the worst came the night my now-husband rescued me from the two men from Tokyo."

"Mrs. Orlando, please tell the court what happened nine years ago, on September 29, in the penthouse of your father's hotel in La Jolla."

"I overheard my father that morning instructing Lyle to allow the clients to go further than any had done before. I was being punished for something. I don't remember what now." She had no recollection other than that threat and not knowing what it would mean. She hadn't revealed to the DA that he'd branded her to prepare her for these sick bastards, either. While that brand no longer had any power over her, she needed to tell the court about it so they could understand Gentry's depravity.

Her heart beat harder. She reached for a bottle of water and twisted off the cap. After downing it in just a few swallows, she closed her eyes and took a deep breath. Maybe it still held a little more power than she wanted to admit. "I should back up a couple of weeks. In preparation for my being used by these two potential business associates, they…" She glanced over at the jury box. Every face was riveted on her testimony. In the gallery, the room was packed. There were even a few people standing, all waiting to hear every sordid detail.

The DA prompted quietly, "What did they do to you, Savannah?"

"My father branded me."

A collective gasp tore through the room, and someone whispered loudly, "My God!" Many on the jury turned to Gentry as if to read his face and try and tell whether she was being truthful. She couldn't look at him. Didn't want to think about that any longer.

"Where did he brand you?"

She swallowed hard, her face growing wet with perspiration and perhaps some tears. "On my labia." The words came out in a near whisper. "I later learned the brand had partly been done to please these two clients from Tokyo. They must have been extremely important to my father's business. I do remember them taking photographs of the brand."

Ropes. Quirt. Electricity.

"Can you describe the brand?"

"Interlocking letters, my father's initials, GG."

Good girl. Damián's good girl.

"What did those clients do to you that night?"

"I was there to be acted upon. They tied me to the bed, completely immobilized. *Against* my will," she added, facing Gentry, venom erupting from within her for all he'd done to her. Yet his breathing had become faster. He licked his lips, and she nearly threw up to think that he seemed to be getting turned on to hear the details. Was it because she'd deprived him of watching the video of that particular session more than once or twice because she'd stolen the hard drive? What a twisted piece-of-shit bastard.

"What did Gentry's clients do to you with his permission?"

"They used a quirt as a warm-up and then later what I learned was called a violet wand."

"Please describe the quirt and violet wand for those unfamiliar with them." the DA inquired.

She wasn't here to testify as a BDSM expert and wondered if her knowledge of such things would taint her reputation with the jury, but they didn't know she lived a lifestyle that used such equipment in much more pleasant ways. She did want the jury to understand the terms in order to better picture what had happened to her.

"The quirt is like a riding crop, only with a smaller handle and with two falls or lashes at the tip. The violet wand is an electrical device used to stimulate nerve endings on various parts of the skin or as conducted through metal." *And in the hands of my Dom, it's delicious.* "The smaller the tip, the more painful it becomes. My father and Lyle used a particularly small metal tip on the violet wand to brand me."

Savannah's chest tightened as she remembered more of the conversation she'd overheard that morning Damián had rescued her. The floodgates seemed to have opened up since her hypnosis session.

"Earlier that day, Father told Lyle to let these two men do anything they wished short of vaginal penetration. This was a new development. In the past, no penetration whatsoever had been permitted."

"How did you interpret this change?"

"I assumed it meant I would have to do oral, but I wasn't sure what other penetration Gentry was allowing." Would they have raped her anally if Damián hadn't come in to save her?

Oh, Damián, I wish you were here with me now.

But suddenly, she realized she was doing better than she'd expected to. *You're the strongest woman I know.* She hadn't believed his words before but now saw she was going to get through this and be even stronger for having faced Gentry once and for all.

"What made you trust Damián Orlando enough to leave the hotel with him the next morning?"

She touched her collar and smiled. "He ran off the clients, stood up to Mr. Gibson, and stayed with me overnight to protect me at a time when I was at my most vulnerable. Unlike all the men in my past—he spent time with me without demanding or taking anything *from* me."

"What happened next?"

"We spent the day together. He took me to his favorite beach, which also happened to be the one where my mother took me on our last day together. But that night, Damián unknowingly brought me back to my father's home thinking I'd be safe there."

"Did you tell Mr. Orlando what had been going on in your home since you were eight?"

She glanced down at her hands and saw two of her fingers were bleeding. "No." The words barely made it out of her constricting throat.

"Why not?"

"Shame. Fear." She met the DA's gaze again. "Fear not only for myself, but for what they might do to Damián, who was an employee at my father's hotel."

"What happened after you went inside the house that night?"

"Both my father and Lyle were waiting and furious that I had failed to serve my father's clients the night before in the penthouse. They took me to Father's office and took turns holding me down and beating me. When one grew too exhausted to continue, they switched places." Both men enjoyed her struggles and exerting their dominance over her.

"I was tortured that night as well." She refused to let her sadistic father get off hearing her explicitly describe the acts, though.

Gentry shoved his legal pad at his attorney, pointing to something he'd written, but Abbot made no objection.

"Please tell the court in what ways the defendant tortured you that night."

Saying she'd been tortured wasn't enough? *Thank God Damián wasn't in the room to hear these things.*

Savannah drew a deep breath, forcing her mind to remain in the present rather than relive these memories. "They knew how I felt about the violet wand after they'd used it to brand me a few weeks earlier. Just the sound of it terrified me. That night, they took turns holding it next to my ears and making it sizzle and crackle to heighten my fears and elicit more screams during this particular beating. Unlike past ones, this time they not only inflicted extreme pain and bruising, but broke the skin on my back, buttocks, and legs. They inflicted so many gashes that they needed to wait for me to heal before hooking me up with clients again. But I ran away before they could send me back to the penthouse." At least she hadn't had to be with clients again for the duration of her time under his rule.

"After that night, were you ever again forced to serve your father's clients?"

"No."

"Why not?"

"I'd been beaten so badly that I couldn't walk for weeks. The lacerations and severe bruising were visible six to eight weeks later. Perhaps they didn't want to have a client alert authorities to abuse." As if these clients had any ounce of human decency in them. In the end, it was a blessing.

"Objection. Speculation.

"Sustained."

"What kept you from seeing the defendant's clients after you healed?"

"I pretended to be more debilitated than I was for a month or so after I'd healed. Then I was able to find the strength to escape on Christmas Eve that year." All because of Damián's precious gift to her—Mari.

"How were you able to endure all these years of torture and abuse, Mrs. Orlando?"

She sobered, pausing a moment to gather her words. "I'm not sure. I almost didn't survive it. Before meeting those last clients, I had made the decision to take my own life as soon as I returned to the house." She'd had nothing to lose or to live for then.

"What stopped you from committing suicide?"

"Partly, meeting Damián Orlando and his kindness to me, but it also took me a little while to sort out what my future could hold if I was to escape. During those initial weeks after the beating, I'd been barely able to get out of bed, much less follow through on a suicide plan." She chose not to mention her pregnancy, not wanting those listening to cheapen what she and Damián had shared that day.

"Then memories of my day with Damián seeped back into my consciousness." Savannah smiled and glanced at her wedding band, thinking of the man who'd become her rock. "I'd never met anyone like him, a man who showed respect for me and my body."

Returning her gaze to the DA, she added, "It had been so long since I'd seen even a glimpse of humanity. Having seen that decent people existed in the world, I chose life and ran away from my father's house, taking refuge at a church in Solana Beach. I didn't return until I was kidnapped this past March."

The DA let the words sink in a moment. "No further questions, Your Honor." The DA took her seat.

"Does the defense wish to cross-examine the witness?"

When Abbott made no move to stand and go to the podium, Gentry began whispering frantically at him. He stabbed the legal pad in front of him where she'd seen Gentry scribbling notes during her testimony the few times she'd looked his way.

"No questions, Your Honor."

Gentry's face grew a mottled red as he stared in her direction. She didn't break eye contact with him, standing up to him without cowering, until the judge said, "The witness is excused."

She took a deep, cleansing breath, stood, and started back to her seat. It was over. At last.

Gentry continued to stare her down as she returned to the gallery, a last-ditch attempt to make her believe he still had power over her. But those days were gone. He meant nothing to her. As soon as she could get out of the courtroom, she'd drive to San Bernardino and put today's ordeal behind her. She also couldn't wait to tell Damián and Adam how she'd done. Adam wasn't just her husband's surrogate dad but also the only man who'd ever been a real father to her.

Gentry would have no control over her body or mind ever again.

She'd faced down the monster who had made her cower in fear so many nights—and days. And she'd won.

She wasn't certain if the final words the jury heard from her would be enough to sway their opinions, or if some would discount her testimony altogether because of the way Gentry had tarnished her image with his lies. But with an oddly relieved heart, Savannah returned to her seat in the gallery.

Alone. If Damián had been here, she might have collapsed against him in tears of relief and joy. Instead, she held her head up and stared down the man she'd once called her father.

She'd handled herself fairly well throughout the trial, only losing her shit—well, her lunch—once during the trial. How would the jurors read her responses? Too much emotion? Not enough? Ice princess? Wounded princess?

She sagged against the back of the chair, suddenly spent. She needed a break but didn't want to miss any of the proceedings.

As if the judge had heard her silent plea, he adjourned for fifteen minutes. Savannah was out of the courtroom in a flash. After taking care of her primary need, she walked over to the sink to wash her hands. Then she wet a paper towel with cold water, dabbing it on her face to cool down.

Staring at herself in the mirror, she was surprised to see that the eyes staring back at her weren't those of a victim but of a victor. She'd stared down the evil that had fathered her and won.

Now her thoughts turned to where Adam and Damián were. She hadn't been able to think much about what they were going through today but hoped they were being treated with the respect American veterans and heroes deserved.

They'd understand that she'd needed to keep her focus on what was happening in this courtroom. As soon as possible, she'd head to San Bernardino.

Back in the courtroom moments later, the judge asked, "Do the People wish to call any other rebuttal witnesses?"

"Yes, Your Honor, but he isn't available this morning. I wonder if we might adjourn until after lunch. I will make every effort to have him transported here by then."

Who was she talking about? When the DA had told her this would be the end of her going up on the stand, Savannah had assumed that also meant the end of testimony and rebuttals. Apparently not.

"Who is the witness?" the judge asked.

"Lyle Gibson."

Her heart jumped into her throat. Again? There was plenty more he could testify about, but much of it would incriminate him, too. However, he'd already incriminated himself earlier in the trial by describing his part in the night Maman and John were murdered. That he'd been in her father's life that far back had surprised Savannah, who didn't remember him before the year he'd been her handler. He had to know any number of other secrets he could tell. What were the chances he'd be honest?

If the DA was calling him, did that mean he'd agreed to corroborate some of the things Savannah had refuted on Gentry's account? Only time would tell.

But first, she had some things to take care of during the lunch break to expedite getting Damián and Adam out of jail as early as possible, so she hurried out the moment court went into recess.

Chapter Thirty-One

After the court adjourned for the day five hours later, pride and self-confidence swelled in Savannah's chest as she descended the courthouse steps and made her way to the rental vehicle. She'd proven to herself today that she could stare down George Gentry and eviscerate him—alone—without letting him make her cower in fear. She'd never want to go through that again, but knowing she could if need be was empowering. Gentry thought he'd destroyed her safety net by having Damián and Adam arrested and removed from the court today. But he would fail due to Damián's and her preparation for the trial.

The look on Gentry's face when she refuted his fictional version of what had happened on her eighteenth birthday, as well as the other lies in his testimony, was priceless. If steam could have poured from his eyes and ears, it would have. Savannah smiled. A great weight had been lifted off her. She felt like Mulan after a decisive battle.

You can never hurt me again.

Even now, her mind reeled from what Lyle had revealed in his rebuttal this afternoon. She couldn't wait to tell Damián, but her focus had shifted to getting Damián and Adam out of jail.

During the lunch break, she'd called an attorney to make them an appointment for tomorrow. At the advice of the office's paralegal, she'd transferred twenty-five thousand dollars from savings to her checking account to cover their expected bonds. Savannah wanted them out of there—tonight. She'd also grabbed a quick bite knowing Damián wouldn't be happy with her if she skipped a meal.

Finally making her way north, using the hands-free Bluetooth in the SUV, she'd called the attorney's office once more to check on things.

Damián and Adam still hadn't been booked, due to a large number of arrests today. The paralegal on the phone assured her she could post bond after hours, just as soon as they were assigned booking numbers. But she wouldn't be able to see them until they were released.

Today had been one of the longest days of her life. Yes, she'd endured far worse in the past, but that was before Damián had become such an important part of her life. Tonight, she needed Damián's arms wrapped around her while lying in their bed at Camp Pendleton. If ever she expected the return of her nightmares, it would be on this night. The shadowy memories that had been lurking at the edges of her memory these past months—and for years before that—had taken shape and been unleashed full force.

Not to mention that the trial wasn't over yet. But they were so close.

Once again, she turned her thoughts to what Damián and Adam had faced today. Damián hadn't shared a lot about his juvenile detention incarceration with her, but today had to have brought up some bad memories for him.

If she was able to bail them out tonight, they could be back in the courtroom with her tomorrow morning for closing statements.

The San Bernardino criminal defense attorney she'd hired had given them an appointment for late tomorrow afternoon. She hoped the jury in Gentry's trial would be in deliberations by then so she could join them.

And God willing, she'd be in the courtroom to see his face when the verdict was read. She should call the DA to find out more about what to expect in the coming days, but right now, her focus needed to be on her husband and Adam.

She was ready for it all to be over so they could go home. She'd never been apart from Marisol this long. While their evening video chats helped, it just wasn't the same.

Parking as close as possible to the Central Detention Center, she followed the paralegal's advice and stowed her cell phone, along with Adam's and Damián's, in the glove compartment before waddling to the judicial center and up the stairs as quickly as a woman eight months along could.

She cleared security quickly, but Damián and Adam still hadn't been booked.

The security person who checked her bag said they would be in a holding pod with other unprocessed detainees until booked. She hoped they were at least together so they could provide moral support for one another.

Her heart ached for them. Especially for Damián, who would be beside himself worrying about her and have not a care at all for the legal problems the two of them faced. She wanted to put Damián's mind at ease and begged the clerk to pass along a handwritten message to him but was told it was against protocol.

Determined not to return to San Diego County without them, she took a seat on a bench near the metal detector entrance to wait. Surely they'd be booked soon.

"Ms. Orlando."

After waiting forty-five minutes, she turned toward the desk to see who had called her name. The young woman smiled sympathetically, probably only seeing the poor pregnant woman waiting to bail out her husband. While Savannah needed no one's pity, this woman stood between her and Damián, so she returned the smile.

"Yes?" she asked, returning to the desk.

"Mr. Orlando and Mr. Montague have been booked." She jotted down some numbers on a pad of paper, tore the top sheet off, and handed it to Savannah. "Here are their booking numbers. Take this to the clerk's office and you can post bail."

Adam's bail had been less than Damián's, but after giving the woman in the clerk's office her driver's license and a personal check to cover both of them, she was told to have a seat again to wait for their release.

Anxious to be reunited with Damián, she kept her eye on the door she expected them to come through any moment.

*   *   *

Damián had gone through several scenarios today of how Savannah's rebuttal might have gone. Was she okay? And what about the baby? He should have been there to protect them both, to rub the stress out of Savannah's back and neck before and after she went on the stand, to support her from across the room as she took down the *maldito bastardo*.

If anything happened to her or the baby, he'd rip Gentry's fucking balls off this time and cram them down his goddamned throat.

"Stop worrying," Dad said. "Savannah's strong. And smart. She won't do anything to jeopardize this pregnancy or the case against Gentry."

Damián glanced over at him. Guilt over dragging Adam into this ate at him, too. "You ought to be home with Karla and the babies, not holed up in this detention bay with me."

"Stop worrying about me, too," Dad said quietly. "Think of the stories we can tell our friends when we see them again. Two married guys don't usually get this much excitement in their lives."

"I could do with a lot less excitement." He ran his hand thru his hair and loosened it from its tie. "I don't see how you can make light of this," he whispered. "What if that bastard succeeds in putting us both away?"

"Who would a jury believe? A soon-to-be-convicted double murderer or two U.S. Marine heroes?"

Damián grew even more serious. "I don't feel like much of a hero today. I should be with Savannah." He didn't want to say anything incriminating in here, but it had been his idea to torture Gentry that day. If their cases went to trial, he'd take the heat for it.

"Neither one of us is going to be convicted for something we didn't do." Thankfully, Dad was aware of the potential for jailhouse snitches and spies and wasn't admitting anything. "Gentry filed these asinine charges because he wanted us out of the way so he could torment Savannah again. What evidence would he possibly have?"

Damián nodded. He couldn't picture Gentry presenting his mangled balls as evidence, so what could he possibly have on them? And even if he did bare it all, he'd have to prove they'd been the ones to do it.

He'd wasted enough time on Gentry's sorry ass. "How do you think she held up?"

"Knowing Savannah, she cut him off at the knees."

Damián grinned at the image. "Sure hope so."

"Montague, Orlando," came the voice of the detention guard. He opened the bay door and waited for them.

What now?

"You've both been bailed out and are free to go. Just be sure to return for your preliminary arraignment hearings Monday."

Savannah!

They gathered their belongings from where they'd been secured, dressed, and were shown the exit.

Damián scanned the waiting area until he saw Savannah sitting alone nibbling on her lower lip. When she glanced toward him, her eyes brightened with unshed tears, and her face lit with a tremulous smile. She looked fragile, yet there was an air of confidence he hadn't seen before. Or was it relief? He raced across the room to her and wrapped her in his arms.

"I've missed you so much, *bebé*." He couldn't wait to ask how it went today, but right now, he needed to hold her. They'd only been apart for ten hours, but every minute seemed like days.

Reluctantly, he took her by the arms and put some distance between them so he could look at her. "Are you okay?" They laughed when they realized they'd both asked the same question. "You first," he said.

"I'm fine. I just want to get out of here so we can talk."

"That sounds like a great idea," Adam said from behind him. "Let's go."

Adam had them ensconced in the backseat together within five minutes while he drove toward the base. Savannah, next to Damián, rested her head on his shoulder; he slid his arm around her back to pull her body closer.

"Tell me everything, *querida*." He placed his palm against her belly. "How's the baby? What happened after we left?"

"I gave my rebuttal." She sat up straighter, beaming at him. "I didn't break down. Not once."

Damn. "I wish I could have been there to watch you take him down."

"No regrets, sweetheart. It wasn't your fault you weren't there, and to be honest, I actually think I needed to face Gentry by myself like this. Yes,

I was terrified out of my skull." She held up her hand and pointed to her wedding band in the dim light. "Look at how I mangled your family heirloom trying to remain grounded the way you taught me by rubbing my ring." She gave a lopsided grin and a shrug.

"I'll fix it when we get home." He clasped her hand in his, pulling it against her baby bump under his hand to connect their circle. "*Jesús*, you sure squeezed the hell out of it." He chuckled so she wouldn't think he was upset about the ring.

"But it did its job, Damián. I didn't even realize it was bent until the drive up here. But it kept me in the moment. I remembered everything we'd worked on, and I stayed calm. I told my story! All of it."

His chest nearly burst with pride for his warrior *princesa* and her increased strength.

"At first, I avoided making eye contact with Gentry. Then something clicked into place. I stared him down as I told what happened. Damián, I actually saw fear on his face at one point. Imagine, Gentry afraid of *me* for a change! The power shift was monumental. I held all the cards for the first time…ever."

"I wish I could have seen it, but I'm so proud of you, *bebé*!"

"Oh, Damián, it was so freeing to confront him after all these years. And to come out the winner? Priceless. At least, I hope the jury sends his ass to prison for the rest of his life after all they've seen and heard. You should have seen him practically go after Sullivan at one point. That woman has some definite Domme tendencies, if you ask me."

"I'm so fucking proud of you, *querida*. You're one kickass opponent."

"Let's just say I wiped the smirk off his face that had been there since he'd gotten you and Adam arrested. I refused to back away from the ugly details, too. And the session last night made it so much easier for me to provide realistic details to this sordid birthday party. Oh, and then there's Lyle!"

Fuck. She'd had to face both those dicks today?

What had she endured alone while he sat in jail unable to help? "Why was he called back in there?"

"After I finished my rebuttal, Lyle took the stand again and gave his rebuttal, refuting many of the things Gentry had lied about concerning him, too."

"Did he disrespect you in any way? Because if he did…"

She shook her head. "I'll admit that, at first, having to share air space with him again so soon left me in a sheer panic." She swallowed. "But you'll never believe what evidence Lyle's been sitting on all these years."

"What?"

"He produced the signed, original contract in which my father had spelled out all the evil things he was going to allow his associates to do to me."

"Where'd he been keeping that piece of evidence?"

"His lawyer's office. I guess he knew he'd need collateral when dealing with someone as ruthless as Gentry." She swallowed before continuing. "He even told the court he had audiotapes of several incriminating conversations with my father in which Gentry instructed Lyle as to what he was or wasn't supposed to let the clients do to me. It was pretty clear he hadn't been as clueless of what was going on as he tried to let on in his earlier testimony."

"Shit. Never thought I'd have anything good to say about Gibson, but good thing he didn't trust Gentry." The two had been thick as thieves for more than a decade, but apparently neither one trusted the other.

She smiled brightly. "I stared both of them down. At one point, Lyle even stumbled on his testimony, because I actually intimidated *him*, too." She giggled, and he couldn't help but relax with a smile of his own.

Her eyes opened wider. "Oh, wait! How could I forget! Remember how I was given some kind of white pill the night of the birthday debacle?"

"Yeah."

"Lyle testified that it was Ecstasy. So that explains the burning sensation and my acting wildly out of character that night."

Fuck them both. He hoped their time in prison ended with them being the bitches to their worst nightmares for what they'd done to a sweet, innocent girl. "Even though you didn't need us, I'm still pissed I didn't get to watch you in action."

Sitting in the drive-through lane to pick up a late dinner, Dad turned around to Savannah, saying, "Told that husband of yours to stop worrying. Let me go on the record, too. Hon, I'm proud as hell of what you accomplished today."

"Damián made me stronger, Adam. Made me believe in myself."

Damián and Dad both shook their heads.

"No, *bebé*, you've always been incredibly strong. All I did was help you find focus and to overcome feeling exposed in front of strangers when sharing your story."

"Don't be modest. You taught me I can control my fear and how much power, if any, I'm willing to allow others to have over me." She stroked his arm, needing even more closeness with him tonight. "You also helped me find my voice, Damián. Without that night at the club on your Alive Day and the countless reminders to ground myself in the moment, I don't know that I could have done it otherwise. Stop beating yourself up about not being there. You can't help that Gentry filed trumped up charges against you two."

Damián turned to glance out the window as Dad pulled into a parking spot. But she was too astute to miss his avoidance tactic.

"*Did* you two do what he accused you of?"

He opened his door and helped her out. "We'll talk about this tonight." Wanting to shift the focus back to her, once inside the elevator, he turned to her. "I'll never forget how you showed that *cabrón* what you're made of, *querida*. I'm so fucking proud of you."

"Will one or both of you ever tell me what exactly happened after my rescue?"

They exchanged glances again before Damián shrugged. "Let's just say we made sure he wouldn't rape anyone else for as long as he lived."

Her eyes opened wide as saucers as she looked from one to the other then a slow smile curved her lips. "Thank you." She gave them both a hug, kissing Dad on the cheek and Damián on the lips. "I'm behind you both a hundred percent. Whatever you choose to do, I'll be there for you the way you've been there for me."

Dios, could he love this woman any more than he did in this moment?

Chapter Thirty-Two

The closing statements were given Friday morning, revealing no surprises. While the jury deliberated, Savannah, Adam, and Damián met with their defense attorney in the afternoon. The attorney mostly rattled off routine procedural information about what to expect at Monday's arraignment. Sounded like it could be months before they'd need to come back to face charges. The attorney assured them she'd probably be able to plea to lesser charges, but both men wanted to plead not guilty at Monday's arraignment. She vowed to work hard to have the charges dropped or reduced before they would go to trial.

"After the holidays," the lawyer began, "I'll approach the DA's office in San Bernardino. By then, Gentry's verdicts will have come down and sentencing will have taken place. I'll see what I can do to get the charges dismissed.

"Sounds good," Adam said. "We'd appreciate anything you can do to make that happen."

With Christmas only ten days away, the three spent most of Saturday shopping for Marisol and the triplets. Adam decided they were so close to the trial's end that he would just wait and fly back with them after the verdict came in.

Adam had to be missing Karla and his kids as much as she and Damián missed Marisol. They'd practically cleaned out the MCX at Pendleton, knowing they couldn't get prices like those back in Denver.

Then there was the Corps factor. Savannah found a T-shirt for Marisol that read: *Marines make the best daddies*. She had to get it but didn't want Damián to see it ahead of time. Pulling on Adam's sleeve, she whispered when he leaned down, "Could you create a diversion so I can buy this without him seeing?"

"Sure thing." He looked for Damián's whereabouts and glanced out the windows. Adam smiled, took Damián by the arm, and pointed outside. "Hey, son, remember those days?"

Damián groaned. "Don't remind me, I had the hardest time learning to tie the double fisherman's knot, and that's the one the instructors always demanded of me."

Curious herself when she should be taking advantage of the subterfuge, Savannah looked outside to see a group of Marines running along the street with rope bundled at their lower backs.

"Did you guys keep a list of our weaknesses or something?"

Adam's laugh carried through the store as she hurried to the counter to pay for that and an adorable jumpsuit for the baby with a cover—as Damián called his cap. It was a miniature replica of a Marine's dress blues. She couldn't wait to see it on the baby—boy or girl.

Shopping had given her a mental break from the trial, but her stress returned as they sat over lunch at Iron Mike's SNCO Lounge. The beautiful views of the Pacific Ocean captivated her until she began kneading the muscles in her lower back to relieve some cramping that had begun in the past hour.

"You okay, *querida*?"

"Just some back pain. Not as bad as with Marisol, annoying nonetheless."

"Why don't we head back to the lodge after this?" Damián asked. "I can give you a massage."

Savannah smiled at him. "Sounds divine. I think I'm shopped out anyway. I can order the rest of the presents online this weekend and probably still get them in time."

Her belly suddenly became hard again, and she pushed the rest of her meal away. This one seemed more intense than the Braxton-Hicks contractions she'd been having for months. Wiping her mouth, she set the napkin beside her plate. "I need to make a pit stop before we head back."

But when she tried to stand, the intense pain in her pelvis nearly took her breath away. Seeing her wince, Adam and Damián both jumped up to help her. The abdominal cramping wasn't letting up, either.

"You okay, *bebé?*"

Unable to speak, she nodded, but when she attempted to stand upright again, a stitch in her side doubled her over.

"Sit down, hon," Adam said, guiding her back into the chair.

"Should we call a doctor?" the server asked.

Shaking her head, she gritted out, "No. I just stood up too fast." Only it didn't feel like the usual stitches she got from doing so in the past.

"Call her an ambulance," Damián told the server who hurried away. "*Querida*, we're going to the emergency department to get you checked out."

Adam threw some bills on the table to cover lunch and the tip. "Hang on, hon. We'll have you checked out in no time."

"But it can't be that. It's too early!" Why was this happening now? The worst of the trial stress was over. They'd been enjoying a quiet lunch together. She had no warning signs for premature labor, but what if the baby came now?

"Eyes."

Nearly paralyzed with fear, she didn't respond until Damián cupped her chin and forced her to face him. "Slow, deep breaths, *querida*." Until he mimicked what he wanted her to do, she had no clue.

"Breathe in," he continued to coach. She did. "Breathe out."

In. Out. Damián continued to breathe with her. With each respiration cycle, she became more relaxed. She couldn't keep the baby inside her if she lost her shit.

By the time the paramedics arrived at the restaurant and began checking her vitals and asking questions, she'd mostly calmed down. While Damián stepped back to let them do their work, she kept her eyes on him, more as a comfort than because he hadn't released her from the Dom command yet.

In a matter of minutes, she was lying on her left side on a stretcher with her head tilted at a comfortable angle being transported to the nearby Naval Hospital Camp Pendleton.

The contractions—she couldn't pretend they were anything else—

were nine minutes apart. Surely they would be able to stop them. "I'm only at thirty-five weeks," she reminded the paramedic seated beside Damián.

"Don't worry, Savannah. This hospital is the best. They'll take good care of you and your baby."

He made it sound like she was having this baby now, but no way could that happen! She turned to Damián and, for the first time, saw a glimmer of worry in his eyes.

Please, get us to the hospital faster.

* * *

This can't be happening! One minute, they're enjoying lunch, and the next, Savannah might be in labor. Damián held onto her hand in the labor room she'd been taken to almost immediately. Another contraction started showing on the monitor.

"Eyes. Breathe with me, *bebé.*" Thank God they'd taken a few child-birth preparation classes, or he wouldn't have known what to do as her coach. How long before the doctor showed up? He wished they were back in Denver where Doctor Palmer could take care of her. She knew everything about Savannah's pregnancy. To her credit, she'd already forwarded the medical records to the hospital so the obstetrician here would be able to have all the information at his or her fingertips.

The labor and delivery nurse had checked her out and said there was no sign that her water had broken and she was only one centimeter dilated. When the doctor showed up, he assured them that, as long as she didn't dilate farther, they didn't think she would deliver. He ordered some IV fluids with medication to help stop contractions and, as a precaution, some other meds to help develop the baby's lungs, just in case she did deliver this weekend.

Shit just got too real, too fast. Seeing Savannah lying there made him feel so helpless, but there wasn't anything he could do but hold her hand, brush the hair from her forehead, and talk with her. Only he didn't know what to say, so he lowered his head to the bed beside her hip and prayed.

Por favor, Dios…

"I think the contractions stopped," Savannah said, and he jerked up his head to make eye contact with her. Her nurse stood beside the bed checking her vitals.

Had he fallen asleep? What the fuck? Savannah had her hand woven through his hair. He glanced over at the monitor. "Are you sure?"

She nodded and smiled. "It's been almost an hour, and I haven't felt any more."

"I think you're right, Mrs. Orlando," the nurse said as she checked the monitors, "but we'll want to keep an eye on you for the next twenty-four hours before releasing you."

After the nurse left, he placed his hand on her belly. "I'll stay with you, *bebé*, and I promise not to fall asleep again."

Her sweet laugh absolved him. "You didn't fall asleep until the contractions stopped—and I'll admit that I dozed off, too. You helped keep me calm just being here with me."

Maybe he'd been of some help. *But fuck*. He'd better be more present when they were dealing with actual labor. He couldn't let her down.

"I want to go home."

He glanced over at the monitor. "The nurse said tomorrow afternoon."

"No, I mean *our* home. Denver. Right after your arraignment hearings Monday, let's leave."

"What about the jury and hearing the verdicts read?"

"I don't care anymore. I've gotten my satisfaction, as you Marines like to say." She smiled. "Telling my story in front of Gentry and the jury was what my soul needed most. I've done all I can do to find justice for my mother, Grainger, and myself. I'm ninety-nine percent certain he'll be found guilty, but if he isn't, then I want to be far away from him when he's set free. It's over, Sir."

He hoped she wouldn't regret the decision but was glad she wanted to go home, too. "Whatever you want to do, you know I'm totally behind you."

"Obviously, being out here isn't good for me or the baby anymore." She placed a hand on the baby bump and interlaced her fingers in his.

Dios, they *had* come close to disaster today.

"Besides, nothing pisses off narcissists like Gentry more than indifference and having people ignore them." She grinned. "So regardless of the outcome, I'll extract a little more vengeance simply by going home before the jury returns a verdict and not giving him another chance to glare at me or try to upset me, not that he could win that battle anymore. I don't think I'll sway the jury with my absence. At least, not if they come up with a decision before they return to the courtroom."

He turned his head to kiss the palm of her hand. "Okay, I'll go find Dad and ask him to get us on the earliest flight possible after our Monday morning arraignment hearing. You need your rest most of all."

"Hand me my purse, please, and I'll leave the DA a message explaining what happened. I'm sure she can excuse my absence from the sentencing phase. If my rebuttal and testimony didn't tell the judge and jury how adversely affected my life has been because of that monster, then nothing will."

He stood and leaned over her, their gazes locking. "You continue to amaze me, woman." He kissed her gently on the lips, afraid anything else might trigger another contraction. "I can't wait to see what the next eighty years with you will be like."

Savannah laughed. "Me neither!"

"Just expect me to still be chasing you around the house, or wherever we're living then, to get into your panties."

"I'd be disappointed if you weren't, Sir."

Chapter Thirty-Three

Savannah fluffed up her Christmas Barbie's dress, fighting the bombardment of memories from the morning she'd received this doll from Maman. She was supposed to be wrapping presents for Mari, José, and Teresa, but her attention kept wandering back to the doll that had miraculously found its way back into her possession after all these years. She planned to give her a place of honor on the mantel this year but didn't want to part with her just yet. Holding the Barbie made her feel Maman's presence again.

"This is the last of it," Damián said as he entered the room carrying a pile of games and toys they'd hidden in the closet over the past few months whenever they'd found something for one of the kids. Well, mostly Marisol and José. Teresa had outgrown toys, so hers came in smaller packages these days. "I'll help you wrap, if you'd like. But don't expect mine to look as pretty as yours."

She smiled at him in his ridiculous Santa hat with *Feliz Navidad* printed in glitter around the white band. "No, I can manage. I've just been daydreaming." She set the doll up on the mantel next to a clear bowl filled with colorful glass ornaments. "Between the trial aftermath and staring at this doll, my concentration skills are nil. So you get the job of thwacking me with your evil stick, Sir, every time my focus wanders from my task at hand."

"I think I'll be the one to decide the implement, *savita*." Despite his stern Dom voice, he grinned and winked, a salacious gleam in his eye. "But you don't have to ask me twice to assert my responsibilities as your Dom."

She didn't intend to let her mind wander anymore, because she seriously didn't care much for that evil thing, which made it the perfect deterrent.

Chiquita nuzzled at her ankle. The dog had been very clingy since they'd returned from California. Savannah indulged her with some extra love, digging her fingers into the fur on Chiquita's head and massaging it much the way she loved having Damián do hers.

"Tell me what else I can do to speed things along? I don't want you up all night wrapping presents."

"You could grab me another roll of superhero paper for the rest of José's presents."

He went to the upright plastic bin that held wrapping paper for all occasions and brought her the roll she'd requested before sitting down beside her. "I'll help hold down the paper while you tape it shut."

They worked in silence a while before her gaze wandered to the Barbie doll again. Maman's smile had been so wide that last Christmas together when Savannah had opened that present—

Snap.

A sting against her upper arm brought her instantly back to the present. "Ow!" She reached up to rub the spot where Damián had flicked her with his middle finger.

"I had to improvise since I don't have the evil stick on me."

"Oh, I already forgot." *Be careful what you ask for, Savannah.* "Sorry, Sir. I promise to stay focused from now on." Maybe if she kept him busy, he wouldn't notice any more lapses. "Why don't you put these presents under the tree and bring me the Mulan gift box so I can assemble Mari's last gift?"

Morbid thoughts penetrated Savannah's mood of what the words *last gift* would mean if, by some cruel twist of fate, this *became* the last gift Mari received from her mother. Her gaze darted to the Barbie then away before Damián caught her. Had Maman any inkling that her life would be cut so short when she'd given Savannah the Christmas Barbie? Tears burned her eyes at the thought of Mari growing up without her, whatever the circumstances.

Maman and John, I hope you can both rest in peace now that your murderer has been convicted.

Next week, she was supposed to be back in the Vista courtroom for Gentry's sentencing, but instead, she'd prepared and mailed her victim's statement. The judge and jury had already heard her testimony concerning the horrors of what she'd endured at Gentry's hands and what losing her mother at such a young age had meant. She wasn't going to put herself through anything more, even if Doctor Palmer allowed her to go back to California after going into premature labor ten days ago. Savannah was done. He'd been found guilty on all charges. Now, she only hoped he'd be put away for the rest of his life, but there was nothing more she could do to guarantee that outcome.

Savannah refused to think about Gentry another minute. Even with a sentence that included parole, Gentry would be in his nineties or beyond before he'd be eligible for a hearing, and not likely be a threat to anyone but himself. If he didn't die from unnatural causes once word got out to the prison population what he'd done to his daughter all those years.

Snap.

How had Damián returned so quickly? "Sorry. I was thinking about the sentencing next week."

"I'm proud of you for choosing not to be there."

"For the first time I can remember, I can live my life without looking over my shoulder or worrying about what he might do to me or my family. I've gotten my closure and peace of mind." There was still the matter of the charges brought against Adam and Damián, but she wouldn't think about that on Christmas Eve.

She'd better finish up here and go to bed. Marisol would be up early. And Savannah's arm was going to bruise if he flicked her in the same spot many more times. Of course, she could avoid that fate by improving her focus and staying in the moment.

She accepted the special box she'd found in SoCal last week. Mari would want to jump right in and play when she opened the gift, so Savannah removed the first Mulan figure from its packaging.

Damián sat beside her again and reached for the box containing Mu-shu, the dragon. "Let me help." He'd always had an affinity for dragons, apparently, given the one that had been tattooed on his chest and bicep.

One by one, she and Damián freed Li Shang and numerous figures from their boxes and Savannah tucked each carefully inside the vintage box. They fit snugly, but it would give Mari a nice carrying case for them all. She might want to take them with her to play with José, Grandpa, or Tía Grant sometime.

"She is going to love playing with them." Savannah smiled, picturing the scene.

"I can just imagine José charging in and wreaking havoc with Marisol's carefully planned campaigns, though," Damián said.

She agreed. "We're in for some epic battles." Their daughter was definitely a strategist, not to mention competitive with her cousin. She'd want to do more than simply recreate the battle scenes from the movie.

Savannah stifled a yawn, hoping Damián wouldn't notice. She wasn't finished yet.

"Time for you to get to bed." As if Damián ever missed a thing.

"I won't argue with you there. Help me carry all these presents to the tree."

"Go. To. Bed. I'll finish up down here."

This would be their first Christmas in their new home, and they'd be joined by Rosa, her two kids, and Mac for dinner tomorrow. She wished for nothing more this Christmas than to be surrounded by her family.

*   *   *

Damián didn't expect Savannah to slap his hand as he pulled a piece of crispy skin off the roasted turkey he'd just removed from the oven. The skin was always his favorite part. She'd rubbed it with chili powder and cayenne pepper, so it had just the right kick for his taste buds.

"Okay, your work in here is done, my dear," she said. "I'm sure you can find something to do besides pilfering turkey in my kitchen."

He popped one more piece into his mouth and smiled at her while chewing slowly without an ounce of remorse. When she shook her head and rolled her eyes, he leaned in and nuzzled her neck, placing a kiss just below her even more delicious earlobe. "Anybody ever tell you you're sexy as hell when you're annoyed?" he whispered.

"You think I'm sexy no matter what mood I'm in."

"*Lo sabes.*" *Yeah, baby.* "When did Doctor Palmer say we could have sex again?"

Because of her premature labor scare, they'd been told no sex and very few orgasms until she was halfway into her thirty-seventh week. "New Year's Eve."

He groaned, even though he knew exactly how long they'd have to wait. Both of them had been counting down the days since they returned from California. This was worse than any sex/orgasm deprivation Damián had inflicted on her as her Dom. Ironic that, when she was ready to resume her sex life after these sporadic two months, she'd be thwarted by something other than a lack of libido.

Damián wrapped his arms around her belly to encircle their baby. "I can't wait to show my woman how much I love her."

"Well, eventually, people are going to want to eat. I've put a lot into this meal and don't want it to become a disaster."

Savannah had insisted on preparing the spicy turkey and sides the way he and Rosa remembered them. She also wanted to introduce their daughter to more of her family's heritage. Although she'd invited Rosa in to advise and help prepare some of the dishes, she'd declared after an hour or so that she had it all under control and sent her in to be with Doctor Mac and the kids.

He didn't like Savannah overdoing it like this, but she'd told him this morning this would be her Christmas gift from the heart to him. With Savannah's inheritance, she could buy him anything he'd ever want or need, but instead, she wanted to give of herself. How could he say no to such a thoughtful present?

Still, he'd done all he could to help her out, lifting the turkey and doing early-morning prep work. Luckily, Damián had given her the best possible Christmas present this morning. If Mari hadn't jumped out of bed before Savannah had a chance to relax in the massage chair, she'd have tried it out at home by now.

But it was ready and waiting for her upstairs. He and Doctor Mac had just carried the chair to the bedroom and set it up. As soon as the meal was over, he'd order her to spend at least an hour relaxing in it.

Savannah told him she had another Christmas present for him that he'd have to wait to open in the privacy of their bedroom. He couldn't wait to find out what it was. Just the thought of what it might be had him grinding his hard dick against her ass. She relaxed with a sigh, melting back against him. Her natural submissiveness only inflamed him more. He'd promised her he wouldn't come until she could, and this forced celibacy was killing him, too.

"I'm not going to have dinner ready on time if you don't give me a little space to move...*Sir*," she added with zero reverence. Not that he gave a flying fuck about protocols. Didn't need them to know she was his in every way that counted.

When he answered by cupping her breasts, she hissed. They were so damned sensitive again. He grinned. She'd have his balls in a vise if he pinched her nipples and messed up her blouse if they leaked. But he also didn't want her to have to run upstairs and change before dinner, so instead, he merely brushed his thumbs over her nipples.

"Damián, please," she begged. "Don't do this to me."

"Do what?" He squeezed her breasts and bent to trail more kisses along the column of her neck.

"Get me all hot and bothered when I know we can't do anything about it for nearly a week."

His right hand trailed over her belly and down to her mound.

She darted a glance to the door. "Damián, if Mari or someone comes in and finds us like this..."

"Like I said, they'll see that I can't keep my hands off my woman. Besides, Marisol's too busy executing her next campaign against José and, surprisingly Teresa, with those Mulan action figures to pay us any mind for a while. And Doctor Mac and Rosa are deep in a discussion about improvements to make at the clinic."

"They're both so passionate about the work there, especially for the migrant and uninsured communities."

When Savannah started to turn around to face him, he held her in place with his left hand around her tits, cupping one, while his right one slipped inside her stretchy pants. Much easier than getting inside her old tight jeans.

She braced her hands on the counter, and her head lolled back against his shoulder giving him even better access to her neck. He nibbled at the same time his finger stroked her swollen clit.

"Oh, Damián." She moaned, becoming a little breathless, and suddenly he, too, wished he hadn't started something they couldn't finish. "Don't tease me like this. You know what the doctor said. A few more days."

"She said no sex and limited orgasms until New Year's Eve. While I want to bury myself so deep inside you, *querida*, you can taste me, we aren't going that far. Just relax and enjoy." Pushing her panties aside, his middle finger slid along her cleft and curled inside her wet passage. He shifted his hand until he could reach up as far as his finger would go.

"Oh, yes! There!" She moaned low in her throat, her response spurring him on. With his thumb on her clit and his middle finger stroking her G-spot, her knees buckled. Holding her more securely with his arm, he brought her closer to the brink. They couldn't safely count on more than a couple more minutes alone.

Her mewling whimpers turned to a groan when he pulled his hand out of her pants. "I think I hate you for doing this to me, Sir."

He guided her body around and pressed his hard-on against her swollen belly. "I nearly came in my pants, *savita*. This is the definition of torture. But I don't regret a thing." With her eyes on him, he inserted his wet finger into his mouth and licked it clean. "Mmm. Delicious."

Her pupils dilated as she smiled back. "That wasn't part of the meal I'd planned as your Christmas gift, but glad you enjoyed it." Her hand started to reach for his engorged dick, but he took a step back.

"No, *bebé*!" He'd cream his pants for sure if she touched him. "We talked about this last night. It's not fair for me to come if you can't. Besides, I want more than two minutes. Six more days, *querida*"—he tapped her pussy lightly—"and then you're all mine."

She placed a chaste kiss on his lips before pulling away. "If I'd known you had ulterior motives for helping me, I might have asked Rosa to stay in here longer."

He grinned as she looked down at the wet stains over each of her breasts. "Damn it, Damián! I'm leaking! I need to go upstairs and change my blouse." She wriggled away from him. "I'll put double pads in my bra this time, in case you turn me on too much over dinner."

Damián laughed heartily as she made a beeline toward the bedroom, taking the back stairway so as to avoid their guests.

He needed to start making plans for New Year's Eve now. First up, finding a babysitter for Marisol. The last thing he wanted was any interruptions.

Chapter Thirty-Four

Savannah poured the guava jelly over the sweet potatoes in the casserole dish, and Damián returned it to the oven. Rosa had shared their mother's recipe, and she hoped it turned out as close to Mrs. Orlando's as he remembered from his childhood. He said he hadn't had any since she died, not even at Rosa's.

She was trying a lot of new recipes this year, from the spicy turkey to roasted green chile cornbread dressing. This past weekend, Megan had given her some fresh green chiles from New Mexico that her brother Patrick supplied her with on a regular basis. Damián preferred those over jalapenos or whatever could be found in local supermarkets.

Everyone from Aspen Corners and Fairchance to Denver had gathered at Adam and Karla's over the pre-Christmas weekend to celebrate the end of the trial and the holidays before they all dispersed to spend Christmas and New Year's with their parents, children, and/or siblings. The Montagues would be spending the rest of the year at the family's historic cabin in the Black Hills where Adam and Karla had honeymooned a year ago. Angelina's restaurant was closed, and they were in Aspen Corners with her mother and brothers. Luke and Cassie were joining them for dinner today. Megan and Ryder were in Chicago with her mother and brother. Ryder's sister had flown in from Santa Fe, too.

She checked on the dressing in the stoneware bowl warming in the oven. The meat had been resting long enough. "Are you ready to carve?" She and Damián had opted out of doing the ceremonial carving at the table, so she'd set out two platters on the counter—one for white meat and one for dark.

"Absolutely. I can't wait to taste this bird."

"Again, you mean?"

"That was only the skin. And if it's any indication, this is going to be the best turkey I can remember." He told her how his mother's employer gifted the family with a turkey every Christmas. "Often she couldn't begin our dinner until she'd come home from working half a day at the house in Rancho Santa Fe. She worked at least part of every day of the year" His bitterness at how she'd been treated remained raw for him to this day.

Damián sharpened the carving knife and picked up the meat fork to begin. She enjoyed having Damián helping out. There was something so special about this meal. Tears pricked her eyes as she thought about giving him a gift that would evoke memories of happy childhood Christmases.

Savannah removed the casserole from the oven. "Is this how you remember it looking?" The glazed sweet potatoes did look delicious to her.

"I remember the smell more than how they looked, and you've transported me back to Eden Gardens, *bebé*." He placed a kiss on her cheek. "*Muchas gracias* for your beautiful gift, *querida*." His accent sounded stronger. The food must have transported him to his mother's kitchen.

With a burst of giggles, Marisol and José ran into the kitchen, followed by Chiquita who made her way to her water bowl and lapped noisily. "Maman, Aidan said their parents went on a cruise, and they don't have anyone to have Christmas dinner with. Can we invite him and his brothers to ours?"

She tried to remember any child from school or the neighborhood named Aidan. Had Mari talked with him while walking Chiquita earlier today? Mari wasn't supposed to use her cell phone except in an emergency.

But that was neither here nor there. Why would the little boys' parents go away and leave them alone, especially at Christmas? She might have to file a complaint with protective services for child neglect unless one was old enough to take care of his younger siblings. Foremost, she needed to make sure they were safe.

"Sure! Why don't you ask them to join us? We have plenty of food."

"Awesome! I'll go tell him!" Mari and José ran out of the room with

Chiquita in fast pursuit. "Don't forget Chiquita's leash!" she called after them. A few seconds later, the front door slammed. So Aidan must be a neighbor nearby. Savannah had been so consumed with everything going on since they'd moved in here that she really hadn't taken the time to get to know their neighbors as well as she should have. After the baby arrived, she'd remedy that.

"I'll carry these platters out to the buffet," he said, lifting the foil-covered dishes and heading for the door.

Checking her list to see what else needed doing, she said a selfish prayer hoping everything would taste as good as he remembered. She turned around to see Rosa standing in the doorway. "Do you need any more help, Savannah?" she asked.

"I think we're about ready."

"It smells like Mamá's kitchen in here." Her sister-in-law's smile faded, and she stood wringing her hands nervously. Was something wrong? "I wonder if you have a minute," she asked meekly.

"Absolutely! Come in, Rosa." She placed the lid on the sweet potatoes and returned them to the warm oven until Damián could carry them out.

"I just have to tell someone," she said, sitting on one of the bar stools. Savannah took a seat beside her.

"What's up?"

"It's Robert." Again, Rosa played with her hands—no, one finger in particular. For the first time today, Savannah noticed she wore a new ring, entwined hearts with two small emeralds.

Before she could ask, Rosa shared, "He gave me this ring for Christmas and said it's a token of his promise to me."

Wow! Things were moving faster for the two of them than she realized, practically under Savannah's nose at the clinic, although she really hadn't been around there much this month. She placed her hand under Rosa's and pulled it toward her for a closer look. "It's beautiful!" Savannah wasn't quite sure what the promise was or where their relationship was headed, but would let Rosa tell her story without peppering her with questions.

"Honestly, Savannah, he actually asked me to..."—she turned her

gaze toward the door to make sure they were alone, Savannah supposed—"marry him while you were in California. But I told him I wasn't
ready to take that step. While he's been wonderful to me and my children,
I'm not sure I can trust any man in that way ever again."

Poor Rosa. Her ex-husband, Julio, had done a number on her and her
children.

"But this morning when he came to pick us up, he pulled me over to
the Christmas tree and gave me this ring." Rosa stared at it in silence a
long time before meeting Savannah's gaze again. She had tears in her eyes.
"I'm afraid, Savannah. I trusted Julio, and look what he did to Teresa."
Not to mention José's beatings and all the beatings and rapes Rosa had
endured.

Savannah was living proof that a person could survive a lot and still
find love again. She hoped Rosa would experience the kind of love
Savannah had for Damián someday, but just as no one could have
convinced Savannah by words alone, Rosa would have to find that
conviction in her own heart. Still, she stood and wrapped Rosa in a
mama-bear hug, whispering, "Doctor Mac isn't Julio. He's a gentle, kind
soul. I would say you can trust him based on all I know about him, but
you'll have to go with your gut."

Savannah pulled away, cupping Rosa's chin, and stared into her big
brown eyes. "Take things as slowly as you need to. If it's meant to be, he'll
still be there if and when you're ready for something more. And it sounds
to me as though he's willing to wait until you're ready. I think this promise
ring makes perfect sense. It will be like a symbol of protection for you and
keep unwanted advances away." Savannah had worn a fake wedding band
for years in an effort to do the same thing.

"Yes, he said that he would always be here to protect me and my
children. And that he chose emeralds, because the stone means positivity,
hope, and loyalty. But everything is happening so fast."

Savannah had fallen in love with Damián in less than a day. "Rosa, I
know how hard it is for you to trust a man after what you and your
daughter have been through, but give him time to prove to you that he'll
stick around and be a good father and husband." A promise ring was the

perfect choice for someone still skittish about relationships, and a way to help Rosa see him in a different light than as the physician she worked for at the clinic.

"The *muy grande* question is whether I can work for him while dating. What if things don't work out?"

"You've been dating?"

Rosa nodded. "We actually started seeing each other outside the clinic before Thanksgiving."

Ah. "I thought I saw some sparks flying across the table."

Rosa grinned sheepishly. "I wasn't ready to say anything yet. I wanted to see what Damo's reaction would be if he saw me with Robert, but I didn't want to jinx the relationship, either." She sighed. "I'm not sure how far I can go in an intimate relationship." Her eyes opened wider, and she splayed out her hands, palms outward. "Not that we've slept together or anything. I won't commit a sin for any man."

Rosa followed her faith much more strictly than Damián or Savannah did. While Savannah had found sanctuary in the church after escaping Gentry and Mari attended parochial school, they weren't devout. Of course, they did go to Mass most Sundays for Mari's sake.

"Trust your instincts and your heart, Rosa. You'll know when the time is right to move to the next step. Whatever that might be. But having the love of a good man, an honorable one like Mac who will love, protect, and defend you no matter what, well, there's no other feeling like that in the world." Something occurred to her. "Does Damián know things are getting serious?"

Rosa shrugged. "He didn't notice the ring, if that's what you mean. But I think Robert might be talking with him about me now. He's old-fashioned and thinks he needs permission or something."

Savannah knew Mac better than Damián did. She wondered how Damián would take to another man coming into Rosa's life. Savannah grinned. This might be interesting to watch. It was a good thing Robert McKenzie had patience. He also seemed a bit old-fashioned, which should work well for what looked to be the start of a long, slow courtship.

The timer chimed. "I think we're about ready."

"How can I help?"

"If you could ask Damián and Robert to help clear the entertainment center, I think we'll move the buffet there, and we'll use the folding table for the kids." Trying to add three more people to the dining room table would be a tight squeeze. "Then send everyone in to grab a dish, and we will be ready as soon as Mari returns with Aidan and his brothers."

* * *

Damián started toward the front door to call for Marisol at the same moment he saw several tall shadows silhouetted against its stained-glass oval window. Once upon a time, he'd have worried it might be a threat to Savannah. After checking through the peephole, he opened the door, surprised to find Marisol and José standing in front of three tall boys who looked to be in their late teens.

At his furrowed expression, Marisol quickly explained. "Daddy, this is Aidan and his brothers." *This* was Aidan? She pointed to the boy on the far left when she said his name. He looked familiar. Sandy blond hair. Kind of a beach bum look, although he'd bet ski bum was more accurate, given they were in the Rockies of Colorado.

"If there's been some misunderstanding, sir," Aidan began, "we'll be fine with our frozen pizzas."

Damián glanced at the other two slightly shorter boys—who must be twins, with their identical hair color and facial features—then back at Aidan. Remembering his manners and that this was Christmas Day, he said, "No, everything's fine. Come on in." Wait until Savannah met Marisol's "little" friend. "*Feliz Navidad.*"

Where the hell had Marisol met Aidan?

Then it hit him. They were the college boys living in the house next door. All three kept odd hours, and Damián hadn't done much more than give a casual wave whenever he'd seen one or two of them in the driveway or backyard. He wasn't even sure which ones he'd waved at.

Marisol took Aidan's hand, making Damián more than a little uncomfortable, and led him into the living room where the smaller folding table was being converted from the buffet to a seating arrangement for up to six. Savannah had tossed a green tablecloth over it, and Rosa and Doctor Mac were placing folding chairs around it.

Marisol introduced everyone else to Aidan first and then to his twin brothers, Finn and Tyler.

One of the twins said, "I hope we aren't putting you out, ma'am." They'd been taught their manners from someone.

"Oh, no!" Savannah assured them, graciously. "I hated hearing you might be having Christmas alone, although I must say I was expecting children closer to Mari's age." She gave an uncertain smile to the boys who towered over them both, all three exceeding six feet in height.

Aidan cleared his throat somewhat nervously. "Marisol and I got to know each other over the back fence when she was outside with Chiquita. I'm a pre-vet student."

"Aidan loves dogs, too, Maman," Marisol said.

"No wonder you two hit it off," she said, her smile slightly less worried.

After the handshakes and greetings were done, Damián glanced over at Teresa, who seemed indecisive about whether she wanted to stay at the table with the adults or join Marisol and the boys.

One of the twins—he truly couldn't tell one from the other—gestured toward an empty chair, and Teresa accepted it, smiling shyly as she thanked him.

Cool it, Uncle Damo. It's not like his niece just agreed to date the boy. She'd only accepted an offer to sit at his table.

While Teresa had been out with Jonathan a few times since their first date over a month ago, she'd told him about her difficulties talking with him about anything other than music. Maybe she could practice her conversational skills today in a safe setting with Aidan and his brothers.

Rosa and Doctor Mac had carried in the remaining side dishes and placed them on the credenza that would now serve as a buffet after they'd moved the stereo equipment to the floor. "I think everything's ready," Savannah announced. She asked Rosa to say grace then said, "Just grab your plate and get in line, everyone."

"Sit down, *querida*." Damián wrapped his arm around her waist and guided her to their table. He wanted her off her feet as soon as possible.

"But I need to make sure our guests have everything first!"

"Sit. Down. I'll bring you your plate," Damián insisted as he pressed her shoulders until she was seated. Growing up, Mamá rarely sat down to eat until everyone had finished. He didn't want Savannah to sacrifice her own health and well-being that way, to say nothing of the baby's. Especially after she'd slaved on the meal all morning. The kids went next. Then the other adults followed.

"Everything's delicious, Savannah," Rosa said as they dug into the food. "Your turkey and dressing remind me of Mamá's, too."

"*Sí*," Damián chimed in. "Thanks so much for preparing this feast for us." He'd nearly choked up when he tasted the green chile dressing, catapulted back to Mamá's table.

"I'm glad everything turned out right," Savannah said, smiling. "I wasn't sure how anything was supposed to taste."

"Just the way you made it," Damián said, leaning over to give her a peck on the cheek. Even that innocent contact made him hard. *Dios*, he was going to explode before New Year's Eve got here.

When he turned his gaze to the other couple at the table, if he could call them that, Rosa and Mac exchanged a smile. It made Damián wonder how serious this was becoming. The good doctor had told Damián earlier this afternoon that he was interested in dating Rosa when she was ready. She must have told him her story about Julio, not something she shared with everyone. Mac promised to watch over her and the kids as a second protector. Since Rosa spent so much of her time in the clinic, it gave Damián a sense of relief knowing that he didn't have to worry about her as much. Not that Julio could hurt her or Teresa again, unless some asinine parole board let him out sooner than the twenty or so years he was sentenced to before being eligible for a parole hearing.

Damián had a sense that Mac would be good for Rosa. He wanted her to find real love, the same kind he shared with Savannah.

"Aidan, do you wanna walk Chiquita with me after dinner?" Marisol's voice drifted to him across the room, making Damián shift his gaze over Rosa's shoulder to the other table. "She likes sniffing around the neighborhood."

"Sure thing. I'll need a walk after eating so much, but I can't stop. It's been a while since we've had a home-cooked meal."

Savannah bent closer to Damián's ear and whispered, "I think our little girl might have a crush on Aidan." She didn't sound any happier about that fact than Damián was.

While Aidan merely smiled at the hero worship in Marisol's eyes before taking another bite of the turkey, Damián decided he might need to have a talk with the boy to make sure his little girl's heart didn't get broken.

A year ago, he'd only just discovered he even had a daughter, and this Christmas, he was worrying about her having her heart broken by a boy. What the fuck happened to enjoying watching her grow up slowly?

"Who's ready for dessert?" Savannah asked.

A collective groan came from the adults, while Marisol and José shouted, "Cookies!" *Buñuelos!*" at the same time.

Savannah had baked mouthwatering Mexican wedding cookies, which he'd sampled last night and again this morning. And Rosa fried out-of-this-world *buñuelos* using Mamá's iron rosette. This had to be the best Christmas he could remember in a long time, mainly because the Orlandos were all together, including Marisol, whom a judge had legally given the surname in September. And, of course, the love of his life, Savannah.

Savannah laughed. "Kids—and boys—they're on a tray over there. Help yourselves. We adults will hold off until later and let the meal settle first."

But as soon as the meal was over and the conversation had died down, his first priority would be getting Savannah into that chair for a nice, long massage.

"Robert, why don't we take a walk around the neighborhood with them?" Clearly, Rosa had overheard them, too, and found a way to chaperone Marisol without seeming to be doing so.

"Thanks, Sis," he whispered, leaning toward her.

She smiled back at him, speaking in a lowered voice, too. "Just wait. It only gets harder."

Man, he was going to have his hands full protecting Marisol over the next twenty or thirty years. Fuck, who was he kidding? The rest of her *life*.

Chapter Thirty-Five

O n New Year's Eve, Damián surprised Savannah with dinner at a trendy local restaurant she'd told him about months ago. With the university on break, it seemed a good time to try it and avoid the noisy crowds.

Damián lifted his water glass, and she did the same. "To George Gentry's never seeing more than an hour of sunshine a day for the rest of his sorry life."

"Hear, hear!" Both took a sip. He'd prefer toasting with a beer but didn't want to partake if she couldn't join in with a glass of her favorite wine. The baby would be here in less than a month, if born by his or her due date.

In addition to welcoming in the New Year, tonight they celebrated the much welcome call from the DA two days ago telling them the judge had given Gentry the maximum sentence for each of his convictions. They'd tried to keep talk of the trial away from Marisol, and with her being off school all week, this was the first chance they'd had to talk about it.

"As much as I would have hated to put you through more, *bebé*, I wish we could've seen the look on his face when the sentence was handed down." He probably thought his privileged status would get him off.

"The DA said he kept scanning the gallery as if he thought we would show up any minute. And that he was screaming obscenities at the jury as he was led away in handcuffs." Savannah beamed. "That would have been priceless to see."

Damián nodded.

"Even though he's technically eligible for parole someday, I don't think he'll outlive two consecutive twenty-five to life sentences plus ten more years for the murders, much less the twenty additional years tacked on for kidnapping and abusing me. He might have made a pact with the devil decades ago, but I doubt he'll live to be a hundred and fifty."

Savannah had a glow about her that conveyed how much peace the news had given her.

"You hardly moved an eyelid while you slept last night." He'd watched her half the night to make sure he could pull her out of a nightmare or PTSD episode quickly, much like Dad used to do with him when he first moved to Denver.

"Knowing he'll never come near us again is the best way to start the year."

After taking a sip, they continued to dine on the Mediterranean fare. Not his favorite cuisine, but tonight was about pleasing his wife. Besides, he'd get to eat what he really wanted later tonight.

"What are you grinning about?" she asked.

Leaning toward her across the table, he whispered, "All the things I'm going to do to your pussy when I get you home."

Her intake of breath told him his words had caught her by surprise, but then she smiled. "I'd ask you to tell me about them, but I know you like to both surprise and embarrass me, so I'll just let my imagination fill in the blanks."

"Not embarrass, *bebé*," he said, grinning. "Challenge social norms, maybe. But I can't control what embarrasses you."

A blush crept into her cheeks, visible even in the candlelight. Even this conversation seemed to have that effect on her. *Dios*, he loved her like mad.

They both passed on dessert, and he settled the bill quickly with cash. Standing, he held out his hand to her. "Let's go home."

As they made their way into the house after dinner, he couldn't help but notice a bounce in her step. And why not? A huge weight had been lifted off her shoulders—his, too. He'd never known Savannah when Gentry wasn't a threat to her safety and wellbeing.

Please let her be at peace the rest of her life.

Damián followed Savannah up the stairs, his eyes fixed on her sashaying ass. He'd been hard for days—okay, weeks. The moratorium on sex had been lifted by the doctor at her check-up yesterday.

Finally!

Marisol had been at Rosa's all day and was excited to ring in the New Year with José and Teresa. The only bells Damián wanted to ring were Savannah's. From the touches and looks she'd given him at dinner, Savannah was ready, too.

At the top of the stairs, he moved ahead of her and took her hand as he led her into the bedroom.

"Where should we start?" Savannah asked. He didn't detect any hesitancy whatsoever. "The bed? Massage chair? Shower?"

Damián turned her around to face the bed, wrapped his arms around her, and pulled her ass against his erection. "We'll get to all of those places and more, *savita*, before the New Year arrives, but I've been waiting all week to get back to where we left off in the kitchen on Christmas Day." He nuzzled her neck, and she moaned, pressing into his body in surrender. Working his lips from her earlobe to the juncture of her neck and shoulder, he planted kisses on her sweet-smelling skin.

"Oh, yes!"

One of his hands moved up to pinch her nipple, and her hips jerked against him. His other hand lowered to her pussy but was hampered by her pants. Time to take this to the next level. He pulled away with a mix of reluctance and anticipation. "Strip for me, *querida*."

Savannah took a step toward the bed before turning to face him. The sultry smile she gave him almost made him lean forward and yank her clothes off on his own, but he controlled his libido, knowing how much hotter it would be watching her slowly unbutton her blouse.

Her bra came into view as she slipped her blouse off her arms to puddle at her feet, and he'd waited long enough. He closed the gap between them to unhook the clasps. Sliding it down her arms, he stared at her swollen, darkened nipples and areolae. Even their shape had changed to better accommodate the baby in a month or so. But he didn't want to think about the baby right now.

"Lose the pants."

She held onto the bedpost to steady herself and shimmied the stretch pants over her belly and down her legs. Leaning her hips against the mattress, she let him remove them the rest of the way. The only thing between him and her pussy... that thong. If he'd known she'd been wearing sexy underwear tonight, he'd have rid her of her slacks at the front door and watched her ass as they went up the stairs.

As if you needed them gone to picture her ass.

He slipped his hand between her legs and shoved the scrap of satin aside, no deterrent to his determination. Gliding his middle finger along her slit, he was met by her readiness. "So wet, *bebé.*"

"For you. Only for you."

He slid one finger inside her then another, pumping in and out of her soaked pussy.

"Oh!" She closed her eyes and leaned back on her elbows, moaning. "Oh God, it feels good to have you touching me again."

"Let's get rid of this thong. And from now on, I want your pussy either bare or wearing a thong until I remove it or instruct you to do so. I've been turned on by you in one ever since our hypnosis play at the club on my Alive Day." Sliding his fingers out of her, he helped her straighten up and clenched one ass cheek in each hand, squeezing before slapping her left one.

"Yes, Sir." Her voice had become breathy. "Glad you like them. I feel sexier when I wear them, too."

"An added bonus." Hooking his thumbs in the sides of the thong, he grazed the sides of her hips and thighs as he rid her of the scrap of material. Stepping back, he stared down at her tits and mound and nearly lost it.

"So fucking beautiful."

"Please let me help you undress, Sir, so I can have equal time." She grazed her fingernails down his chest and over his abs, until she reached for his belt buckle and undid it.

Holding his hands at his sides, he gave himself over to her. Ignoring his shirt, she slowly slid the belt from its loops and tossed it on the bed. Next, she unbuttoned and unzipped him. His raging hard-on sprang out, having nothing to confine it, and she slid the pants off his hips, lowering herself with them until she knelt in front of him with his cock pointing at her face.

"Oh, what have we here?" She hadn't been in such a playful mood in months. *Dios*, she was going to kill him tonight.

Hooking her thumbs through two belt loops, she slid his black jeans to below his knees and let them rest there while she took his erection into her hands. She didn't use a lot of pressure. Instead, she skimmed her fingers and thumb softly up his shaft until she came to the plum head where she let her thumb glide back and forth in his precum. She didn't even flinch at the wetness like she used to. Another trigger she'd conquered.

But he wanted to make it special for her first. He reached for her arms to lift her to her feet again, but she wouldn't budge. Instead, she looked up at him and nearly made him come all over her face. "I've wanted to do this since Christmas, but you wouldn't let me. I owe you a blowjob that comes from my heart."

She didn't have to say *after the last one*. He'd been reluctant to ask her for one. Honestly, even after their talk when he collared her. He'd hated what she'd done to herself.

"*Please*, Sir."

How could he say no when she begged him like that?

Momentarily unable to speak past the lump in his throat, he helped her to her feet. Together, they removed his pants the rest of the way. Crossing to the bed, he grabbed his pillow and returned to drop it on the floor between them. "I won't be able to enjoy you giving me head if I'm worrying about the pain in your knees."

Her face broke out in a smile as he lowered her to the pillow. "Thank you, Sir." Without hesitation, she wrapped her lips around his cock and flicked her tongue against the tip of his knob, lapping as more precum seeped against her tongue. Inch by inch, she drew him inside her warm mouth, grazing him with her teeth just enough to make his balls jump, either from excitement or fear.

She added her hand to pump the lower half of his shaft, simulating the feel of her tight pussy. It didn't take any arm-twisting for him to relinquish any remaining control to her.

More vigorously, she bobbed up and down on his cock, each thrust taking him a little deeper. He grabbed her hair and wrapped it around his fists, setting a new pace for her. When she looked up at him and smiled a deliciously slutty smile, he almost blew his wad down her throat then and there.

My Princess Slut.

Time to slow this down. He didn't want to be the first to come. He tried the slower pace, but she kept burying his dick farther down her throat. When he hit the back of it, he waited for her to pull off him, but she swallowed the head of his dick instead. Fucking swallowed it!

"Jesús!" Her throat squeezed him as tightly as her pussy would later tonight.

She stilled, holding him at the back of her throat and swallowed around him again. He remembered the last time she'd deep-throated him and was determined to pay attention to her responses better this time, hard as it might be.

Moaning as she released his shaft made him think she'd reached her limit. But then she cupped his balls and gave them a little squeeze. When his cock jerked, she took him even deeper. He closed his eyes and tilted his head back to savor the moment a little longer. When his balls tightened, though, he tugged by her hair to ease her off of his dick. She'd brought him to the brink so fast. He had to remind himself they had all night.

"Ay, güey, savita! Your mouth—and throat, *Dios!*—are fucking amazing. But if I don't stop you now, I'm not going to be able to bury myself inside you for at least another hour."

He couldn't miss her groan—sounded like disappointment—as he lifted her to her feet again. She brushed tears from her eyes. Concerned, he cupped her chin, searching her eyes. "Everything okay?"

She smiled. "I just need to work on my gag reflex some more. You said you wanted me to set some empowering resolutions for next year. Maybe that can be one of them, Sir."

"Sounds like a plan, *bebé*." He glanced over at the chair. "Why don't we move this over there?"

He removed his shirt. At last, both of them were completely naked.

He took her hand and led her to the massage chair, grinning like a lovesick fool. "Let me help you into it." Damián held her arms and torso steady as she bent over and took her seat like a queen ascending the throne. "Sink back into it."

Once she seemed settled, he reached for the remote and turned on one of the settings he'd pre-programmed to focus on her ass and pussy. He'd been waiting to put the chair through its paces. He stepped back to assess her position.

Turning off the vibrations momentarily, he positioned her legs between the massage pads then tilted the chair back into the zero gravity setting. Doc Palmer had said it would be the safest angle to use, and he had programmed the preset already.

Her eyes opened wide in wonderment. "That's amazing! I haven't had the pressure off my lower back in forever."

Now he wished he'd given her the chair as an early present, but that couldn't be helped now. He spent the next twenty minutes or so showing her a number of settings for various massages and relaxation techniques the chair could help her with.

She looked sheepishly up at him. "Sorry, I know I'm supposed to be thinking about sex right now, but I can't get over how good this thing feels."

"I want you to enjoy a massage first. But if it's sex you want, there's a function for that, too." He pulled out a rubber ball he'd stashed earlier in the chair's side pocket. Unlike the one he'd used at the club, this one had its own vibrator inside, with a series of bumps on its surface for added friction. While this chair was a higher-end version of what the club had purchased—destined to be used more as far as non-sexual massage and relaxation—he expected the pressure on her clit to have similar results.

"Open for me, *savita*."

She did so, as far as the chair allowed, and he took two fingers of his other hand to spread her lower lips open and expose her clit. Positioning one of the ball's soft bumps directly against her bundle of nerves, he turned on the vibrator.

"Oh. It won't take much of that to get me off, Sir."

Just you wait.

Damián set the function to medium, and the look of pleasure on her face told him he'd hit the right spots. After a minute or so, she sighed and closed her eyes, letting the sensations pulse throughout her body. Watching her enjoying herself made his chest swell with pride.

That wasn't the only thing swelling. He took his cock in one hand and stroked it as he watched her. Too late, he remembered the recovered memory of her eighteenth birthday, but before he could release himself, she opened her eyes. They zeroed in on the hand stroking his cock, and he prepared for her to sink into a flashback or be triggered. Instead, she licked her lips.

Damián wasn't finished demonstrating the chair, though. He turned the remote to full speed. Her hands gripped the sides of the chair, and she squirmed against the ball bouncing on her clit. "Yes! Oh God, yes!" She closed her eyes, and he watched her getting closer to the brink. When he dialed back the vibrator in the ball, she met his gaze. "Damián, you've outdone yourself this time. I might never want to leave this chair."

"Oh, you'll leave it if you want to enjoy that orgasm you're working toward." He paused for a beat to build up her hopes. "But you do not have permission to come yet."

Excitement in her eyes was followed by frustration. "*Por favor, Señor.* It's been so long."

Dios, he loved that she was begging him for it. *Enough already.* He couldn't wait another minute to take her.

When he turned off the chair and removed the vibrating ball, she groaned. "I can see you're going to want to use that setting when you're home alone while Marisol and I are out of the house, which is fine. That's why I got you the chair—to relieve stress." He held up the ball. "But you're *only* going to use *this* on orgasm mode with your Dom's permission. *¿Comprendes?*"

"You, Sir, are evil."

He chuckled, stroking himself again, watchful for any sign she'd been triggered by his action or her position. But she seemed too lost in the moment to care about the past. Moving the chair to the upright position, he impatiently waited for her to regain her equilibrium. "My dick needs to bury itself inside you. Now. And it's not going to happen with you in that chair."

As he helped her out of it, she placed a kiss on his cheek and wrapped her arms around him. "I love you so much."

"I love you, too, *mi* Savannah."

Guiding her to the bed, he grabbed two pillows and laid them near the edge. He kissed her, pinching her nipple with one hand and stroking her clit with the other. The kiss was far from tender. Thank God. When she gripped his cock, he nearly exploded. Supporting her upper body, he helped her bend forward at the waist and lower her head onto the pillows.

She tilted her face to the side. "Please, hurry."

Topping from the bottom? That wouldn't do.

"Who's in charge in this bedroom, *savita*?"

"You are, Sir."

"Let's try and remember that so I don't have to swat that pretty little ass of yours with my tawse."

The glazed look in her eyes told him she was ready for anything he cared to dish out. "I wouldn't mind that, either." Taking her wrists, he bent her arms at the elbows and let her hands rest naturally on either edge of the pillow. "Comfortable?"

"Yes, Sir. Well, everywhere but my pussy. It's *very* uncomfortable. So's my clit."

Savannah's rediscovered sexuality was going to be the death of him yet.

But what a way to go.

*   *   *

Savannah's entire body quivered as he placed her in the position that she loved the most lately, with the trunk of her body and her belly hanging freely, far enough away from the mattress that her abdomen wouldn't be shoved against it when he entered her forcefully. She did so like it rough when he had her at a fever pitch like this.

Judging by how easily Damián's fingers slid through her folds, she was dripping wet. Would he make her wait long? His throbbing hard-on told her he was equally anxious for their time together. It had been forever.

Damián's warm body pressed against her butt. "Spread your legs wider for me, *querida*." She did and immediately felt his erection gliding up and down her slippery folds before flicking against her swollen clit.

"Your clit is hard for me," he said. "Your pussy so wet." She heard the pride in his voice. He knew without a doubt that he'd made her that way.

He stroked her back and sides in several deep, smooth motions until his hands came around to cup her dangling breasts.

"Ready?"

"Oh, yes." She couldn't wait to have him inside her. He surprised her by pinching her nipples. "Oh, fuck!" *Did I just say fuck?* Not that Damián hadn't said it many times, but it wasn't a word she used much, if ever. But they were more sensitive than they had been a few weeks ago. "I mean, God, that hurts!"

"I thought you said you were ready." His fingers massaged her tender nipples, shaking off the residual pain.

"I thought you meant for you to come inside me." While she no longer had triggers, he usually asked first, just to be sure. "My mind had been focused on that, not my nipples."

His chuckle reverberated through her back and butt. Without further ado, he stood up, grabbed her hips, and drove himself inside her, filling her with one stroke. A grunt emitted from her throat involuntarily. Grounded in the moment, she let the sensations of her throbbing nipples and having him buried inside her take over. Grabbing the pillow with both hands, she held on as he pounded into her, increasing the force, depth, and speed with each thrust. When his finger flicked her clit, she nearly exploded.

Did he realize how close she was to coming? "Permission to come,

Sir?"

"Not until I say so." *Rat bastard.* He enjoyed controlling her orgasms and making her go out of her mind before he gave her the release she craved.

He rubbed his thumb against her puckered star, and she clenched him even tighter. "Wait, Sir. I'm not sure—" Her pussy muscles clamped around his fingers.

"I'm not going there tonight, *bebé.* But we *will* try anal after the baby is here. You'll need some preparation with butt plugs first."

Again, she spasmed against his cock at the thought. The idea definitely intrigued and excited her. There were so many things she had yet to explore with him.

But right now, all she wanted to do was come. Squeezing her eyes shut, she decided not to play fair. She tightened her vaginal muscles each time he pulled away, as if to hold him there. Kegels. She almost giggled to think how much more prepared she'd be for this delivery than she had been for Mari's.

"Keep that up, *savita,* and I won't last much longer."

Good! She panted, as if doing her no-push Lamaze breathing—or mile twenty-five of a marathon.

Wait for him. Wait for him. Wait—

"Now, *bebé.* Come with me."

He pinched her clit, and she nearly flung him off of her. "Dear Lord!" But the discomfort quickly dissipated as her body convulsed in an intense orgasm that rolled over her in wave after wave, not letting up until the last ounce of energy had been drained from her body.

"Fuck, woman! So fucking sweet! I've missed this." He rarely expressed himself when he came, so he must be feeling the intensity as well. Like a deluge after a long drought.

When guilt entered into her thoughts, she pushed it away. She'd changed. Her inhibitions and triggers were a thing of the past—well, she hoped so in the case of the latter, but triggers were unpredictable. But she hadn't flashed back to her eighteenth birthday, even though Damián had been stroking his erection in a similar manner. All she'd seen was her husband and how aroused he was watching her naked body. *Progress.*

She groaned and tried to avoid his fingers when her clit began to feel overstimulated, but he released the nub and slowly rubbed her lower lips before slapping her butt a couple of times for good measure after pulling out. He helped her to stand upright again and immediately yanked the extra blanket off the bottom of the bed to wrap it around her.

When he lifted her in his arms, she screamed, "Put me down! I'm not as light as I used to be." The stare he gave her made her stomach drop into her pelvis. "I'm sorry, Sir. I just don't want you to hurt yourself." *Or drop me.* But she should have known he wouldn't endanger her or the baby. He seemed totally steady on his feet.

Her body began shaking before he set her down beside the chair he used for cuddling and for aftercare. He smiled and placed a sweet kiss on her lips before he sat and pulled her onto his lap. Cocooned in the blanket and his arms, she let all the feelings wash over her.

"That was intense," she murmured.

"Tell me about it."

Her trembling lessened as they came down off their high. Hearing him say it was intense for him, too, confirmed that the two of them were totally in sync and growing stronger than ever.

"And after I let you rest up again, my tongue and mouth are ready to worship your clit and pussy like I've never gone down on you before."

"I'll hold you to that." She giggled at the pun. "I wonder if it's just because sex while pregnant is hotter. If so, it almost makes me want to get pregnant immediately after this one."

He chuckled, his chest vibrating against her cheek. "You know I'll do everything in my power to accommodate your every wish, my Princess Slut." The way she craved sex these days, she certainly was living up to the nickname he'd given her. "But why don't we wait and see what sex outside of pregnancy is like, *querida*, for, oh, say a year or two? There are lots of other positions and techniques we can explore when we aren't constrained by the fact you're pregnant. We've hardly begun to enjoy that chair's versatility." Not to mention continuing to explore her own sexuality. Who knew what all she hadn't tried yet? The possibilities seemed limitless.

"Well, if you insist." She smiled, thinking about the lifetime they hoped to have together to explore each other's bodies and sexual interests. "I love you more each day, Sir Damián."

"And I love my little Savannah with every breath in my body."

She closed her eyes. Life couldn't get any better than this.

Chapter Thirty-Six

The sporadic Braxton-Hicks contractions she'd been feeling for months intensified not long after Damián left for the shop that morning. Having seen Doctor Palmer yesterday and hearing she hadn't dilated any farther since her premature labor a month ago, she wasn't worried about an early delivery. She'd been at two centimeters for more than a week when pregnant with Mari. This baby would most likely come closer to the due date, which was still almost two weeks away.

But the pressure grew stronger all morning, and the contractions started to become more regular. Still too far apart to call Damián home. He'd told her he had to overhaul an engine, which would take all day. She didn't want to worry him unnecessarily. If her water broke or the contractions became regular, closer together, and harder, then she'd know it was time to get serious.

These were nothing like the ones she remembered having with Mari, though. She decided to go about her normal routine, putting on some soup for lunch for her and Mari. Her daughter would stay busy watching Saturday morning cartoons for at least another hour.

Savannah slowly climbed the stairs and straightened up their bedrooms, pressing her hand to her lower back when another contraction almost took her breath away. But when it passed, she felt fine.

Back downstairs in the kitchen, she ladled out two bowls of vegetable-beef soup and set Mari's beside her peanut-butter-and-strawberry-jam sandwich. "Time for lunch, Mari," she called.

A trickle of wetness escaped her panties and ran down her thigh. Great. Probably leaking urine. Small wonder with all the pressure on her bladder. She hadn't taken a bathroom break in more than an hour.

After getting Mari settled at the table, Savannah went back upstairs to change her underwear then joined Mari, who was staging a mock battle between Mulan and Li Shang, two of the action figures she'd given her for Christmas.

"Would you like me to play one of the parts?"

"Sure! You can be Mushu."

Savannah picked up the dragon and pretended to cast a spell on the two soldiers when a severe cramp seized her abdomen and robbed her of breath.

"Maman, are you all right?"

No words would come out, so she nodded vigorously, but this one felt more like active labor than practice contractions. She hadn't been timing them yet, but glanced at the clock on the microwave. Perhaps she ought to do so, though, before calling the doctor or Damián.

Not wanting to alarm Mari with the severity of the pain, she gritted her teeth and forced a smile. After another moment, the intensity decreased enough for her to say, "I'm fine. Now eat your lunch."

Mari gave her side-eye glances as she chewed a bite of her sandwich, her somber expression telling Savannah the little girl couldn't help but be worried. She took on the self-imposed role of protector when Damián wasn't here. Savannah wanted to calm her fears, but something wasn't normal about these contractions. She might need to take Mari and the pets to Adam and Karla's on the way to the hospital, so she sent her out to walk Chiquita. It took a few minutes before Savannah was able to stand to clear the table. Suddenly, a gush of warm liquid poured down her leg onto the floor.

Her heart rate kicked up a notch—okay, maybe ten. Having her water break was a surefire sign that, within twenty-four hours, she'd be holding her new baby. Time to call Damián to let him know to finish up whatever he could and head home, but first, she'd clean up this mess. She wouldn't ask Mari to do so.

Retrieving a roll of paper towels, she pulled off a huge wad and awkwardly knelt down to soak up the fluid. A wave of dizziness overcame her, and she grabbed a table leg to keep herself from falling over. Soon after it passed, the next contraction cramped her abdomen, cervix, and back at the same time, doubling her over and taking her breath away once more. She lowered herself onto her side. A feeling of intense fullness in her vagina left her writhing on the floor.

"Mari!" She gasped for air. "Come quick!"

No response. *Damn.* She must be outside still. Savannah had left her phone on the table. She lay there several interminable minutes until the front door opened and Chiquita came bounding in to wait at her food bowl.

Savannah screamed, "Mari! Maman needs you!"

The little girl came rushing into the room with leash in hand and Aidan close behind her. "Maman! What's wrong?"

"Call Daddy! Hurry, Princess." She pointed toward the table, unable to speak as another contraction hit her. They were practically on top of each other now, maybe five minutes apart.

Aidan knelt beside her to take her pulse. Did a pre-vet student know anything about human pulse rates?

He pulled out his phone. "I'm going to call 911 so we can transport you safely to the hospital."

"Oh, that's not necessary. Damián's only fifteen minutes away."

When she heard Mari leaving a frantic message on Damián's voicemail, though, she nodded at Aidan. "Go ahead and call." She didn't want Mari traumatized by watching her *maman* giving birth on the kitchen floor.

Savannah hoped Damián wouldn't freak out when he heard Mari's frantic message about the baby coming early—in their kitchen. He must have gone out for lunch. She knew he wouldn't answer his phone while riding his bike.

"Dispatch, my neighbor appears to be in labor. I'm a volunteer firefighter here to assist in whatever way you tell me. I've had some paramedic training."

Aidan was a firefighter, as well as a pre-vet student? No time to process it all right now. She was simply thankful he was here.

"Yes, ma'am," he said into the phone, giving their address. He held the phone away from his mouth and asked for her due date, then relayed the information. "January 26th."

This couldn't be happening. Not on her kitchen floor. Thank goodness she'd mopped the floor last night. It had at least been clean before her water broke.

"Marisol," he said in a loud, authoritative voice, "go get all the pillows off the couch and your parents' bed. And hurry!" Thank God he was taking charge of the situation and giving Mari something to do besides watch in stunned silence. They hadn't planned on having Mari witness the birth of the baby, only to have her come in later as the new big sister to hold her first sibling. But nothing was going as planned.

Damián, come home. We need you.

Aidan gave Savannah calm assurances that everything would be okay, easing some of her panic.

"Mrs. Orlando, the 911 dispatcher wants to know if you can feel the baby's head outside your...body." Did he just blush?

"Lots of pressure. Not sure." She found it difficult to breathe. No longer embarrassed that she was doing this in front of her teenaged neighbor, she pulled up her dress and felt inside her soaked panties. "No. Nothing yet." *Thank God.* She didn't want to give birth on the floor. Surely either Damián or the EMTs would arrive in time.

"Good," she heard the dispatcher say as she moved her panties down to her thighs and Aidan took them the rest of the way off. She was beyond being embarrassed about that, too.

"Mrs. Orlando, they don't want you to push until the EMT or paramedics tell you to. Understand?"

"I'll try not to." But the urge to do just that became unbearable minutes later.

"I have to push! Now!"

"Try taking short bursts of air, rapid breaths," he relayed from the dispatcher. Over the next few minutes, a flurry of activity had Aidan lifting her up and Mari placing pillows under her back and head to get her into a more upright position.

Aidan told the dispatcher he was going to get the things she asked for and would be turning over the phone to her eight-year-old daughter. He instructed Mari to sit beside Savannah to provide additional support. "Marisol, stay on the phone until I get back." Aidan asked Savannah, "Where do you keep your clean towels?"

"Upstairs hall closet."

He ran off in a flash.

While Mari was putting up a strong façade, her subdued demeanor alerted Savannah that she was stressed. "How are you doing, baby?"

"Me? I'm okay." She paused before adding, "I don't like to see you hurting."

"Oh, don't worry about me. Just wait until you meet your new baby sister or brother."

When another contraction hit, Savannah feared that might happen even sooner than she'd like. She fought the urge to push. The dispatcher must have heard her groans and heavy breathing and struck up a conversation to distract Mari, doing a great job at calming her.

The rumble of Damián's hog reverberated through the house as he pulled into the garage. Tears ran down her cheeks. *He's home!*

"Savannah!" he shouted as he came into the house.

"We're in the kitchen, Daddy!"

Savannah's gaze shifted to the doorway, and when he filled it, she let out tears of joy. He quickly assessed the situation and knelt beside her. Mari handed him the phone. "The 911 lady wants to talk with you, Daddy."

"Thanks, *Princesa.*" He gave her a quick peck on the cheek then spoke into the phone. "Hello. This is Savannah's husband, Damián Orlando."

As the pain ebbed a bit, Savannah said to Mari, "Why don't you go see if Aidan found everything he needs? Then I want you to go back to the living room and watch for the ambulance."

Mari jumped up and scampered off, probably more than a little relieved that she wasn't in the thick of things any longer.

Now if only they could get to the hospital before the baby came.

* * *

Damián nodded as Marisol did as she was told. He hoped his daughter would think that everything was under control, even if it wasn't. To the dispatcher, he asked, "What can I do to help?"

Given instructions to wash, Damián ran to the sink to scrub his hands. He couldn't believe what he'd walked into. Checking his messages after his lunch break, he'd freaked out when he heard Marisol's voice on the phone. He'd jumped back on the bike and hurried home—to find this.

Kneeling beside Savannah, he whispered, "*Querida*, I got here as fast as I could." He kissed her forehead, noticing the perspiration on her upper lip.

"You're here now. That's all that matters." She sounded nervous but wasn't freaking out as much as he was. He trusted her to tell him if she was. And while he counted on Savannah's past delivery to give her an edge when the time came, neither of them had predicted this birth scenario.

To the dispatcher, he said, "I'm ready."

"Here are the towels," Aidan said as he ran into the room.

What was Aidan doing here? Hell, thank God he was here, if he could help. "Thanks, Aidan. Set them on that chair."

"I still need a shoelace, sir."

Damián didn't have any shoes with laces and couldn't remember any being on Savannah's or Marisol's shoes, either.

"How about your wristband, sir?" Aidan asked.

Damián glanced down at the leather band Tracy Miller had made for him. Somehow, he didn't think Tracy or her dad, Sergeant, whose name had been inscribed on it along with Damián's, would mind if he used it for this. And if the dispatcher was okay with used shoestrings, then his leather band couldn't be any more unsanitary.

"Good thinking," he said as he removed it. Had Aidan already been here when Savannah went into labor? It was about the time Mari took Chiquita for a midday walk.

Damián just hoped the dispatcher would tell him what to do with all this stuff when the time came.

Worried about Marisol, he suggested that Aidan stay with her. As the boy nodded and went into the living room, Damián remembered his training as her coach and the advice he'd gotten from Dad, who hadn't been able to help Karla with her contractions after they'd discovered the third baby and whisked her off to have a C-section.

Jesús, what if Savannah had complications, too? Where were the fucking EMTs?

Savannah's scream nearly tore out his gut. "The baby's coming!"

"Are you sure?"

Savannah glared at him, letting him know in no uncertain terms she knew more about what was going on than he did.

"Tell her not to push yet," came the voice over the phone simultaneously with Aidan's from the living room.

Maybe you *should tell her.*

Wait, he turned to see Aidan returning. What did he know about childbirth?

To free up his hands and so everyone could hear, Damián placed the phone on speaker and set it on the floor near her head.

"Savannah, breathe in then out. Don't push before the EMTs arrive." *Please don't have this baby on my watch.*

"But they…aren't…going to…get here…in time," Savannah spit out the words through clenched teeth, fighting to keep the baby from coming out. What if she couldn't wait? "I need to push!"

"Short bursts, Savannah," Aidan coached.

"Damián," the dispatcher's voice came through the phone, "I need you to look and see if you can see the crown of the baby's head."

Savannah spread her knees and lifted her dress. He leaned down. At the opening of her vagina, he saw tufts of wet, black hair in about a two-inch radius. "I see the baby's black hair!"

Holy fuck! The enormity of what was about to happen hit him like a sledgehammer.

"Okay, if the baby's crowning we aren't going to be able to wait for the EMTs. Savannah and Damián, are we ready to bring this baby into the world?" His *no* and her *yes* coincided with each other. The dispatcher may have gone into cheerleader mode, but he wasn't ready for this!

Savannah met Damián's gaze, tears welling in her eyes. "It's almost time to meet our baby." He searched her eyes. She seemed more relieved now than she had been when he'd arrived, but then her face contorted again in pain.

"When you feel the pain of each contraction, Savannah, I want you to take a deep breath, hold it, then push as you bear down with all the strength you have left."

Damián's throat closed with emotion. Why couldn't this moment have happened in the safety of a hospital with a trained physician on hand? He might fuck this up.

Get a grip. You aren't going to screw the pooch.

He took a hand towel from the ones Aidan had brought down, wet it under the faucet, then washed the sweat from her face.

"That feels wonderful." She sighed.

"Tell me when you have the next contraction, *bebé*."

"Oh, you'll know." She didn't smile, but he could tell her sense of humor was intact.

"Damián, are you still there? How's she doing?"

"*Sí.* Nothing much changed."

Next, he massaged her belly, needing something to do while waiting. When her uterus hardened beneath his fingertips, he told the dispatcher, "Okay, I think she's starting another contraction."

"Remind her, when the pain starts, she needs to take a deep breath, hold it, and push," the dispatcher instructed.

Fuck. Shit's about to get real.

"Breathe, Damián," Savannah coached, trying to smile. How could she smile at a time like this? She truly was the strongest person he'd ever known. "I've done this before. Everything's going to be fine."

Great. She was coaching him now! *Get your ass in gear, man.*

As the contraction built, she let out a moan. Damián lifted the cloth off her forehead and tossed it onto the table.

I've got this.

When Savannah grimaced with its intensity, Damián commanded her attention to try and keep her relaxed. "Eyes, *savita*." After she locked her gaze with his, he added, "Deep, cleansing breath in, hold it, then push."

She nodded.

When Damián gave the go-ahead, she filled her lungs and pushed with all her might as if willing that baby to leave her body. Seeing Savannah in such extreme pain ripped his heart out, even if the outcome would be a joyful one.

"Okay, relax when the contraction ends and wait for the next one," the dispatcher said. How many more before they got the baby out? Was there any harm if the baby was stuck in the birth canal? How could it breathe? Or did it even need to yet?

"A couple more like that, and we'll have the head out. Do we know if it's a boy or a girl?"

"Not yet," Damián answered, but he didn't care which it was, as long as the baby was healthy. His parents had lost young babies. How they'd been able to survive such a loss, he couldn't imagine. But that wasn't going to happen on his watch.

"Damián, as the baby's head comes out, I want you to support it with gentle pressure. Don't pull, just support. Let the baby come out more with each contraction. Do you have that?"

"Yes, ma'am."

"We don't want the baby to pop out too fast."

Did he have any control over that? Or anything, for that matter?

"Damián," the dispatcher said, "take a look now, and tell me how much of the head has crowned."

He didn't know exactly how to describe it. "Maybe enough to be covered by a baby baseball cap. I don't see the ears yet."

"Okay, I need you to reach your fingers in around the neck to make sure the cord isn't there."

The blood pounded in his ears as his finger probed, hoping he knew what a cord was supposed to feel like. "I don't think it is."

"You'd know if it was there. I think maybe one more contraction, a good push, and your baby's head will be out."

What about the rest of the baby?

Savannah met his gaze momentarily before steeling herself on the next contraction. Then she pushed the baby's head from her body. Damián stared at what he held in his palm. *Holy fuck!*

"Okay, I have the head in my hands." *Jesús*, this was surreal.

"Wonderful. Now, we need to quickly clean any mucus out of the baby's mouth and then nose before he or she takes a breath."

Aidan reached in and, with the corner of a towel, cleaned them both expertly. The kid's hands were steadier than Damián's, for sure. "How'd you know to do that?"

"I'm a volunteer with the fire department," he said. "We take classes in childbirth, just in case of calls like this."

"No shit?" What were the chances?

"When you see the shoulders," the dispatcher continued, reminding him what they needed to be doing, "have Savannah do the same inhale then push during each contraction. With your hands, use slow, gentle pressure and support to the baby's head. Gently rotate the body if it helps to ease the baby out. Repeat with the same pressure to the hips, if necessary. Do you understand?"

"Support the head, shoulders, butt. Got it." He turned to Aidan. "You ever delivered a baby?"

"Only in mock childbirth training exercises."

"Well, you're still ahead of me." Recognizing Aidan knew something more than he did provided a small amount of relief.

The dispatcher gave a rare chuckle. "You make a great team, guys."

Remembering who was ultimately in charge, he smiled at Savannah. "I'm so proud of you, *savita*. Once again, you amaze me with your strength and self-control."

"I don't feel like I'm in control."

"But you are. She said just a few more pushes and you'll be holding our son or daughter."

"I feel another one starting," Savannah announced.

"Now, Savannah," the 911 operator said, "I want you to give me another hard push. We're almost there. Inhale then push as hard as you ever have."

Savannah grunted as she gave it all she had. She must be exhausted but didn't give up.

"That's it, *bebé*. You're doing great. Keep pushing."

Everything happened in a blur at that point. After the shoulders were delivered, the baby slipped into his waiting hands—a blood-splotched, wet, beautiful, squirming little human being.

His eyes blurred, and Damián grinned like a total imbecile as he looked at the baby and then back up at Savannah.

"Don't pull away from Savannah's body or tug on the umbilical cord," the dispatcher cautioned. "Do we have a girl or a boy?"

For the first time, he looked away from the baby's head and down to the…penis.

"It's a boy!" Damián said. The tears spilled down his cheeks, and he nearly burst with joy—and more than a little relief.

After a short pause, she added, "Okay, we still have a few more things to do, Damián," the dispatcher said. "Do you have the shoestring and clean towels?"

"*Sí*, ma'am. We have everything ready."

"After the cord stops pulsating, one of you can tie the cord." Aidan nodded toward Damián. With eyes stinging, he nodded.

Aidan covered his hands with one of the fluffy towels. "I'll place the baby on Mrs. Orlando's abdomen first." Aidan moved in as close as possible before Damián carefully placed the baby in the boy's large hands. Savannah welcomed him onto her belly, stroking his wet head.

Removing his wristband, Damián spoke in the direction of the phone. "The cord's stopped pulsating. We're ready."

Following the dispatcher's instructions, he tied the cord before his eyes filled with too many tears for him to see. Damián blinked before meeting Savannah's gaze; she was in tears, too.

She let out a nervous laugh as she smiled at Damián. "I wanted to give you a boy this time but was afraid to say anything and jinx us."

"You know I'd have welcomed a girl or a boy, but it'll be nice to see what it's like raising one of each."

Best of all, Damián would be there for this boy from the very beginning, unlike with Marisol. He wouldn't allow himself any regrets about that anymore, though. He'd simply take each moment from this day on and make the most of it with his entire family. Another Orlando to watch over.

They were a family of four now. *Un-fucking-believable.*

The baby let out a wail, and Marisol came into the doorway. She took one look at the baby and then at the cord protruding from Savannah's vagina before turning a little green.

Damián needed to get her out of here but calm her down first. "Marisol, everything's fine, but I need you to keep watching for the ambulance. I'll let you see your baby brother in a minute."

Hearing she had a brother lit up her face again. Her squeal of delight brought a smile to his and Savannah's faces, too.

With adrenaline still pumping but no mission to accomplish, Damián spoke to the dispatcher again. "What do I do now?"

"Just keep him wrapped, skin on skin with Savannah, if possible. He'll lose heat fast."

"I hear sirens!" Marisol shouted from the living room.

About damned time.

"I'll stay on the line until the EMTs come in," the dispatcher said, "but congratulations, Damián and Savannah. You both did great! You, too, Aidan!" She paused and asked, "Savannah, honey, how are you feeling?"

"Tired. Sore. Elated."

"I'll bet!"

"And how are you holding up, Damián?"

"My baby's fine. And so's my wife. I'm fu—fantastic." Probably best not to let any F bombs go in this moment. But he did feel fucking fantastic.

"You should be proud of yourself. It's not every day a man delivers his own baby."

"I'm more proud of my wife. She did all the hard work. And I had a lot of help from Aidan and you, too."

"They're in here," Marisol said. Two fire department EMTs entered with a stretcher and equipment.

"Aidan!" the first EMT said. "If we'd known you were here, we wouldn't have hurried."

Aidan laughed. "I've never been so happy to see your ugly face, Brent. I'm just glad this wasn't too different from what we learned in training."

Damián wouldn't have wanted to change a thing about what had just happened, now that the baby was safely here.

One EMT checked Savannah's vitals while the other cut the cord, covered the baby with a heat-reflective blanket, and assessed the baby's condition.

Damián moved up closer to Savannah's head, on the other side from where the EMT knelt. He stroked her hair, brushing it away from her damp forehead. "I can't believe he's here."

"Which hospital were you planning to deliver at?" the EMT interrupted. They answered simultaneously. "Great. We'll transport you there," he said to Savannah. Then to Damián, "You might want to call her OB if you haven't already done so."

"Is everything okay? She wasn't due for two more weeks."

"Looks good. We can deliver the placenta here or after we reach the hospital, but you did a good job, brother."

Damián leaned over Savannah's face. "We all did. But I'd rather get her safely to the hospital, if that's okay." He didn't want anything to mar this perfect delivery.

"That'll be fine," the EMT said.

Damián placed a kiss on her lips before the EMTs transferred her to the stretcher, placed their baby boy in her arms, and rolled her out to the ambulance. He held her hand until they loaded her in the back. Knowing there wasn't any room for him, he assured Savannah, "Marisol and I will meet you at the hospital, *bebé.*"

Watching the ambulance drive away with Savannah and their newborn in it wrenched his heart.

"Come on, *mi muñequita.* Let's see how fast we can get to the hospital."

Chapter Thirty-Seven

"I know we didn't want to choose any names until he or she was born," Damián said, "but do you have any idea what we're going to name him?"

Savannah hadn't a clue, but before she could answer, the nurse came in to check her vitals and press on her uterus again. Had Damián come up with a list yet? She'd been so consumed with the trial, Christmas, and then her final weeks at the clinic before maternity leave that she hadn't given the baby's name much thought. How sad was that?

She stared down at the sleeping face of her son, and her chin quivered. He had jet black hair, like his Daddy and Mari, and such long fingers.

"Oh, Damián, isn't he beautiful?"

Damián brushed a lock of hair away from Savannah's forehead, and she looked up at him. "*You're* beautiful, too, *preciosa.*"

Savannah blinked away the sting in her eyes and wrapped her free hand behind his head to pull him closer. Their lips met in a brief but poignant kiss.

"I love you, Damián."

"And I love you more each day, *querida.* Thank you for my two beautiful children."

About an hour ago, they'd sent Mari home to Adam and Karla's for dinner, but they all should be back soon. Savannah blinked away happy tears. What did the future hold for the four of them?

Just take it one day at a time.

Maman had given her similar advice so many times when she'd been wishing her life away, anxious for a birthday or Christmas to come. "Isn't he the most perfect little boy you've ever seen, Maman?" she whispered. Damián had grown used to her conversations with her mother.

She cleared her throat, not wanting to dwell on her loss today. No doubt Damián was wishing his parents had lived to see their grandchildren, too. But Savannah took comfort knowing her mother's spirit was here with them—and his parents, too, no doubt. Perhaps even John Grainger was at her bedside with Maman.

"You're going to have a waiting room full of visitors tonight, but I don't want you to overdo it," he admonished, one hand stroking her hair and the other the baby's.

"Don't worry. I'll give you a wink when I need a nap. Maybe we'll limit them to fifteen-minute visits tonight. I'll let you police it." While she was getting better about asserting herself, this evening, she just wanted to chill.

"Before everyone returns from Adam and Karla's," she asked, "shouldn't we talk about what we're going to name this little guy? Have you come up with any names you like?"

He bit the inside of his lower lip. "How would you feel about my mother's maiden name for his middle name?"

"Diaz." She used it with the one she'd thought of, and it sounded so perfect.

Time to see what Damián thought of her choice. "I love it. And…I was just thinking about recognizing Aidan for being a part of bringing him into the world. But two Aidans in such close proximity might be confusing, especially for Mari. How would you feel about using his surname, though? A word that also holds special meaning to me after what I went through last year." She glanced down at the baby. "How does Justice Diaz Orlando sound?"

He repeated it aloud a couple of times then nodded with a smile. "*Bueno*. It's strong." He said it again out loud. "Sí. It's perfect, just like you." He leaned closer and captured Savannah's lips in an open-mouth kiss that left her uterus clenching. "Ouch. No fair! My hormones aren't my friends right now."

He chuckled. "Sorry. I'll try and keep my hands and lips off you for a few weeks."

"Wellll," she said, drawing out the word and giving him a sly grin, "the nurse said any activity that makes my uterus contract is good, so that I can start getting it back to its normal shape and size. And you definitely make my girly parts spasm, Sir."

His low growl had her clit spasming now. How long did Doctor Palmer tell them they had to wait to have sex again? And what might they get away with short of intercourse in the meantime?

The world faded away to only the three of them for the next few minutes. She would have to get used to calling him by his proper name now, rather than Baby Orlando.

Savannah didn't know how much time passed with them simply staring at and touching their precious baby when she heard Damián's phone vibrate. He pulled it out.

"Dad says they're back and wants to know if it's a good time to bring Marisol back in."

"Text him a photo."

She smiled, bending toward the baby so he would be included, and gave a thumbs-up. While Mari had seen the baby already, no one else had yet. Savannah was ready to show off her little man to the family. "Tell everyone to come and meet the newest addition to the family."

"I'll bring them in." Before he left, he whispered to the baby, "Justice Diaz Orlando, be good for your *maman* while I'm gone."

Alone again with her baby, Savannah turned once more to the sleepy little boy lying skin to skin against her bare breast. She kissed his forehead and whispered, "I'm so happy to have you in my arms at last, Justice Diaz Orlando."

In some ways, the pregnancy had seemed longer than Mari's, but that was all behind them. While this scene with just the two of them reminded her of the way it had been after Mari was born, Savannah reveled in the knowledge this period of aloneness was temporary. They would have Damián in their lives forever—or as long as God willed it. She wouldn't have to face everything on her own again.

She heard Mari's chatter a few seconds before the door opened and she came bounding into the room and up to the hospital bed. Adam and Karla followed.

Mari's gaze was fixed on the sleeping baby on Savannah's chest, his head covered in a crocheted skull cap. Savannah briefly pulled the sheet away for her new visitors to inspect him for the first time.

"He's so beautiful, you guys," Karla said. She cleared her throat, and Savannah saw her eyes had brightened. For Adam's sake—and Karla's—she hoped her hormones weren't going to go haywire. They already had their hands full with the triplets who weren't even walking yet.

"Isn't he?" Damián grinned from ear to ear.

Adam clapped him on the back. "I still can't believe you delivered your own baby."

"Neither can I, Dad. Neither can I."

Karla moved closer, leaning over Mari for a better look.

"He's still red," Mari whispered, as if afraid to awaken or insult him.

"That's normal for the first few hours, sweetie. You looked like this, too." Actually, it was uncanny how much they looked like twins, just born eight years apart.

"Now that you mention it," Damián said, "he does look like Marisol's baby pictures."

Mari reached out tentatively to touch his cheek, and he opened his mouth to begin rooting for a nipple. Savannah smiled and adjusted his head to help him find it. Even though he would only get colostrum now, it was never too early to start practicing breastfeeding.

"What's he doing?"

"Learning to eat. My body will make milk for him for as long as he needs it, and he's getting his first lesson in how to find it."

"Wow," she said in awe. "That's totally ah-mazing."

"Have you chosen his name yet?" Karla asked.

"We were actually talking about that before you came back. Justice in honor of Aidan Justice, who helped deliver him, and Diaz for Damián's mother's maiden name."

"Justice Diaz Orlando. I love that!" she said.

"I think we should have named him Aidan," Mari announced.

"We did name him for Aidan, just used his last name instead. It might get confusing, *Princesa*, with two Aidans living so close to each other," Damián explained.

Mari's idol-worship of Aidan once concerned Savannah, but after what he'd done for her in her kitchen this afternoon, the boy had won her undying respect and gratitude. As far as how he acted with Mari, he treated her more like a little sister than anything.

Of course, she still had regular talks with Mari about good touch and bad touch and that no matter who made her uncomfortable or crossed the line, she was to tell Savannah or Daddy about it. And if she didn't want to talk with her parents, she could talk with Tía Grant or Grammy Karla or any adult she trusted, because sometimes it was easier to tell a non-parent.

Savannah didn't want to be hypervigilant but also wouldn't pretend that sick, perverted individuals didn't exist in the world. At least she'd had a hand in putting one of the worst monsters away for life. Damián had also had a talk with Aidan about making sure he didn't overstep Mari's personal boundaries. Sad, but necessary in today's world—not that it was anything new.

Hoping to move from her gloomy train of thought, Savannah asked, "What do you think about being a big sister, Mari?"

She cocked her head as she continued to scrutinize the tiny baby. "He's not much fun now, but I'll help you take care of him, Maman. When can he crawl like Rori, Pax, and Kate?"

"Not for at least six months. Remember, your aunts and uncle are almost eight months older than our baby. But watching Grandpa and Grammy's babies, you'll always know how to help your brother get to the next phase. And I'm sure he'll like having you play with him eventually, but for the next few months, don't forget that he's just entered into the world. He has so much to become accustomed to."

"Is he gonna sleep all the time?"

The baby had dozed off again when he hadn't gotten any satisfaction from her nipple, but he'd remained latched on. She'd have to keep her nipples well-lubricated with olive oil, which Anita had advised her to use with Mari. Those tiny jaws and gums could be brutal.

Savannah tried not to grin at her daughter's disappointment. "Yes, I'm afraid newborn babies are like kittens. Remember how much Boots used to sleep when you first got him?"

"He still sleeps a lot."

"Not nearly as much as he did a year ago, though."

Mari hitched the corner of her mouth. "Can I go back out to the waiting place with everybody?"

Savannah smiled. "Sure. Who all is out there?"

"Marc and Angelina, Ryder and Megan, Rosa, and Grant."

"Who's watching the triplets?" she asked Karla.

"Luke and Cassie. José's there, too."

Savannah's eyes filled with tears. God, she loved being a part of this family.

"Would you like to hold him?" she asked Karla.

"Would I ever!"

Savannah bundled the diapered baby in the receiving blanket so he wouldn't be cold, and Karla scooped him up. "Oh. My. God. I can't believe how light he is! How much did he weigh?"

"Seven pounds, twelve ounces, so not as light as you think," Damián said. "And nineteen and three-quarter inches long."

"I guess I'm just used to my three who are all closer to nineteen and twenty pounds each now."

She remembered how fast Mari had grown and understood completely.

"Can I get up there with you, Maman?"

Savannah patted the mattress, and Marisol scrambled up, laying her head on her mommy's breast much as her son had done moments ago. Was she feeling a little insecure about her place in their hearts?

Savannah stroked her hair. "Your little brother is going to love having you for a big sister. But you'll always be our little girl."

Damián must have noticed, too, and added, "We loved you first and will never stop loving you. Having a new baby in the family just helps our hearts grow bigger."

"I'm glad." Savannah couldn't see her face but heard the smile there. "I can't wait 'til he comes home. Can I hold him?"

"Sure," Savannah said. "Sit on that chair over there, and Grammy Karla will bring him to you."

Adam brought a spare pillow over to place behind her. "You'll put your arm on the rest here and be sure to keep his head steady." The man certainly had come a long way with babies since his own had arrived. Seeing the grandfather he had become to Marisol did Savannah's heart good, too.

Karla handed Justice to his new big sister, and Savannah watched Mari's eyes grow wider as she looked at him in awe. She babbled to him in a low voice for several minutes and held him as if he were a raw egg she was afraid to break.

Damián leaned down to kiss Savannah on the forehead. "How are you doing, *bebé*? Tired?"

"Getting there, but let me visit a little longer with Adam and Karla and spend a few minutes with everyone else waiting out there."

He nodded. "But when I think it's time for you to get your sleep, I'm going to send everyone home. You've been through a lot today."

She loved how he took care of her, first and foremost.

"Okay, I'm done holding him," Mari announced.

Karla asked Adam if he'd like to hold the baby. "Absolutely." He lifted Justice out of Mari's arms. Savannah smiled, remembering how reticent he'd been with his own babies during their first few weeks, but now he was an old pro.

"Hey, buddy. I'm your Grandpa Adam. Welcome to the world." Seeing the tough former master sergeant cooing at her newborn son brought tears to her eyes.

Savannah noticed Damián seemed close to breaking down, too. Despite his equally tough exterior, he wore his heart on his sleeve for his family.

Adam came to her bedside and handed the baby back to her. "You've given the family a beautiful new addition, Savannah." Adam placed a fatherly kiss on her forehead, and tears sprang to her eyes again. So many feelings for this man. He'd been there for her countless times since she'd come to Denver and had even come out to California to testify and provide moral support during the trial.

"Thank you, Ad—" She stopped, unable to continue. "Would you mind if I call you Dad, too?"

His eyes had gone a little misty, too. "I'd like that a lot, hon."

Karla cleared her throat before speaking. "Why don't I go out and see who else wants to come in for a brief visit before we leave and let you get some rest, Savannah?"

She nodded, unable to say anything.

Adam and Karla left minutes later with Mari. Damián gave her a chaste kiss on her lips. "I'll be right back with more visitors."

No sooner had he left the room than Savannah's eyelids grew heavy. She heard rather than saw the door open and close. Positioning the baby between her breasts, she fell asleep.

* * *

Damián returned to find Savannah sound asleep. After letting in Rosa, Marc, and Angelina to take a peek at the newest Orlando, he thanked them for coming and promised to let them hold Justice next time.

Damián planned on spending the night with Savannah and would make sure she slept. He couldn't do a lot for the baby right now except change his diapers and bring him to her whenever she wanted to hold or feed him. He sat and stared at them for a long time then heard a light tap at the door.

Dad peeked his head in. "How are you holding up, son?" he whispered.

"Other than overwhelmed and totally blessed?"

"It's one of the greatest feelings in the world, isn't it?" he said as he sat down next to Damián.

Everyone else had gone home, but Dad had promised to stick around to keep him company, at least until Savannah woke up. He'd watched over Damián many a night during some of the darkest days of his life. He'd taught Damián a lot about living, too.

Damián didn't want to lose his shit in front of him, but the enormity of what had happened today suddenly hit him like a helmet to the face. His leg began shaking the way Grant's sometimes did.

Dad chuckled. "Take a deep breath before you pass out on me."

Damián filled his lungs several times. "He's so little. I can't believe a few hours ago he was inside Savannah's belly and now he's a living, breathing human being who I need to protect more than ever."

"I know where you're coming from. Been there, done that—and not all that long ago. At least you only have one helpless baby to deal with at a time."

One was more than enough.

They sat in silence watching Savannah and Justice sleep for a long time before Adam broke the silence. "He sure got your black hair. And look at that fist he's making."

Damián chuffed. He'd been known to put his hand through a wall— or a face—a few times, not that he intended to exhibit those behaviors in front of his newborn son.

Justice's tiny fingers held onto Savannah's ring for dear life—the same one Damián had inherited from his parents and had given to Savannah on their wedding day. Justice would gather strength from the Orlando women who had worn this ring over three generations. Tears stung his eyes with thoughts of his *mamá* and *abuela*.

"What if something bad happens to him? What if I'm not there for—"

Dad squeezed his shoulder. "You'll be there. You're one of the most responsible family men I know. As for protecting them, just remember your training, take precautions, and love them to death."

"Death is the last thing I want to think about today."

Dad clapped him on the back. "Then stop getting all maudlin on me. All you need to be thinking about now is that precious gift you've been given—three of them, actually. The three biggest threats to your family— Gentry, Gibson, and Julio—have been neutralized for the next decade, if not for the rest of your lives. And you know we'll all have your backs until we're old and decrepit. Then we'll have the next generation to take care of us in our old age—a lot sooner for me than you." He shook his head as if he couldn't quite figure out how he'd grown older. "Pax and Justice will kick the asses of anyone who messes with any member of our family."

"Don't count Marisol out—and I have a feeling you'll be teaching your own daughters how to protect and defend, too, when the time comes."

"Yeah. Guess that was a little sexist." He chuckled unapologetically. "You and I sure chose some kick-ass women to share our lives with. I won't underestimate *any* of their children."

With Savannah sleeping, Damián went to the bed and carefully lifted the tiny bundle off her chest, careful not to disturb her sleep. She opened her eyes briefly then smiled and went back to sleep.

Like Karla, Damián couldn't believe how little the boy weighed. Cupping the back of Justice's head, he returned to the chair next to Dad's and held him out in front of him so that they could have a closer look. Justice stared right back at him. Weren't they supposed to be practically blind at this age?

Dad cleared his throat. "I will always be eternally grateful for the help Aidan gave our family today. That's one fine-looking boy you have, Damián. In no time at all, our sons are going to be playing baseball together and fighting over girls."

"Soccer. I want him to play soccer," Damián said firmly.

"Let me enjoy him as a baby a few years, you two," Savannah said. Damián turned to find her smiling at them. "And your daughters might want to be on a soccer or baseball team, too."

Seeing humor and love on her face, he grinned back at her, surprised she'd overheard them. "Quite true, *querida.*"

"Point taken," Dad chimed in.

Her gaze drifted to Justice, and she sobered. "I just don't want our children to grow up any faster than they have to."

"I'd better head back to the house." Adam stood. "I wish you all every happiness there is. God knows, you've earned it."

Damián stood and returned the baby to Savannah's chest before approaching Dad and wrapping his arms around him in a bear hug.

"Proud of you, son."

Damián's eyes burned with unshed tears. "Love you, too, Dad."

After he'd left, Damián turned to Savannah and pulled his chair closer. His stump hurt like hell, but he wasn't leaving their sides tonight to go home and take care of it.

"I love seeing you with Justice Diaz in your arms," she said.

The little boy squirmed. "Do you think he recognizes his name already?"

She laughed. "More likely, he recognizes our voices."

Damián shrugged off that explanation. This boy was going to be smarter than Damián ever was. When he stared into their eyes, he already looked like he had the answers to every question known to man.

Savannah patted the mattress, and he sat down beside her. "I can't believe we made another perfect little person."

"We do make beautiful babies, don't we?" she agreed.

He cupped her cheek. "That we do, but let's not make another one for a while."

She laughed. "There's only one surefire way to avoid a pregnancy."

"Forget that. If God gives us another baby in nine months, we'll welcome him or her just like we did this one."

"Remember, I won't get the go-ahead for sex for at least a few weeks. And I do intend to plan the next baby, which will be a first for us."

Damián grinned. "We're passionate people. What's wrong with that?"

Savannah laughed. "I can't believe we're even talking about future kids when I just delivered our son."

Damián glanced at the clock. "In some ways, it seems longer, but, in others, like it just happened an hour ago." He bent down to kiss her lips. When she grabbed the back of his head to deepen it, his tongue entered her warm mouth to tango with hers. Pulling away, he met her gaze again.

A few minutes later, she seemed to screw up her courage to move then grimaced as she turned onto her side. "Do you need something for pain?"

She shook her head. "It mostly goes away as soon as I stop moving."

"Don't be macho. If you need something, ask for it."

"Look who's talking. I can often say the same to you. Like today.

You're favoring your leg. Go home and give your stump a rest. I'll be fine."

He glanced down at Justice again. "I don't intend to leave here without both of you. I've gone a lot longer without babying my foot."

"I still can't believe how long you hid your amputation from me when I first arrived. For months!"

"Let's not talk about that time anymore. In the morning, Dad's going to bring over the packed bag we left at home. Marisol's going to be fine at Rosa's until we get home."

"They said I might go home in the afternoon."

"So soon? Is that wise?"

"Maybe not for new mothers who don't have a support network, but I think they saw that I'm going to be surrounded by people who will make sure I don't overdo it."

"Damn straight you will." He sobered and leaned closer. "You amaze me every day, *preciosa*. Watching you giving birth—*Madre de Dios*. And I'm not sure exactly where the transition phase I was dreading happened, but thanks for not ripping my throat out or something."

She laughed. "I didn't want to scare you off."

"If helping you give birth on our kitchen floor doesn't scare me off, nothing will. I'm yours forever, *querida*."

Epilogue

One last time, Damián tightened the bolts into the flanges and attached the stripper pole into the bedroom ceiling. He couldn't wait for Savannah to come home and see it but wanted to make double sure it was safe for her. Savannah was at Karla's with the kids and Cassie, no doubt baking a cake for tonight to celebrate Damián's twenty-ninth birthday.

He'd spent the week in the shop degreasing the galvanized pipe, making sure it had no nicks that could cut her, preparing the base and ceiling mount blocks, and then spray-painting it a brass color. Luke had joined him a couple of hours ago to help with the installation. Good thing, because it quickly turned out to be a two-man job. They'd even had to jump in Luke's truck to return to Damián's bike shop to cut the pole a half an inch shorter due to a slight miscalculation. Finally, the two of them had managed to mount it to the ceiling and floor in the bedroom.

Damián stepped off the ladder and stood back to survey their work. He couldn't wait to see Savannah using it. While she'd found a pole-dancing exercise class at a downtown gym, it was difficult for her to find time to go. Besides, he didn't get to watch her moves at the gym.

"Dayum. That might be the best birthday present you'll ever get," Luke said.

Damián had to agree. With Savannah's increasing lack of inhibition, this would definitely be a gift enjoyed by both of them.

But it wasn't quite shiny enough after they'd handled the pipe. He glanced around the room. "Hand me that furniture polish."

He'd just finished applying the polish, which should be dry by the time she'd try it out tonight after the kids went to sleep, when the front door slammed. "Fuck. They're home early. I need to keep her out of here before she sees it."

They started hastily gathering up their tools to clean up the area, expecting her to head to the kitchen to hide his cake first.

"Damián, I don't want you to come down—"

Too late. Savannah stood in the doorway when he and Luke looked up, her mouth open. Her eyes lit up, and she smiled. "Damiàn! I love it!"

Without warning, she took a running start toward it.

"No! Wait!" Before he could stop her, Savannah grabbed onto the pole to spin herself around, but the still-wet polish made it too slippery. She lost her grasp, and her back crashed into the wall with a thud. She slumped to the floor. Damián's heart stopped as he raced to her.

"*Bebé*, are you okay?"

"Don't get up right away, darlin'," Luke cautioned, cupping her chin. "Follow my finger." She seemed to follow it to the left then back to the right just fine. "Tell me how many fingers you see," he said, holding out two fingers in front of her.

"Six?" She looked a little dazed and sounded confused.

Fuck. Thank God Luke was a search-and-rescue volunteer and knew what to do. While Damián had taken first aid and CPR classes for the shop, he couldn't think straight right now. "Shouldn't we get her to the emergency department so they can check her out?" What the hell had he been thinking to polish the pole like that? She might have broken bones, maybe even a concussion. *Fuck, fuck, fuck.*

"I'm joking, Sir," she said with a grin. "There were only two fingers. I'm just trying to hide my embarrassment at such a lame attempt to mount the pole."

Someone was asking for a good spanking. "That's nothing to kid about, *savita*."

"I'm sorry." She turned her focus back to the pole. "Help me up so I can regain some of my dignity."

Each man took one arm and lifted her to her feet. She seemed steady enough, but Damián wrapped an arm around her lower back, just in case.

"Where are the kids?"

"Karla's. I...needed to pick up something before we head back over for your party." Her attention returned to the new addition to their bedroom. "I can't believe you installed a dance pole for me, Damián. I absolutely love it!"

So it's a dance pole to her, huh? "Don't try to do anything on it until I can wipe off the polish. I don't want you to get hurt any worse."

"Nothing's hurt but my pride right now." She turned to him and gave him a hug. "Thank you so much! You're a man of many surprises."

"I remember a time when you didn't like surprises."

"There once was a time when I didn't like a lot of things—but I've changed, thanks to you."

"That you have." He couldn't resist another kiss, deepening it when she opened her mouth to him.

The roar of a familiar hog pulling into their driveway captured their attention. Luke must have left them alone sometime during their kiss. Damián and Savannah crossed the room to see who'd just pulled up. *The fuck?*

"Sounds like the Harley I've been restoring the past couple months."

"You recognize them by their sound?" Savannah asked.

"No doubt about it with that one." He'd recognize the sound of that particular engine anywhere. "Let's go downstairs." He took her by the hand but preceded her on the stairs, in case there were any residual effects from her fall.

As they walked out the front door, he wondered if he was finally about to meet the mysterious client who'd relayed him instructions through the shop's foreman. Damián had worked on the custom detailing, painstakingly restoring it to the same specs as the one he'd owned before joining the Corps. Maybe the owner had come over to personally thank him, but he wasn't supposed to pick it up until tomorrow. The shop was closed on Sundays. Was there a problem?

"Dayum. Nice bike," Luke said, standing in the driveway grinning at Damián—obviously not the new owner of the bike.

The man on the Harley unstrapped the helmet's chin strap and slowly removed it.

"Dad?" He'd bought a Harley knowing Karla's aversion to them? No wonder he'd wanted to hide his identity. Damián never would have taken the job if he'd known the bike was for Dad.

"You did a great job, son. That's the smoothest ride I've ever taken."

Damián closed the gap to stand near the front tire. "What are you thinking? Karla's going to kill you if you bring that home."

"You're right. So I thought maybe your garage might be the perfect place for it." Dad pointed toward the garage behind Damián.

"No way, man. I'm not going to help you hide something this big from Karla. She'll have both our asses when she finds out."

"I can only imagine," Savannah agreed.

What was Dad thinking?

Dad sobered. "Well then, that presents a problem."

Damn right, it does. But it's not my *problem.* "I'm not in the bike sales business. You're going to have to find a new buyer on your own."

Dad swung his leg over the back of the bike and lowered the jiffy stand. "I think that can be arranged." He walked toward them and handed the keys to Savannah, who accepted them.

Damián glanced her way and found her smiling. At him. He looked between her and Dad, who was also grinning ear to ear now, before returning his gaze to his wife.

Savannah held the key out to him. "Happy Birthday, Damián."

What the everloving fuck? "Are you saying, *you're* the client?"

She nodded, tears brimming in her eyes before two streamed down her cheeks. He closed the gap, took the keys, and wrapped her in his arms.

"I guess I managed to surprise you. I couldn't have done it half as well without Dad's help. I'd even gone upstairs earlier to make sure you didn't come down before we could pull it off."

"*Sí*, did you ever. All this time, I was working on my own bike?" He still couldn't figure out how she'd pulled it off.

"I knew you'd put just as much love into a client's bike as your own, and I so wanted to replace some of what you lost because of…well, everything that happened back then."

Damián couldn't speak for the lump in his throat, so he simply held on tight until Dad cleared his throat and Damián did the same. Pulling apart, he gazed into Savannah's eyes.

"I love you, *bebé*. Not because you gave me this awesome birthday present, but because of who you are and the precious gifts of Marisol and Justice that you've given me."

"Stop. You'll have me crying all night if you keep this up. Why don't you take your newest baby for a ride?"

"Not without you."

Her eyes opened wider. "Really?"

Adam—*Dad*—handed her the helmet he'd worn. "I'm sure the girls have everything under control back at the house. I can hop a ride with Luke back to the shop to get my SUV, and we can meet you two at my place for the birthday party after your ride."

"Sure thing," Luke said.

How much of this did he know about?

Savannah looked longingly at the bike.

Dad commanded, "Go!"

She turned to Damián. "Can we? I've been dying to get on a bike with you again for months."

Looks like both of them had given the other a gift with mutual satisfaction. "Sure."

"Give me a minute to run and change into something more appropriate first." She set the helmet on the seat of the bike and ran into the house from the garage.

"Stay off that pole!" he shouted before she'd opened the door to go inside.

She turned toward him. "I promise to wait until tonight."

"Pole?" Dad asked after she'd gone inside.

"Yeah. Luke and I just installed a stripper pole in the bedroom so she can start working out on one again."

"I'm sure that's not the only reason you got her one."

"Well, it is my birthday." His gaze turned toward the bike again. "I had no idea she was cooking this up right under my nose. She's planned this for months, even when she had all that shit on her plate with the trial."

"You've got a keeper there, son."

"Damn right I do. She's full of surprises."

"Just like Karla. I don't think either of us would want to change a thing about them, though."

"Fuck, no."

*   *   *

Almost a month later, Savannah put the finishing touches on her waterproof mascara. She had a date with Damián tonight and wanted to look her best. Rosa was taking care of Mari and J.D. She smiled thinking how quickly her little boy had picked up a nickname. But Savannah and Damián had learned the name Justice sometimes confused people, and Justice Diaz was a mouthful, so they'd started using his initials.

Damián would be home any minute. She should be elated, but her thoughts kept returning to the envelope on the credenza downstairs from the San Bernardino District Attorney's office. Would it contain good news or bad? Was there news about the charges filed against Damián and Dad? Their lives were starting to become blessedly normal after so much trauma and aggravation. Would that trend continue?

When the front door slammed, she shoved the wand into the mascara tube and headed toward the hallway. He'd started up the stairs when she stopped him.

"Wait there. I'm on my way down." The sooner they got this out of the way, the sooner they could move on to their date. When she reached him, she kissed him, his lips firm under hers before he opened to her.

He pulled away and smiled at her. "I love coming home to you, woman."

"I love these days when I'm here to greet you when you come home." Thoughts of the letter on the credenza tempered her enthusiasm. "Something came for you in the mail today. I think you should look at it right away."

"What could possibly be more important than getting ready for our date?"

Without answering, she led him over to the basket that held the day's mail and picked up the letter on the top of the stack. "This, I'm afraid." *Really afraid.*

He checked the return address first, and Savannah felt his body stiffen. "I'll deal with it later." He set the letter back on the credenza and cupped her face. "Tonight, I have a date with a beautiful *chica*, and I don't want anything to put a damper on it." He kissed her, nibbling at her lower lip until she opened for him. While he managed to distract her for a few moments with a toe-curling kiss, when he pulled away, her thoughts returned to the unopened letter.

"Sir, I don't know if I can concentrate while worrying about what's in that letter. If it has to do with those charges, then Dad probably got one, too. In case we should run into him tonight, I think we need to know what it says."

He sighed, staring at the letter again as if it contained anthrax. "I won't lie to you. I'm worried, too. Open it for me?"

She nodded, drew a deep breath, and picked up her mother's letter opener. Savannah held her breath as she extracted the letter from the envelope. It was printed on stiff bond letterhead, and the DA's return address and California State insignia were emblazoned across the top.

"Dear Mr. Orlando..." she began, noticing that Damián was fiddling with his wristband. Thank goodness the staff at the hospital realized how important it was after seeing the engraving and took great pains to get it back to him. It was even more important to them now, having helped them care for their son in his first minutes after birth.

Focusing again, she continued: "I am writing to inform you that the charges against you in the case of..." Savannah rattled off the legalese, anxious to get to the point of the letter. Her hand began to shake. The thought of having Damián undergo a trial that might land him in prison in California made her sick. Gentry deserved what they'd done to him and more for the years of torture and abuse he'd subjected her to.

Damián took the letter from her hand, as if to spare her the bad news. "Here, let me." He scanned the letter quickly to find where she left off.

"Because the complainant who brought the charges against you has been convicted of two counts of murder and other felonies, the District Attorney's office has dropped all charges against you with prejudice."

Dropped the charges? "Thank God!" She threw herself at Damián and wrapped her arms around him. After a moment of celebration, she pulled away. "But what does *with prejudice* mean?"

"*No lo sé.*"

"Let me Google it." She pulled her phone out of her pocket and looked up the legal term. After only becoming more confused as to whether some of the definitions applied in this case, she found a simple one that seemed to fit. "This sounds like the best answer." She read:

In the formal legal world, a court case that is dismissed with prejudice means that it is dismissed permanently.

Oh, please, let that mean what it sounds like.

"It goes on to say that a dismissal with prejudice means that the case is over and done with. The courts can't come back later and attempt to bring up these charges again." She lowered the phone and met Damián's gaze. "It's over, sweetheart."

Within seconds, they were in each other's arms, tears streaming down her cheeks. "I can't believe how everything is falling into place so perfectly."

"This calls for an even bigger celebration tonight," he announced.

She released him and stared into his eyes. What did he have planned? "I didn't know we were celebrating; I thought it was just a much-needed date and adult time."

He gave her an enigmatic smile that made her even more curious, but he didn't say anything more. Instead, he held up the letter again. "I can't believe they dropped the charges." He read a little farther down the page, and his eyes opened wider. "Un-fucking-believable."

"What?" Her heart pounded harder in the moment it took for him to answer her.

"Says here they didn't want to bring two war heroes up against a man serving time for a double murder and kidnapping and battery convictions."

"Wow." She nearly collapsed in relief. "I can see how it might look bad for the DA's office." She wasn't sure she should ask, but this time, curiosity did get the best of her. "Sir?"

He set the letter back on the credenza. "*Sí, bebé?*"

"We didn't talk about this in any detail the night I bailed you out, but what exactly did you and Dad do?"

His face remained grim for a moment. Then he smiled. "I made sure my girl got the justice and retribution she deserved. I didn't trust the court system to take care of that for me."

Savannah's heart pounded so loudly she almost didn't hear the end of his declaration. "So you did do the things mentioned in the charges? Physical things, not just threats?"

He nodded.

Dear God, if this had gone to trial, there was a very good chance they'd both have lost and been sent to a California prison for many years.

"What were you thinking? You risked your freedom."

He shrugged. "It was the right thing to do."

"So in effect, you branded him."

"That's one way to put it."

She could never condone vigilante justice—not out loud, anyway— but hearing that the two of them left their mark on Gentry's offensive anatomy provided Savannah that last measure of justice she hadn't gotten through the trial and sentencing. Behind bars for what would probably be the rest of his life, he would have a constant reminder of the man he'd first tried to ruin then attempted to kill during the raid on the cabin.

Justice had definitely been served.

She launched herself into his arms again. "Thank you, Sir, for protecting me and our children and for making sure that fucking monster never hurts anyone again."

*   *   *

Damián pulled up outside the Masters at Arms Club after dinner. Seeing the lights shining through the windows to the great room,

Savannah couldn't hide her surprise. "It's Thursday. The club isn't open tonight."

"I've got connections."

Of course, he did. Tonight promised to be even more fun than she'd expected, not that they didn't make the most of the equipment showing up in their home—like the massage chair and dance pole—for times when they could be alone. She certainly enjoyed the array of opportunities for fantasies to come to life—and for Damián to wield his eight-foot bullwhip—when they played at the club, especially on private nights like this apparently was.

He took her hand and led her through the kitchen door and straight down the hallway past the theme rooms and into the great room. To her further surprise, she found an assembly of all the owners plus Ryder and Megan, the club's newest members, who'd signed the contracts to join soon after the Alive Day commemoration last November. Damián and Savannah hadn't gotten to the club much since then, but according to Karla, they only drove the two hours to play here on special occasions.

She wondered what was up. When all eyes and smiling faces turned toward her, she began to think she was somehow the guest of honor. She cast a puzzled glance toward Damián, who squeezed her hand and propelled her toward the circle of chairs.

And then she remembered. He'd told her she'd have her own Alive Day commemoration. She did a quick mental check of the date and realized this was the day they'd rescued her from Gentry's last attempt to abuse her. This time, he'd have probably killed her if they hadn't gotten to her in time.

"You don't have to give me an Alive Day." She still didn't like to take away from what the commemorations meant to military heroes.

"I told you we would do this, and we will." There was no room for discussion. He took a seat and pulled her onto his lap before the others took their seats. The other submissives chose to sit on the laps of their Doms, too. Only Grant sat by herself yet in the group.

"Savannah, I've told you hundreds of times that you're the strongest person I know," he began. "But—"

When his voice broke, she caressed his cheek. "Sir, you don't have to—"

He pressed a finger to her lips to silence her protest. "*Savita*, I've watched you blossom over the past year. Learning to trust me—as well as yourself—was a huge step. I love your strength, your power, your newfound freedom. Mostly, I love you for who you are. And you have no idea how proud I am that you wear my collar as well as my ring…"—he tapped each one before continuing—"…and with them, you accepted my love, guidance, and protection."

It was Savannah's turn to have her throat close up. She cleared it, uncertain what she would say until the words started to pour out of her. "Sir, you and your family"—her hand swept the circle taking in everyone present—"accepted me unconditionally and have been there for me every step of the way. But you, Sir, did so much more than rescue me from a monster a year ago today. You helped me reclaim my body, my sexuality, and my sanity."

She took a deep breath before she could continue. "Being your submissive empowered me in ways I never imagined such a role would. You showed me that I am the one in control. I call the shots, although I also have learned to enjoy surprises and know when to go along for the ride." She grinned at him before sobering again. "But I decide whether we continue or end an activity. And you stopped immediately when I used my safeword the last time we were here, on *your* Alive Day." She hoped they wouldn't stay away so long between visits now that she wasn't pregnant.

"Thank you for entrusting yourself to me, *savita*, and for being honest with me about when you had been triggered and unable to continue. That alone instilled much more confidence in me and the future of our dynamic."

She kissed him, long and deep and hard, hoping this little chat would end soon so they could pursue a scene, just the two of them. Someone cleared their throat, bringing her back to the group. Turning to them, she said, "And each of you played a part in my healing, too. From taking me into your home a year ago, Adam and Karla. To Dad…"—she was still getting used to calling him that, but it became more natural every day—

"...you being at the courthouse meant so much to us both."

"Hon, I can hardly remember a time you weren't part of our family. And the way you've helped Damián push his limitations aside and take on new challenges—like learning to ski? Well, you already had a place in my heart forever, but you earned my undying gratitude, too."

"And you've always felt like a sister to me, Savannah," Karla added. "Your strength and courage lift me up, too. I want to be like you when I grow up." She giggled, and Adam stroked her arm.

Savannah swallowed past the lump in her throat. "I'd better finish what I want to say before you all have me in tears." She turned toward the lone female Marine in the group. "Grant, you leave me feeling safe and protected. And you've done an amazing job with Mari's martial arts training. Your special skills were an integral part of the rescue last March, too." She cleared her throat. "You have a strong protective instinct and take your role as club manager very seriously, leaving all the submissives feeling safe." Grant sometimes scared them a little, but Savannah wouldn't mention that here.

"I only do what any manager or dungeon monitor would do."

"As one of the people who plays here, I would have to say you're being too modest."

Grant shrugged, but Savannah didn't want to put her in the spotlight to the point of being uncomfortable. "Angelina, our talks about the lifestyle helped me to understand the ways in which it could help me. Marc, your medical skills kept me alive and relatively pain free that day in the cabin, plain and simple. Ryder and Megan, the gentle and attentive ways you helped Sir make me comfortable after I triggered during the wax play scene last November meant so much to me."

She smiled at them then Damián. "Without the support of your extended family to help us through our many struggles this past year, we'd have had to endure them alone. I know we would have, but we're so blessed that we didn't have to, thanks to your—*our*—amazing family."

"*Bebé*, how could you not be a part of us? You fit in perfectly."

She couldn't resist another kiss, this one leaving her hot and bothered and ready to move on to the rest of the evening. "Sir, did we come here to play?"

He chuckled. "We can play here or at home."

"Or both."

The grin on his face widened. "That can be arranged. It's your night. What would you like to do?"

"Wellll, I'm no longer pregnant."

He patted her almost flat belly. She'd been working out daily this past month on her dance pole and getting great results.

"Did you have something in mind already?"

She nodded. "I'd love to try wax play again, Sir, just not limited to my feet this time. But, even though I don't think white wax would still trigger me this time, I don't want to tempt fate."

"Good idea. There are plenty of colors to choose from." Damián turned to the men and women seated in the circle. "Thank you for all you've done to make Savannah, me, and my new family welcome. But now, if you'll excuse us, I think we'd all like to have a little time to ourselves and to take advantage of the club while we're here."

"You get first choice," Dad said. "Which area or room would you like?"

"I stored the burner and wax supplies in the medical room," Damián said.

"One of my favorite rooms, Sir." She especially remembered the time he first taught her to pleasure herself while strapped to that table—the same night he'd introduced her to the evil stick and the more pleasurable uses of the quirt and violet wand.

"Sounds good to me."

She stroked his cheek. "How did I ever come to deserve someone as perfect as you, Sir?"

He chuffed. "Somebody's perfect, all right," he said, "but it's you, *querida*, not me. I knew it the moment I laid eyes on you at the hotel's restaurant in La Jolla and never stopped believing that, even when we were apart."

Savannah blinked away the tears. To be loved so strongly and steadfastly by this man had helped to heal her many wounds. Their future would be what they made of it—and judging by the love and support that surrounded them, good things were headed their way.

Books by Kallypso Masters

Rescue Me Saga (Erotic Romance)

Kally has no intention of ending the *Rescue Me Saga* ever, but will introduce some new series with new characters in the years to come. The following *Rescue Me Saga* titles are available in e-book and print formats on my web site and at major booksellers:

Masters at Arms & Nobody's Angel (Combined Volume)

Nobody's Hero

Nobody's Perfect

Somebody's Angel

Nobody's Lost

Nobody's Dream

Somebody's Perfect

Rescue Me Saga Box Set Books 1-3 (always e-book only)

Rescue Me Saga Box Set Books 4-6 and Western Dreams (always e-book only)

Rescue Me Saga Extras (Erotic Romance)

This will be a series of hot, fun, short-story collections featuring beloved couples from the *Rescue Me Saga*.

Western Dreams (Rescue Me Saga Extras #1)

(Contains new scenes with Megan & Ryder and Cassie & Luke)

Roar
(a *Rescue Me Saga* Erotic Romance Spin-off)

(Erotic Romance with Secondary Characters from the *Rescue Me Saga*. *Roar* provides a lead into the upcoming trilogy with Patrick, Grant, and Gunnar's stories. No clue when that series will be written. Kally is waiting for Grant to open up.)

Bluegrass Spirits (Supernatural Contemporary Romance)

(Contemporary Romance…with a Haunting Twist)

Jesse's Hideout

Kate's Secret

kallypsomasters.com/books

About the Author

Kallypso Masters is a *USA Today* Bestselling Author with more than half-a-million copies of her books sold in e-book and paperback formats since August 2011. All her books feature alpha males, strong women, and happy endings because those are her favorite stories to read, but that doesn't mean they don't touch on the tough issues sometimes. Her best-known series—the Rescue Me Saga—features emotional, realistic adult Romance novels with characters healing from past traumas and PTSD, sometimes using unconventional methods (like BDSM).

An eighth-generation Kentuckian, in spring 2017, Kally launched the new **Bluegrass Spirits** series, supernatural Contemporary Romances set in some of her favorite places in her home state. *Jesse's Hideout* (Bluegrass Spirits #1) is set in her father's hometown in Nelson County and includes a recipe section with some of Kally's treasured family recipes, most of which are mentioned in the story. *Kate's Secret* (Bluegrass Spirits #2) takes place in horse country outside Midway in Woodford County. Local flavor abounds in both novels.

Kally has been living her own "happily ever after" with her husband of more than 35 years, known affectionately to her readers as Mr. Ray. They have two adult children, a rescued dog, and a rescued cat. And, as her friends and fans know, Kally lives for visits from her adorable grandson, Erik, who was the model for the character Derek in *Jesse's Hideout* and Erik in *Kate's Secret*. (He insisted on having his real name used in the second one!)

Kally enjoys meeting readers at book signings and events throughout North America and is on a mission to meet with at least one reader for a meal, signing, or other event in all 50 states. She's staying closer to home these days, but expects to have KallypsoCon in Virginia or Maryland in 2019. To keep up with upcoming events, check out the Appearances page on her web site! She's always open to having signings in her home state of Kentucky, too!

*For timely updates, sneak peeks at unedited excerpts, and much more, sign up for her e-mails or text alerts on her website at **kallypsomasters.com**.*

To contact or engage with Kally, go to:
Facebook (where almost all of her posts are public),
Facebook Author page,
Twitter (@kallypsomasters),
InstaGram (instagram.com/kallypsomasters)
Kally's Web site (KallypsoMasters.com).

And feel free to e-mail Kally at kallypsomasters@gmail.com, or write to her at
Kallypso Masters, PO Box 1183, Richmond, KY 40476-1183

Get your Signed Books & Merchandise in the Kally Store!

Want to own merchandise or personalized, signed paperback copies of any or all of Kallypso Masters' books? New *Bluegrass Spirits* series items will be coming soon, but there's already a line of t-shirts and other items connected to the *Rescue Me Saga* series and KallypsoCons. With each order, you'll receive a sports pack filled with Kally's latest FREE items. Kally ships internationally. To shop for these items and much more, go to kallypsomasters.com/kally_swag.

And you can also purchase any of Kally's e-books directly from her now, too! Just click the "Kally's Shop" link for any of the books listed on her website. Or go here for a complete list of available titles. New releases will be published exclusively in Kally's Shop at least two weeks before being available on other retailer sites.
kallypsomasters.com/buy-direct

Roar (A Rescue Me Saga Spin-off)

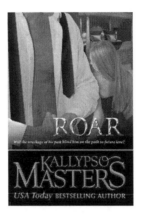

A tragic accident left his beloved wife just beyond his reach, haunting Kristoffer Roar Larson for four years until a chance meeting with Pamela stirs feelings best kept buried. Her assertive alpha personality coupled with her desire to submit and serve fascinates him. Will he allow her presence to shine light once more into the dark corners of his life?

Dr. Pamela Jeffrey thrives on providing medical assistance to those in war-torn corners of the world until a health scare grounds her stateside. While pursuing her deepest secret desire, she encounters Kristoffer, who reluctantly agrees to help prepare her for a future Dom. The bond deepens between them as does her desire for him to be that man in her life, but Kristoffer cannot meet all of her needs. Can she be satisfied without regrets with what he can propose?

As the undeniable connection grows between them, feelings of betrayal take root. How can Pamela convince him he deserves another chance at love? Will Kristoffer be able to fully open himself to the ginger-haired sprite who makes him question everything he once believed? Or will he lose the woman teaching him to live again as surely as he lost the person who first taught him to love?

NOTE: While this book is a standalone, it includes secondary characters from the Rescue Me Saga, including Gunnar Larson, Patrick Gallagher, and V. Grant and there is a scene in the Masters at Arms Club.

Reading Order for the *Rescue Me Saga & Extras*

kallypsomasters.com/books

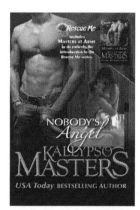

Masters at Arms & Nobody's Angel (Combined Volume)

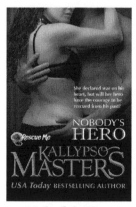

Nobody's Hero

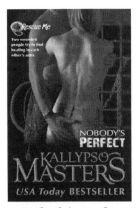

Nobody's Perfect

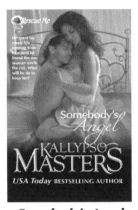

Somebody's Angel

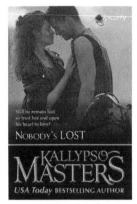

Nobody's Lost

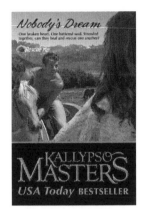

Nobody's Dream

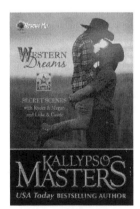

Western Dreams

Somebody's Perfect

Bluegrass Spirits
(A Supernatural Contemporary Romance series)

From the *USA Today* Best-Selling Author of the *Rescue Me Saga* comes a new Contemporary Romance series with supernatural elements set amidst the many flavors of Kentucky. In *Bluegrass Spirits*, Kallypso Masters distills love and happily ever afters—with a little matchmaking guidance from loved ones on the other side. While there will be updates about earlier couples in each subsequent story, each novel can be enjoyed on its own.

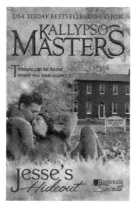

Jesse's Hideout

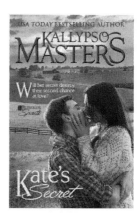

Kate's Secret

Made in the USA
Middletown, DE
23 June 2019